This book may be kept

~~~AYS

T H E

S I L E N T

P E O P L E

BY WALTER

the silent people

M A C K E N

The Macmillan Company,   New York

"We are the silent people.
How long must we be still,
to nurse in secret at our breast
an ancient culture?

Let us arise and cry then;
Call from the sleeping ashes
of destiny a chieftain who
will be our voice.

He will strike the brass
and we will erupt
from our hidden caves
into the golden light of newborn day."

FLAN MCCARTHY

part one

chapter 1

HE MOVED THROUGH the fair. It was early October. The midday sun was shining brightly from its low arc behind him. The small street-town of Fáirche, shaped like a Y, was as congested in its heart and its extremities as a colony of ants under a stone. There was a faint passage in the center where he threaded his way. His eyes were shining. He was very pleased. He was very interestd in all that went on around him. Even so, his tongue and palate were exploring and savoring with exquisite care the small penny piece of white bread that he had bought at a stall. That expenditure had exhausted his finances, but he thought it was worth it as he chewed and swallowed, oh so carefully.

There was more room to move at the crotch of the Y. He stood here, his bare feet widely spread, catching the last crumbs of the bread from his fingers with the tip of his tongue. The peddlers had their stalls set around in a ring and a gentle breeze from the west was stirring the gaily colored ribbons tied on slender sticks and erected high to be seen, and to flutter, so that they would arouse desire for possession in the hearts of the girls.

He smelled around him. Very mixed up. Pleasant and unpleasant. There were pigs with ropes around their hind legs, squealing each time they tried to move away and got a chuck from the rope. Small black cattle, meaty after the summer mountain-feeding. Most of the houses were low and thatched, huddling close to each other for consolation, and from some of them loud noises came, as the successful sellers tippled away a little of their money. All round him men were spitting and cursing and arguing. They had sticks in their hands and they would emphasize their points by beating the stick on the dung-covered road, or hitting the bony hip of an inoffensive cow who would jump and move and cause all the closely packed animals to jump and move too, men with bare feet pushing at them and pulling back in case they would step on their toes. It is not pleasant to have the hoof of a beast rest on your bare toes.

Most of the women and girls were around the stalls. The older women had baskets covered with white cloths. They had eggs and yellow butter wrapped in cabbage leaves in the baskets.

A girl called to him. She was small-sized so she hopped up and down like a jumping rabbit.

"Dualta! Dualta!" she called.

Smiling, he made his way over to her.

She was standing in front of the ribbon stall. It was a gay stall filled with colored ribbons and rosary beads and pictures and glinting knickknacks.

"Dualta, my darling," the black-haired girl said to him, catching his arm. "Will you buy me a blue ribbon?"

"Oh, Sorcha," he said, "at this minute I couldn't buy enough ribbon to color the left leg of a sparrow. And even if I could, what would your father say?"

"My father loves you," she said. "He would welcome you to our house." Her face was close to him.

"Don't be teasing," he said. "Your father has so many in his house now that the dog has to leave his fleas outside the door."

"We could live together up the chimney," she said.

"How could we make love in a chimney?" he asked.

"Who said anything about love?" she asked. "We would be just chimney friends."

They laughed. She pressed his arm. She looked down at her feet, raising the hem of the heavy petticoat.

"These cursed shoes are killing me," she said. She had quite small feet. The shoes were heavy, but shapely and very new.

"Why have you to be elegant?" he asked. "Why didn't you leave the shoes at home? You'll spend hours scouring the fair off them."

"I have to get a husband," she sighed. "They won't look at you any more unless you are wearing shoes." He laughed. "Well, it's true," she said. "You are not civilized if you do not have shoes."

"I'd take you without them," Dualta said.

She sighed.

"You would be a good husband," she said, "if you weren't seventeen and if you had something to offer. What have you to offer."

"Beauty," he said, joking, lifting his face, "one shirt, one smallcoat, two trousers, books, words of love, a stout body and two good feet." He stamped his feet in the mire. He splashed. She screeched and pulled back from him.

"You'll ruin my clothes," she said. "Come over visiting to-night. We will have fun. Propose to my father for me. Let's hear him wriggling out of it, praising your uncle Marcus."

"I'll do that," said Dualta, "I'll give him a few more gray hairs."

"I have here the smallcoat of a noble lord," a loud voice suddenly shouted in English. It brought a hush over the fair. They turned their heads. It came from a beefy man standing on a box at an old-clothes stall. He was holding up a coat of red cloth with brass buttons on it. "You can dress and go and dine with the Lord Lieutenant in it. You can drive the cows in it. You can go to Mass in it. You can get married in it. You can be buried decently in it. You can hand it on as an heirloom to your great-grandchildren. What am I offered for it? Who'll propose sixpence for a start?"

Sorcha and Dualta laughed. Most people didn't understand the English but the peddler mimicked all the virtues of the coat.

"Sorcha! Sorcha!" a voice was calling.

"There's my mother," she said. "I will go to her. Don't forget to come over. There might be a stray fiddler from the fair."

"I'll come," he said. She left him.

He was making his way to the stall of the old books when his eye was attracted by the peddler holding up a little girl figure, gaily bedecked with greens and yellows. There was a little handle on it and he was twisting this and the little figure was going through the most extraordinary movements, legs flailing, arms flailing, and the little brass decorations on it were attracting rays of the sun and glinting. It was fascinating. He stood there watching, smiling, absorbed. He didn't see the horseman coming from his right, impatiently forcing his way through the crowd.

He was a tall young man sitting very straight on his horse. The horse was a heavily built fawn-colored hunter with pink nostrils. The man carried a tapered flexible whip in his right hand. It was loaded with lead shot and as he moved he used the whip on animals who blocked his way and, indeed, flicked it occasionally at a human back that was turned to his passing. Both animals and humans winced under the flick of this whip. His coming brought silence and when he had passed the taken-up talking was not as loud as before. He was followed by a beefy rough-faced man on a plodding farm horse and other men who carried sticks and whose feet and bodies were splashed with mud. Some of them carried dead hares whose broken necks were dangling.

The horse and man were finally blocked by the figure of young Dualta standing there smiling at the dancing doll. The horseman regarded the face of the youth. Light brown waving hair growing long, a thin sensitive nose and red lips pulled back over white teeth. An intelligent face. The horseman waited. He wondered what was making the boy so absorbed. He didn't look. His stomach was sour. His eyes were red-rimmed and bloodshot from last night's prefair session. Suddenly a wave of distaste and frustration came over him. He raised the whip and harder perhaps than he had intended, he brought it down across the face of the youth.

One moment Dualta was dancing in his heart with the little doll girl, his mind fitting a fiddler's tune to the gyrations of her limbs and the next moment he was in agony, a searing pain shooting through his whole head as the blow of the whip opened the cheekbone near his eye.

He gasped with pain and bent forward, his hand covering the pain. He squeezed it. Then he turned to look for the source of it. He saw the grim young face looking at him from the horse, lips tightened in a handsome face. Of course Dualta knew him. He was the Half-Sir, the son of their landlord, a young hard-drinking reckless-riding, reckless-living young man. He knew who he was and yet he did what he did, because he was flaming with anger. The polished riding boot was near to him. He caught it and he heaved with all his strength and the young man flew from the saddle and landed on the other side. He landed where the dung of the fair was deepest, and he landed on the side of his face. Dualta ducked under the belly of the horse. He wanted to lay his hands on him. The horse reared as Dualta reached for the man. The horse was frightened and ran, and the Half-Sir's foot was in the stirrup and the horse dragged him along the ground, scouring the street with his body and head. You could already see the stains on his red coat, the brown splashes on his white breeches.

The onlookers were petrified.

Dualta wasn't satisfied.

He set out after the frightened horse, but hands caught at him. He was aware of a great silence and confused shouting, and he fought against the hands that held him, shouting "Free me out! Free me out, I tell you!"

But they didn't free him. His squirming body was passed from hands to hands. Rough powerful hands, one of them was even clapped over his mouth to stop his shouting.

Then he was inside a house where it was almost dark, just lighted by the flare of the turf fire in the open hearth. There was a powerful smell of whiskey and the crowded bodies of men.

He heard the voice speaking urgently.

"Easy! Be easy for God's sake! Easy! Easy!" The cloud left his head. He could see. The face of Sorcha's father.

"You saw what he did to me? You saw what he did to me?" he asked.

"Dualta," said the strong gray-whiskered face, close to his

own. "You have no time. What have you done, boy? Listen! Are you listening?"

"Yes, yes," said Dualta, rubbing his hand on his cheek, seeing the scarlet blood then on the palm.

"Little time, Dualta. Get out the back way, and flee home, boy. See your uncle Marcus. He'll tell you what to do. The others may not know it was you. But they'll know soon enough. You hear, Dualta, you have no time. Go! Are you easy?"

"Yes," said Dualta. "I'm easy now."

The back door was opened and he was pushed out. He stood there bewildered for a moment. What had happened to him? He had been so happy. The yard was small. It was filled with chickens and ducks. The ducks looked at him with their heads on one side and quacked doubtfully. The wall wasn't high. He leaped over it and crouched on the far side. He was still bewildered. He looked at the Mount, towering up in front of his eyes. They lived on its left shoulder. He would have to go there. There were many green fields and hedges between him and home, many open spaces where a running figure could easily be seen. He could hear uproar now in the street. I can sort it out later, he thought. Now I must go home. He ran straight across the field in front of him and then breaking through a fuchsia hedge in the next one he ran left, knowing that he was hidden for the time being from searching eyes.

The people gained as much time for him as they could. The Half-Sir's men had run after the horse. They had to pacify it, stop its rearing, hold its nostrils, while the others freed the young horseman. He wasn't a pleasant sight. The side of his face had hit stones. His beautiful clothes were soiled and filthy. He was standing for some time on his feet. His legs were trembling.

"Who was it? Who was it, sir?" he heard them asking.

"A boy," he said. "Some boy. He had brown hair and white teeth."

He turned and went back abruptly. The men with the sticks followed him. He stopped near the place of the dancing doll.

He looked around him at the heavy faces. They were as blank as white walls.

"Who was it? What was his name?" he asked in a loud voice. He picked a specific face. He went closer to it. He pointed a finger. "I give you two seconds to tell me his name," he said.

The man shook his head.

"I do not understand. I do not understand the English," he said in Irish.

"Farley!" the Half-Sir shouted then, and the thickset man who had been riding the rough horse came close to him.

"Ask him! Ask him who it was," he demanded.

Farley broke into Irish.

"Who was it? Who was it did it to the master? Do you want us all in trouble?"

"I don't know, Farley," the man said. "I saw nothing. I was in the other place drinking a happorth of whiskey. I came out when I heard the ree-raw."

"He doesn't know," said Farley in English. "He doesn't know, sir. He wasn't here."

"Well, ask somebody else! Ask somebody else! Some of them know. They couldn't all be as blind as they are stupid. Ask them!" He was pale with anger.

Farley asked. But nobody knew. Nobody had seen anything. They weren't there at the time.

"I'd love to do something to them," said the Half-Sir. "They know damn well. Here, Farley, who in the whole place has a young man with brown hair and a thin face. He's tall and well set up."

"Unless it's the nephew of the schoolmaster Marcus," said Farley. "Maybe it was him. If he isn't here. Did you leave a mark on him?"

"I left a mark on him."

Farley shouted in Irish.

"Is Dualta O Duane here at the fair?"

There was no answer. It was so silent you could hear the song of the birds. Farley and the Half-Sir looked at each other.

"Right! Bring my horse," he said. "We will go and have a look at this Dualta and if he's the one, he'll show it and by God he'll pay for it!" They brought his horse. He got into the saddle. He looked down at them. Their faces were blank. As stupid looking as bloody bullocks he thought. Then he brought the whip down on the horse's flank and the horse ran. A path cleared for him like magic and he galloped down the bad road toward the Mount and his retinue followed after him roaring and shouting, and all of the mass of people looked after them silently. Sorcha was biting her knuckles and there were tears in her eyes.

Dualta approached the village from the south. It was easy to take advantage of the many folds in the fields as they crept up the Mount. Some of the fields were soft with grass, some of them had the stubbles of the cut oats on them, and they were hard on his feet. Others had wide beds of dying potato stalks, where tall fading thistles grew among the stalks and pierced his legs. Beyond the fields there was a patch of cutover bog with sedge and coarse grass that was slippery from the recent rains.

When he came within sight of the village he went on one knee, breathing hard, and looked at it. Below, the street-town seemed empty but he couldn't see into the streets of it, just the dots of people who remained on its outskirts, but at the demesne side of the town he saw horsemen galloping on the road and men running after them, and beginning to jump walls and cross the fields to keep up with the horsemen.

The doors of the houses in the village were closed. So unusual that. Some child must have got ahead of him running the straight way. There were about ten houses, built in a semicircle around a sort of green where a few pigs wallowed. The houses were built with their backs to the north, seeming to be half set into the stony ground. Some of them were straw thatched, some sedge thatched. One or two of them were stone built, packed with lime-mortar. The others were built from dobe mud. Half of them had chimneys from which smoke was lazily rising. From the others smoke came through the unglassed windows. His uncle's house was at the apex, higher on the hill, looking down at all the others. The door was open. But he didn't want to go directly to it. He felt he didn't want to pass by the closed doors, the green bereft of children. He went to the left, working his way to get to the back of his uncle's house. From here the Mount started to rise to its high swelling proportions. Panting from his exertions he reached this height and sank down behind it. By putting his head over the top he could nearly look down into the chimney of his uncle's house, but he ducked again quickly when he saw the horseman rounding the hill and galloping toward the green.

The Half-Sir pulled up outside the house of Marcus. Behind him Farley was beating the slow plow horse to come close to him. Already some of the field runners were closer than he. They formed around the horseman who was calling, "You inside, come out here! You, whatever your name is, come out here!"

They waited.

"Come when you are called!" shouted the horseman impatiently.

There was a movement in the doorway and then a big man came out into the sunlight.

He was wiping his hands on a rag.

His shirt sleeves were rolled over big arms. His corduroy breeches were neat over gray woolen stockings and heavy brogue shoes. He had a strong sunburned face with muscular jaws. His spiky hair, once ginger in color was going gray. He looked at the horseman with calm eyes.

"You are Marcus the schoolteacher?" he asked.

"I am," the man said.

"You have a nephew?" the other asked.

"Yes," said Marcus.

"Where is he?"

"He is not in my pocket," said Marcus.

"Be careful of your speech," said the Half-Sir, his hand tightening on the whip.

"I am," said Marcus.

"See if he is in the house, Farley," said the man. Farley got off the horse. He went toward the house. He looked at Marcus, who was taller than he. Marcus stood blocking him for a moment and then stood aside. Farley went into the house. They waited. He came out. "There is no one there," he said.

"When your nephew comes here," said the Half-Sir, "I want him. If he has a mark on his face he is in the worst trouble he ever was in."

"What is he supposed to have done?" Marcus asked.

"You'll find out soon enough," said the Half-Sir. "Farley, divide the men up. Send some of them to block the way to Cong. Let others of them shut off the road to Connemara and Mayo. In the meantime I'll go home and collect some hunters, and dogs. You hear that, schoolteacher?"

"I hear that," said Marcus.

"Then heed it," said the Half-Sir. "He won't get out of here. I'll pluck him out of the bottle. If you have sense you will find him and bring him to me. That way he might find a little mercy, but if I have to hunt him and find him he will never forget it."

He turned his horse then and went away. Farley talked to the men with the sticks and they split two ways, one party of them going north and the other south, straight across the land. Then Farley followed his master and Marcus was left looking after them.

He stood there for a moment thinking, and then he turned abruptly and went into the house.

Dualta waited until he could hear no sound, then he eased himself over the height and slithered down. He was behind his house, hidden from view. He stayed there a short time, and then walked carefully around the blank wall, which held neither back window nor back door, rounded the gable end, looked, and walked swiftly into the house.

Marcus was doing a strange thing. He was taking books from a shelf over the fireplace and putting them into a sack. There was only the light of the fire in the kitchen and the opaque light that came through the window which, instead of glass, held a stretched, scraped sheepskin fitted in the frame.

Marcus turned when the light from the door was blocked.

"Come in closer," he said in Irish, "until I look at you."

Dualta did so.

"You have a mark on your face," said Marcus.

"I have a mark on my face," said Dualta, putting his hand up to feel it tenderly and wondering that he was still consumed with rage.

chapter II

I T WAS A ONE-ROOMED house. The floor was the rock of the hillside. It had been chipped and leveled and worn smooth by the passage of feet for many years. There was a wooden box pegged to the wall that held a few crocks, a few plates. The chimney was of wickerwork plastered over with mud, and whitewashed. The two beds were bags of straw neatly folded and placed in the corner with two brown blankets draped over them. There were two long crudely built forms for the scholars. That was all.

When Marcus had the books put into the sack, he went over to the wooden box and started to place the crockery carefully on top of the books.

Dualta said to him, "What are you doing?"

Marcus said, "I'm packing."

Dualta said wonderingly, "Where are you going?"

Marcus looked over his shoulder at him. Then he put the sack on the floor and came over to him.

"Dualta," he said, "what have you done?"

"He hit me," said Dualta, "I only tumbled him off his horse."

"You only tumbled him off his horse," said Marcus. "Ah, well, that's not much. He's only the son of the landlord."

"Was I to stand there and be beaten and do nothing?" Dualta asked.

"That's right," said Marcus. "You should have tumbled him off his horse in your head, Dualta."

"Am I a slave?" Dualta asked angrily. "Are we all slaves?"

Marcus considered this.

"What is a slave? If you remember what I have taught you,

there was a slave once called Spartacus. He didn't think he was a slave. You know what happened to him?"

"This isn't then, it's now," said Dualta. "There's no man on God's earth going to hit me as if I was an animal."

"That's grand," said Marcus. "So you are free. You did what you had to do, and now I have to pay the price of your victory."

"It's nothing to do with you," said Dualta.

"There are some potatoes boiled in the pot," said Marcus. "You better eat a few of them. You haven't much time."

"I'm not going anywhere," Dualta almost shouted. "I'm staying here."

Marcus looked at him.

"Do you know what will happen to you?" he asked.

"I don't care," said Dualta. "If I have to die, I will die. They won't take me without blood. I tell you. There's law. He hit me first."

Marcus rubbed his big hands over his head. He sat on a form.

"Listen to me, Dualta," he said. "There is law. Maybe it's good law, I don't know. But you cannot interpret it. I cannot. They are the people who say what the law means. They are the magistrates. They are the ones who say what right is. Right is on their side. Nothing else matters. They take you. They will beat you within an inch of your life, and then they will transport what's left of you for seven years to Australia. Maybe you want to be beaten. Maybe you want to go to Australia. If you do, all right, all right. As long as you know."

He got up and went back to his sack.

"But I don't understand," said Dualta almost plaintively. "What has it got to do with you?"

"I'm your uncle," Marcus said. "What do I own? I own nothing. I built this house but it isn't mine. I grow potatoes in a two-rood field but it isn't mine. Use your head. I'm going because I have no option. If I don't go I will be put." He looked at the bewildered face of his nephew. He went over to him. He put a hand on his shoulder. "You should have accepted the blow, Dualta. We have no weapons, except patience and suffer-

ance, and talk about tomorrow. Dualta, go and eat some potatoes."

Suddenly the anger left Dualta. He felt cold. He felt miserable. He crouched over the black pot where the potatoes rested
in their split jackets. He reached for one. It was hot. He threw
it from hand to hand to cool it. He looked at the big back of
Marcus. He felt his stomach falling.

"Will we go together then?" he asked.

Marcus paused before he answered him.

"No," he said. "We have to part, Dualta. I will go back to
my brother in Connemara. I will go along the spine of the
Mount where I can be seen. They will be sure I am going to
meet you. It might draw them away from you. You will have to
go down to the big lake and cross at its narrow part and get to
Galway and go south."

He watched Dualta's bent head. He was easing off the skin
of the potato with his thumbnail.

"I have another sack. I will put your possessions into it and a
few potatoes to carry you."

He took Dualta's folded clothes from the windowsill, his cloth
breeches and stockings and the smallcoat and two shirts, and a
pair of brogue shoes from the corner.

"The best thing about being a slave is that you have so little
to take with you when you go," he said cheerfully, watching the
bent head of his nephew. He placed the sack beside him.

"I have two implements," he said then. "We will share them.
The spade for you and the manure fork for me." He laughed.
"See, with this spade I give you a livelihood. Here is a spade
and go into the great world and make your fortune." He tied
the ends of the sack around the handle of the spade, left it
against the wall. Then he went to where his smallcoat was
hanging from a peg. He put it on him and the battered beaver
hat. It sat rakishly on his spiky hair. He felt in the pocket of
the coat and pulled out a small leather purse. He opened it
and tumbled the coins it contained into the palm of his hand.
He put some back into his purse. He went down to Dualta.

"Here," he said, holding out his hand to him. He put money

into his palm. "Pocket that," he said. "It's just three half crowns, half of what I possess."

"I cannot do this," mumbled Dualta.

"You have to," said Marcus peeling a potato and biting into it. They ate.

"Hurry now," Marcus said. "Get movement under you. We haven't long to wait."

Dualta stood up.

"Keep high enough on the Mount where the horses can't climb," said Marcus. "Don't let the dogs get the wind of you. Move down toward the fall of night, and get across and hide in the hills on the other side. You hear all this?"

"I do," said Dualta.

"Then get up and go now," said Marcus.

"This is not right," said Dualta.

"Will you go for the love of God, Dualta?" asked Marcus.

Dualta went to the spade. He raised it, pushed the sack down and put the spade on his shoulder. He went to the door. He looked at the village. There was no sign of life in it.

"Like rabbits," he said aloud bitterly. "You see them on a sandhill darting into their burrows at the sound of a footfall."

"Don't blame them," said Marcus. "They are holding on to life."

Dualta paused. So many things in his head he wished to say to this man who had been his mother and father for so long.

Dualta said, "God be with you, Uncle Marcus," and went out the door and turned right and scrambled up the place behind. Then, not turning again, he speeded his pace and moved toward the towering bulk of the Mount.

Marcus stood there motionless, looking at the blank doorway. He felt like wailing. But that wouldn't do. Soon now, Dualta would have to go someplace. He was too bright to stay with his uncle. Marcus had taught him most of what he knew himself except the wisdom and acceptance that comes with maturity. He remembered him after the 1817 famine and fever had hit them. Dualta was the only survivor of his house, mother and father, sister and brothers, all gone. Nine years ago, a thin fever-wracked boy not a pick on him, just eyes like the beginning of a fish. Marcus had brought him from there to here and he was as his son. A picture in his mind of the famine funerals then, the women wailing, their thin screeching piercing the sky.

He shook himself. This wouldn't do. He wrapped the blankets around his sack and tied them neatly with a few whangs so that he could carry them hanging from his shoulder like a peddler's budget. He lifted the potato pot and the wooden water bucket and carried them outside and left them in front of the house. The neighbors could have them, he thought, first come lucky. Then he went back and looked at the inside of his thatch. He got the manure fork, raised it and pushed away some scraws from the blackened wooden supports until he could see the straw of the thatch. He poked at that with the fork until he broke through and he could see a little sky. Then he upended one of the forms. It was long. It reached to the opening he had made. He put the other one on top of it. At the foot of these he emptied the bed sacks and piled the straw around them.

Then he went to the door and looked down. He couldn't see, but he could hear the barking of dogs and the voices of men, so he went back and, using the fork, he carried the live burning turf of the fire and laid it on the straw. It smouldered and sizzled and burst into flame. When the flame rose and started to lick at the wood of the forms, he shouldered his budget, hefted his fork, sternly quelled the outrage that rose in him at what he was doing to his little home, and then he went outside, pulled the door closed behind him and stood there waiting for the horsemen and the pack of dogs that, shouting and barking, had turned into the approach of the village.

Only the one horseman came toward him. The dogs surrounded the horse's legs. Many breeds, brown and white beagles and one or two deerhounds, big, shaggy, friendly fellows with lolling tongues and also some of the local collies who had joined the dog pack.

Marcus looked at the Half-Sir. He didn't try to hide the distaste he felt for him. It didn't matter any more.

"We know now it was your nephew, schoolteacher," he said. "We found somebody not unwilling to talk."

"Even Eden had serpents," said Marcus.

"So where is he?" the man asked. He had changed his clothes, Marcus noticed. But the side of his face was pitted and sore looking. His eyes were glinting.

"You go and find him," said Marcus. "He is one, you are many."

The man dismounted angrily, swinging his whip and facing Marcus. He was surprised then to find that the other man topped him almost by a head. He saw the smile on the face of Marcus.

"I have a mind to chastise you for your nephew," he said.

"You better forget it," said Marcus. "He was a boy, I am a man. If a boy could do what he did to you, what could a man do?" The prongs of the fork were winking in the sunlight. They caught the eye of the Half-Sir. He looked at the eyes of Marcus. They were cold eyes and anger was beginning to peep from them. The Half-Sir didn't feel self-assured. He turned and waved at the horsemen behind him. "Come here," he called. There were five of them. They came, flogging their horses, pulling up and stopping, the horses rearing.

"What's to do, Charles?" one of them asked. They were young men. The Half-Sir looked at Marcus.

Marcus said, "You feel safer now."

Said Charles to them: "He knows where his nephew went. Will we beat it out of him?"

A young fair-haired man frowned distastefully.

"You do it, Charles," he said. "You beat it out of him."

"That's right," said Marcus, "you do it, sir."

"I want you to hear this," said the Half-Sir. "This man is hereby evicted, and anyone who shelters him will suffer his fate. You hear that, schoolteacher?"

"I do," said Marcus as suddenly from behind him there was a loud swoosh and the roof of the house turned into a high blaze, roaring and smoking into the blue sky. The horses shied. Their riders pulled them back. "I must have forgotten to quench the fire behind me," said Marcus. "In that field there are two roods of potatoes. They are yours. They will pay my rent. I owe your father nothing then."

"Where is he? Where is your nephew?"

"Find him," said Marcus.

"Come on, Charles," the fair-haired one said. "What's the fun if we know where he is? He has to be somewhere on the Mount."

Charles looked again at Marcus, then at the burning house.

"We'll find him," he said. "There's no place in Ireland that will be safe from me."

Marcus said nothing. The Half-Sir mounted slowly as if to show that he was not afraid of turning his back on the big man, then men, horses and dogs raced to the opening into the village where they paused, split in two and turning right and left headed toward the sun to scour each side of the Mount.

Marcus stood there.

When the noise was ended, some of the doors of the village opened and children appeared from them. They looked frightened. They came a few yards from their doorways and looked back at the burning house and the man standing there. They kept looking at him.

He recognized them. All faces and shapes of heads that he had rapped knuckles on; girls with long hair tied with ribbons, boys in petticoats and boys in ragged breeches and worn shirts, they just stood there solemnly looking at him. Suddenly, the lids of his eyes were hot. He had liked here. He had liked what he was doing. He had liked the people. Why, oh why, Dualta, couldn't you take a blow from a whip?

He raised his hand in the air to them, and then he scrambled up the height behind the house. They watched him until he had disappeared and then silently they moved up toward the burning house. Here and there in the doorways some of the women appeared and watched their children sadly moving to the pyre of the house of their learning. The face of the descending sun was smudged by the black smelly smoke that filled the air.

chapter III

ON THE SHOULDER of the Mount, some hundreds of feet short of its peak, Dualta lay full length in the crudely built sheep shelter and looked out through the gaps in the stones. The sun was getting low. The sky was the burnt golden color you would see on the top of a wood-mushroom. He could see back beyond the farthest mountains. They seemed small from here although they were bigger than the Mount. The sides away from the sun were colored a deep purple and the lakes between them were like shimmering sheets of silver. And out beyond them was the sea and its islands. If only he was a bird and could fly. The horsemen and the dogs were below him to the left.

He turned on his side and, looking up, saw his uncle Marcus slowly climbing to the peak of the Mount, moving slowly and methodically, the way he did everything. Dualta knew that the hunters were watching him. Uncle Marcus knew they were watching him, hoping that he had a place set to meet Dualta. If they kept watching him they might leave gaps through which Dualta could slither.

His uncle Marcus had reached the crest and was walking there silhouetted for all to see, bravely, almost swaggering you thought, with the fork on his shoulder and then he bent and moved and shouted and fired a stone and Dualta almost smiled to see the two hares racing away from him, down the Mount in the direction of the dogs.

He watched closely.

He saw one of the dogs raising his nose into the air. He saw him getting the scent and then he was off baying and the whole pack of dogs followed him. The horsemen whistled and called but the dogs paid them no heed. Very few dogs can resist the scent of a hare, so the horsemen had no option but to follow them. It was bad ground for the horses; thin soil over a covering of shale, but they slipped and recovered and chose their ground and raced up the Mount after the dogs.

It was Dualta's chance and he took it. He crossed down behind them, having taken one more look at his uncle on the Mount. He chose the ground that gave him cover in its folds, and ran swiftly. He was thinking: This crowd will go around the Mount, but the others will come this side from the north of the Mount, so I must get to the river before that. He took chances. Out in the open places he raced down the side of the hill with the strides of a giant. If one of the horsemen had turned his head, he would have been seen and captured. Because he was reckless he got away with it. In his heart he didn't really care if they did find him. He would hurt someone before they subdued him. He thought of the face of the Half-Sir and he hated him, blindly, grinding his teeth, gripping the handle of the spade, seeing the iron of it cleaving skulls. And he was ashamed of this feeling too, that he should be capable of it, and blaming the Half-Sir for having engendered it in him.

When he reached lower ground he was safe from being seen for a while, shut off by a satellite hill that tried ambitiously to rear itself from the boggy ground. Ahead of him were green fields rendered lush by the river that flowed through the valley. He rested here, breathing hard. The sun was lower. It was sending up giant despairing rays from behind the mountains. The clap-light was about to fall, and in October it fell fairly swiftly, but over his left shoulder there was a giant harvest moon, a huge yellow globe like a big turnip. This did not please him. He crossed two fields, jumping the low stone walls and then sank down when he heard the hurrooing. He dared to look. Both parties had joined, and now spread out arclike, covering a wide area and coming down the river valley scouring it like a flood.

Now what do I do? he wondered. Should he give himself up and take what they have to give, looking at them scornfully, bleeding defiantly, like the great Irish heroes of the sagas? Who would care? Who was there left to make a great poem about him? Who would care to make a poem about him, an obscure youth, even if there were any great Gaelic poets left, which there weren't, his uncle claimed, only proud beggars who turned thin jingles, as weak as water spits? He laughed a little thinking of himself as a great hero of a new saga. What would it be called? The Boy and the Beagles. He looked high up for his uncle then, but there was no sign of him against the sky. So he was on his way. He had done what he could.

There was a wall near him running down the incline toward the river. He reached it. It barely covered him as he crouched and ran down beside it. The river was wild and deep after the recent rains. It was a very clear color, sort of gray. He was away below where it could be crossed with dry feet. So he didn't hesitate. He went into it. It was deeper than he had thought and the current was stronger, but he kicked with his feet and grabbed the fading rushes on the other side. He pulled himself into there. He could feel the gray sticky mud around his legs. His body was warm from the running, but it was soon cold. He held the sack free of the water, but he had to sink it when he heard the sounds coming nearer. So now everything was wet. He sat in the mud. He could feel it oozing through his clothes. He thought of being dragged from the mud like a rat. Would they shake him to get the mud off him before they beat him?

He turned to look up the river. He saw them. The dogs and one horseman. Not the Half-Sir. Coming very close. Could the dogs smell his head? Would they get his scent from the place where he had entered the river?

They might have if a hare hadn't burst from a form almost under their noses. He felt like getting up and cheering. Baying and shouting and cursing that faded away. He gave them time to depart before he dragged himself from the mud. The far bank of the river was high. He crawled up there and looked over. There were two horsemen this side. They were looking after the baying dogs. They paused and consulted and then went away toward a sort of road below and the rude bridge that crossed the river. As soon as they left, he left, straight away from the river, running across the fields where the ground rose on the other side, rising to a range of hills that ran down to the spot in the big lake where he had to go. He gained the shelter of these hills and finding a patch of fading heather he rolled in it as a horse rolls in sand, kicking and rubbing trying to squeeze away the mud and the wet and the bleakness.

He looked for his enemies. They had been going in the right direction, away from him, but now they had all turned and were coming back this way. Whether they had lost the hare or turned him, he didn't know. The horsemen on the road had turned too and were coming back. He scrambled over to the sun-side of the hill and started running. He ran toward the spot where the road was curving madly like a worm impaled on a hook. This was his last fling, he knew. He would have to reach this before them or he was finished. He was young and he was strong but there wasn't much breath left in him. And he was hungry. He was conscious of all these things. The blood was pounding in his ears. But he reached the furze-lined road and broke through and gained the other side in a few leaps and rolled and tumbled down the far slopes and lay there completely exhausted, a long briar tendril wrapped around one of his legs and lacerating it. Above him he heard the sound of the horse hooves on the rough stone road.

He got to his feet. Tenderly he unwrapped the briar from his leg. It was dark down here now but there was a long path of moonlight on the water of the great lake. He limped down to the shore. He was walking in the curve of a bay. His feet crushed the wild mint and waves of it rose to his nostrils. He saw the wooded point out from him and he stumbled toward it. He couldn't be seen, but that did not make him safe. There was no inch safe now for him on this side.

When he reached the point and looked at the short stretch of water between him and the other shore he knew that he couldn't swim that far. It was only a few hundred yards, but he was too tired and he had never swum that far before. So wearily he went back into the wood. He searched it in the moonlight until he found a fallen tree that would suit him. Lying there for a year or more, it was well rotted, the middle part broken away, but its core was sound. He managed to raise it on his shoulder and stumbled with it to the shore. Much of it fell away, rotten, but enough remained. He waded with it into the deep water. He got it under his oxters, held the spade and the sodden sack free of the water and kicked out with his feet. The water was calm. There was little wind. In about ten minutes he was free of the path of moonlight and yard by yard the dark bulk of the far shore came nearer to him.

He thought of the giant pike of the lake about which the fishermen told such tales. He wondered if one of them would come up for a look and snap off one of his feet. This made him laugh weakly. It's just the proof of how unsafe land animals feel once they are on the deep water.

The shore came closer and closer until he felt stones under his feet when he let them down, so he freed himself from the almost sinking log and stumbled and fell and rose again until he felt the coarse sand and then his heart sank as the bulk of a big man rose from the gray rocks where he had blended and came toward him. He had a big stick in his hand and he spoke in Irish and he said: "Well, boy, it took you a long time to get here."

Dualta just dropped the spade and sack and sat down drearily on the sand.

chapter IV

DUALTA SAID: "Weren't they cunning to send you to wait for me here? I didn't grant them that much brains."

"Who's this you talk about?" the man asked.

"Them, over there," said Dualta nodding his head at the opposite shore, looking innocent and pleasant under the subtle moonlight.

The man spat.

"The curse of the devil on them," he said.

Dualta was surprised. "You mean they didn't plant you?" he asked.

The man laughed. "The only one who will plant me is the gravedigger," he said. "Stir yourself from that. You must be wet. You'll die of the fever."

Dualta rose to his feet. Now he felt his whole body shivering. "I don't understand. I thought you were one of them."

"I was at the fair with a little pig," the man said. "I saw. It was a brave but foolish thing you did. When I came home I climbed the hill behind. It was good. It was like a story you can see. You on the Mount and the horses and the dogs. I could see it all until the sun went under. I saw the way you were moving. I would have crossed to you with my old thing of a boat, but I was afraid they would see that on the water and be guided to you. So I waited."

"But how about your gentlemen? Won't they know?"

"Let them scratch their own skin. Come. The house is a piece away. The walk will warm you. I will carry your spade." He took it from him and set off walking. Dualta followed him. The wet clothes were cold on him but his heart was warm. He felt like laughing. If this wasn't a trick? Could there be such deceit in such an open countenance? He stopped still. He could run away. The man had close ears. He turned and looked at the stopped figure. He seemed to divine the thoughts of Dualta.

"No, no, man," he said. "It won't do. You will have to take to people. Would I betray you? My name is Joyce."

"It is a good name," said Dualta.

"Our portion of it was never dirtied," said the man.

"Over there nobody raised a hand or a voice for me," said Dualta, "only my uncle."

"He was a good man," said Joyce, "and it was his duty. Why should the others pay a penalty for your spirit?"

"You are," said Dualta.

"Not me," the man laughed. "I teach foxes their tricks. Your passing will leave no more on me than a soft summer wind on the water. Come with me, for God's sake or you will perish with the dampness."

He turned then and walked on.

Dualta followed him, calling out: "Forgive it to me that I doubted you. I am not wise."

"Who is?" the man asked, raising his voice. "Máirtin is my name."

"My deep thanks to you, Máirtin," said Dualta.

"Save your wind," said Máirtin, "it's a stiff climb and you must by this time be weary."

It was a stiff climb, through deep heather and fading thick sedge and soft places where he sank to his shins in brown slime and only with an effort plucked his feet free. He was tired, so the climb took it out of him, but at least it warmed his body and set his clothes steaming. The thickset barefooted man ahead of him walked casually as if he were on a level place with a fair surface.

Dualta was pleased when they came into a declivity where a house was built beside a tumbling mountain stream. The moon shone on the whitewash of the house and the spilled waters of the stream flashed like precious stones. Behind the hill was a cliff, deeply indented by the stream.

Máirtin waited for him at the door of the house. He saw

that the house had no chimney, just a hole in the thatch through which smoke came and was flattened by the twirling currents of air.

"You are welcome," Máirtin said when he reached him. "Go in and stand in front of the fire."

Dualta ducked his head and entered. The place was lighted only by the flames of a roaring turf fire on the open hearth. His nose was assailed with smells, smoke and children and, yes, pigs. There was a sow lying on straw in a corner on his right, penned in by birch poles on short trestles. He looked around. He saw many eyes glinting at him. His eyes became accustomed to the light and he began to pick out the children. Very small, and up. They all seemed the same. He could tell their sex only if they had grown a little big for their tattered wool petticoats. A bigger girl with a dress and a barefooted woman standing near the fire lifted the lid off a steaming potato pot.

"God bless all here," Dualta said.

"You are welcome," the woman said, straightening up.

Máirtin spoke from behind him.

"This is Dualta, the nephew of the schoolmaster," he said. "He is as wet as a trout. Pull the clothes off him, Máire and let him stand in front of the fire."

"God bless us," the woman said, "he looks drowned. Go away children. Pull down, Dualta."

Dualta was embarrassed. He heard Máirtin chuckling.

"Go back up in the room, girls," he said then, "and let the man dry out without your eyes on him."

Four persons detached themselves from the shades. They disappeared behind an opening near the hearth. He heard murmured words and giggles as they vanished. He started to strip himself. It was wonderful to feel the warmth of the fire on his body. Máirtin took his wet clothes and hung them from the iron crooks in the hearth. They began to steam like himself. Then he felt the woman rubbing at his back with a coarse cloth. He was embarrassed. She was clucking with her tongue. "How will you live?" she asked. "You're destroyed with the dampness." He relaxed.

"Here," said Máirtin, "will we empty the sack?"

"Do that," said Dualta, "the things in there must be destroyed too." Máirtin loosed the neck of the wet sack from the spade and reached for the contents. Very pitiful. His extra clothes, his shoes and a pair of woolen stockings. Máirtin hung them all, shaking his head. Then he took out two books. They were wet but one of them had leather bindings and that had saved it. Máirtin looked at them. "This is the English writing is it?"

Dualta looked. It was a copy of Goldsmith's *History of England, Rome, and Greece*. "It is," he said.

"You read and write then?" Máirtin asked.

"My uncle is a schoolmaster," said Dualta.

"That's a wonderful thing, powerful," said Máirtin. "We have no teacher here yet. Some say the priest will get one soon. If you had time you could teach us all to write, or maybe just the little ones. We are ignorant. It is very sad. Maybe the young ones will be better off?"

"Maybe they are better off now without it," said Dualta.

"No, you are wrong," said Máirtin. "This is an English book too?" He was holding up a wet book. The pages were stuck. He was gently releasing them.

"Yes," said Dualta. "That's one about the travels of Gulliver."

"I've heard some of the stories of him," said Máirtin. "The old mother knew a lot of tales. She is dead now, God rest her."

"You are well dry at the back," said Máire, handing him the cloth. "Now rub yourself. I will turn out the pot."

He took the cloth and rubbed himself. He felt better.

"You will be like this Gulliver yourself now, I'm afraid," Máirtin said. "You will have to travel farther than malice."

"Wrap yourself in this and sit," said Máire. She put a thin blanket around his shoulders and at his legs he felt the round cut from a tree. It was seasoned and worn smooth and was a good stool. He pulled the blanket around him and sat.

"You can come down now, girls," Máirtin called. "The man is visible."

They came down from the room huddled close together,

shyly as if he were going to murder them. The other small ones had come closer to him, sitting on the stone floor, their eyes glinting.

"How many have you?" he asked.

"Nine, thank God," said Máirtin. "Four girls and four boys and big Paidi that's out visiting. He's tracking a girl but she'll have none of him. He has nothing and her father has six cattle."

"Maybe the girl prefers Paidi to the cattle?"

"She does not," said Máirtin. "She has a head on her shoulders. Sell trout and eat salted herrings."

Máire was turning the drained pot of potatoes onto a flat round cish. They steamed in their big pile. Some of the jackets were open invitingly.

"You must be weak with the hunger," said Máirtin. "Take up and eat." He blessed himself. Some of the small children were already reaching. They had to pull back their hands reluctantly and bless themselves and listen to their father thanking God melodiously for the pot of potatoes. Then they grabbed.

The potatoes were red hot. They had to dance them from hand to hand as they skinned them. Máire put a tin of course salt beside the kish and handed Dualta a tin mug of buttermilk. He bit into the potato and supped the buttermilk. Bit and supped. Bit and supped and he was as hungry as an animal, but had to restrain himself from eating too fast.

"Paidi will miss his meal," said Máire.

"Let the girl pay for his company," said Máirtin.

The children laughed and the girls giggled, but nobody stopped from reducing the big pile of potatoes. The sow behind them woke from her snoozing and grunted hungrily as the smell of the fresh boiled potatoes reached into her subconscious.

Dualta felt warm, and safe, and the happenings of the day no longer seemed such a nightmare.

He woke with a start, frightened. Over his head in the loft, a cock was crowing. It was a weird sound in the enclosed space of the kitchen. He heard a voice calling and arms reaching with a stick. There was an indignant fluttering of wings, a seeming waterfall of feathers as the cock and the chickens flew down from the loft and were chased protesting like titled ladies into the dawn. All this he could see without opening his eyes. He felt very tired still. He heard the sow protesting then and grunting like an old gentleman as she too was driven from the warm place and out the door. The straw and its covering where he slept were warm. Beside him the four little boys were sleeping, head to toe like oat sheaves in a cart. They looked very young and innocent, their hair tousled, their young faces and brows untroubled.

Then he saw Máirtin at the door. He came over to him.

"You are awake," he said. "Rise up fast. There are boats crossing the loch." Dualta felt his heart sinking as he pushed aside the blanket. The little boys slept on. He put the blanket back over them. He was wearing his own dried shirt. It didn't take him long to get into his breeches. "I have all ready for you," Máirtin was saying. "All packed away. Paidi is keeping an eye on them. We have some cold potatoes that will take the edge off your hunger as you go. I will call him. He will be with you."

Dualta didn't answer him. Máirtin went out the door.

Máire who had been listening to them, suddenly sat on the stool and dropped her head in her hands. He could see long streaks of gray in her brown hair. She wasn't an old woman. Her shoulders were heaving.

"Tell me, what is wrong?" Dualta asked. "Have I upset you?"

She shook her head.

"Paidi is going away," she said.

"He will be back at Christmas," said Dualta.

"He will be missed," she said. "He is very lively."

"It's not as if he was going away forever," said Dualta. "You have eight others."

"That makes no difference," she said. "Miss one, miss all. Each one is a new bit of your heart. When he goes it is taken away."

Who would feel like that for me? Dualta thought.

Máirtin was at the door again.

"Are you all but ready?" Máirtin asked.

"Yes," said Dualta. He looked at Máire. She had blue eyes. One time she must have been beautiful. She had regular features.

"I thank you," he said to her, trying to express all that he felt in a few words. "May you be blessed." He went to the door and into the light. The sun was barely over the horizon. Here they were shut away from its light by the hills behind. He saw the young man running toward him. He was jumping wet places like a goat. A big young man with thickly muscled bare legs, unruly brown hair, big white teeth in a generous mouth, and well worn patched clothes.

He stopped in front of them.

"They are halfway across," he said. "You must be important, Dualta. They want very much to get close to you. Maybe they want you to marry one of their daughters. Did you injure her?"

He thought this was funny. He laughed, slapping his thigh.

"You better go if you are going," said Máirtin. He spoke gruffly. He didn't meet his son's eyes, Dualta noticed.

"Yes," said Paidi. "I will get my things and say farewell to the family. Are the young ones awake?"

"They seem to be still sleeping," said Dualta.

"That's as well," said Paidi, "otherwise they would be making noises like bonhams. Anyone would think I was going away forever."

"If he didn't go and earn a little at the digging," said Máirtin, "how would we pay our rent? Isn't it better for him to go for a little than for the lot of us to be tramping the roads forever?"

"Paidi will get you across the hills," said Máirtin then. "He is to meet other diggers on the far side and you can travel south together."

"That will be good," said Dualta. "They say down there that there are men who are not afraid of their landlords. They even kill them."

Máirtin was silent.

"Take it easy," he said then. "You are too young to feel that way. There is great talk of a man called O'Connell. He is only a Munsterman but there might be some good in him."

"I have heard of him," said Dualta. "He talks. He doesn't do anything."

"The gift of the talk might be better than a charge from a gun," said Máirtin.

Paidi came running out of the house with a spade on his shoulder and the bundle tied to it.

"Come on," Paidi called. "Are we to be here all day? Shouldn't we have miles of the road over us by now? Women and children! Listen, I leave you well, Father. I will be back with the Christmas and some gold guineas in my pocket. You hear."

"I do," said Máirtin. "Don't stand there talking about them. Be off with you and may the luck rise with the both of you. Here's your spade and things, Dualta. I nearly deprived you of them."

"Come on! Come with me!" said Paidi, suddenly moving away. Dualta looked at Máirtin.

"Thank you from my heart, Máirtin," he said, and then followed after. Paidi set a murderous pace. He jumped the stream from rock to rock, his bare feet gripping the wet stones like suckers. Then he turned right and started climbing the hill. He looked back once. Máire was at the door and the girls were clustered around her like chickens. They were waving their hands.

"You'd think a man was going away forever," Paidi was saying. Then he said no more. The climbing took all of their breath and attention. Halfway, they rested. They sat in the heather. They could no longer see Máirtin's house. They could see the edge of the lake and the place where three boats were pulled up on the shore. Below them they saw groupings of houses clustered together in valley villages, up on the sides of hills, away from the good lands below, where they had been forced to carve fields from stony ground and boggy land.

"You needn't worry," said Paidi, "in a good cause, the biggest and most expert liars in Ireland live down there."

"How did they know I crossed?" Dualta asked.

"Somebody on the other side must have seen you," said Paidi. "We better get over the crest. The lads will be waiting on the road on the far side. You won't be alone any more, Dualta. We'll get through to the south, don't fear. I wouldn't mind if we had to spill a bit of blood doing it either." He looked back once more and was sorry he had done so. Some of the young ones had climbed a shoulder of a hill and were standing there waving. You could see sadness in their waving.

Paidi turned away and began furiously to climb the hill.

When they topped the great hill and before they moved down they could see a thousand lakes stretched at their feet. Paidi searched the ground below with his eyes. Dualta could make out the winding ribbon of dirt road going in and out between the lakes like a snake. Paidi shouted. He professed to see a cluster of men moving on the road. Dualta couldn't make them out. Paidi said, laughing, "You wouldn't do in the Revenue," and set off running.

It took them nearly an hour to reach the rough road below where ten young men were gathered waiting for them. As they came in sight, they shouted and waved calling: "Run! run, you devils!" and Paidi and Dualta looked at each other and smiled and started to run. It was hardly fair. Dualta was slender and less heavy. If you roll a light rock and a heavy rock down the side of a hill which gets below first? I don't know, but Dualta was the first to reach the road.

"Oh, you are getting weak, Paidi," one young man said. "It must be all the courting."

They laughed at this.

Paidi, almost breathless, said: "This is Dualta. He is coming with us."

They welcomed him. They were roughly dressed in homespun clothes. They carried spades, and some of them had their shoes tied around their necks. They were well burned by the sun. One of them was sitting at the side of the road tying a rag on a bloody big toe.

"Were you dancing, Fursa?" Paidi asked him. They laughed.

"I hit me toe against a cursed rock," said Fursa. Tenderly he patted the brand new shoes hanging around his neck. "Wasn't it a damn good job I wasn't wearing my new shoes."

They laughed hilariously at this old joke and then in a group they hefted their spades and their sparse possessions and set out for the distant town, the bottleneck leading to the south.

It was a fine day and the sun shone on them.

chapter V

THEY WERE SITting on stones outside some of the thatched houses in the liberties putting on their shoes when they saw the long procession coming from behind them. They had been about five hours walking, but Dualta had felt the road short on him. All the diggers were young. The eldest of them wasn't yet twenty-one. They were lighthearted and they joked and they sang and they told stories about the odd people in their own places. They talked about how much they might earn in the south. Some held that they might get up to tenpence a day. Others were more pessimistic. They thought maybe fivepence with a meal of potatoes. Fursa said it was a pity they couldn't have made the trip in August when they could have gone to Dublin and crossed to Scotland. He said one of theirs who had to return because he had lost three fingers with a carelessly swung sickle had been making over a shilling a day, and after paying his way on the boat, he had two pounds fifteen shillings when he got home. Wasn't this wealth in a short time?

"He had to walk and work for it," said Paidi.

Tomás Mór was walking carefully on the road trying to get the feel of his shoes. He was hobbling.

"God, they are killing me!" he said. "They are murder. I'll never abide them. Curse them! I'll take them off again."

"You won't," said Fursa. "Do you want to make a disgrace of us walking the town in your bare hooves? Don't they think little enough of us as it is?"

Dualta tentatively walked himself. It had been many months since he had worn shoes. They were made big for him, but the woolen stockings and the pressure of the hard leather were compressing his feet so that they felt like hot coals.

"Watch what's coming up the road," said Fursa. "What's happening?"

They looked. The procession stretched in a long file. It was headed by a carriage drawn by two horses. Behind that were men on horseback, then people walking and a few common carts with people sitting up on them, more people walking and the rear was brought up by farther men on horseback.

"I declare it must be an election. There must be an election in town," said Fursa. "Hey," he called to a man across the street leaning on the half door of his house. "What's up in town. Is there an election?" The man cupped his ear with his hand. Fursa went halfway across to him. "Is there an election, I asked?" he shouted.

"Oh, yes, yes, yes," said the man. "Why don't you talk proper Irish?"

Paidi laughed. "You hear that, Fursa," he said. "Take the turf out of your mouth."

"I've a good mind to go over and break your mouth," said Fursa to the man.

"What you say?" he asked.

"I hope it's an election," said Tomás Mór. "We might get a few free drinks by stealth."

"I said I'd like to give you a kick in the belly," said Fursa whose face was red. The rest of them laughed watching his rage.

"I don't understand a word you're saying," the man said. He was genuinely exasperated.

"You ignorant bostoon!" Fursa shouted.

"Ah," the man said, "I know what that means. You can't come from the bog and talk like that to your betters. Get on about your business or I'll go over and chastise you."

Fursa was dancing with rage in the middle of the rutted road.

The carriage was level with him. It slowly passed by. There was an upright gentleman sitting in it. His hands were resting on a stick. He had a tall gray hat on him. He kept his eyes strictly in front of him, never looked out the window.

Then Paidi started calling sheep. "Ma-a-a! Ma-a-a-a! Ma-a-a-a!" The rest of them took it up too. People came to the doors of houses grinning to see what it was about, and they too started calling sheep.

Dualta watched the leading horseman. You could recognize the agent and behind him the bailiff, attended by satellite bailiffs with thick blackthorn sticks in their hands. They were walking. There were at least thirty people walking or riding the carts. These didn't like the calling. Some of them flushed. Some of them just looked straight ahead. Some of them dropped their eyes.

Dualta felt sorry for them. It wasn't their fault. They were the forty-shilling freeholders, who were neither free nor holding anything. They did look like sheep, gathered into the fold, tended by shepherds who told them there was an election and when and how they were to go and who they were to vote for. It was as simple as that. If they didn't do what they were told, their houses would be pulled down about their ears and they would be given the road. Dualta wondered what he would do if he were a forty-shilling freeholder. It didn't mean anything anyhow. It was just a device created by the landlords to make things look good. The more freeholders they had who they could make vote in the right way, the greater their chances for patronage in a sea of corruption.

They weren't all meek. One big walking man shook his fist at them and would have come to them if his wife wasn't pulling at his elbow. Three of the bailiffs came out of the line and walked toward them, waving their sticks.

They contented themselves with saying "Hold your tongues, you!" because they were faced by twelve healthy young men with spades whose digging edges were sharpened by stones. Someday, Dualta thought cynically, these same young men would be in the shoes of their fathers and they too, however full of bile, and whatever dignity and pride they had to swallow, would join in the landlord's procession to the polling booths.

"Leave them be," Dualta suddenly said, loudly.

The others looked at him wonderingly. But they stopped.

But what they had started continued. The chorus of ma-a-a's went with the procession all through the west liberties, by the collection of thatched houses, right up to the three-story stone houses built this side of the bridge.

The diggers, walking carefully and painfully in their shoes, shouldered their spades and walked toward the bridge after the voters. From here in, the whole place was as packed with people as a potato pit with potatoes. There was hardly room to move. One or two dray-type carts with goods on them were having a hard time getting through the crowds. The drivers were standing lashing the patient horses and cursing at the people. Plodding horses with panniers were everywhere, their owners shouting to let them through, let them through. You could distinguish the country people from the townspeople by their ruddy faces and heavy-type clothes. Many town children, badly clad, barefooted, dirty-faced were eeling their way, shouting and begging with dirty little palms upturned, and even stealing. Dualta saw as they grabbed a cake from a stall and ran. There was no order at all. It was all confusion. Somewhere up ahead of them brass instruments were blaring. Lots of men were drunk, singing to the sky with their heads back. His nostrils were brutally assailed with unaccustomed smells so that he had to pinch them. Not that that did any good. The road and pavements were badly potholed and had been filled with rubbish that was tramped down and exuded very unsavory smells, particularly once they had passed the clean torrent of the river piling under the bridge.

Here there were many drunken men wearing colored favors in their hats and waving black sticks. They started to shout at the carriage ahead and at those following the carriage. "Go home! Go home! ye cowards! Ye traitors! Ye dirty vote-sellers!" Many worse things, and cabbage stalks and dirt were flung from the side.

The bailiff came back on his horse to them. He looked at them.

"Do you want a free drink, some free food?" he asked.

"Ah," said Fursa, "you are talking to our bellies."

"Go each side of the people then," the bailiff said, "as far as the booths and we'll fill them for ye."

Fursa looked at Paidi. They grinned. They nodded. "We're your men," said Paidi. "Hey, lads. Split up, each side of the freeholders and guard them with your lives. We don't know who they are voting for but sure they came from the west side of the bridge."

They laughed and split into two sizes and using the handles of their spades freely they walked as a guard each side of the people. They were nearly all tall young men and strong men. When the others maa-ed they meigled. When the others waved their black sticks they swung their gleaming spades which were longer and had a farther reach. They drew on their deep knowledge of the language to return a double curse for a single one, a scorching obscenity for an insulting one. It was a wonderful bedlam of noise and counternoise, with the citizens straining their necks to see and people leaning precariously out of the narrow windows of the tall-storied houses to cheer and counter-cheer and sometimes throw things onto the gathering below.

Dualta felt excited with it. The streets were so narrow and the houses so tall that the sound reverberated all over the sky. He got glimpses of the shop windows through the narrow panes. He got glimpses through the arches into the Spanish-type court-yards, men thronged and jammed into the tippling houses, the smell of spices and horse dung and sweat and dirt and harness and oil and smoke. He had never been in the midst of so many people before. He felt choked, smothered, blocking the blow of a blackthorn stick with the handle of the spade, laughing into a suffused drunken countenance. When he was called "You Connermara pig!" he would answer "You Galway gurnet!" and whether his insulter came from Galway or not, it seemed to infuriate him. One of them appealed to God in heaven and then jammed his beaver hat down on his own face. But they were all sturdy and they kept the barrier, so that the freeholders they were protecting became bold and hurled back insults too, and rose in their carts and made speeches to the sky. And all the time Dualta knew that the gentleman in the carriage ahead of them was sitting with his face to the front and his hands on his stick and he might as well be anywhere but where he was for all the attention he was paying to the mob.

After some time they made their way into the open space where the booths were. Here it was not as noisy. Disdainful soldiers sat on horses and looked down from their eminence. Elegantly dressed ladies sat on seats on the steps of the court-house and watched the confusion as if they were at a playhouse. Satins and curling hair and flashing teeth and smooth men in expensive breeches with tall velvet collars and gleaming hats tilted over one eye. The soldiers held the opening into the square so that they left the main noise behind them, and the horsemen dismounted, and the men came down from their carts and they went into the booths and publicly and in a loud voice announced who was their man, and God help them if they forgot who he was, as some of them were inclined to do, never having met him and knowing nothing about him. Some of them had taken the time to have his name written on a piece of paper which they looked at before they called out his name confidently as if they were in the room the day his mother was delivered of him. Dualta saw little of this. He was eating cold beef, a thing he had not done for many a year, and mutton, and eating great chunks from a white loaf, and flagons of Persse's porter and glasses of Joyce's whiskey, he who had never drunk anything stronger than buttermilk, but his life was so changed, and he felt that it was changed for good here in an alien place smoth-ered with people, where it was hard to breathe and impossible to think, where his heart was aching for the slow philosophical speech of his uncle Marcus, the scholars chanting, the evening he had missed in the house of the father of Sorcha, the laughter and the sly humor and the fresh wind blowing on the Mount and the sight of the sun on the waters of the lake, all that, all that behind him, hatred in him for what had made him leave it, fear in him of what was before him—lost he was like a feather on an outgoing tide, like a thistle on the wind, like a call in a valley deriding you as it receded, so sad that he sat and rested his back against a stall and cried, silently, the tears running down his face, inside he cheering at himself remembering what they said that a man was soft in drink.

Paidi's face learing at him. "Get up! Get up! Dualta. See what I have found for you!" Paidi not drunk. His eyes clear. Shaking his head. A girl with red hair and white skin, looking at him, a frown between her brows. He is only a child, what have ye done to him? Not a child. A man I am. We are slaves. You hear that. Look at those stupid people walking into those stupid booths and voting for men they never heard of. Is this the action of free men, or is it the action of slaves?

Paidi saying I didn't know he knew books so well. Get up and we'll go to the dry lodgings. This is Ellen. She pities you. She will get us dry lodgings where they stay themselves in Crotty's of Gut Lane. Isn't she decent? Come, come, Dualta, my father would kill me if he saw I had done this to you. Come let us help you.

I need no help from anyone. I am on my own. I can rise to my own feet and walk. All the things I can weep for too, singing in my head.

Paidi calling: Come on, men, come on we are going to the lodgings, gather yourselves and follow after us.

Walking. Paidi's strong hand under his elbow, and a soft arm holding his other arm. Sometimes his arm hit against her soft breast and it only made him want to cry, bringing back to his mind in a vague misty flash the time he had a mother, that he belonged to somebody.

There was the press of people again, the loud shouting. The cursing, forcing their way through throngs and multitudes. Shouting and cursing. What was the world coming to? Where was the place that there was only the cry of the curlew, the blackbirds frightened clack at the going down of the sun. Connemara cattle! Galway gurnets! Clashing of wood on wood and shouts and screams of laughter. This was what elections meant, where simple people chose honest men who would represent them in the corporation or the faraway dream land of London where their representatives would go in order to bring in more Coercion Acts, or something else that would bind them deeper to their chains. Where all these thoughts came from, liberated from a bottle, or from the austere style of the poets talking of long times ago when men were free and had access to the boards of their lords to argue and declare their freedom and their rights. He remembered no more.

chapter VI

They stood for sale in the market place of the southern town on a warm autumnal day.

It was an uneasy town.

They had seen the posted notice on a tree as they were coming in that morning. On top of the notice was a crude drawing of a coffin.

Underneath the coffin was written in the two tongues:

> This is waiting for any Digger
> who hires himself for less
> than ONE SHILLING per day.
> signed
> Captain White

They were staring at it when one of the new police came from the town and tore it from the tree. He was a smart-looking man with his flat conical hat. There weren't a lot of these new police around. They were already beginning to be called Peelers on account of the man who had created them. They were sent to act as the leaven in the dough of the baronial police known as the rough-and-ready boys. This one had been a soldier, Dualta thought. He walked very straight.

He said to them, "You know what this is?"

Of course they looked at him stupidly with their mouths half open.

So to their surprise he broke into fluent Irish.

"You do not accept this," he said. "You will go in and hire yourself at the prevailing rates and you will not allow yourselves to be intimidated by anyone. You will be protected."

"We thank you," said Dualta, so he marched away from them, before going, turning to point to a most official-looking notice farther on. Instead of a coffin this had a crown on the top of it, but it more or less meant the same thing, that under the Insurrection Act of such a date and the Coercion Act of such another date, this district was under military law. You were to be at home at such a time and not abroad at such another time, not to gather together in groups of more than two or three.

"Between the Whiteboys and the Kingsboys," said Dualta grinning, "I can see we are going to have a hard time."

Paidi was uneasy.

"Maybe we ought to pass this town by, Dualta," he said. "Why should we want trouble? I just want to make a few pounds in peace and go home."

"There aren't a lot of towns left, Paidi," said Dualta. "And the season is getting late. I like the look of this town. Let us go in and see what happens."

"I don't like police," said Paidi. "I don't like soldiers. I feel toward them as a fisherman feels toward a redheaded woman or the blacksmith feels toward the tailor."

Dualta laughed.

"Come, Paidi," he said. "Don't you feel the blood quickening in your veins? Here we will have a combination of work and danger."

"Maybe it's what you are looking for," said Paidi. "But I want none of it. I would like to make my own trouble, not to have it ready made like a suit of clothes."

Dualta set off walking toward the old west gate of the town. Paidi caught up with him.

He noticed the silence in the marketplace. That was unusual. Marketplaces are always full of sound, people calling and shouting, cursing or singing. But here sound was muted. They passed by long rows of thatched cottages, some of them very dirty looking. There were many puddles in the badly paved road. They could hear the sound of their own shoes on the stones. You could trace the silence to the soldiers who sat on trained horses, unmoving, silent except for the noise the bit made when a horse occasionally shook his head, or to the armed rough-and-ready boys who moved in twos or fours, armed, not erect figures like the Peelers but slouching, untidy, some of them fat, looking around them with suspicious eyes.

The silence reminded Dualta of the mountain. Mostly on account of the rain, mountains sing. There are always streams rushing down the sides of them, bubbling and gurgling their way, goughing out a bed. So it is a strange thing to walk a mountain in a drought, going after sheep or herding heifers to the new sedge. The silence is almost shocking, like this market-place now.

They came to the hiring place. They could recognize it from the way the cold sun was reflecting from the brightened blades of the spades of the diggers.

They joined this group of men, who looked at them silently, with no animosity, or no friendliness either, for that matter. Dualta tried to think of where they had come from. It was hard to tell. He knew there was no Connachtman among them. But that was as far as he could go. He marveled at the antipathy to the Connachtmen they had met on their way. Near Galway it was fear of the Connemaramen; farther south it was the Connachtmen. He supposed it was natural. Bands of men going and coming from the harvest were well behaved in places, but sometimes when they had money they got drunk in the dry lodgings, and they sang wild songs and they danced wild dances and they cried, and sometimes they made love with their wild magic to the girls, and when they departed, sometimes in the dark of night, without paying the twopence for the shelter, they left behind them curses and tears.

He thought of his companions. One by one or two by two they had dropped off. Most of them he had liked. One or two of them he had not liked. They were brutal, almost primitive, illiterate. These were the ones that would fight at the drop of a hat over nothing, their faces red, their eyes with red anger in them. Paidi was different. He had to be as the son of his father. Dualta was sure he could have hired himself before this, but that he wanted to be with Dualta. Did he promise his father some such? Did he think Dualta wasn't able to look after himself? He felt older than Paidi, although he wasn't. But he liked his honesty, the purity of his joking, his deference toward women; he the man with the reputation he had among his fellows. Paidi was a good man. Dualta hoped that they would not be parted.

But they were, of course.

A large man with a roll of fat on his neck and very plump cheeks. It was somewhat like buying a bullock you were suspicious of. This man walked around the thinning group of diggers, in front of them and then around the back of them, sizing them up. The only thing he didn't do was to poke their buttocks with his stick. Paidi caught his eye. Paidi wasn't tall, but he was powerfully muscular-looking. How many baskets of potatoes could you dig in a day? They had boasted about their prowess on the road, claiming feats of digging that would shame Fionn Mac Cumhail. How much turf could they cut in a day? How much hay could they lay with the scythe? Paidi never boasted. Just he would say: "Oh, a fair amount, a fair amount!"

"Come here to me," the man beckoned Paidi. He went to him.

"You will dig for me?" the man asked.

"For how much?" asked Paidi.

"Eightpence," said the man.

Paidi opened his blue eyes wide. "Oh, I would be afraid," he said. "We read a notice on a tree. They said they would fill the coffins with men that worked for less than a shilling a day."

"The curse of hell on them!" said the man. "It's easy known that they don't have to hire anyone."

"Maybe they wouldn't put their own people in coffins," said Paidi, "but I'm a stranger. They would plant me and sleep easy. I will give you value for your money."

The man looked at him.

"A shilling less twopence for food," he said. Paidi thought over that. He nodded. "All right," he said, "if you will hire my friend."

"Who is he?" he asked. Paidi pointed him out. "He looks thin," the man said. "Would he have the staying power? He looks more like a clerk."

"He's stronger than a dray horse," said Paidi.

"I don't want another digger," the man said. "I'm a poor man. Come with me," he said in a loud voice. "I will give you a shilling a day." This for the benefit of the listeners. He walked up to Dualta. "Your friend wants you," he said. "You only look like a boy to me, so I will give you boy's wages and food."

Dualta smiled.

"Judging by the look of you," he said, "the food would be thin."

Surprisingly the man laughed. His belly shook.

"Wit is a poor digger of potatoes," he said. "I don't want you but your friend wants you. I cannot pay two men's wages."

"I will wait," said Dualta. "Go with the man, Paidi."

A cloud passed over Paidi's open countenance.

"Who are you?" Dualta asked the man.

"I am Heffernan," the man said. "I live near the cross of the Hanging Tree, six miles to the northeast of the town."

"See, Paidi," said Dualta. "I know where you are. On the Sunday sometime I will seek you."

Paidi didn't want to leave him. He thought how much he had enjoyed the company of Dualta, sharing the knowledge he possessed that he had plucked from his ability to read. Many things, true companionship. Paidi thought, this is fine, but how can the poor afford pleasures? He should have hired himself out days ago. Each day he didn't work was so much less to pay the rent at home. And they were so depending on his labor. He decided.

"I will be seeing you so. You will trace me?" he asked.

"I will," said Dualta.

"I have a cart the other side of the town," Heffernan said. He walked away almost waddling. Paidi shouldered his spade. He looked quickly into Dualta's eyes, and then dropped his head.

"I will go," he said. "I will see you."

"With the help of God," said Dualta. He watched him as he turned away. Paidi walked slowly and then quickened his pace with determination. He didn't turn his head. Soon they were lost to sight. Dualta looked at the sky. It was coldly blue with flecks of fine weather clouds traced all over it. It's as well to be without Paidi, he thought. Now I have no props at all. I am on my own. It is better to be this way. You cannot afford to become fond of people. Opposite him a hill rose high over the roofs of the thatched houses. It was a tall hill with the wide river at the foot of it. It could remind him of home if it wasn't a cultivated hill, right up to its peak, a verdant hill, fully clothed with green fields and tall timber.

The Bianconi car passed him, on its long trip to Limerick. It was a silent journey for this car. Normally there was great noise and confusion when the Bianconi cars passed, plagued with the shouts of about fifty beggar boys, nearly naked, pleading with their hands out and practiced tears in their eyes, the driver cracking the whip and shouting, the people settling into their precarious perches, the ladies in the long seats holding onto their bonnets, the jingling of the harness. Now it passed by in silence, and even the horses seemed to be trotting carefully and decorously.

There were many gentlemen in the town. They rode their horses and they were all heavily armed, pistols sticking out all over them, and behind, their bullyboys walked or rode carrying sticks or blunderbusses over their shoulders. Something is really stirring in this place, Dualta thought, if only I could get to the heart of it.

"You there, come here," he heard a voice calling. He focused his eyes. There was a horseman in the middle of the road pointing at him with a whip. He was a young man, well dressed, white breeches of broadcloth pushed into black polished boots with the tops turned down. Bile rose in Dualta at the sight of him. He could have been the Half-Sir. Dualta didn't move.

"Do you hear me talking to you? Come here!"

Dualta didn't move. He saw the anger rising in the young man's face. Very quickly he was off his horse, the reins trailing and he was approaching Dualta with determination.

"When I call, come to me, do you hear?" he was saying as he came forward. He was not deterred by the sudden flashing of the eyes of the boy facing him nor of the way his knuckles had whitened on the handle of the spade. I will let him hit me, Dualta thought, and then I will split him with the spade.

The form of the policeman stepped between them.

"Is there anything wrong, sir?" this man asked. He was the one who had torn down the notice.

"I called this thick," said the gentleman, "and he spurned me. If you stand aside, Sergeant, I will teach him manners."

"Sir, things are tense in this town today. It would be better for the peace if you decided to be reasonable." He looked at Dualta. "I don't think this fellow understands English," he said.

"Yes, I do," said Dualta. "You are mixing me up with my friend. He did not understand English. I do."

"Why didn't you answer the gentleman?" the policeman asked.

"I am not a dog," said Dualta. "He beckoned as if he was calling his dog."

"You are for hire, aren't you?" the young gentleman asked angrily.

"Yes," said Dualta.

"Well, then," he said as if this was the end of the argument.

"I have to like the looks of the people to whom I will hire myself," said Dualta. "I don't like your looks."

The young man's face became suffused with anger. Dualta's face was white under the sun color and his eyes were sparking. The young man suddenly looked around him and was upset by what he saw. They were deeply surrounded by a ring of countrymen. It seemed to have happened in a moment. Tall men and short men and young men, with impassive faces, just looking at him. They were completely hemmed in. The ring around them was at least five men deep. At the outer ring some of the rough-and-ready boys were trying to force their way into the center, but were unable to make their way through the solid mass of bodies.

"If you desire to hit me with that whip, just do so," said Dualta.

The policeman looked around him.

"Now, now," he said. "No need for that tone, I'm sure. The gentleman had no intention of hitting you."

"Certainly not," said the gentleman. "Why should I soil my whip?" He was brave enough. He started to walk through the crowd of men as if they weren't there. They opened a lane for him. He reached his horse. He mounted. He stood looking down at them. They all stared back at him impassively. He was daunted. You could see that. He would like to make a gesture but he couldn't think of one. So he brought the whip down viciously on the flank of the horse. The horse whinnied and reared and then galloped.

The policeman said to Dualta, "You are a lucky young man."

Dualta said, "Why do you say that?"

"Many reasons," said the policeman. Then he turned to the crowd. "Go on now! Go about your business. Break up this crowd. It's against the law."

Gradually the mass moved, drifting away until Dualta was left with the policeman and the three or four rough-and-ready boys ruefully regarding the Sergeant.

"You could be a dead young man now," said the policeman. "Watch yourself. Keep out of trouble. It's possible that the young gentleman will be back with friends. I would advise you to change your position."

"I will stay where I am," said Dualta.

"I told you," said the policeman and walked away. The others followed him, looking like mongrels trailing a greyhound.

Dualta was looking after him when a voice said, "Has no man hired you?"

Automatically, as if he had read it, Dualta said: "No man, Lord."

Then he turned to look at the voice. He was looking at a tall man with a deeply lined face. He wore no hat. He had white hair that looked too old for his face. It was a strong face, with two lines of bitterness cutting between his nose and his chin. His eyes were a very pale blue and his eyebrows were black. A strange interesting-looking countenance.

"You are a young man of learning," he said.

"I have some," said Dualta. He noticed they were talking Irish. Sometimes he found it hard to understand the Irish of the south. They put the emphasis on different parts of the words and almost sang some of the vowels, elided more, thinned others. But this man spoke very clearly.

"Do you seek trouble deliberately?" he asked. "Do you wish to embrace it?"

"No," said Dualta. "He reminded me of somebody. My good sense deserted me."

"You are not without courage," said the man.

"What is courage?" Dualta asked.

"Facing your oppressors with a straight back," said the man. "That is courage. But it must be done at an opportune time. You are free to be hired. Will you hire yourself to me?"

"What is the rate?" Dualta asked.

The man laughed.

"I don't know," he said. "Whatever you are worth. Maybe nothing. You will get opportunities to fight oppression. You will be able to hit back? Does the thought of that please you?"

"It does," said Dualta.

The man held out his hand. "My name is Cuan McCarthy," he said. "You will have to trust me."

Dualta felt the hard hand that firmly grasped his own. The look of the man was open and direct, and held promise. Of what? Dualta didn't know, but his pulse tingled.

"I am your man," he said.

"Come with me," said Cuan. "I have a spare horse which I purchased today. That will be your first job, to ride it, without a saddle," he added.

"My seat would not know the feel of a saddle," said Dualta. "It was educated to the bare back of a pony."

The man smiled.

"We will go the back way," he said, "because the policeman was right. Your antagonist will return. We will leave him to weep."

He turned abruptly and walked away.

Dualta hefted his spade and followed him and his heart was beating faster than usual.

part two

chapter VII

THE WOMAN SAID, "Are you ready?" "Yes," said Dualta dipping his quill in the inkhorn.

"The first one to Tooley," she said. "Write that he has only hours to withdraw his bid on the land of the Ryans. You know how to say it."

Dualta wrote:

> "Tooley. You have been warned.
> You have only hours left.
> Go now, and withdraw your bid.
> You know the consequences.
>   Captain Right"

Nothing disturbed the silence but the scratching of the quill on the paper. Dualta considered it. He decided to leave it bare without any flourishes. He rose from the table and carried it over to her. Before he handed it to her he held it in front of the fire to dry, careful that the thin ink didn't run. She took it. She was sitting beside the fire. Her head bent over the letter. Her hair was uncovered. She was an enormous fat woman. Her hair was still black. It was parted in the center and pulled back. It gleamed. She had a good forehead. From below her forehead her face started to swell. Then her body, all the way down to her ankles. She had small feet. They were encased in boots that would barely fasten around her ankles. He watched her as she read. Her face didn't register anything.

"Now the other," she said as she folded the letter carefully.

He went back to the table. He thought, tickling his lips with the goosequill. This one would have to be different.

He crossed a cross with a cross three times on the head of the paper. That looked spiky. Then he wrote:

"Hanley: This is the last warning.
Go, or you will sleep in the
Embrace of the Briars.
Captain Rock"

He smiled as he read that. He thought of Hanley, Wilcocks' bailiff, a white-skinned man, with soft hands and a comfortable stomach. He thought of him being stripped naked, of the six-foot hole being dug in the earth, filled around with briars and the soft body of Hanley being forced into this bed. He had a bald head. It would be gleaming whitely in the light of the torches. He would undoubtedly scream as the briars tore his soft flesh. He would be terrified at the thought of the briar-bed. Dualta thought he could afford to smile. Because it had never been done on anyone around here yet. The threat of it was sufficient as soon as the word of its having been done to someone somewhere else, sometime, percolated into the valley. He wondered if anyone had ever slept in the briar bed. He was assured that they had done so in other places. But as far as Dualta was concerned it was a game. He loved writing these threatening letters.

He went and handed it to her.

She read it and laughed.

"That will frighten Hanley," she said. "He is soft. It would do him no harm to get a few briar thorns into his softness. We will add to the letter with a bit of action. He is already afeared. I would say that he is ready to go."

He was glad that she was pleased. She was a formidable woman. Perhaps it was the fatness of her that never allowed an expression to move the heaviness of her countenance. The small hands, the small feet looked innocuous, Missis Annie, widow woman who ran a small shop at the cross roads in the valley. She had small even teeth and when she smiled she looked so jolly.

"How long have you been here now?" she asked.

"Say six months," said Dualta.

"We will have to get another writer," she said.

"Why so?" he asked. "Am I not satisfactory?"

"Oh, yes, dear," she said. "But they get to know. You can tell a man from his hand. If it is too well known, someday you will write and somebody will see and recognize, and they will say: Oh, that is the hand of the young Connachtman that works for Annie. You see?"

"Yes," said Dualta.

"But you will advise," she said. "Some of your imaginations would chill the blood of an eel. Go see if there is any sign of McCarthy."

Dualta went to the door.

It was a good sheltered valley, covered off by the Knockmealdown Mountains, and if you were high enough you looked left and saw the Galtees away off, and when you looked right you could see the Monevalagh, with the Comeraghs behind them. He supposed that was why the people were fighters. The men all seemed to have long jaws that could clamp shut like the grip of a vise. The valley itself was rich and lush, cultivated almost to the peak of the hills, a thing Dualta could never get used to. But if you looked closely you realized that all the houses were pressed back up into the high ground. The river that bisected the valley had rich fields on either side of it, and these rich fields seemed as if they had inexorably pushed back the houses and the smaller fields, pressed them and forced them back up the hills, while on the far side of the river a three-story stone house, with pillars at its great front door, lay snug in the middle of a park field of thirty acres. The sun was shining on it now. The river was gleaming, the fresh leaves were peeping on the great trees in the parkland. Behind the house he could see the carriage houses and the hay barns and the horse stalls. He thought: if the little houses and fields had been pushed back over the years, they were now reaching out and bit by bit trying to embrace part of what they had been deprived of, and the rich lands were shivering.

"You are looking at your future home," said the voice behind him.

"What's that?" said Dualta. He turned and saw Cuan. "I never saw you coming although I was on the watch for you. What do you mean, my future home?"

"You are going to live there," said Cuan.

"I am?" asked Dualta. "I suppose I'm going to marry Wilcocks' daughter?"

McCarthy laughed.

"Don't be that ambitious," he said. "No, we have been gradually reducing his workmen as you know. So we are going to send you to work for him. He will be pleased to have you. He would be pleased to have a cripple not to mind a strong man."

"Do you wish to make me a Trojan horse?" Dualta asked.

"The very thing," said McCarthy, "the very thing. Come in and we will talk to Annie."

They went toward the house. Then Cuan's eye was caught by the movement in the valley. "Stop," he said. They turned and looked. On the road behind the big house there was a cavalcade of men moving. The dark-clothed ones were on horseback. They were armed. There were other horsemen and walking men with implements on their shoulders. Cuan walked quickly to the door, "Come out, Annie," he called. "They are going to knock Morogh Ryan." He came back and stood beside Dualta. His fists were clenched, Dualta saw, and the jaw muscles were bulging on his face. His eyes were slitted as he watched. The bitter lines near his mouth were very deep.

"He is for eviction?" Dualta asked.

"He is," said Cuan, "he is for eviction."

"He is a weak man," said Dualta. "He was bound to go to the wall someday."

Cuan turned on him. "Whose fault?" he asked. "Whose fault? Because he is weak all the more reason that he should find true justice. A strong man can look after himself. Your day will come! You talk like that and your day will come too, then you will look around you and you will find no pity."

Dualta remained silent. Morogh Ryan bid for land at a very

high price. He had five acres. He paid a rent of five pounds an acre. That was twenty pounds. Even with his potatoes and his bit of oats and his cows and his pig, it was not enough to pay the rent. Because he was a lazy man anyhow, and he grew weeds. You didn't need to be a prophet to know that he would one day fall. It was part of life. He wasn't a good man with land. He should never have bid for what he couldn't afford.

"You can't understand," said Cuan. "You are young. You dismiss men like straws. It's not the men. It's the system. Morogh has five children. What will become of them? He will go into a town and at the outskirts he will build a wretched shelter. He will beg and look for odd jobs and he will scour rubbish heaps. Unless God is better to him than now, he will have to sell the small bodies of his daughters for a stone of potatoes. Yes, he is a weak man, is Morogh."

Annie was standing beside them. Her arms were folded. They watched it all enacted. The people converging on the house. There was no wall around it. Just a rough yard in front with the manure heap piled high near the door. There was smoke rising from the thatch. The sun didn't glint off the windows because they held no glass. They saw the figure of Morogh at the door, and then his wife, and the children emerging like rabbits out of a burrow. They saw the hands waving. It didn't take long. They saw the hooks tied to ropes thrown over the thatch and the men straining, like the rope-pulling teams at the harvest sports, and then there was a crack, audible even to them watching and the roof collapsed. It was a one-roomed cottage. The supports of the thatch were gone, just one or two blackened beams crooked and exposed and the marks of the fire on the inside of one gable. That was all. Smoke started to rise from the ruins as the fallen thatch fell on the still burning turf fire. It smouldered and burst into flame. Dualta's heart stopped at the sight. It brought back to him the sight of the death of the house of his uncle Marcus. But that was free. That was done by a free man. This was different.

They remained.

"We are not men," Cuan was saying. "We should be all

over there, every man of us with pikes and pitchforks and sleans, all in one mass to prevent them from doing this."

"What good would it do for everyone to die?" Annie asked. "That would please them. They could clean out the valley at one stroke. No. It is better to repay."

Then after a pause she said: "Well, Tooley will pay for this. Tooley will pay!"

"Tonight, Dualta," said Cuan. "You will come. It's about time you saw the result of your letters. It might restore some of your pity for the poor."

"I'm not wanting in pity," said Dualta.

"We'll see," said Cuan. "We'll see!"

They took soot from the chimney of Cuan's house and they rubbed it on their faces. Then they took the prepared rush torches, unlighted, and went into the night. The horses were tied at the back of the house. They mounted them and gave them their heads, because it was the dark of the moon. The stars were obscured by clouds.

Dualta was excited. These were the sort of actions he had wanted. Mounted men in the night, soot, torches, the sound of a shod hoof hitting a stone. The horses seemed to know where they were going. They left the rough road and descended the hill. The bushes blocking the gaps into the fields had all been removed. The horses seemed to find their way to the gaps as if it were broad daylight.

There was a sheen on the river, hardly perceptible. You could hear the gentle rustling of the dead rushes, and the scamper on the water of a frightened water hen. The horses bent their heads, widened their nostrils and scented the water before they crossed. It was quite deep but the ford was hard underfoot. Dualta felt the water kissing his shoes. They labored up the other bank and trotted to the fields on the far side. In about ten minutes they came to the grove of willow trees. They couldn't see but they heard the movement of horses pacing and being quieted; the slap of a hard palm on the neck of a horse; uneasy horses whining and being gently shushed.

They stopped there. Cuan spoke, "Are we all here?"

"We are all here," a voice answered him. "Don't light the torches until we are about the house," he said. "Did men bring the kettles?" "They will be at the place," he was answered. "The police are all gone," said Cuan. "They had to escort that dangerous criminal Morogh Ryan out of the valley." There was a snort of laughter. "When the flames go up, flee, and let the horses loose on the hills. Go to bed. We move. Now!"

Dualta felt the excitement now. The fact that you could not see added to it. Hearing voices out of the darkness. The smell of the horses. Being surrounded by men you knew but couldn't recognize. He thought: Maybe I should have stayed at home and organized something like this for the Half-Sir, but at least now I know. Now I know how it is done. It will give you a feeling of power. That you were hitting back; that you were concealed and free from discovery. You were an anonymous freedom-fighter under the soft spring cloak of darkness.

First the horses walked and then when they had negotiated the fields and felt their hooves on the rough road they trotted, and then somebody shouted and they ran. The sound of twenty horsemen on the road was exhilarating. It was dangerous. Men and horses all around you. Tossing manes and squeals and shouts. One or two dogs started to bark.

Then they were there, just when his blood was being warmed.

There were other horsemen waiting.

"Spread around," said the voice of Cuan. Dualta stayed where he was, facing the house. He saw the horsemen moving out on either side. There was a faint reflection from the whitewashed walls of Tooley's house. "Light up!" said the voice of Cuan. On the left there was the splutter of an expensive matchstick and then a torch flared and from the one torch others were lighted until a ring of flaming torches lit up the house in an unnatural glow. Inside the kitchen of the house a dog started to bark.

Cuan called: "Come out, Tooley! Tooley, come out!"

There was a silence then. Nothing but the dog barking and the hissing of the torches. Dualta imagined Tooley. Tooley would be frightened, he thought. It was a wonderful way to frighten a man.

Cuan didn't give him long. His voice was hard. "Come out, Tooley!" he called. Dualta tried to imagine Tooley, waking up. His realization. How his stomach would contract with fear. He would reach for his breeches, hurriedly pull them on, pull back the bolt on the door.

A baby started to cry in the house. Dualta's heart sank. A baby! But Tooley was a comparatively young man. He was bound to have a baby. It didn't matter. The door opened and Tooley came out. Shirt and breeches and bare feet, his brown curly hair tousled. He was a big man. His chest was stretching his shirt. He had a big jaw. He blinked in the light of the torches. He didn't seem very afraid. He didn't seem as afraid as he should be.

"What do you want?" he asked.

"You were warned, Tooley," said Cuan. "Many times. You were told not to bid for Ryan's land."

"I need Ryan's land," said Tooley. "I have ten children. The five acres I possess are not enough. Ryan was lazy. I want that land to live."

"You pay no attention to the wishes of the people?" Cuan asked.

"Who are the people?" asked Tooley, his big fists clenched. "If they are men let them face me, not writing letters behind closed doors like timorous women. I have a right to live. I have a right to feed my children. I have a right to better myself. And that I'll do, if all the cowards in Ireland were gathered out there, skulking behind torches."

There was a movement to the right of him. A horse and rider came into the light. Dualta saw an arm raised. He saw the heavy stick fall on the side of Tooley's head. He heard the sound of the blow. Tooley shut his eyes. That was all. He opened them again. The horseman fell back. There was the sound of a scream as Tooley's wife came from behind him. She held his arm.

"Tom! Tom! Tom!" she said. He put a hand on her hand.

The blood was flowing freely from his forehead down the side of his face. But he kept looking at them and his eyes were brave as ever. Dualta felt his stomach heaving.

"Bring the kettles!" Cuan called. "Get your children out of the house!"

"What are you going to do?" Tooley asked.

"We are going to burn you out," said Cuan. "You were warned."

Tooley was going to protest. Was he going to beseech?

"Brave men," he said. "O, the brave men of Ireland! Burn me? I'll build again. A hundred times. If you want to drive me out of this valley you will have to kill me."

"Men like you have been killed before," said Cuan.

"From the back of a bush," said Tooley. "From a drain, from a ditch, where rats lurk. Is there a man that will face me in the daylight among you?" Furiously he wiped the blood from his eye.

"Put the coals in the thatch," Cuan called coldly.

Dualta saw the men with the swinging kettles. They were glowing from the live turf sods they carried. He saw them being extracted glowing from the kettles and being stuck under the straw thatch. There were about ten of them. They started to burn, to smoke, to glow.

Tooley's shoulders slumped. Then he went back into the house. His wife followed him. They brought out their children. One of them was a baby in arms. Two more were barely able to walk. They were frightened, the young ones, and crying. They made up for Tooley. Some of the bigger children started to bring out pieces of things from the house, hurrying them away. Tooley himself and his wife. The horsemen didn't help. Dualta wanted to get down and help, but he knew now that it was forbidden.

The horsemen waited there until the thatch was well alight. The Tooleys rushed in and out faster and faster as the flames caught hold. The horsemen waited there until they saw pieces of flaming stuff falling into the inside of the house, until there was no hope of it being saved and then, on Cuan's one word, they turned away from there. The torches had sizzled to death, but there was plenty of light from the burning house.

Dualta kept his head down. There was plenty of light now to recognize people. But he didn't want to. He didn't want to know who they were. He looked back once. Tooley was standing up as straight as a good mountain ash tree, looking after them. There was anger in his face and a touch of helplessness, but no fear at all, Dualta thought, no fear at all.

He followed after the silent horsemen.

chapteR VIII

DUALTA WAS lying on the thick branch of a chestnut tree that spread like the rafters of a roof over the muddy avenue. It was night. The light of the moon was filtering through the bare branches. The brown sticky leaves of the chestnut tree were at the bursting point. He could barely make out the shape of Cuan sitting behind the bole of a tree on the other side. He was cradling the pistol between his knees.

He heard a hiss from Cuan, stiffened on the branch and took a tight hold of the stick in his right hand. He listened. At the far end of the avenue, the sound of a horseshoe hitting a stone. So Hanley was on his way.

Later he heard the tiny whistle that Cuan emitted.

Dualta waited for the shot from the pistol. When it came he leaned down and hit at Hanley's beaver hat with the stick. It was a good bit of timing. The horse shied; Hanley half fell off. Then he got to the ground, and leaving his hat and his horse and everything else, he set off running up the avenue. He was shouting: "Ah! Ah! Ah!" as if all the devils in hell were after him.

They found their horses where they had left them. They got safely through the woods and into the hills. The horses knew their way. They were sure-footed. The excitement died for Dualta. He ceased to chuckle over Hanley. Besides, Cuan was dour. He didn't want to talk about it. It was nearly dawn when they stood on the last hill that led down to the town. They could see the dark bulk of it below, and the gleam from the broad river.

"What is our real reason for coming here, Cuan?" Dualta asked.

"We are going to look at a hanging," said Cuan.

"A hanging!" Dualta exclaimed, and his heart sank.

"That's right," said Cuan. "In case you think it is all for fun, like games played on a corpse at a wake."

"Do I need to be convinced?" Dualta asked.

"You do," said Cuan. "You are jibing at going to Wilcocks aren't you?"

"It's too much like being a spy," said Dualta. "I am a faulty person, I know, but I like to be in the open."

"You'll see what happens to people who are in the open," said Cuan angrily.

"I don't want to see men hanged," said Dualta. "You go and I will wait for you."

"Why are you afraid?" Cuan asked him.

"Not fear," said Dualta. "It's not decent to watch men dying."

"There has to be a purpose in the things we are doing," said Cuan. "It's not just ideas in a thinking head. There must be reason. This is a reason. It is the working of landlordism. They insisted on a Coercion Act. You have to see the fruits of this, if you want to know what we are fighting about. Have you ever watched people dying?"

"Yes," said Dualta, tight-lipped.

"Well this is no different," said Cuan. "You can even pray for them and for yourself that someday you too won't decorate a rope. This is a country where you can see innocent men dying with a look of bewilderment on their faces. No man minds dying for something he has done. It must be a terrible thing for a man to die when he has done nothing."

"Who are they?" Dualta asked.

"They are the two men who are supposed to have shot Riddler the bailiff," said Cuan.

"Did they shoot him?" asked Dualta.

"One of them did," said Cuan, "but the other knew nothing about it."

"They wouldn't hang an innocent man," said Dualta.

Cuan laughed. It wasn't free laughter. He jogged ahead. Dualta followed him reluctantly. They came down from the hill on to the long dirt road that wound its way to the town. It was a spring day. You could see the green grass shooting through the yellow-tipped frostbitten grasses of the fields. The woodbine in the hedges was in leaf as it twined its deadly tentacles on everything within its reach.

I must see more young people, Dualta thought. I have been too long with older people. They will sap the youth in me. I will wake up one day and find that my youth is past and that I have not enjoyed it at all. Suddenly he thought of Paidi. That's it, next Sunday he would set out early and travel to the place where Paidi was working, at the village of the cross of the Hanging Tree. He thought of Paidi. Eat, sleep, joke, talk to the girls the language of understatement and flattery. Bailiffs, Coercion acts, vengeance, freedom, all passed over Paidi's head. He thought of making money to bring home for his people. That was all. And laughing when the occasion arose, that was all. Dualta felt guilty that he hadn't gone across to see him. But he was so busy, and Paidi and what he was doing were as far apart as day and night, day and night.

There was silence in the town. It was like the silence that had enwrapped it when he and Paidi had come to the hiring fair.

There were not many people in the poorer parts of the town. The doors were closed. That was not usual. Some children playing in the dust, thin dogs barking at the two horses as they passed. They stopped at the big shop where Annie got her provisions and they walked the horses into the yard. The boy there took them and led them into a stall. "Big day? Big day?" he asked. "That's right, Murt," said Cuan. He gave him a list. "Get that filled," he said, "and load it on the horses." "Right, man, right," said Murt taking it. "I'll see to that. Are ye going to look?" "Yes," said Cuan. "I'd go meself," said Murt, "if I wasn't as busy as a flea on a dog. Funerals or hangings, you can't keep up with the custom." "Lucky for you," said Cuan, and they walked toward the square.

When they turned into the better street and walked toward the square, they saw that it was crowded. Well-dressed people.

WALTER MACKEN

In the square itself there were carriages drawn up. Dualta was sickened to see that there were some women in the carriages. There were some country people. Not many. There was a double line of soldiers facing out from the gallows. The only raucous sound was the call of the chapmen selling their penny broadsheets, The Seven Champions of Christendom, Irish Rogues and Raparees, the Life and Adventures of Captain Freney, The Battle of Aughrim, Hibernian Tales, and others about murderers, grave robbers, the battle of Waterloo. They were appropriate tales for a hanging.

Anyhow, Dualta was thinking, I don't have to look. I can close my eyes. Every man is provided with curtains over his eyes if he wishes to use them.

"See," Cuan was saying, "how they conduct everything with panoply? Even the sordid business of hanging, they give it color and form."

"Why do you say that one man is innocent?" Dualta asked.

"I know," said Cuan. "I have talked with the people from the place. I know the other three men who were there. This young man happened to be in the wrong place at the wrong time. He was heard talking to the older man by an informer. He recognized him by his Connacht accent. Like yours. It could have been you. We didn't get the informer. They sent him out of the country, better guarded than the jewels of a king. We hope that someday somebody will catch up with him. Even if they do not, he will get a crick in his neck looking over his shoulder for the rest of his life. The innocent young man was coming home from courting a girl."

The countrywomen with the cloaks had gone on their knees. They took rosary beads from their pockets. There was a stirring among the soldiers, a stiffening of their backs. Their hands tightened on their guns.

Dualta felt his left leg trembling.

The two men mounted the gallows from behind. Their arms were bound. There was a priest out in front reading from a black book.

Then he could see them. It was to be a double hanging.

The squat pleasant-faced hangman stood between them. He had his coat off. His arms were bared. The man on the right was a big-chested, gray-haired man with a determined face. His mouth was clamped shut. His thick neck was bare. He was a muscular man. He looked rocklike. The young man had curly brown hair falling down over his forehead. His hair was being moved by the gentle wind. He was low-sized, powerful-looking, but his mouth was open and he was crying. Tears were pouring down his cheeks.

Dualta felt as if he had been kicked in the heart.

"Paidi!" he called. He felt a strong grip on his arm.

"Shush, Dualta," said Cuan. There were heads turning.

"It's Paidi, Paidi," said Dualta. The blood had drained from his face. He made a move to shove through the people. Cuan held on to him. "Be easy, Dualta," he said. "Be easy." "But it's Paidi," said Dualta.

Paidi hadn't heard him.

Dualta felt his whole body drained. He was shocked all over. He couldn't move now even if he wanted to. But it couldn't be Paidi. If you knew Paidi. This couldn't be Paidi. Paidi wouldn't even be bothered holding a gun. He wouldn't know what side the ball came from. Scream now about a miscarriage of justice. Who do you scream to? Cold-faced indifferent officers of martial law, taking damn good care that somebody hangs to try and break the conspiracy of silence? But he's too young. He isn't even twenty. Is he the first to go like that? What about his mother and father and all those kids waiting for him to come home in the glen in the hills near the great lake? Well, it's waiting they will be. They would have lost him anyhow to a woman sometime. They won't even know properly. Read the papers in the English tongue. He had read them himself. But you don't think of people's proper names when they are written in English and they are Irish in your head. You don't even recognize the words.

He stood there helpless, unbelieving, rooted, trembling, drained, what will I do? who will I go to? but these things don't take long. Before his horrified eyes, the living ones fell and the bodies swung, and there were still tears on Paidi's dead cheeks when Dualta turned away and groped his way free of the square and stumbled down the street. Free of the crowd he leaned against a house and vomited. He wished to die. He groaned and went on holding his stomach with his arms.

I am the one, he thought. I betrayed him. I didn't go near him. This would not have happened if I had gone to see him, talked to him. He could never face his people. Paidi would not have come this far south if it wasn't for Dualta. Keep an eye on him, he could hear Paidi's father say. Stay with him until he is settled. And what had been Dualta's thanks for his kindness? Oh, great God, he groaned.

He blindly recognized the place they had left the horses. He went in there, and into the horse stall, and sat on hay in the corner and buried his face in his arms. The horse stirred and widened his nostrils and sniffed at his hair.

A long time, a long time before the blood came back to his body.

He knew Cuan was there. He knew he had been there for some time. He didn't talk. Somebody had to talk eventually.

"I didn't know you knew him, Dualta," he said. "I didn't know."

"We came together from Connacht," said Dualta.

"I'm sorry. I'm truly sorry," said Cuan.

"The men that were there, they knew he had nothing to do with it," said Dualta. "Cuan, why didn't they come forward and say so?"

"They would have hanged too," said Cuan. "They wouldn't have saved Paidi. Just five dead instead of two."

"I would have come forward," said Dualta. Cuan was silent.

"What will happen to his body?" Dualta asked.

"That will be taken care of," said Cuan. "The people over there will look after it. I'm truly sorry, Dualta. I didn't know. If I knew we would never have gone."

"I might never have known if we hadn't gone," said Dualta. "There are so many hangings."

"That's right," said Cuan. "There are so many hangings."

He was silent. "I will see to the goods and we will go home," he said then. "I will tell you when all is ready."

Dualta dropped his head in his arms again.

He heard Cuan's call, and rose and went stiffly into the yard. He had to shade his eyes from the light with his arm. The horses were heavily burdened. He had difficulty getting on his horse's back. Then they headed out of the town.

He knew none of the way they went. His horse just followed after Cuan's.

He thought, I was worrying about my youth. Paidi is gone out like a light, just like a light you quench, and not in fair time. So now you know what murder really is, whether it is by the hand of a civilian or by the hand of rulers with all the outward show of justice and impartiality. This was no law. It was law without reason or hope for the people who came under its shadow.

I have lost my youth well and truly now, he thought.

Only one sentence he spoke.

"I will go to Wilcocks, Cuan," he said.

"Listen, Dualta," said Cuan, "I didn't mean . . ."

"I will go to Wilcocks," he said.

Cuan was silent.

chapteR IX

H_E DISDAINED the back avenue into the house. He went to the main wrought-iron gates. They were double gates, as tall as two men and a half, yet they opened easily. Inside the gate was the small squat house of Bullock, the English field bailiff. Dualta walked past. There was smoke from the chimney. The door was open. He was waiting for a shout, but none came. He supposed that Bullock was in the fields.

It was a pleasant avenue. It was shaded by poplar trees. To his left the great open fields sloped to the river. Their vastness was broken in places by towering beech trees, some copper-colored, some green. Red cattle grazed the fields or rested in the shade of the trees. The whole valley was hazy in the June sun. From here you could see the whitewashed houses well up in the hills. He supposed they could look menacing enough if you were afraid of them.

The drive wound pleasantly. The trees ended and the drive opened into a large semicircle in front of the house where the carriages could turn. The drive was well kept, hard ground-in gravel, that had been well scuffled of grass and weeds.

He stood there and looked at the house, a solid three-story stone-built house with a pillared doorway with very tall eight-paned windows on each side of the doorway and slightly smaller windows on the top floors. He noticed that the bottom windows were ready to be barricaded, the heavy iron-bound shutters were there ready to be hung on the great spikes that had been driven into the stonework. Wilcocks' was the only place in the area that hadn't been barricaded, but apparently Hanley's leaving had made him feel cautious. Many big houses had been surprised. Arms had been stolen, servitors beaten. The front door was big and solid, the panels carved from the thick timber. It was oil-polished and gleamed dully in the sunshine.

He stood there for a little longer, and then, hefting his bundle on the spade handle, he walked around the house toward the back quarters. The house was as broad as it was long. At the back there was a great cobblestoned yard closed in on all sides by two-story slated stables and carriage houses. The yard was empty. They were all in the fields. All but the turf boy who was attending the fires under the two great pots of boiling potatoes. One was for the pigs and the other was for the workers. The boy stood and rubbed the turf smoke out of his eyes. Dualta nodded at him and then went in the open back door into the kitchen.

It was a huge kitchen. Great copper pots and pans, burnished bright, hung on the walls facing him. There was a big rough table sitting in the middle of the flagged floor. Rough chairs and two enormous kitchen cupboards groaning with their weight of delf and jugs and plates and mugs. There were two girls cleaning vegetables at the table and a great big fat woman with bare feet cutting into a joint of meat with a bloodied knife. The girls saw him first as he blocked the light. They looked up at him, their knives held in midair. "God bless the good work," he said politely. Then the fat lady turned. She hadn't small eyes like Annie, he noticed. She had big eyes in a red face. She could be cranky, he thought, so he smiled at her and softened his eyes. He knew that he wasn't ugly and that his smile could be a useful weapon. Its effect on the girls was immediate, but it brought nothing from the fat lady but a grunt.

"It's a grand sight," said Dualta, "to see three beautiful maidens around a table." The girls giggled. The fat lady was not amused. She looked him up and down from toe to crown. His shoes were polished, his hose was neatly darned by himself, his breeches were corduroy but new and the belt that held them up was new. His shirt was clean, his jacket fairly respectable and his hair was shining. He was newly shaved. He knew all this. So he showed her his teeth again in a pleasant smile.

They were good and white, from the application of a mixture of soot and salt rubbed on with his finger.

"We don't feed the beggars until night," she said, turning back to her meat cutting.

"Do you insult everyone that comes into the house?" he asked.

"It depends what they come for," she said. "What's under you?"

"I am looking for work," said Dualta.

"We have enough maidservants," she said.

"You might be deceived by my delicate build," said Dualta. He rolled his eyes at her significantly. She laughed. He was getting on with her, he thought. Charm Biddy, they said, and the house is yours.

At this moment he was pushed from behind by a large hand. He staggered over to the table. The coarse voice had said, "Out of my way." He turned to look at the giant who came in. He was carrying a bale of cut logs on his shoulder. He went toward the huge fireplace and dropped the bale with a terrible clatter into the great chest.

"Christy," said Dualta grimly, "if you weren't as big as you are, I'd make you pay for that push."

Christy looked at him. Then he scratched his curly hair and pointed a large finger at him and said, "Dualta!"

"The light dawned," said Dualta.

"You know this fellow, Christy," Biddy said.

"That's Dualta," said Christy. "He's from Annie's."

"I'd have told you, Biddy," one of the girls said, "if you gave me a chance."

"What are you doing out of Annie's?" Biddy asked.

"She put me," said Dualta sadly.

"Did she catch your hand in the money box?" she asked rudely.

"No," said Dualta. "But I'm a Connachtman."

"I can tell that from your speech," she said.

"So people didn't like me," said Dualta.

"I don't wonder," said Biddy.

"I like Connachtmen," said the tall girl. "My name is Nora, Dualta."

"Hello, Nora," said Dualta.

"I liked you, Dualta," said Christy after thought.

"Thanks, Christy," said Dualta. "I liked you too before you pushed me."

"You were in the way of the door," said Christy reasonably.

"Ah," said Dualta.

"I heard about you," said Biddy. "You were good at sums, people said, and the writing. It's a wonder Annie let you go. She can't write her own name."

"Reading and writing and arithmetic," said Dualta. "I can write love letters or begging letters, but I'm better at love letters. I can multiply and divide and subtract. I can dig as many potatoes as any man. I can cut five carts of turf in a day. I can mow a meadow. I'm one of the best men that ever came into this district, and the poor creatures in the valley don't know it."

"You have the gift of boasting anyhow," said Biddy. "What do you want here?"

"I don't know," said Dualta. "I was going home, and then thought I'd stop and see if you people would have any use for me. Would it be too much to ask if I could see himself, then?"

Biddy was wiping her hands on her apron. She was looking at him shrewdly.

"I'll see," she said abruptly. "Keep an eye on him, you, and don't let him steal anything." She went out a door.

"She likes you," said Nora. "Sit down, Dualta."

"How do you know she likes me?" he asked.

"The way she talks to you," said Nora. He sat near the table. He looked at Nora. She was a dark-haired girl, with black eyes.

"I'd hate to hear her so if she loved somebody," said Dualta.

"But why are you leaving Annie, Dualta?" said Christy. Dualta looked at his puzzled face and thought it is only the really simple people who go to the heart of the matter.

"People up there don't like me," he said patiently. "Some of them are a queer lot. Very suspicious." Silence descended on them for the moment. He broke it. "Who is the little one?" he asked. She was a small fair girl. She blushed easily, like now. "That's Teresa," said Nora. "You won't get a word out of her. I hope you work here, Dualta."

"Is there room for me?" he asked.

"They've lost a lot of people," she said. "Even Teresa and myself got letters."

"Oh," said Dualta. He had written them himself. It was odd to see an anonymous Nora Criodan and Teresa Flannery becoming real in front of his eyes. "They didn't frighten you?" he asked.

"Not me," she said with determination, "but Teresa was crying. She's soft."

He looked at the blushing Teresa. What a nice manly occupation, he thought, writing letters to frighten girls.

"I got no letters at all," said Christy.

"They were probably afraid of you," said Dualta.

"I'm not afraid of them," said Christy.

"Best of men," said Dualta.

"All right," said Biddy from the door. Dualta was startled. With her so silent bare feet, he hadn't heard her coming. "Come with me now," she said, "and don't forget to keep your tongue in your mouth."

He rose. "I'll leave this," he said about the spade and his bundle. Nora took them. "They'll be in the corner for you," she said. "I hope you are lucky."

"So do I," he said. He followed Biddy. They came into a large hall that stretched from here to the front door. It was a big hall of polished wood and paneled walls. The staircase bisected the hall. It had slender railings and a polished mahogany hand rail. There were rugs made of sheepskin on the floors. Dualta walked on the tips of his toes. This was the first time he had ever been in a house like this. Back in his own place, the nearest he had come to one was peeping in at it from the railings of the front gate. The colored glass at the sides of the front door threw dancing reflections on the floor. He thought those were pretty.

Biddy opened a door. "Wait in here now," she said.

"Thank you, ma'am," he said and walked in.

There was a carpet on the floor. His feet made no sound.

"Don't touch anything," she said, and closed the door after her.

He drew in his breath. It was a library. They were leather-bound volumes with gold-leaf lettering. He swiveled his head as he read the titles. All the knowledge that a man could want was here—Dryden, Scott, Shakespeare, encyclopedias, *Costumes of the Nations, Wild Sports of the East,* Pinkerton's *Voyages,* Blagdon's *India,* Byron, Johnson, Swift, Paley, Goldsmith, Hume, Gibbon, Pope, Hogarth, books on travel, bound editions of magazines, poetry, Greek books, Latin books, volume after volume. Enough to make you groan at the sight of them. So many you wanted that it would take a whole lifetime to get hold of, one by one, time by time, in cheap battered and bowdlerized editions, sold as waste by the chapmen.

There was a table used as a reading desk. There were account books open on this. There was a quill pen resting in an inkwell. It was as if a presence had been and gone. An elusive scent. He thought that Wilcocks would hardly use scent, or would he? What did he know about people like Wilcocks, just to see him from a distance riding his horse and spit in the dust as he passed?

There was an English magazine open under his eyes on the table. He looked at it. A whole page was taken up with a funny drawing. The blood rose in his face as he examined it. It was an Irish drawing, the man in the middle waving a shillelagh, a man in tattered clothes with the face of an ape, a small pug nose, red-faced. Other people reeling drunk, waving kegs. All of them had apelike faces. The women had apelike faces. So had the children. The women were ugly, with dirty clothes, streeling hair. The children looked like the demons he once saw carved on old churches in France, from a drawing. Not one of them had a redeeming feature. He tried to read the caption. It was a strange mixture of English that the Irish were supposed to speak, like the hieroglyphics on an Egyptian tomb.

He thought of all the people he knew. He tried to place them beside this crew of subhumans displayed as typical. His resting hand on the desk clenched into a white fist.

That was the way the girl saw him as she came into the room. The white fist, the muscles bunched at the side of his jaw, a scar on his cheekbone that was standing out whitely against his suffused face. His nostrils flaring. She was surprised. She walked behind him and looked down at what was obviously moving him. He didn't know she was there.

"You don't approve of the cartoon?" she said.

"Are we apes?" he asked. "We are not animals. We have souls. We are like other human beings. We can laugh and cry. We can love and hate. Do we speak with stones in our mouth like gobbling turkeys? Have we fallen so low that this is the way we are seen? Even by our enemies?"

Then he realized. The tension left him. He smelled again the scent that had been in the room with him before. He turned. A girl with calm brown eyes was regarding him. She was well dressed. Superior cloth. Her skin was very smooth. She was half laughing at him, watching his face composing itself. He had given himself away. She watched the life going out of his countenance, the secret look that she was so used to, veiling his thoughts. She was Wilcocks' daughter, of course. Not very often seen. Home this last year from being educated in Dublin and London and France. Not home long enough for people to get to assess her. They said she was all right. She was kind. She helped the really poor without ostentation, and without forcing tracts on them villifying the Blessed Virgin.

"I'm sorry, Miss," he said. "You caught me when I wasn't looking."

"I caught you when you were looking," she said. She moved to the table. She sat down behind the account books.

"You haven't answered my question," she said. He was trying to think of her name. He had overheard it. A strange name because it didn't fit her and who she was. An Irish name, of all things, tied on to such an ascendancy name as Wilcocks.

"I cannot answer it, Miss Una," he said. He thought of it in time. What do I do now, he wondered? Do I revert to being humble and ingratiating and secret? She was a very good-looking girl. She looked very Irish, dark with the creamy white skin so many handsome Irish girls wore unconsciously. He could think of Irish girls in the hills better looking than her, if they had the polish and attention of the toilette.

"Why?" she asked.

"I am on the wrong side of the road," he said, recklessly. "You are in a better position to answer it than me."

She looked at him.

"All right," she said. "It's really very simple. It is induced by fear."

"I don't understand that," he said.

"You ridicule what you fear," she said, "in order by laughing at it to make it appear innocuous." She watched him thinking over this. He looked at her with closer attention.

"Why?" he asked.

"Well," she said. "You are many, we are few. There are a few thousand people who own the whole country surrounded on all sides by millions and millions of people who do not wish them well. Is this true?"

"It could be," he said cautiously.

"All you have to do now is look up at the houses on the hills looking down at us here to feel this. We are one against how many? Particularly now, with violence. So you see, we are afraid. It has always been the same. There is violence and savage repression, leading to horror and a guilty conscience, so you will always find that, at times of acute violence, the ridicule becomes sharper and uglier and more depraved. It will continue. You will have to put up with it. It is part of life now."

"Does a thing like that make you laugh, then?" he asked. "Does it amuse you?"

"No," she said. "It makes me sad."

What kind of a girl is this one at all, he wondered? She saw his wonder.

"I surprise you?" she asked.

"Yes," he said.

"Not everybody is an enemy, you know," she said. "There are people on the other side who think, if they are educated. They don't at all feel that the Irish people are near apes. You don't look like an ape yourself. You are one of the people. What is your name?"

"My name is Duane," he said. "Dualta."

"Your speech is not Tipperary," she said.

"I am from Connacht," he said. "I am from the mountains."

"I detect pride in your attitude," she said.

"Every man is proud of his own place," he said, "if he is a man."

"Why did you leave it then?" she asked.

"The young landlord hit me with a whip because I was in the way of his horse," he said, putting his hand up to the scar, "so I tumbled him from his horse and had to take off and run." He was more than surprised, he was amazed at his own frankness.

She saw the flash of hate in his eyes at the remembrance.

"Do you consider then that all landlords are to be equated on the same level as the one you tumbled?"

This was shrewd. Actually he had never thought about it much. He had never tried to find out. What opportunities had he for finding out?

"I don't know," he answered.

"You were right to tumble him," she said. "I would have done the same myself. All men are entitled to personal dignity."

"You look young," he said, "and you talk with age, and I'm sure you would have given him a bad time if you were me." He laughed. He had a picture of this girl with the determined chin punishing the Half-Sir most vigorously. She laughed too, as if the same picture had flashed into her mind. Dualta felt the sharpness of the whole thing easing away from him in the laughter.

They were laughing like this when the door opened again and Wilcocks came in. It could only be he. His eyebrows rose at the sight of his daughter laughing freely with the young countryman.

"Well," he said loudly, "what about him?" Dualta stopped

laughing. The girl didn't stop abruptly. She allowed the laughter to taper away. Dualta saw a strong tall man with gray hair and a moustache. He had a strong face. The girl saw the curtain coming down on the face of the young man.

"He can read and write," she said. "Are you a good hand at accounts?" she asked.

"Yes," said Dualta. "I can do accounts."

"Why did you leave Annie?" Wilcocks asked. He came into the room. He stood facing him, his hands behind his back. "She is a decent woman. She gets a lot of custom from us. Why did you leave her?"

"It was best," said Dualta. "The people did not take to me because I was a Connachtman."

"A bunch of bloody scoundrels," said Wilcocks. "But we'll weed them out." He went to the window. He looked up at the hills. "We'll weed them out," he said, "if I have to knock every house in the valley." He turned back. "Can you use a gun?"

"No, sir," said Dualta. "I cannot. I never handled one. You know what would happen to one of us if we were found with a gun?"

"Quite right too," said Wilcocks. "They'd have us all shot in our beds. I suppose you are the wrong religion?"

"I am a Catholic," said Dualta.

"Well, I hope you are a better one than some of them in the valley," said Wilcocks. "What do you think, Una, is he all right? Will he do?"

She didn't say so immediately. They waited.

"Yes, Father," she said. "I think so."

"Right," said Wilcocks. "You can help with the accounts. Since these scum drove off my bailiffs, we are short-handed there. Also you can look after my daughter when she is abroad. You will learn how to use a gun. And use it if you have to. You can help other ways too. We are short-handed. We'll give you fair wages, and you can sleep in the house. I have a feeling. I don't like the feeling I have. They are up to something out there. But I'm able for them. They will be sorry people. Right, Una, I'm going out. Look after it. If you are satisfied that's all right with me. Dammit, you are turning out better than if you were a son. What's his name, did you say?"

"Duane," said Una.

"All right, Duane. Do right by me and I'll do right by you. And don't be afraid. That Hanley fellow was like a fainting girl. One shot at him and he's running like a rabbit with a thistle in his scutch."

He went out abruptly.

He left a bit of his heavy personality behind him.

She rose. "I'll show you the house," she said. "You will have to see to it that the shutters go up on the windows. They are very slow."

"Am I a guard of the body, then?" he asked.

"I can take care of myself," she said. "But it is as well to take precautions." She went out of the room. He followed her. She showed him the main rooms below. She enjoyed at second hand his scrutiny of each of them. They were furnished with many beautiful pieces. She noted the way he walked softly. Upstairs she showed him a room where he would sleep. It was in the attic. There was a skylight through which he could examine the stars. It reminded him of the room in Galway where he had waked after the drinking. An iron bedstead and a few chests. It was full of June sun reflecting off the white walls.

He said: "Why are you called with an Irish name?"

She answered. "One time my father was very Irish. He read all the old legends and the sagas. He married a girl from Limerick. He met her at a hunt ball. She was a Catholic, but she changed for him. He had a very strong personality. He was a very good-looking man." That accounts for it, he thought, the Irishness of her. What other grand lady like her would bother to go the rounds of the house with a new man?

"You do not come here to hurt us?" he heard her asking then. "You have not come here with a different purpose?" He kept his muscles from stiffening. She was a very shrewd girl. It was a few seconds before he turned to face her, a look of puzzlement on his face.

"I would never hurt you, Miss Una," he said.

"Not me," she said, "us. All of us." She had a very direct look. Her eyes were deep-sunken ones, seeming to be looking at him from a long distance.

"I will never hurt you, or yours," he said.

She looked at him again for a time, trying to get behind the completely sincere-sounding voice of his.

"All right," she said. "You can get food in the kitchen. I'll send for you when I want you."

Then she left him. He looked after her for a long time.

That night he lay on his bed and he looked at the stars with his hands under his head. He thought: Well Cuan, I have done what you wanted, and I hope it will be as easy as you think. He thought of the crying Paidi with his broken neck and his jaw tightened. He couldn't sleep. Eventually he rose and put the mattress on the floor. That was better. He slept then and before sleeping decided that he would have to be very wary of the girl with the direct eyes.

chapteR X

He WENT TO THE carriage house. He grabbed the small light two-wheeled cart and pulled it into the yard. Torpey put his head out of the horse stable looking at him sourly. He was an ugly man, Torpey. He wasn't surprised that Una preferred to have himself with her instead of the dour man who seemed to be able to talk nothing but horse language.

"Harness up for Miss Una," said Dualta. He went to help him. They chose the honey-colored mare with the white tail and mane. Whatever else, Torpey kept the horses in great shape. Torpey put on the harness and led the horse outside.

"You go?" he asked Dualta.

"I go," said Dualta. Torpey grunted. He didn't like Dualta.

"Careful," said Torpey. "Watch. You look out. Mind the mare."

"I'll mind her," said Dualta. "It doesn't matter if I break my neck?"

"No," said Torpey.

"That's what I thought," said Dualta.

He got into the padded seat, held the reins, clucked his tongue at the mare and drove her sedately out of the yard and around to the front of the house. The mare waited patiently. The front door was open. Wilcocks appeared there. He shouted from the steps. "What's up, Duane?"

"Miss Una is going out, sir," said Dualta.

Wilcocks came down a few steps.

"This bloody O'Connell," he shouted. "You see he is getting nearly a thousand pounds a week out of this Catholic rent?"

"It's a lot of money, sir," said Dualta.

Wilcocks came down another few steps.

"The bloody demagogue'll buy the whole country," he said.

"I didn't know the country could be bought, sir," said Dualta.

Wilcocks peered at him under his heavy eyebrows. Then he hooted with laughter. But he sobered.

"Sometimes you might be too bright for your own good, Duane," he said. "What do the people see in him? They are flocking after him like dogs in heat. You watch that fellow, Duane. He hates us all. He'll drag the whole country into the mud."

Dualta was about to say that most of the country was in the mud anyhow, but he held his peace. Wilcocks was using Dualta as if he was addressing the nation.

"They are even inviting him to London," said Wilcocks. "Imagine that. An ignoramus like that in London! What's the Government thinking of over there? They should clap him in irons. Imagine consulting O'Connell. Are they gone mad?"

"He has become very powerful, sir," said Dualta.

"A sorry day, dammit," said Wilcocks. "Before we know where we are we'll have men like Christy making maiden speeches in the House of Commons."

A picture of Christy standing up in the House of Commons addressing the people there came into Dualta's mind. He had to laugh. Wilcocks watched him. He was pleased with his laughter. "Well, it could happen," he said. "You mark my words. They should have confined that fellow to the Kerry bogs that spawned him. Ah, hello, dear, you are off again?"

This to Una who came into the doorway, pulling on long gloves over her bare arms.

"Yes, Father," she said. "I won't be long."

"Be careful, Duane," said Wilcocks. "I don't like things. Keep your eyes open. Things have been too quiet in the valley."

"I'll be careful, sir," said Dualta. He could have told him that while his daughter was with him, she was as safe as if she was in a vault in a bank.

"Right," said Wilcocks. "O'Connell in London, by God! Catholic Relief. What's coming over them?" He turned back into the house again. Dualta helped Una into the cart, and mounted himself.

"Where to, Miss?" he asked.

"The same place, Dualta," she said.

He clucked at the mare and they clopped sedately down the drive into the avenue of the poplars.

He always felt very content with her. She had that effect on people. She was a calm girl. He had driven her to many balls and feasts. He had noticed the way she attracted the young bucks. She was a good-looking girl and when she was dressed up in special finery, she attracted them. When they came to say good night to her, he might not have existed. They didn't even see him, no more than they saw the drivers of the other carriages. But she did. Inquired if he had enjoyed himself.

Sitting beside Una now, smelling the sweetness of her, his conscience troubled him. He told himself that in this he wasn't entitled to a conscience.

She said, "Would you change your religion, Dualta?"

He was startled from his thoughts.

"That's a queer question," he said.

"Why is it queer?" she asked. "You would be considerably bettered if you became a Protestant, wouldn't you?"

"Yes," he said. "There are better jobs open, security. I would be favored. Why do you ask this?"

"You don't seem on the surface," she said, "to be a very good Catholic, so why shouldn't you embrace something that would improve your life?"

He glanced at her. Her face was almost expressionless. She wasn't looking at him.

"How do you know I am not a good Catholic?" he asked.

"I don't," she said. "On the surface you don't appear so. You don't go to Confession, do you, very often?"

He didn't. But he wondered how she knew. He couldn't go to Confession. If he went to Confession he would have to tell about the depredations he took part in, and be asked how he was going to make material reparation for the injuries he had caused. He was very uneasy.

"I didn't notice you trying to proselytize before," he said. "Why do you start on me?"

"No," she said. "It's not that. I am just asking you. Would you change your religion from indifferent Catholicism to indifferent Protestantism?"

"No," he said.

"Why?" she asked.

"I haven't thought about it much," he said. "Just that it's there."

"I see," she said. "I just wanted to know."

"Are you any wiser after my answer?" he asked.

She laughed.

"I don't think so," she said, and then she grew silent again.

He clucked at the mare, slapped the reins on her rump. She was inclined to laze if she thought you had forgotten her.

Three miles from the house they came to the place of the assignation. This was the fourth time he had come here with her. She had been on her own too. There was a gateway that led into a small wood of pine trees, young ones planted about twelve years. There was a path that wound through, and it ended up at the river where it tumbled over a fall of about twenty feet. He got down and opened the gate and led the mare inside, walked her about ten yards until she was hidden from the road and could graze the sparse grass that grew beside the rutted track.

He helped her down.

"Thank you," she said. She was thinking deeply, he thought. She didn't give him her courteous smile and admonition about waiting for her. He wondered if that released him from the implied promise of not following as he watched her slim figure going down the track, her hands holding up the skirt so that it wouldn't sweep the dust.

He sat down to think about it. He plucked a blade of grass and chewed it. He thought it had a pine taste, and wondered if the mare noticed this and if it made the grass tastier or not.

He thought she must be meeting a lover. This thought disappointed him. She didn't seem to be the sort of person to do

things under cover. But perhaps if her lover was a young im-
poverished man? Most of the landlord parents set great store
on who their daughters married. They had to have some money
as well as class. It just wouldn't do for Wilcocks' daughter to
marry just any young man, he knew, but also he had thought
that she was the kind of person who, if she fell in love, would
just trot out the young man to her father and say, "Here is
your future son-in-law." She had a determined chin. He knew
so little about their lives. In their own way they secreted themselves from the watching eyes of the servants they possessed.
Normally it would have been all one to him. Let them be
born; let them marry; let them die; time, place or person, what
was it to do with him? They were a strange race beyond his
ken. But you couldn't be meeting a person like Una, doing
things for her, laughing with her, joking, talking, and not permit a part of you to show, and also to get to like her very
much. He had to admit that. It was a dangerous thing to do.
After all, these people were his enemies. Wasn't he fighting
them? Didn't he wish to injure them? So it was a dangerous
thing to permit yourself to begin to like them. Where would
that leave warfare?

He got to his feet and set off through the woods.

It's part of your job, he told himself as he placed his feet
cautiously on the pine needles, moved from tree to tree, drawing near the eternal booming of the waterfall. She might be
seeing an Army man or even a policeman. She might be a sort
of spy, a calm kind person outwardly who was undermining
the conspiracy in the valley, getting ropes ready for the lot of
them.

He knew this thinking was ridiculous, but it eased his conscience at the thought that he was going to spy on her. After
all, she hadn't said that he was to wait for her. He had kept
his curiosity in check before. But she had told him to wait
then. Today she had said nothing.

The nearer he came to the waterfall, the lower he got to the
ground. Close to the river the trees were sparser and the ferns
were thick and tall and beginning to turn golden. The at-

mosphere was very oppressive. The clouds were very low. The heavens were due to open.

He parted the ferns in front of his eyes and looked into the glade.

He saw the broad back of a man. He was sitting on a fallen tree trunk, a black-clad back, with light-brown hair tied. She was standing up. She had her gloves off. She was kneading them and slapping them. She would walk away from him toward the brink of the fall, and she would seem to be outlined in the spray that was rising from the pool. She would spread her arms, and stamp her foot. She came back. She was appealing to him. She sat beside him on the log, half facing him. He shook his head. He now got up and walked to the edge of the fall, then he turned and walked back toward her. He was talking, expostulating, and as he turned and faced him, Dualta saw that he was a priest. He didn't know him. He wasn't either of the two priests in the valley. It was no love scene he had come upon. He could hear no words, nor did he want to hear any, as he started to withdraw, just a word here and there over the sound of the water. The priest was urging her to be patient over something, not to press things to an issue. That's all he could make out as he withdrew, ashamed of himself, thinking that if she had made up her mind to do something, even the priest had a poor chance of persuading her to the contrary.

But why a priest? he wondered. Why a priest? What was wrong with her? Meeting a priest in secret? It's none of my business, he thought. What business is it of mine? He thought what a low opinion he had of himself at the moment. Now he knew and he would do well to forget it as quickly as possible. But he wondered how the priest had come, so when he reached the mare he cut off right into the woods, and smelled the brown horse before he saw him, a light horse saddled and tied to a tree. The horse saw him. He was nervous. Dualta made soothing noises with his mouth and his lips and the horse calmed. Then he turned and made his way back to the mare. He rested his back against the bole of a tree and chewed another blade of grass while he waited for her.

She came. He thought she looked pale. But it may have been the odd light in the sky.

"Enjoyed yourself, Dualta?" she asked automatically.

"Yes," said Dualta, "the grass tastes of pine." She looked at him. She laughed. "How good to be free of care," she said. "Let us go."

He led the mare out of the wood onto the road. He helped her up into the seat, mounted himself and set off down the road. They cleared the wood. The river on their left was gleaming dully as it wound its way from the valley. The leaves of the trees were turning. It made the whole place around them look lush, and heavy with wealth. It had been a good autumn. The harvest would be good.

She said. "Have you got to like this valley?"

He said: "Yes. It grows on you."

"But you wouldn't exchange it for your own place?" she asked.

"No, Miss," he said. "I don't think so."

"It's my place, this," she said. "My valley. I know parts of it you will never see. When I climb the hills and look down at it on a clear day, my heart is bright. It's where I was born. It means a lot to me."

"I know it does," he said.

"It would be very hard to lose it," she said.

"Are you going to get married?" he asked.

"Married?" she inquired. "Oh! You think that? No. Not at the moment. You don't lose things if you get married, you gain them."

He stayed silent.

"Times I was away," she said, "in all those wonderful cities, I thought of the valley. It is like your religion. You find that the valley is rooted in your heart. I thought how later, when it was mine, the things I would do to improve it."

"No more evictions?" said Dualta trying to keep feeling out of his voice.

It silenced her. She looked at him.

"Your English has improved since you came to us, Dualta.

Lots of the Irish intonations are gone out of it. Do evictions hurt you?"

"I only remarked," he said.

"I thought of lots of things," she said. "Many things. It is not good to plan too far ahead. You never know how your plans will be changed or diverted."

"Are all your plans changed then?" he asked.

She thought.

"Yes," she said. "I'm afraid so. You will know soon enough. I'm afraid everybody will know soon enough."

She sighed.

chapter XI

SHE HESITATED at the door of the living room where she knew he was. She leaned her head against it, and put her arm to her breast to ease the thumping of her heart.

For she knew her father.

He was a just man, if you were just with him. You knew where you stood with him. If you were his enemy, that was that. He was built on kindness and fairness, but also built-in prejudices that were as strong as the faith of a saint. She loved him, but his own love was inarticulate. He regarded softness of expression as a concession to Irish romanticism. One must be a realist. A few soft romantic words were for the bedchamber, if gruffly enunciated. When he had been a major of the yeomanry, he had been at his happiest. He was built that way, or at least that was the way he had made himself. His one concession to romanticism had been falling in love with Una's mother, and he had fought all opposition as if he were conducting a war until he had got his way. But on many things his mind was closed and this saddened her. She thought her interview could have only one result. Anything else, knowing her father, would amount to a miracle, and in this case there could be no miracle. She knew what she was up against, and also she knew herself.

She opened the door and went in.

He was sitting in the leather-covered chair reading a book and smoking a pipe. There was a whiskey decanter and a glass on the small table by his elbow. It was getting dark in the room. The two big windows let in light but the sky was not light-giving. The oak logs resting on the iron in the fireplace were flaming well. She looked at all those things because she didn't know how she would begin.

He looked up.

"You are back, Una," he said. "I was afraid you would be caught in the weather. The break is coming."

"I got back," she said. "The break is coming."

She sat on the arm of the chair on the other side of him. He looked at her. She looked at him. He thought that he had a very pretty daughter, but a sad one.

"Did somebody take your toy?" he asked smiling. It was a sentence taken from memories of her childhood.

She considered this. "Yes, I think so," she said. "Somebody took my toy and presented me with a sword."

"That sounds serious," he said, chuckling.

"Father," she said. "Talk to me about my mother."

He was surprised. His eyebrows rose. He took up a glass, sipped at the whiskey. "Why," he said, "you know everything about her already."

"All I really know," she said, "is that she died when I was thirteen. That is nearly seven years ago. Her memory is fading from me. I remember she was dark and she had a soft laugh."

"Yes," he said, clearing his throat. "She had a soft laugh. She was a gay, attractive person, your mother Kathleen. Not as serious as you, you know. You got a bit too much of me in you, I'm afraid. You could have done more with her lightness of heart."

"Why did she die, then?" she asked.

He thought. She could see that the thinking hurt him.

"She got this damn fever that was going then," he said. "She used to bring food to some of the tenants, the poorer ones. And medicines. She brought them laughter too. All that is forgotten now, the scoundrels, even forgotten her name and the things she did for them. They killed her, you might say, by accepting her kindness."

"How did you persuade her to marry you?" she asked.

"What a question," he said. "Dammit, I was well set up then. I could stand in a mirror with any man. I wasn't a gay dog, but I liked life and I knew what I wanted. So I went after her."

"But she was a Catholic," said Una.

"Yes," said he, "she was filled with that superstition. We were in what people call love. She was necessary to me, and I was to her. One of those things. No helping oneself. Never met a woman before or since like her. It was once for all, you see. Of course her people were against me. So were my own, for that matter. But I wanted this girl and I got her. She never saw her people again."

"Wasn't that hard on her?" Una asked.

"It wasn't my fault," he said. "They told her if she married me she was cutting herself off from them. She had a terrible time deciding, but then there was no help for either of us, once this thing had us in its grip. So they cut her away as if she was a rotten branch on the family tree. They are a hidebound and stubborn lot, these Irish Catholics once they take a few steps up in the world."

She stood up. Her back was to the fire.

"Father," she said, "I am afraid that you will have to cast me off too."

He put down the glass slowly.

"What do you mean?" he asked.

"Father," she said, "I am going to become a Catholic."

She watched the changes appearing in his face. Her legs were trembling. Saw the dawn of the knowledge and the shock, as if he had been kicked, and then his face went pale. Later she knew that it would go red.

"Do you know what you said?" he asked.

"Only too well, Father," she answered.

"You are not joking," he said. "This is not an Irish sense of humor."

"No, Father," she said.

"What are you doing to me?" he asked. He got up. He walked to the window. He looked out at the lowering sky. Already in the distance there was the low murmur of far-off thunder. Not a leaf was moving on a tree in the calm sticky air. His hands were clenched behind his back. She could see that the knuckles were white. Then he turned back to her.

"You are of mixed blood," he said. "My father was right. I didn't think so. Someday you will have to pay. We must be calm. Tell me quietly how this stupid notion came into your head."

There was a shake in her voice now. She was afraid of his desperate calmness.

"My mother taught me to pray when I was small," she said.

"If she taught you the Catholic way, she was a traitor," he said. "Do you hear that?"

"You cannot drive out a deep-rooted belief merely by saying that you no longer believe in it," said Una.

"She swore it on the Book of God," he said. "She swore it by her own soul. Are you putting your mother in Hell?"

"No," she said.

"She had abandoned their superstitions," he said. "She never met them again, never mixed with them again. She gained truth and love by doing that. Why would she try to pervert her own daughter? Are you making her out a monster?"

"I only said she taught me to pray," said Una.

He calmed himself. He turned away from her. "What then?" he asked.

"In Paris, in London, in Dublin," she said, "I studied as you know, and I read and I met many people. They were all only milestones on the road back to the religion of my mother. I didn't want it. I fought fiercely with every notion of it that came into my head. You don't know. You will never know how hard I fought against it. But now the fighting is over. I am going back. I am telling you before I do so."

There was silence from him. He dropped his head. He rubbed his forehead with his hand.

"How can I help you?" he wondered. "If a cow wanders into a bog hole, I can help her. If a mare is covered with mud, I can wash her. What am I going to do with you? Because I could never believe that you could become involved with your logical mind in a religion of superstition and idolatry. Good God, a daughter of mine!"

He walked away again. Then he turned and came back to her.

"Think of what you are getting into, for God's sake," he said. "Look at this O'Connell, the leader of the Catholics, vulgar, foul-mouthed and unscrupulous, backed up by those ignorant power-mad priests. He is an apostle, with them, of sedition. They are consumed with hatred for the established social order, the Established Church and the British Constitution, ready to overthrow it with a convulsion of society, at the first opportunity. Are these the people with whom you want to cast your lot?"

"Father," she said. "I know only a few priests. I found them good and holy men and more than literate. I am not going into politics. I am merely becoming a Catholic because my soul is telling me to."

"Oh, no," he said. "There is more to it than that. You are abandoning your own class. What do you think has made us what we are? Our faith in the Protestant religion. Our knowledge of its truth. Once you change sides you are in politics. You have gone over to the enemies of your own class. Do you realize how they hate us and our holy religion? Do you realize the terror they have brought again and again on this land in order to eradicate it? Have you thought of the thousands of martyrs who have died for the Protestant faith?"

"There have been many deaths on the other side," she began. He cut her off.

"See, already you are beginning to think on the other side," he said. "I can see that you are perverted already." She noted now that his face was red. He had passed away from paleness. There was sparking anger in his eyes. It made her calmer. The trembling went out of her limbs. He pulled open the door of the room. He roared out there in the hall. "Come here all of you from the kitchen! Come here! Biddy, Nora, Teresa, Duane, Christy! Come here, whoever is in the kitchen!" He came back in. He was glaring at her, as if she was a stranger who had deeply wounded him.

"You haven't thought," he shouted. "You haven't the least idea of what you have let yourself in for. I pray to the great God to enlighten you to what is before you if you step into the gutter. Because into the gutter you are going. Has anyone in this life deliberately chose to go down instead of going up?" He went to the door again. "Come on," he shouted. "Hurry up! Come when you are called!"

He was like the major again. He was barking out orders as

if he was talking to a troop of soldiers dragged from the bowels of the hulk ships on the Thames, she thought. She was very sad about it.

They shuffled in uneasily, Biddy and the girls. The girls were nearly wringing their hands. Dualta came after them. He was in his shirt sleeves. He had been eating. Christy, large and lumbering and barefooted, with brown tree bark clinging to his shirt and his hair, little Mocky, with his boy's dirty face, and his ragged clothes, his feet bare and discolored with brown dried bog mud.

"Stand along in a line there!" he shouted at them. "Go on now! Stand in a line there and let her see you."

They were red-faced, sweating, embarrassed, moving from foot to foot. Una felt their humiliation but could do nothing about it. Dualta wasn't humiliated. He was very interested. She didn't look at Dualta. He saw her standing straight at the fireplace, pale, her hands held in front of her.

"These are a cross section," Wilcocks was shouting, "of your traveling companions. A much better section than what you will meet. These are your brothers and sisters. Look at them! Embrace them! Kiss their feet!"

He was in a towering rage. Dualta thought: He should have let us all dress in our Sunday clothes before this presentation.

"Your mistress wants to join you," the Major was saying to them in a barracks-square voice. "She wants to be one of you! You hear that? Aren't you flattered, that she has become perverted? She will partake of your rags, your dirty thatched churches, your diseased confessionals. Aren't you pleased? That she is to become one of you?"

"Father!" said Una.

"Not to me," he said turning on her. "Don't say that word to me. Say that word to one of your greasy priests in a curtained fetid box. Don't say that word to me. Don't say that word to me ever again!"

Dualta felt sorry for him. He could see the hurt behind his anger.

Una spoke firmly.

"You can go now, Biddy," she said. "Thank you for coming."

They looked at Wilcocks. He had turned his back on them.

"I am sorry," said Una. "I am very sorry." They didn't know what to do. Dualta decided. He turned to the door and went out. They followed him. They went back bewildered to the big kitchen. They sat in silence, their ears strained. Nothing came to them except the sound of the distant thunder. Outside, big separate drops were falling on the dried earth, tapping it playfully, building up to the force of the storm that was driving them ahead of it, like silver sentinels.

"That did no good," said Una. Her father's back was turned to her. He didn't answer her.

"I know how you feel," she said.

"You do not," he said.

"I can only do one thing," she said, "leave you." It was a kind of question with her, not a statement. It remained tense on the air, unanswered. "I will collect a few of my possessions," she said, "and I will take myself out of your sight." He didn't answer. "Is it any use telling you how sorry I am?" she asked.

"Sorrow!" he snorted. "You have ended my life and you are sorry. You have debased me. If you do this thing now to me, there are not enough tears in the whole world to wash it away from me."

"I cannot turn back," she said. "It has been too hard coming this far. I have to go on now wherever it leads."

"As you wish," he said coldly. He came back. He sat in the chair. He poured a drink from the decanter. He took up his book. His hands were trembling. She had her hand up to her mouth. She had to press her nostrils to stop from crying. She walked to the door. She turned there.

"I will go to the town," she said. "Can I have Dualta to drive me there?"

"As you wish," he said, indifferently.

She went up the stairs slowly. She rubbed her hand on the polished banisters. She looked at the oil paintings that hung on the walls. In her own room, she got the small trunk from the wardrobe. She had it ready. All these actions had been gone over in her mind many times. She knew it would have to end like this, so she was prepared. She knew everything belonging to her that she would require. It was all soon packed. They filled the trunk, but she was leaving a lot behind her. She stopped thinking of that, in case she would cry.

She went downstairs then. She walked to the kitchen. She walked in on their silence. It was becoming very dark. She could barely see them in the light of the fire.

"Dualta," she said, "would you get the carriage horses harnessed? I want you to drive me to the town. Christy, would you come to my room and bring down my chest?"

Christy looked around him, waving his arms helplessly. Then he shuffled past her. Dualta rose and went out. She looked at Biddy and the girls.

She said: "I'm sorry my father did that to you. He is upset. You must forgive him. I won't say goodbye," she said. "I am sure we will meet again sometime." Biddy was on the point of crying, so she left hurriedly.

In the hall she got her cloak, and two hatboxes. She walked to the front door with them. She left them there. Then she went up the stairs again. Christy was outside her door with the chest on his shoulder as if it was of no weight. "Leave it below at the door," she said.

She looked around her room. It was such a nice room. It was unlikely that she would ever see the like of it again. She took a small tin handcase by its leather handle and she walked out the door. She closed it softly after her.

She went down the stairs very slowly. She had often thought of the way she would come down those stairs on her father's arm, in her wedding dress. Below, waiting, would be the mysterious bridegroom, never possessing a face, everything else but that, beautiful hair, body and carriage. Maybe dim eyes filled with love and rapture, the rooms resounding to the sound of chamber music, the tinkle of glasses, raised voices. The door was open. Christy was standing there. The rain was coming down, the skies weeping bitterly.

She said, "Leave those out too." She could see the wet carriage waiting in the rain.

She went to the door of the living room. She hesitated again. Then she went in.

Her father was where she had left him. The book was held listlessly in his hand. She thought that she had never loved her father more than she did at this minute. He knew she was there.

"Una," he said, "don't leave me." This was what he said. It was not fair. It put the whole guilt on her. It implied surrender. With all her heart she wished that she could do so. She imagined the wonderful joy of their reunion. She also knew that on the one point he would be utterly implacable. That was his way of life. He could see no other. He could understand no other.

There was no middle way.

She said, "Goodbye, my dear father," and then she closed the door and left him. She ran down the steps. She didn't mind the rain. Dualta had the door open for her. He helped her in.

"That was what it was all about?" he asked.

She looked at him blindly. He could already see the tears in her eyes, held back by the tightening of her jaws.

"Yes," she said, "that's what it was all about." He closed the door on her, climbed onto the high seat, fastened his coachman's thick cloak against the beating rain, shouted at the horses, slapped their wet hides with the reins, and pulled away from the house.

The whole sky was black. Sky and earth seemed to have become one black wet moaning mass. The sky in the distance was lightened now and again by the reflection of the lightning flashes.

It's just as well, Dualta thought grimly, as he bent his head to the blast, that she cannot see a thing. It was just as well she could get no long lingering look at the valley as she passed out of it.

"Hup! Hup! Hup!" he shouted at the reluctant horses.

chapter XII

HE WAS PLANT-ing little trees on a hilly place to the north of the house when the word came to him.

It was a word he had been afraid of, and when he heard it, his heart sank.

They were planting the young trees on what had been the holding of the Fortune family. There was nothing left of them now. The house had been leveled, the garden walls had been used to make drains, the ditches filled, and in years to come the four acres would be a thickly planted wood, a pleasant place on the side of the hill. He wondered if in time men would praise Wilcocks for his love of tree planting; if they would stumble on the ivy-covered ruins of what was once a cottage; and wonder in the sun-filtered wood at the grass-covered ridges which had once grown enough potatoes to fill the bellies of ten people. Let the future look after the future, he had thought then, angrily.

It was in a cleft where the stream came over a black rock on its way to the river below that he saw Cuan.

There was room here for six young trees, by the bank of the stream.

Cuan was sitting on the other side, smoking a long clay pipe.

Dualta looked around him. None of the other planters were in his vision. He sat down across the stream from Cuan. They looked at each other calmly.

"Well," said Dualta.

"Tonight," said Cuan.

"Oh," said Dualta.

It was springtime. It was beginning to show in the valley.

"Whaley has gone to the big town," said Cuan. "He won't be back tonight."

Whaley was the new bailiff. He was from England, a place called Yorkshire. He was a stocky man, without fear, and very efficient. If he had no fear, he took precautions. It was impossible to frighten him with letters. He never came within reach of a gun. He was impossible. Dualta liked him. He got things done. Dualta could admire men who got things done, because Wilcocks wasn't as efficient as he had been. In the six months or so since his daughter left, he was drinking more and caring less. The evictions mounted. There had been four. Fortune had been the first of them. Dualta was aware that Wilcocks was striking around him like a wounded animal. He didn't think it fair that the little people should be struck to ease his pain.

"Are you sure this is not too soon?" he asked.

"Are you getting soft on Wilcocks?" Cuan asked sarcastically.

"No," said Dualta.

"The people are too impatient. If he is not struck now, he won't leave a sinner in the valley," said Cuan.

"Are you going to hurt him?" Dualta asked.

"We are going to burn him out," said Cuan.

Dualta thought of the nice house he now lived in going up in flames. He supposed that it was just being sentimental. He didn't like to think of the house going up in flames. This wasn't logical.

"I see," he said. Cuan blew a puff of tobacco smoke into the air.

"Like that," he demonstrated. He smiled.

"Wilcocks must not be hurt," said Dualta.

"Burning will hurt him enough," said Cuan.

"He mustn't be hurt himself," said Dualta. "That will bring terrible things on the valley. They will scour it."

"We'll try not to hurt him," said Cuan.

"I mean this, Cuan," said Dualta.

"Can I account for every man in the heat of the moment?" Cuan asked.

"I don't care," said Dualta. "You'll have to account for them.

You will have to swear he won't be hurt or I won't go on with it."

"Are you gone soft on Wilcocks?" Cuan asked.

"No," said Dualta. "I'm just wise. Leave him alone in his person."

Cuan sighed. "All right," he said. "I'll talk sense to them."

They heard voices behind Dualta. Cuan rose. He tapped the pipe on his heel. "You know everything," he said to Dualta. "Just as it was planned. You are the Trojan horse. Let your belly open at midnight." He smiled. His eyes were gleaming. Dualta felt daunted by the look of him. He nodded his head. Cuan sauntered away. He was out of sight by the time the other planters came level with Dualta.

The cheerfulness went out of him for the rest of the day.

The laborers remarked it. Normally he would be joking with them, aping the gruff overseer. There were twenty-four of them. They were paid five pennies a day and their potatoes hot in the evening. Eleven of them were estate laborers who got no money at all, but paid for their cottage and the few roods of ground for their potatoes by their labor. They were simple men, hard-working, grumbling, keeping themselves away from conspiracies as long as they had nearly enough to eat, a few shillings per year for tobacco, and to buy Sunday clothes for their children. They seemed to demand nothing else of life. This was their lot and until somebody bettered it for them they were going to accept it. They remained unfired by ambition. "He's sick," one said. And another said: "He eat too much from the pickling trough." "He's in love," said another. "He is hungry for Nora," said another. "She would never lie with a foreigner," one said.

He refused to rise. He remained silent, directing them to the lie of the young trees. He himself had been directed by Whaley, in a thick English accent men found it most difficult to understand, so that he had to be drawing his orders on paper most of the time.

They returned to the house as the dusk set in. They washed their hands at the pump in the yard and sat in the covered shed and ate their potatoes from the great pot. Salt and buttermilk

garnished the hot potatoes. It was amazing how soon the great
pot was emptied and the mound of skins thrown into the trough
for the pigs.

So they sat in the shed faintly lighted by the fires under the
pots and some of them smoked their pipes and some of them
chewed their tobacco, until the cold nip of the evening came on
the air and they started to drift away, some to faraway cottages,
some to the estate cottages and the unmarried ones to the rooms
over the carriage houses. He thought of the strength available if
called upon. About ten men. Would they fight for Wilcocks?
They wouldn't fight exactly for him but they would fight for
their five pennies a day and their potatoes. So they would have
to be quietened. That had been arranged for. You couldn't de-
pend on them because they had too many mouths depending on
them already.

He said good night. He went into the house. He didn't stay in
the kitchen to banter talk with them. He went through. They
remarked on this with their eyes. It's very strange behavior for
Dualta, they thought. Then they shrugged it off and went on
with their work. Young people are odd when the spring comes.
They get queer fluxes.

He went to the library. He worked at the books with the light
of a tallow candle mounted on a wrought-iron candlestick. Miss
Una had liked those. She had got the blacksmith to make many
of them almost in his own fancy. He enjoyed this job. He added
many flourishes as he went along.

He was doing only the simple accounts. He tried to concen-
trate on them. The wages book. Biddy a very good cook, £8 per
year, Nora £4, Teresa £3-10, Christy £6, the turf boy, the pump
boy, the cow boy, the carpenter, the blacksmith, the slaughter-
house man, stewards, bailiffs—the estate was a little industry.
Wilcocks fed many mouths. Many would be hungry without
him. But the payment came from the highly priced acres of the
tenants. Here you were up against the sacred rights of property,
embodied, they said, in the Ten Commandments.

He thought, now is the time that I should go around closing
the heavy shutters on the windows. But not tonight. Tonight

he was to forget to close the shutters. That made it very easy for them.

He looked around at the books. All would be gone, consumed in fire. He didn't think that was fair. Knowledge should not be destroyed. That was vandalism. What could he do? Nothing. He couldn't hide them now. They were too many. He thought of the pleasure he had got from reading, and the indignation, nearly all indignation, but a lot of pleasure too, a great lot of pleasure once the English words started to come easy to him. A lot that was beautiful and inspired amongst all the others. Paine's *Age of Reason, Common Sense, Crisis Papers* were there. A few years ago you would have been hanged if you were found with *The Age of Reason.* He wondered what Wilcocks thought as he read it. He could see him getting red in the face and hurling the book at the wall, only to retrieve it when he had cooled off and continue reading it. It was opposed to everything he believed in, but Wilcocks also believed in reading the other side, just to know what they were up to, never for a moment giving a comma of it his consent.

It was a great pity about the books, Dualta thought, sighing.

He was restless. He left the library. He took the candle with him into the hall. He listened. The click of a glass from the drawing room where Wilcocks was. Dualta could see him as if he was there. Looking into the fire. He was not the same since Una left. It had hit him very hard. Dualta knew this well. He felt sorry for him. The trouble was, he might as well admit it, that he liked Wilcocks. Principles to him were things that you stood for, and if necessary died for. It didn't matter if the principles were faulty. Principles were what you yourself held to be the rule of life as you saw it. You stuck to those. He genuinely regarded the lower orders as lower orders, if Catholic, superstitious, obstinate and irredeemable, and only a little raised above the animal order. As such he treated them as he would favorite animals. He was kind, thoughtful (except where the sacred rights of private property might be in danger), generous (within the spoken limits set by the order of landlords, so you didn't raise your workers by a penny a day if a more feckless member of the class couldn't afford it). Beyond all this he liked him because he had a sense of humor, and just because he was likable.

There was the sound of voices and laughter from the kitchen. Dualta went softly up the stairs to his own attic room.

He thought Cuan had chosen his night well. All the defenses were down. They could do what they wanted to do, have come and gone again inside twenty minutes. He sat on his bed. He knew he would have to gather his possessions, because he would have to escape in the confusion. It would be very obvious that he was an enemy in the house. This upset him, this thought. He had eaten the man's food, earned his money, laughed and joked and forced most of the people to like him. What would they think of him after this? What would Wilcocks think of him? What would Una think of him? What did it matter? When you engaged on things like this, you didn't expect to be liked. What difference would it make?

He gathered his belongings. He noted wryly that he had got used to sleeping in a bed. He remembered the story told of the poor cottager who decided to raise his bale of straw from the floor and pegged up a bedstead for himself, four inches off the damp ground. He slept in this with great joy. The next day his horse was drowned so he lowered the bed to the ground again, saying, God humbles those who exalt themselves.

He folded his clothes and his cheap books and his papers into a tidy budget and wrapped them with cord, so that he could bear them on his shoulders.

He sat there for some time, trying not to think at all.

He heard Biddy and the girls going to their attic rooms. Later he heard Wilcocks coming to the landing below and going into his own room. The house was wrapped in silence then. To the rest of them it would be a normal silence, but to him it was the silence preceding death.

He blew out the candle, caught up his budget and went softly down the stairs. He paused outside Wilcocks' bedroom door. He listened. He could hear nothing. This landing was bathed in moonlight. The raiders needed the light of the moon. He saw the closed door of Una's room. He went to it. He opened it softly. He went in. He would watch from there through the large window. He wondered how much time was left, one hour or two. He went back and sat on the bed. It was a curtained bed. The curtain rails creaked as he sat, the silk rustled. He thought of Una. Very faintly he was enveloped in the remains of the scent that was hers. That and tang of dampness. Nobody had been in her room since she had left. It was as it was, just for cleaning.

He thought about her. She was an odd girl. He remembered saying goodbye to her at the town on that wet night when he left her at the inn. He had left her things and then she had taken off her glove and held out her hand to him. He had taken it in his own wet hand. He still could feel the tingle of her soft flesh in his palm. She looked at him. She expected him to say something. He hadn't. What was she to him, or her father? She was disappointed in him. He thought she shouldn't have left her father like that. She should have found some other way. If he had a father he would not leave him.

Now he remembered her more clearly, and his sorrow that she had gone away and he would never know where she was. You got used to her, that was it, he thought, and could imagine how her father had missed her; how much he wanted to give in to her, and how completely incapable he was of doing so. He had never mentioned her name since she left, and probably never would again. He would just suffer her inside him.

He remembered another thing then, the day he came, worming his way in like an eel in a shallow pond, about how he hadn't come, had he, to hurt them. He remembered that. He said no, didn't he, neither you nor yours. Was it a lie, then? If this was patriotism was he permitted to lie? Was it patriotism? How would the burning of this house advance the cause of patriotism? Wouldn't it only retard it? Wouldn't the soldiers and the police and the javelins and the bum bailiffs exact a terrible price from the whole valley?

Would they spare Wilcocks, despite what Cuan promised? There were so many who had been deeply deprived by him. They bore nothing for him but an abiding hatred. If some of these were armed, would they have the patience to hold their hands and let him live? Dualta stood up. He didn't think so. Let him decide now, here at once before it was too late. Did he want to go through with this thing? If he didn't what was he to do, sneak out of the house and leave it helpless and alone, pound his chest in after years and say, I had nothing to do with it? I wasn't there?

On the other hand if he did not approve he would have to do something about it. He couldn't be negative. And if he wanted to do something about it he would have to do it now and do it fast, before it was too late, too late.

His emotions were mixed but his actions were cold and ordered. He went down the stairs quickly. He left his budget handy in the hall. Then he moved from room to room, lifted the window, pulled the heavy shutters close and barred them. The moonlight was shut out, so he had to stumble his way in the dark. At times he was almost in panic in case the dark figures of the horsemen would appear in front of him and the torches break into light. He was haunted by the thought of Tooley and what had happened to him.

His last job was to shoot the heavy bolts on the kitchen door. Christy was there, sleeping in a corner near the fire. He shook him awake. It took a lot of time to shake him awake. He slept as if he had been hit on the head with a block of wood.

"Christy! Christy! Christy!" Got him conscious. "Get into the hall," he shouted. "Into the hall. We are going to be attacked. You hear!" Got him to his feet, staggering as if he was drunk, guided him through the darkness. Left him in the hall, and went up the stairs again on light feet. He went to the room of Biddy. He awakened her with sibilant whispering. Could only see the vague bulk of her in the moonlight. He didn't want her to wake up in terror. "Listen," he said, "there is going to be an attack on the house. Stay where you are and don't move." He closed the door. The two girls sleeping in the attic room. Fear in the whites of their eyes. "Stay where you are. Don't move out of the room." Just in case. If the attack succeeded there would be time to get them out.

He went to a window then on the landing and looked out. He thought he could see the forms of them, converging, terrifyingly ghostlike in the moonlight. His heart was beating fast. One last trip now.

He went to the door of Wilcocks. He knocked. Called "Mister Wilcocks! Mister Wilcocks!" Again and again, his knocking and voice insistent. He heard a reaction. He waited. He heard the strike of the sulfur light and under the door he saw the light of the candles. "Put out the light!" he shouted at once. It went out immediately. So Wilcocks was well awake. He waited. The door opened.

"Well," he said crisply.

"We are going to be attacked," said Dualta.

"Are the shutters closed?"

"Yes."

"Rouse the men in the yard," he said.

"No good," said Dualta. It was a good plan. As they came one by one the houses would be guarded by silent men, the doors blocked with timber, oak pegs slipped into latches. The house would be completely isolated.

"Go down," said Wilcocks. "Light candles in the gun room."

Dualta left him. Who am I betraying, he wondered as he went? I couldn't see it happen to here? What will they think of me? He didn't care. At this moment, he didn't care.

He went down. He collected Christy. They lighted two three-branched candlesticks in the gun room. The light flickered off the oiled barrels of the muskets and the shotguns and the pistols.

"Dualta! Dualta! What's abroad?" Christy was asking. He was hardly awake yet.

Wilcocks wasn't long. His nightshirt was shoved into his breeches and he wore light pumps on his feet.

He was decisive now, anyhow, Dualta thought.

"We will load the guns," he said. "You, Duane, have we much time?"

"We have very little time," said Dualta.

"Here, take these," he said. He gave him three long sulfur matches with a striker. "Go out on the roof," he said. "In the gulley between the two roofs you will find a covered iron pot. Set fire to it. It is a signal light. When they see it help will come. We will load the guns. Take a top window each. Go now."

Dualta left. Climbed the stairs and the attic stairs and forced the skylight window. The iron bar that held it was strong. He had trouble forcing it. It gave to his strength and he pulled himself out. He walked between the valley of the two roofs until he came to the awkward bulk of the pot. He lifted the lid of it. It was stacked with pitch and wood. He paused a moment. Then he pulled himself up the sloping slates until his head appeared over the top. He looked down. There were horsemen on the front lawn now, and their torches were coming alight one after the other, springing up, smoking.

He returned to the pot. One after another he struck the lights and applied them to the stuff in the pot. It was bonedry. Suddenly it went up in flames with a loud whoosh, almost blinding him. A tall dark red flame rose from it and clouds of smoke. He went back to the skylight, dropped through, closed it after him, wondering at the perspicacity of Wilcocks. Who would have thought of a signal fire but he? He was sure now that the barricadoed houses were better prepared than they had thought. This was the first attack on a big house. But for himself it would have been already successful despite all the precautions. He thought that the Trojan horse had turned into a goat, or an ass, or a sheep, or a snake, he didn't know what. But no name would be nice, not even the first one.

Wilcocks was on the landing.

He handed him a gun. "Take the room on the right," he said. "Break the glass if you have to."

There was no need. At that moment they heard the glass of the windows breaking, some from stones, some from shots. He went to the room. It happened to be Una's. As he arrived a flaming torch came through the broken window. He caught it and threw it out again, scuffled the smouldering rug with his foot. Then he went to the window, shoved out the barrel of the shotgun, and pulled the trigger. He took care to aim in the air. From another window he heard the sound of another shot, and the scream of a horse. He peered over the edge of the window. There was a confused milling of horsemen below and shouting. One or two shots from guns. The tops of the trees around about were eerily lighted by the fire of the roof, the tops of them rosy.

Go away now, men! Go away now, men, for the love of God! he urged them in his mind before the others come up behind and catch you. He didn't want that either, you see. He didn't know what he wanted.

He heard the strong voice calling them. That would be Cuan. Ordering over the shouts and the shots, and in another moment the men outside seemed to be obliterated as they threw the torches away from them toward the house, and then there was the sound of thundering hooves on the turf. They were going away, flying in all directions. He sighed. Glad that Cuan had seen sense, cut his losses, escaped before it was too late. This violence was too ambitious. It was too big for small men, bloated with success against much lesser opponents, like Tooley. He raised himself, peering, trying to see as the scattering horsemen ran for the river and the woods, and already from the poplar drive there was shouting and the sounds of horsemen. How much better organized they were than Cuan knew, Dualta thought, as he sat on the floor with his back to the window. He felt exhausted. They had not succeeded. What was success! They had not succeeded on account of him. On the other hand Wilcocks had succeeded on account of him. To whom was the victory then. He couldn't say.

Wilcocks was at the door.

"Are you all right, Duane? I think they are running away."

"Yes, sir," said Dualta. "I think they are running away."

"Let's get down to the hall then," said Wilcocks. "Get the door open. Help is on its way. We might be able to catch some of the blackguards."

Dualta followed after him. He paused for a moment before leaving Una's room. He thought it odd that it should be Una's room. He smelled once more, widening his nostrils for the faint scent of her, but it was completely obscured by the foul-smelling rush-tallow torch that had been a brief lodger.

He went down the stairs listlessly.

Wilcocks was standing in the open door. He held a gun. Christy was lighting the wall candlesticks in the hallway. The place was being filled with light and shadow. Smoke from the dying torches outside was drifting into the hallway like wraiths. He left down the gun, and took up his budget. He knew that now was the time for him to go quietly out the back way and disappear in the woods. But a strange inertia held him. He leaned against the stairs. He couldn't make himself go. He wanted nothing from them, from any of them. He had come to a part in his life when he had taken sides, for no clear reason that he could see, and in this case he couldn't see that taking sides would be of the slightest avail.

So he stood there and watched listlessly, as they came: gentlemen hurriedly dressed, or half dressed, with unshaven faces. Guns and red faces and loud talk. Coming and going, coming and going, and squat men with sticks, shouting and going. Horses, voices, that never came into perspective, gentlemen and burly followers reminding him of long ago when they had hunted him like a hare on the side of the Mount. Just these types of people. They were everywhere. How could you escape from them?

They came into focus when he saw that he was suddenly surrounded by angry faces, with the face of Wilcocks in the middle of them. Not angry, but pale and stern.

"Duane! Duane! Wake up!" he was saying. "You knew they were coming. How did you know they were coming? Speak up, man. How did you know they were coming?"

Dualta looked at them. There were five of them. Three young men and two older gray-haired men, all very disheveled. And they were angry.

"I just knew," said Dualta. "Isn't that enough?"

"No, Duane," said Wilcocks, "it is not enough. If you knew they were coming, you must know who they are."

Dualta shook his head.

"I do not know," he said.

"You are lying," said one of the young men.

"That's right," said Dualta.

"You will have to tell," said Wilcocks. "I am grateful to you.

You saved the house. But this goes beyond loyalty. These men must be found and hanged. You must name them."

"No," said Dualta.

"By God," said the young man. "He will be made to tell."

"Wait a minute," said Wilcocks. "You will have to tell, Duane. There is no escape but to tell."

"No," said Dualta.

"He'll have to be made to talk," said the angry young man.

"You hear that, Duane," said Wilcocks. "This is too serious. You will have to talk."

"No," said Dualta.

Wilcocks looked at him. Dualta met his eyes squarely. Wilcocks held his look for a moment and then his face got red. Like long ago when his daughter faced him. He stepped back. "All right," he said.

Dualta saw them coming toward him, with boots and fists and sticks and even the reversed barrel of a pistol.

He thought: Once before I was hit and I hit back. I will not hit back. If I had not hit back then, I would not be here now. Perhaps, he thought, this will purge me of the distaste I have for myself. Perhaps this will make me one of the people again. How subtle is the temptation of the big house, he thought. You get used to it. Regular food, salt mutton and beef at frequent intervals, a soft bed to lie on, like living in a well stocked fort, while outside the natives scratch for a living in the poor ground. Dimly he could understand how the lost Gaelic poets cried for the departed chieftains, long gone and their boards groaning. Were they bemoaning the lost power of the chieftains or the good living conditions that sapped them and separated them from their own and refined their poetry until it was beyond the understanding of common men?

He thought of this as the first blow rocked all the teeth in his head. If he had betrayed his own people he would accept the pain; he had to pay for it. If this was the way it had to be he would accept it. This was his thought as the kick of the riding boot in his groin brought him to the ground.

chapter XIII

CUAN WAS pleased with his plan, and with the excellent way it unrolled itself smoothly. Once they broke into the estate and fanned out, blinding the houses of the bailiffs, into the back portions to lock the sleeping men in the quarters over the carriage houses, and the house was ringed with determined if nervous men, he felt pleased. In a small way it represented his large dream. This he had thought of many times at night, stirring restlessly in his straw. The world was made up of community cells. This valley was a small one, but only one of many. All were complementary. So what he was doing here in a small way could be built up and spread so that it would take in a whole nation, like a fire in a forest jumping from tree to tree. This was why it drove him to fury to see men content with their lot. He was always angry at the shabby people in the shack towns springing up around the large centers of population, ragged men with large ragged families erecting frail shacks made of wood and mud, begging, half starving, drinking raw whiskey at times to drive away misery, but laughing, lolling in the sun in their rags, cuddling children with ricketty limbs. Why did they submit to this? They didn't have to submit like this.

So his plan pleased him. It was organized. It was drilled. It would be swift, and Wilcocks' house would soon be just a blackened pile. If they took revenge afterwards on the people, so much the better. Out of persecution would come bitterness, a lust for revenge, and Wilcocks' house could be a torch that lighted freedom in the south.

He knew at once that it was lost when the signal fire flared from the roof. He hadn't calculated on this. When the horsemen lighted the torches and he saw the shutters fast closed on the lower windows he knew there was not time. Broken glass in the upper windows, shots, firing, all were no use. It was already too late. He was in a cold rage but his mind worked well.

He galloped among them, shouting: "Get away! Get away! Scatter! Out of the grounds. Leave the horses! Get home on foot!" For there would be pursuit. It was better for the pursuers to chase riderless horses. It would confuse them.

He could feel their disappointment, and worse still he could feel them disintegrating as panic took over from confidence. They milled around. He set his horse and went around the house. The men there were gazing up at the roof. It was reflecting off their faces. He shouted at them. He gestured with his arm. They got his message and set out of the yard. All except one, he noticed as he was about to pull the horse's head around. This was Tom Ryan, a relation of Annie's. He was fumbling under his coat, and took out a package that gleamed whitely and then he threw this on the ground before he turned to move away.

Cuan closed on him.

"What are you doing, Tom?" he asked.

"Annie told me to leave this," he said. "It'll mislead them, she said."

"All right," said Cuan. "Get out of here. When you cross the river get home to bed fast. Let the horse free. Chase him up the hills. Give them something to follow."

Tom dug his heels into the horse's flanks. Cuan bent down from the saddle and swept up the package. It consisted of a bundle of papers tied with twine. He hadn't time, but he moved the pages with his fingers. In the glaring mixture of light, fire and moonlight he could see that the writing was that of Dualta. In one of the sentences he read his own name. They were letters that Dualta had written and discarded, carefully saved by Annie. There was one note from Dualta to himself, their names clear in both of them. He knew he was going pale with shock. He heard shouting from the front of the house. He turned the head of the horse and set out of the yard. The sound of the hooves on the stones ceased and was taken up by the dull clop on the grass of the park.

He swallowed his anger in order to think.

Annie. He was not surprised the more he thought. She had decided to end the affair. There were two strangers in the valley. The affair could not be ended without offering victims. They were the victims. Oh, Annie! Should he be surprised? He peered ahead at the horseman. He thought he saw Ryan heading down for the river, bent low over the horse. From his left he heard the shouts and the sound of horsemen. These would be the ones answering the signal fires. He thought that he might have to face Annie. He wondered if he did face her if he would have the patience not to kill her. The spittle was sour in his mouth. When he got close to the horseman he called, "Tom! Tom!" He saw the man's head turning. He slowed the run of the horse. They were not far from the river.

"Tell Annie," said Cuan, "I got the package."

"All right, Cuan, all right," said Tom. "We must hurry, man, they will be on top of us."

"Tell her I said this," said Cuan. "Remember it. Tell her I said, Let her head never rest easy. Again. Sometime I will come back to face her. You'll tell her this, Tom?"

"Yes, yes," said Tom impatiently.

"It may be tomorrow or next week or next year," he said. "Tell her that, but that I will come back to her and I will reward her. Tell her that. Tell her to keep her head over her shoulder for the coming of Cuan McCarthy."

"Can't you tell her yourself, Cuan," said Tom. "You will be seeing her."

"I will," said Cuan. "Just tell her that I will be seeing her."

Tom slapped the horse's flank with his palm. He jumped and set off toward the river.

Cuan dismounted from his horse. He had the blunderbuss in his hand. He smacked the horse and he set off after the other one, going more swiftly when he was released of his load.

Cuan bent low and set off running across the parkland back toward Wilcocks' house. He was glad of the physical action. It served to calm his hot blood. Who was it had said it somewhere, sometime? Behind this conspiracy there is somebody who is making something out of it. It wasn't himself. He made nothing out of it, only the satisfaction he got from the planning and the dreams. He thought they all felt the same as himself, imbued with love of an ideal to be wrested, however violently, from life. As he thought, he realized what he was getting out of it. From their meager collections they would buy a lease here to save someone from eviction, or they would lease fallow land and put an evicted person onto it. The respectable part of the valley was ringed with places they had bought or rented or leased, and they were all in Annie's name. He knew that now. She was a respectable person, who could be expected to be charitable to those who respected her. She was doing it for the people. But she had built up a creditable number of acres in her own name, which one by one would revert to her. It was as simple as that. She had no charity. She had no honor. She had no patriotism. But she had what she wanted. It was so simple. And he was the simpleton. He and Dualta.

Dualta.

That was the name that was bringing him back.

He threw himself on the grass as he saw the massing of men in front of the lighted door of the house. There were horsemen coming and going. Orders were being shouted. Some of them dismounted, leaving their horses outside. Most of them, to commands, set off into the surrounding areas chasing the sound of the fleeing horse hooves. Why had Dualta failed to open the shutters or save them from being closed? Cuan wanted to know this. Had he been discovered? If he had he was in trouble. It would be easy for Cuan to get away. It was no problem, over the hills and wash out his mouth and the taste of Annie from the clean water of a mountain stream. But he wasn't going to do it. Not until he knew what was happening to Dualta, and why.

He waited patiently. All the horsemen had come and gone. The men had been freed from their sleeping quarters. He saw them coming from the back places, armed with sticks and farm implements, whatever was available, and setting out running like dogs to the heels of the horsemen. And then there was nobody, coming from any direction, just the five saddled horses in front of the open door of the house, moving from the graveled drive to crop grass in the moonlight. He rose and ran swiftly. He leaped the steps and stood beside the open door.

He saw the blood on Dualta's head and he saw him as he fell to the heavy kick.

Then he moved in.

"No more," he said in a loud voice.

The young man who had his boot raised, let it drop slowly as he saw the barrel of the gun gazing at him. Cuan saw the five hard faces looking at him.

"Gentlemen," he said, "move away from him." They were not armed. Except for whips. Their guns were leaning against the stairs. They had pistols in their belts. He waved the gun. They moved back a little. "Are you all right, Dualta?" he asked.

Dualta nodded his head. He rose to his knees slowly, then pulled himself to his feet by grasping the banisters of the stairs.

"Are you coming, Dualta?" Cuan asked to encourage him.

Dualta nodded his head. He straightened up. Then he went to where his budget was resting on a chair. He raised it to his shoulder and then walked slowly toward Cuan.

"Take a gun with you," said Cuan.

Dualta shook his head. "No gun," he said and walked painfully on.

"You can follow us," said Cuan, "but some of you will die with us."

"You can go away," Wilcocks said. "You will not be followed by us. The police will take care of you."

He said this to Dualta. Dualta knew this. He stopped. He looked at him. Was this Wilcocks' way of trying to say something? You never knew with him. "Anything I owe you," said Dualta, "I have paid." Then he walked past Cuan into the moonlight.

Cuan waited a little longer. He didn't trust them. He wanted Dualta to recover and get a little farther away. He looked at the five of them. Wilcocks he knew. He didn't know the others.

They were alien to him. They regarded him with hatred. This pleased him.

When he thought enough time had gone, he stepped back and kept walking back until he was free of the light from the door. The signal fire was dead. The moon was getting low in the sky. He saw Dualta and went to him and put his hand under his arm.

"We will have to hurry," he said.

Dualta tried to break from his shuffle. Into a walk and then into a shuffling run. Cuan kept looking over his shoulder.

He needn't have worried. When he was gone from the doorway Wilcocks moved to it and closed the door.

The others had gone for their weapons. They saw Wilcocks standing in front of the door.

"George! George!" they said.

"No," said Wilcocks. "Let them go. The police will take care of them."

"Do you know what you are doing?" one asked him.

"Yes," said Wilcocks. "He didn't have to tell me. But he told me. Now he can go."

"You are a damn fool, George," they said.

"Yes," said Wilcocks. "Perhaps I am."

But he stayed with his back to the door. He thought about Duane. He decided that he would miss him. He had introduced a note of youth and wit to his house. He was a traitor but he was not all bad. He would miss him as he would a favorite gun dog? He thought not. He would miss him as a person, he thought. Now, but he had been so devilishly deceitful that if the police ever caught up with him and hanged him, he would not weep.

"We will go and empty the decanter, gentlemen," he said. "We have earned it, and confound their politics." He left the door and went toward the drawing room. They looked at one another, shrugged, dropped the guns and trooped after him.

Dualta read the last line of the letters and then slowly tore them into small pieces. He stood up. There was a high wind blowing up here on the Galtee mountains. He let the pieces go and the wind took them and scattered them like snowflakes ahead of it. It allowed some of them to rest on the heather and the soft places before it took them up again and scattered them farther and farther away from his sight. Dualta sighed and sat on the rock.

They had spent the night and most of the dawn laboriously climbing the mountain. They wanted their breath for breathing not for talking. But the talking would have to come, he knew. Cuan had gone to a farther height to try and spot smoke that might be rising from a chimney or a mountain dwelling or from the bothán of a shepherd. Because they were hungry and they had no food.

It was a clear day. He couldn't see all of the valley they had left. But he could see the river and the houses on the other side of it, and where it opened up into the great fertile plain, the winding river and the great fields and the sprawling towns, and the clustered villages. A bird's-eye view. He felt pain looking down. It had held no permanence for him, but it held memories. He thought what a nice peaceful valley it could have been, only for some of the people in it. Like himself say. Annie as well then. Sort of pustules on a healthy body. Not Cuan. Cuan was a dedicated animal. A man of violence. Wherever he went he would bring that with him, but he knew what he wanted and he was prepared to do what he thought was right in order to do it. But he could never be like Dualta or Annie.

He heard his voice behind him.

"Well, and what do you think of that, Dualta?" He came to him and sat on a rock opposite him. His eyes were like sharp needles.

"It wasn't unexpected," said Dualta.

"She had me fooled," said Cuan. "Oh, she had me fooled. She never once was working for the people. That she should have used me, a man of my intelligence. That I should have been used by an illiterate. It's killing me."

"You never asked me," said Dualta, "why the shutters were closed."

Cuan dropped his eyes from him. He leaned on his elbow. He turned his head away.

"So we will part here," said Dualta.

"What will you do?" Cuan asked.

"I will drift home," said Dualta. "I will seek my uncle Marcus."

"How will you go?" Cuan asked.

"I will go to Limerick," said Dualta.

"And walk into their arms?" said Cuan derisively. "Don't you know they will be waiting for you, after this?"

"What will you do?" Dualta asked.

Cuan stood up.

"I will go down into Kerry," he said, "traveling the hills. You can walk on hills from here to Cinnmhara; the Galtee, the Nagle, the Boggeragh mountains, on to the McGillicuddy Reeks. It will take time, but it will be safe enough. The hunt will slacken down. They will forget. I have a job to do in Clare, then and I will work my way into it quietly across the Shannon mouth. You can come with me if you want to. I do not want to press my company on you."

"You might find me unpleasant to travel with," said Dualta. "If I betrayed you once I could do it again."

To his surprise Cuan laughed, a hearty laugh that lightened the somber lines of his face.

"Oh, no, Dualta, if you were going to betray me, you would tell me all about it long in advance so that your conscience wouldn't trouble you afterwards."

"I hope so," said Dualta. "I sincerely hope so. What kind of a job will you do in Clare?"

"Some time ago," said Cuan, "they sent for help. They want two strangers to frighten an agent."

"To kill him?" asked Dualta.

"No," said Cuan, "just to frighten him. Like Hanley. You remember Hanley?"

"You mean the bang and the blow and the scuttling like a hare?" asked Dualta.

"That's it," said Cuan.

"I'll do that for you, Cuan," he said, "to make up to you, but do you know what I want now?"

"What?" Cuan asked.

"I want to be commonplace," said Dualta. "I want to be one with the people. I want to dig and sow and harvest, just being one of the people. You see down there, that was dangerous."

"How?" Cuan asked.

"Soften you," said Dualta. "You get used to living in a big house. I only realized it. They don't try to subvert you. It's just the things that are there. And you say why shouldn't I have them, too? I understand something. I used to wonder, how can they get Irishmen to work for them, to carry out all the dirty things that have to be done, injuring their own people. I know now. You just slide into it, little by little. Living in two worlds. One day you will slide into their world. You won't even know that you have done it. And you will be unhappy. You will be most unhappy, without knowing the reason."

"You have learned something," said Cuan.

"I have learned to take blows," said Dualta. "And that's a big lesson. I learned that down there. If you want to help, you are not to be outside kneading the dough. You must be the leaven inside it. Living with it. Do you understand me?"

"No," said Cuan.

"There are two worlds," said Dualta, "and you must choose which one you are going to live in. I have chosen mine now, and I will not desert it again. I will live in it with all my heart, and someway while living in it I will add to it, and survive in the middle of it."

"No good," said Cuan. "Sink into torpor like the rest? Have faith in God, who hasn't heard the cries of the Irish for hundreds of years? Be reduced to lower than serfs? No. You hit and hit and hit again. Choosing your place. Only by inducing fear will you get alleviation. You're wrong, Dualta. I know what you mean but you are wrong."

"Then you will let me go with you?" Dualta asked.

"As long as you frighten an agent at the end," said Cuan.

Dualta laughed.

"I will do that," he said. "I will frighten an agent before I become part of the people."

"Let us get then," said Cuan. "I saw the soldiers gathering around the house. Soon they will be scouring the hills. They won't like it, but they'll do it, and we have to be far away before they are up on this one."

Dualta rose. He shouldered his budget. He regretted that he hadn't thought to put food into it. He tightened the belt around his breeches. Cuan had gone ahead of him.

"Cuan," he called.

Cuan turned to look at him.

"Do you know," said Dualta, "I'm happy for the first time in a long time." He looked at the prematurely white-haired man standing there outlined against the sky, and he thought: Now I have affection for him.

"It's a queer time to be happy," said Cuan, "with months of walking in front of us and policemen and soldiers on our tail."

"Well, I am," said Dualta, "and I'm hungry too."

"We will find smoke," said Cuan. "Forget your hunger and walk. Time is short for now." He turned and walked away.

Dualta looked down into the valley once again. He could see the town where they had hanged Paidi. This brought a lurch to his heart. And he thought of Wilcocks' daughter Una. He thought she was a nice girl and it's just as well she is gone out of my life, because it wouldn't do at all. It just wouldn't do.

Then he turned and followed after Cuan, the tall, tough heather scratching at his stockinged legs.

part three

chapter xiv

IT WAS RAINING. This was mountain rain, driven by the wind, millions of minute misty drops that clung and soaked you to the skin. Sometimes when the extra gust of wind whipped the mist away, Dualta could see a shaft of sunlight in a valley.

Ahead of him he could see Cuan plodding away, his head bowed to the wind, his short cloak flapping soggily against his legs. He thought that Cuan's shape was thinner than it had been. He knew he was thin himself. Months of mountain traveling, some days with no food at all except edible roots and watercress, other days gorged with the flesh of sheep, which Cuan always claimed he had just seen slaughtered by an eagle which he had robbed of its prey. Dualta smiled now thinking of this, and he would always afterwards refer to unexpected things as gifts of the eagle. But they were healthy. They had no soft flesh left on them. They could race a mountain pony. He thought of the many places they had rested their heads in the months past; stone shelters made by men, or arched rocks in heather wildernesses manured by sheep; crudely built shelters where the herders slept. Once or twice real houses where they slept head to feet, packing a kitchen floor like sods of turf in a clamp. These were good, those houses. They worked in the day for their food and they laughed and sang and danced at night on the mud floors. But always they were pursued by rumors, by men who might have seen a patrol of soldiers, or a troop of police, or even a patrol of Revenue men with their bullies who were searching the mountains for stills. They were always on the move, rarely at rest until your dreams were filled with a tidy cottage with a new straw thatch and whitewashed walls, with the sun shining on it. Ordered gardens and children laughing; going to Mass with the people on Sunday dressed in their Sunday clothes. Just order, a little peace. He didn't yearn for the fleshpots of Wilcocks' house, soft beds and meat and hot baked bread. He would settle for much less than that now.

He nearly bumped into Cuan, who was bent down staring ahead of him. They were on a sort of post road now which would join two towns. It was a strange place for a road, but there it was, a good road, drained at the sides, with not too many pot-holes in its heart. At that moment the mist rolled away, like a curtain being raised, and below them they saw the mountains sloping and flattening to meet the sea. The sea was shimmering, greenly and bluely, shadowed islands were set in it. It seemed to stretch to eternity to meet the white scudding clouds on the horizon. In an inlet below them the new sun made the yellow sands shine. Below on the coast, cliffs and rocks with the sea breaking over them fought for your looking with the belts of forest trees, the green fenced fields.

Dualta suddenly set out running down the coarse ground, breathing in the clean salt-laden air.

He ran a long way and wasn't even breathless from the run, when around the shoulder of the hill came a racing hare and baying beagles and behind them the forms of running and shouting men. He was in the middle of the hare hunt almost before he was aware of it. When the hare saw him, it paused, fatally, because the dogs got to it. It had only time for one despairing cry before it died and then the panting men were there and they were looking curiously at him, and at the figure of Cuan coming down the hill behind him, his cloak on the breeze, like a great flapping black crow.

They were a ragged-looking bunch of men, mostly barefooted, healthy-looking, bright-eyed, and breathing heavily after the chase. All except one who came from behind, a tall burly man, booted to his calves, his neck stockless. As Dualta met his eyes, his heart started to pound slowly, because you couldn't but recognize the face or the figure. It was strange to see the lines drawn in a newspaper or a magazine, the cartooning and caricaturing of the real suddenly become reality before your eyes. There it was, the thick curly hair with the reddish tint, dusted with gray, intelligent blue eyes and an impudent snub nose. He found himself looking at Daniel O'Connell, who came forward to meet him, as curious as a Kerryman, as strange as if a drawn figure had walked out of the pages of a newspaper.

"Well," said the deep voice, clear on the air, "and who are you?"

He spoke in English. Why was this? How did he know that Dualta or Cuan who had now drawn up beside him would know English.

"We are scholars," said Dualta, "traveling for our health."

He wondered if the man would understand the subtle humor. He did and Dualta was pleased. His eyes almost disappeared in a network of laugh wrinkles. He threw back his head and laughed. His whole body laughed.

"Well then," he said, "let us sit and get the benefit of your scholarship. We ignorant Kerry people are always open to enlightenment from traveling genius. Ho, Party," he shouted then in Irish to the huge man near him who was holding the hare and fighting off the dogs. "That is our second kill so we can afford to eat. Call up the rations." There were many rocks in the place, making comfortable enough seats, like a druid's circle. He sat on one, and stretched out his legs. "Where are you from?" he asked Dualta.

"I am from the Corrib country," said Dualta, sitting on a stone out from him, dropping his bundle on the ground.

"A Galwayman," said O'Connell, "and a Connachtman. Where will you meet a Connachtman with learning?" he quoted an Irish proverb.

"Or a Munsterman with honesty?" Dualta quoted back at him.

O'Connell laughed. He was pleased. He slapped his thigh. "Your companion is a dumb man then?" he asked, pointing at Cuan. Cuan did not sit. He rested leaning on a stick he had picked up, one foot wound around it. Dualta glanced at him. His face was set in moody lines. He was looking at O'Connell with a blank face.

"It's many a time a man's tongue broke his nose," said Cuan

adding to the quotations. O'Connell didn't laugh. He kept look-ing at Cuan. He is a shrewd one, Dualta thought. He recognizes hostility. He did not resent it though. He waved his arm.

"Have you anything like that in Connacht?" he asked. Dualta looked at the view his wave had embraced. It was wonderful. The bare places seemed to be covered with small houses with blue smoke emanating from them. They were built for the most part of dry stone walls, so that they merged into the mountains, be-coming part of them. Below them in the great fields were graz-ing animals, looking like carved wooden toys. A few bigger houses in parklands with a river seen here and there through the trees, sparkling. Near one of the yellow beaches he could see a large two-story house at the end of an avenue.

"Is that Darrynane?" he asked.

"Yes," said O'Connell with a satisfied sigh, "that is Darry-nane. A refuge for sinners like me," he added, laughing. "Can you beat that in Connacht?"

"For every beauty you have," said Dualta, "we can show you seven."

"Why are you away then?" O'Connell asked.

"What is love without possession?" Dualta asked.

O'Connell thought over this. "Maybe you have a point," he said, "but what is beauty without life? To be alive is the more important. Better to be alive than never to have been called into being. Aye?"

Dualta agreed.

Party came back. He was carrying a basket. He put it on the ground and knelt behind it.

"Let us eat, in the name of God," said O'Connell. "You look like men who could do with food."

"We ate," said Cuan, "a few miles back in the home of one of your evicted tenants. In a hedge house."

O'Connell looked at him.

"Who is he talking about, Party?" he asked.

"He is talking about Corpán," said Party. "Will I hit this black fellow for you, Counsellor? Corpán couldn't live. If the agent hadn't put him, we would. Let me take one blow at his black countenance."

The Silent People

"No," said O'Connell. "It is more important to eat."

Dualta took the buttered cake and the piece of meat most gratefully. Cuan leaned on his stick and refused. The rest of the men sat down and took potatoes from their pockets, joined with the pieces of whole meal cake that Party gave out to them.

All the time that his strong jaws were chewing his food, O'Connell was examining Cuan and Dualta.

Dualta felt pleasure from the food and the company.

He thought that the reality of meeting a famous man was very different from the hearing of him. He had read his speeches. They seemed verbose, wordy and long-winded. But that was the style of speechmaking. But men who were there said that the way he said them bore no resemblance to the wordy words of them. He could send the blood pounding in your veins with the sound of his voice, his inflections. His speeches were unprepared. He spoke according as the mood of the people made him. Dualta thought that the real man used these speeches to hide behind them. There was very little that wasn't known about him now, on the surface. Because he was educated in France and had been caught up with the Revolution he hated the idea of the spilling of blood. Men thought at one time that he was an agnostic. Not any more. Some said he was a hypocrite. He had killed a man in a duel. When he went to Mass and Holy Communion he wore a black glove on the hand that had pulled the trigger. Was that hypocrisy? He was a great lawyer. One of the few professions open to Catholics, he had made it his own. He drove a coach and four he said, through the perverted laws. Now he was getting a thousand pounds a week from the Catholic Rent. Oh-ho, they shouted! He was earning as much as that at the bar and gave it up to free his country from its shackles, he retorted. You couldn't fight without money, considering the great wealth that was interposed between tyranny and liberty. There was no in-between here. You thought he was an honest man and a sincere patriot and a truly pious Catholic, or you thought he was a deceiver, using public pennies for his own ends, a demagogue, battening on the emotions of a volatile and uneducated people, an impious man using God for his own ends.

Dualta just saw a well-built Kerryman with an open neck sitting mightily on a stone and chewing bread and meat, on the side of a Kerry hillside.

He suddenly stopped eating and started to laugh.

They all looked at him, chewing postponed.

"Ah?" said O'Connell inquiringly.

"Away from here," said Dualta, "you are a great man or a monster. Up here you are just another man chasing hares."

"Is that bad?" O'Connell asked. "Am I not permitted to chase hares?"

"But certainly," said Dualta. "I eat your food. I am only getting part of my own back. I have given about one shilling and tenpence to the Catholic Rent. Now I have eaten it all back again."

O'Connell laughed, genuine laughter. "I hope to get the worth of the food out of you," he said. "Where are you going now?"

"We are going into Clare," said Dualta.

"A good county," said O'Connell. "Your comrade stands and scowls at me like a crane that is going to eat a fish. How have I hurt you, friend?" he asked Cuan directly then. He stood up for it, shaking the crumbs from his clothes.

"In London," said Cuan, "you reneged on the forty-shilling freeholders."

"The forties," said he calmly, "were invented by the Establishment to send their fools into Parliament. They went in droves like cattle and voted for the men they were told to vote for."

"They put the Beresfords out of Waterford," said Cuan. "They are braver people than you think."

"They are much braver than I thought they were," said O'Connell. "That's dead now, that Relief Act. Next time they will be in."

"You hate the men of 1798," said Cuan.

"No," said O'Connell patiently. "I do not. It was a deplorable insurrection. It was instigated by Pitt. They fell for it. He wanted them to. It helped him to carry the Union. Who can forgive them for that?"

"Do the suffering of the people then under the militia, all that slaughter and violation and death mean nothing to you?" He was leaning forward, his face was pale.

"Yes," said O'Connell, "and also this, there should never be militia. There should never be ordinary people with arms in their hands. What can come from that except slaughter and rapine? I saw it in two countries. I am never likely to forget it."

"So we must save our blood?" asked Cuan. "We must never shed a drop of it for our country?"

"Not while I'm here," said O'Connell. "There has been too much blood spilled, without need. Listen, I have called a nation into existence, all of them, not a few here and a few there with pikes in the thatch, but a whole people. I will imbue them like yeast in a cake so that they will rise and swell, and become so peacefully big and cohesive, so morally strong that they will have to be handed what they want."

"You are a dreamer," said Cuan. "Who ever heard of a Kerry dreamer?"

"No," said O'Connell. "It is violent men who are dreamers. You are a violent man. When I was a student, I saw the result of violence. I was down with typhus over there in Carhen when Lord Edward Fitzgerald was arrested for death, and Wolfe Tone captured. These men should not have died. They were too talented. They should have lived for their country. That's how I felt then and how I feel now. It is the way I see it, a great cohesive mass boiling and stirring like porridge in a pot, until it overflows and becomes irresistible. Sometime then, long ago, I made a speech. I said: Moderation is the character of genuine patriotism, of that patriotism that seeks for the happiness of mankind. There is a character that is caused by hatred of oppression. This is passion, the other is principle. There is a great difference. Unreasonable patriotism will always lead to violence. I wish I could make you understand me. I wish I could win you. You seem to be an intelligent man."

Could Cuan see, Dualta wondered, the oddity of this meeting, of a man like O'Connell pleading on a Kerry hillside for understanding from a tall white-haired man whom he had never met and was unlikely to meet again? Could he see this and not understand that O'Connell was sincere. He tried to think of the wealthy landowners he had met. They would not pass five seconds in the company of a man like Cuan or himself. By now they would have set the dogs on them.

"We have never got anything from them," said Cuan, "by being kind and accepting. Nothing has ever come from them except from the point of the pike and the barrel of the gun. Nothing ever will."

O'Connell dropped his arms.

"It will always be the same," he said, "unless I win. If I win, what then? Will you acknowledge that I was right? Are you big enough to do that?"

"If you win," said Cuan, "I will become your bondman. But you won't. You are fighting against history."

"No," said O'Connell, "I am trying to interpret history. You watch."

"I will watch," said Cuan.

O'Connell turned then to Dualta. He smiled. "How about you?" he asked. "Have I sounded a chord in you?"

Dualta thought.

"Oh, yes," he said. "You have played a tune on me. I am your man. Haven't I given you one shilling and tenpence?"

O'Connell bowed to him in mock thanks.

"Did you tell me your name?" he asked.

"No," said Dualta. "I am Dualta Duane. He is Cuan Mc-Carthy."

"McCarthy is a fighting name," said O'Connell.

"So was O'Connell," said Cuan.

"And still is," said O'Connell. "I must go, I see my poor secretary struggling up the hill with a basket of letters on his arm. If you are staying here come down and see me at home. We will talk more."

"We are bound far away," said Dualta.

"I hope we meet again," said O'Connell. "Party, free the dogs and let us try and rise another hare before I am caught with the letters. Goodbye, friend Dualta, and you, McCarthy. I am glad we met. I hope we meet again."

The dogs started howling. The men started shouting. Then they freed the dogs and they scuttled around snuffing and baying and the men followed them. O'Connell set off with his long stride, looking at least ten years younger than his fifty years. Once he paused and turned back to regard them and wave his hand and then he was out of their sight. They stood for some time looking after him, until the whole assembly was hidden by the shoulder of the hill.

Then Dualta turned to Cuan and said, "Well, Cuan, let us be on our way to Clare."

"And a bit of beautiful violence," said Cuan. He kicked at the crumb-littered ground, "to get the taste of false peace out of our mouths."

chapteR XV

THEY STOOD ON the hill and looked down at the valley. The sun was shining from a cloudless blue sky. Wearing only shirts and trousers they had the rest of their clothes and their shoes bundled in their budgets.

"There it is," said Cuan, and he sat on the flat limestone rock. There were plenty of rocks. The hill on which they were was part of a ring that ran around the valley, enclosing it in a rocky embrace. The hills were all stones. Dualta had never seen so many stones in one place in his whole life. The arms of the stony hills ran down to the sea. The valley was about twenty miles across and about ten from the sea beach to where they were. It was a lush enough valley. The pattern was the same. Right in the middle were tall trees through which you could glimpse the gray walls of a big house. On the left nearer the sea there was another smaller one. On the right, high up, there was a third, and down beside the sea was another house standing in the middle of green fields and surrounded by a wall. The cottages were seeming to be climbing the hills, all around the rim of the valley, clustered closely and beside them small patches of potato and oat fields which seemed to have been wrung from the rocks with great agony. They were all dry-stone-built houses with straw-thatched roofs. All you had to do was to pick any field you liked and the stones were there ready for you. Some of them were big and might have to be split with a wedge, but even if you possessed little stone-skill, he thought, you should be able to build a passable house.

Down at the sea the houses were built on top of one another as tightly packed together as a turf clamp. The smoke from their chimneys was lost in the blue of the sky. He raised his eyes a little across the sea to the other side of the Bay of Galway and he could see his own mountains rising mistily out of the earth, like a blue dream.

"I am not far from home now," he said. "If I was a good swimmer."

"You like it?" Cuan asked.

"I like it," said Dualta.

"Like all pretty things," said Cuan, "it conceals ugly things. It is not all smiles. There are slimy things under the stones. The people call it the Valley of the Flowers."

Dualta could see why. The rocks were not entirely without color. They had their own different blue-gray color, and in between them patches of earth, that were carpeted with gentians and wild orchids and some sort of yellow flower he didn't know, trying to remember the plant and flower lessons of Uncle Marcus, who knew all of them and what diseases their roots and leaves were good for.

"Some flowers can be poisonous," Cuan went on. "They call the town below the Town of the Sea. When the wind is north, a bitter wind comes from the bay and scours the whole valley. The house in the middle is the house of Tewson. That is where his man Clarke holds court."

"Is he the one?" Dualta asked.

"Clarke is the one," said Cuan grimly, "Tewson is rarely here. He is what they call an absentee. If money runs low he pays a visit to spur Clarke to greater effort. Clarke rarely fails him. Clarke is a just man, you see. He is a good Catholic who works hard for his master as he is urged in the Gospels. How can he be faulted for doing his duty according to the will of God? Over on the right is the house attached to the glebe lands of the Protestant Bishop. His affairs are very ably conducted by a man called Cringe. He is a good man, to the last farthing. He is a devoted Protestant, as is right, but he cannot see why all those stupid dirty people who are his tenants won't turn and cling to the true faith. The house on the left and its fields are owned by a man named Bradish and his family. He is a Catholic. He bought part of Tewson's place when Sir Vincent was in some scrape with a woman in London and wanted money fast. Bradish is so pleased and grateful for being a landlord of sorts, that he can never cease thanking God for the benefits conferred upon him and licking all the hands of the gentlemen who permit such a strange thing to happen. The house near the sea is the house of an honest man named Donaghue. He was one of the people. He opened a shop. He runs in the mail. Bit by bit he bought an acre here and an acre there. He is sound. He is a man of business. He is building acre on acre. In a hundred years it is possible that his descendants will own the whole valley. He has a son who is as dogged as himself. For the rest, they are just people, good and bad, kind and cruel, cheerful enough, happy enough."

"Are you glad to be back here then?" Dualta asked.

Cuan lay down on the rocks, his hands under his head. He thought.

"I think I am," he said. "I will know better when I see my brother. I was quite young when I left, after all. You cannot erase the memories of your youth. Besides, I'm feeling old. We have traveled a long tiring way. I am not as young as you. Maybe I would try to settle down."

"Why do we see no people?" Dualta asked.

Cuan sat up abruptly.

"I have been wondering that," he said. "They should be everywhere. We shouldn't have been able to poke our nose into the valley without hundreds of eyes watching us. Down there beyond the big house, say halfway between us and the sea, behind the shoulder of the field of the hazel bushes, I think I see a concourse of people. What are they up to then?"

"It must be important," said Dualta, "if they are all there."

"The people of the valley," said Cuan, "are very curious. It need not be important to take them away from home." He shaded his eyes with his hand, peering. He suddenly stood up. He put his fingers in his mouth and whistled shrilly. Then he waved his arm in an inviting gesture. He sat down again. "I saw a boy minding sheep," he said. "Perhaps we will hear from him, if he wants to tell us."

They waited.

They heard the bark of a dog. The dog arrived before the boy. He sniffed in their direction. He was a black-and-white collie. He bared his teeth at the same time that he was wagging his tail. The boy appeared from below them. He came toward them. He stood out from them. He had a long hazel stick in his hand. He was a tall thin boy with very big eyes, tangled hair. His clothes were not good. They could see his legs and his breast through his torn garments. He pulled flowers from their stalks with his toes.

"Who are you?" Cuan asked. He kept his mouth shut. "Are you dumb?"

"Who are you then?" he asked.

"I am called McCarthy," said Cuan. At this intelligence the boy's eyes widened.

"Are you a relation of the File McCarthy then?" he asked.

"He is my brother," said Cuan.

The boy came closer.

"I have heard of you then," he said. "I have heard talk about you."

"Where are all the people?" Cuan asked.

A look of disgust came over the boy's face. He turned his head. "Down there, they are," he said. "They built a house for a new teacher. There will be school now in the valley."

"What!" exclaimed Cuan, "and where is Napoleon then, who had his school in the town?"

"He's not young," said the boy. "He drinks too much, they say. Father Finucane got this new one. He got the people to build a house. Now, even the girls have to go to school."

"Who is this priest Finucane?" Cuan asked.

"He is a young one, a man in place of the parish priest."

"The parish priest is dead then, Father Melican, is that so?"

"No, then. He was hit by lightning one day on the Carn. The horse he was riding was killed. He is not well. He cannot walk but with crutches. So this young man came. He is our misfortune. This house for the teacher and she a woman!"

"Is that bad then?" Dualta asked.

"Who wishes to be taught by a woman?" the boy asked indignantly. "Who wishes to be taught at all? Doesn't my father say that there is more education in the sky and the breeze than in the walls of a house?"

"Who is your father?" Cuan asked.

"He is Bottle Daxon," said the boy. "I am Colman."

"Can you read?" Dualta asked.

"Who needs to read?" he asked.

"Can you add two and two?" Dualta asked.

"Of what need is two and two?" the boy asked.

"Do you forever wish to be as ignorant and stupid as you are now?" Dualta asked.

"Who are you?" the boy asked. "You have the cut of a stranger. I will not be stupid and ignorant. I know more than many people. I can make songs and sing them. You see. I am going now back to my sheep. They are wandering, like you in the head," he added to Dualta and ran down the hill. Dualta laughed and watched him go.

"His father makes whiskey in the hills," said Cuan. "Well, we will push on. We will go to the house of my brother. Let us see if he will welcome us. My goodness, things are changing in the valley if they are bringing in a female teacher. What is the place coming to? No wonder young Colman is filled with resentment." He walked along the hill in the direction that the boy had gone, and Dualta, taking another look at the placid looking valley and the glittering sea, hefted his budget and followed after him.

The priest had called for Miss McMahon at the home of the Bradish family where she had been staying for nearly four weeks. She was not sorry to see him. The house was an undistinguished plain two-story house with a portico held up by greater looking pillars. They were plaster pillars and weathering badly. The house was well furnished but too full of bric-a-brac, imported by Mrs. Bradish, who on her rare trips to Dublin could never resist the blandishments of the fakers. So thought Miss McMahon. Mrs. Bradish was a rotund apple-cheeked woman who talked incessantly. She had been a Miss O'Brien and in some vague way had tacked herself on to the famous O'Briens who since the time of Brian of the Tributes, the King, had ruled large parts of Clare, fighting, killing, changing their shirts, apostasizing to hold their lands, persecuting, tormenting or rewarding the inhabitants, turning out bishops, priests, soldiers, cowards, traitors, duelists, a proud gang of saints and sinners, just like all the other clans who had held on to their possessions since the coming of the Norman invaders. Her husband was a second son from a Roscommon family, less distinguished than in Mrs. Bradish's saga. He was a bluff hearty man who trod the safe road of neutrality in all issues, keeping his head down when the arguments flowed. His wife knew every family in Ireland, who they married, when they were married, the issue of the marriages, their scandalous or heroic deeds in war and peace. She kept a book on them, all these items clipped from the newspapers. It went back many years. She was delighted when they were invited to balls in the bigger houses. Miss MacMahon imagined she would be too cloying, too sweet, too agreeable on occasions like that. Miss MacMahon regretted that Mrs. Bradish had this effect on her, because she was a kindly and hospitable woman. The two girls, Helen and Margaret, were silent girls in their early twenties. Their mother was pushing them so hard at second and third sons of families, that Miss MacMahon thought they would end up unmarried if they didn't break away from her mismanagement of the mart.

They were in the hall, sitting, waiting. All Miss MacMahon's truck was waiting on the steps of the portico. Mrs. Bradish was fussing.

"But are you sure, Miss MacMahon, that you won't take the carriage? All that truck. What will people think?"

"They would think less of me," said Miss MacMahon firmly, "if I arrived in a carriage. My lot is set among the people. It is what I want. There is little use starting off on the wrong foot."

"But how can you be so brave?" said Helen. "You will be living in that house, on your own."

"You will have to do your own cooking," said Margaret.

"On an open fire," said Helen.

"Really, Miss MacMahon, it is ridiculous," said Mrs. Bradish. "We would be most happy if you stayed here with us, and went down to the wretched school every day. What they want with an education anyhow, I don't know. What will they do with it?"

"Like the rest of us," said Miss MacMahon firmly, "they will be better people for it."

Bradish grunted.

"It's debatable," he said. "All the same, young woman living alone. There are some bad characters in the valley."

"I have yet to find a really bad one," said Miss MacMahon.

"But that was Tipperary, not Clare, dear," said Mrs. Bradish. "They are wilder here you know. Very temperamental, Terry Alts and Lady Clare. All those secret societies. So frightening."

"O'Connell and the Catholic Association stirring everyone up," said Bradish. "Be quiet, I say, and everything will come to us. Nothing will come from agitation."

"I know very little about politics," said Miss MacMahon. "All I want to do is to teach children, to make them better people. That's all."

So she was overjoyed watching through the open door when she saw the cart, a common cart with block wheels, coming up the short drive from the road. There was a big fair-haired man clicking his tongue at the horse and beside him the young priest was sitting, his black clothes looking heavy in the sunlight.

"He has come," she said, rising. "I cannot tell you how grateful I am for your hospitality. If I had ten tongues, I couldn't thank you enough."

"Say no more about it," said Mrs. Bradish, "I only wish we could hold on to you. We will all pray for your safety."

Miss MacMahon laughed.

"Really," she said, "I am only going a few miles you know. I am not going into the heart of Africa."

"There are worse places than Africa," said Mrs. Bradish darkly.

How little they know about their own people, Miss Mac-Mahon thought. Because they don't really try to know them. They shut themselves up in a cocoon of safety. In their own way they too possessed closed faces like the country people.

She walked out to the steps. The priest waved his arm at her and jumped lightly from the cart. He came toward her. He was a young man with a freckled face, and reddish hair.

"You haven't changed your mind have you?" he asked as he came toward her. He was serious about it, she saw.

"Why would I do that?" she asked. He heaved a sigh, took her hand.

"Thank God for that," he said. "It seems too good to be true, that was why I called up bogies. Good day, ma'am. Goo'day, Mr. Bradish, and ladies," he said, waving his hat at them. "I am sorry to rob you of such an attractive guest."

"No sorrier than we are, Father Finucane," said Mrs. Bradish. "Really the whole thing is ridiculous you know."

"Not to us," said the priest, "not to all the future geniuses that Miss MacMahon is going to turn out of the new school."

"You can return to us at any time if you are disillusioned, Miss MacMahon," said Mrs. Bradish.

"Thank you kindly," said Miss MacMahon, walking down the steps.

"All this, Miss?" the fair-haired countryman asked.

"All this," she said smiling.

"This is Moran McCleary," said the priest.

"I'm pleased to meet you," said Miss MacMahon holding out her hand. He looked at it and looked at her and then took it in his own hand, a hard hand, as hard as bogdeal. He smiled at her then. The heart of Miss MacMahon warmed.

They said goodbye again as Moran piled the stuff on the cart. It left only enough room for the seat in front. Father Finucane helped Miss MacMahon up to the seat. Not much help indeed. She clambered easily. She could nearly hear Mrs. Bradish tut-tutting.

"You drive, Father," said Moran. "I'll walk and pick up any that drop."

The priest took up the reins. He clucked at the horse with his tongue, remembered to turn and wave at the doubtful people on the steps, and then the cart pulled away. Miss Mac-Mahon took a peep to see if they were out of view, and then she relaxed, sighed, took off the hat, held it in her lap, shook her dark hair in the gentle warm breeze, and said, "Thank God!"

"Oh-ho," said the priest. "G'wan up, Liz," slapping the reins against the back of the horse. The horse ignored him, setting a pace and keeping it. "They are good people. They mean well," he added then.

"They are like Job's comforters," she said.

"Do you really and truly understand what you are doing?" he asked.

"I thought your friend Father Joe explained it all," she said.

"So he did," said the priest. "My God, those days in Maynooth, we didn't know how happy we were. We were not like doctors. It was all theory. Imagine a doctor who never saw the inside of a body until after he was qualified. But you are different. You were brought up well. You have traveled. Do you know what the job you have taken on will be like? Do you know how you will have to live? Such a vast change for you, it will be. The things you have to put up with. Good God." He rubbed his hair with his hand distractedly.

"Father, do you want a schoolteacher?" she asked.

"You'll know how badly," he said. "There is such a terrible hunger for education among the people. What had they? They had Napoleon. He was a soldier with Wellington. He lost a leg at Waterloo, hence the name. Fourpence a day pension. Just enough to keep him in drink. ABC, two and two make four, the towns of Spain and France and southern rivers. That's his limit, that and a bunch of hazel rods to beat their backs, and only boys. What a godsend you would be! But it's so hard."

"You do not trust me, then?" she asked.

"Oh, yes," he said. "But I am afraid you will not be able to stay with us. That frightens me. To give a cup of hope and take it away as soon as their lips are about to touch it."

"You'll have to have faith in me," she said.

"Your pupils will pay you a penny a week," he said. "I will try to scrape maybe ten, twenty pounds a year from the parish funds. You have no funds of your own?"

"Very little now," she said.

"So you will be as poor as anyone else in the valley," he said.

"That's all right," she said. "I don't eat much."

"But it's not right," he said.

"What is right?" she asked. "I want to do it. That's all. I cannot explain it. This is what I want to do. I talked it over with Father Joe. What can I do that is really necessary? What is the greatest need? Education is. I am trained. I have knowledge. I can teach. I will be helping. I will feel that I am helping. It is as easy as that."

He looked at her, the straight nose, the firm chin.

"It won't be easy," he said. "It will be terribly hard."

"That is for me to worry about," she said. "I hope I am not as weak as you expect me to be."

"I do not think that," he said. "But I want you to know this. I have to say it to you. The first moment you feel that it is becoming an unbearable burden, I want you to come and tell me. Don't fight it. Just come and tell me."

"I'll do that," she said.

"You are so young and pretty, damn it," he said exasperatedly. "You don't belong to all the things you will have to live amongst. Tell me, if you feel you have to dedicate your life to educating the children, why this way, why not a convent of nuns? They are doing such great work, slowly but surely. How they would have welcomed you!"

She laughed.

"I don't want to be a nun," she said. "I am a woman. I want to get married someday and have children. I do not want to remain a virgin. Now, are you satisfied?"

He threw back his head and laughed.

"Oh, rich," he said. "You will have wonderful opportunities in this valley of finding a rich husband. Maximum income ten pounds a year and a pig to pay the rent. Don't you know that all the gentry will frown on you for what you are doing? Don't you know you have no more chance of being invited to their dinners and balls and parties now? You throw in your lot with the people and you have thrown the rich men's board out of the window. You have become a servant. Do you realize that?"

"Yes," she said firmly.

"What am I?" the priest asked wonderingly. "The devil's advocate? I have said all on his side. Now on the other, let me rejoice. I will pray for you every day. I will thank God for you in the Mass. You will find your rewards much greater than you imagine. You are on the side of the angels. We have a real teacher in the Valley of the Flowers for the first time in seven hundred years. Praise be to God!" And then he did a strange thing, he stood up in the cart, and he waved his beaver hat three times around his head and he shouted in a loud voice, "Yoo! Yoo! Hu!"

He startled the horse. He startled the birds. Moran behind laughed heartily at the sight of him. Miss MacMahon laughed too, clapping her hands. He sat down again grinning.

"Did they not teach you decorum in Maynooth then?" she asked.

"They did, in faith," he said, "but sometimes it is as well to forget it. Now we are coming to the cross, so we will have to behave ourselves like decent people. Miss MacMahon, put on your hat. Moran come to the horse and lead him with sedateness. The people will expect gentility from us, and the behavior of gentlemen." He settled his heavy hat on his own head, a bit rakishly because his red hair was thick and it was a hot day. Miss MacMahon, still laughing, put on her own hat and tied the ribbons under her chin, and smoothed the folds of her satin dress. Moran licked his hand with his tongue as he went to the horse's head and smoothed down his hair with the lick. Then they turned into the road that led from the town into the valley, turned away from the town, and from here on the people were waiting for them, thin at first, and then thickening at the approach to the new school which was built in the field of the hazels on a site generously provided by the Bradishes.

They were dressed in their best clothes, she could see, the men had shining shaved faces. Some wore hats, and if they hadn't hats they had their hair flattened to their skulls with mountain water. All the best dressed people were in front showing off their new clothes with the tailor's crease still in them, corduroy or broadcloth of wool with ducktailed coats and the girls were colorful in greens and reds, their hair gleaming, and all the children were waving branches of trees, and everyone was taking the fill of their eyes of the new teacher. They shouted "Fáilte don Gleann, Miss," welcome, welcome to the valley as she passed, and with her limited Irish she could hear a few things like, Man, she is a fine piece. She is as young as a girl. Where did Father Finucane find a lady like that? She'll never stick it. She was conscious as the cart passed of them falling in behind, and it was a big concourse of cheerful talking people that debouched into the yard in front of the school where the cart stopped and Father Finucane jumped down.

The school was gleaming newly. It was built of dry stone. The split limestone was newly blue. There were two windows and a sound door, all new and the thatch was last year's oat straw and still retained a little of its golden glow.

The priest helped her from the cart. She was a bit bewildered now. So many faces. So many people. Young girls looking at her very frankly. Young boys looking at her out of the sides of their eyes. Out of the anonymous crowd then emerged a face under a thatch of curly gray-black hair. A big face, fat, pitted with small pox marks, with a huge bulbous nose and side whiskers, a vast face with missing teeth already rolling out sonorous praises from a thick-lipped mouth.

"This is Mister Shields, Miss MacMahon," Father Finucane was saying, "our former teacher now retired after a lifetime of endeavor."

"Forcibly retired, ma'am," he was saying, "under force of circumstances after the labor of years during the course of which

I fought for King and country under the eye of my friend Wellington, giving the man sound advice on several occasions, doomed thereafter to twack the backsides, if you will excuse the phrase, of the thickest-headed louts that ever God put into a valley. I am most pleased to meet you and if at any time, as one confrere to another, you wish to be advised by an older mind of the things necessary to the educational elevation of as rude and ignorant a people as God ever put on the face of the earth, all you have to do is send for me, and I will come at speed, waving my most precious possession, a thing of which I am proud and gratified."

At which he lifted his peg leg, in case she would miss seeing it, and the people laughed. Apparently they liked to be insulted by Napoleon.

She met other people. She shook their hands. But there were too many of them.

Her things were taken from the cart and carried into the house. There was a bit of ceremony. There was no key, but a hasp and staple that was closed by a wooden peg tied to the doorpost. The peg had been made a bit thick and it took a lot of dramatics and a little mild cursing before it was plucked from the hasp and she was ushered into the house.

It was very bare. But there was a fire burning in the open fireplace. Long benches of new timber were against the walls. In some triumph she was shown the other room, a small room behind the fireplace where there was a peg bed raised four inches from the ground, a sort of mattress made from intertwined rods, woven like the reeds in a basket. A new small table and a new chair. She met the carpenter. She thanked him for his labors. He beamed on her and rubbed the wood softly with his hands.

They said goodbye to her, and she said how wonderful they were to have done all this for her, how she was looking forward to meeting the children in the new school. Many people thought there should be a dance and a bit of drinking to celebrate the event properly, but didn't like to suggest it because she looked like a lady, and they went away one by one commenting on her appearance and wagering on her chances, praising her or shaking their heads, and eventually she was left with Father Finucane.

She looked at him helplessly.

He said: "I told you!" He indicated the place with his hand. "It was a triumph for them," he said. "They put a lot into it. They built it in a week of hard work. It looks very bare. You will put the shape of a home on it. There is no window glass or they would tax us."

She nodded her head.

"I will go," he said. "Tomorrow I will come back and we can arrange when the classes will begin."

She nodded.

"All right," he said, "God bless you."

She nodded.

"I told you it would be hard," he said.

She nodded again.

"Well, I'll leave you," he said.

She nodded.

He felt helpless, so did the only thing he could do. He went out of the place and closed the door softly after him.

Miss MacMahon looked at her piled truck in the middle of the earthen floor, and the bareness of her new domain, and the shafts of sunlight through the small windows, and then she sat down on one of the new benches, and she started to cry.

chapter XVI

UALTA FOL-
lowed Cuan. It
was a stony way,
even if their bare feet were hardened, the soles covered with
quarter inch of calloused flesh like the finest of impervious
leather, it was still painful to stub a toe against a sharp stone.

Then Cuan stopped and Dualta came close to him. They were
looking down on a narrow valley sheltered only by the hills.
It was only a few hundred yards across and the same long. Down
its center ran a stream that disappeared into a gaping cave before it could tumble down the hillside. He noticed all over the
Burren that streams were being slugged like that, as if a giant
were lying beneath the hills with an insatiable thirst and ever
open pores. This side of the stream there was a house. It was
hard to see it in the welter of rock, since it was rock itself, and
the thatch was aged and its color blended with the surround-
ings, the green parts of it being like lichen. But there was a slow
smoke coming from the stone chimney. On the other side of
the stream a few roods of earth had been cleared, walls built
around the patch and the potato stalks were green and healthy.
Apart from that healthy patch, the floor of the small valley was
covered with boulders that had been deposited when the stream
was in flood.

"It is a hard place for a poet," said Dualta.

Cuan grunted and started down.

The door of the house was unpainted and sagged. The windows had no frames. Cuan had to lift the door from the earthen
floor to get into the place. Dualta followed him.

"Are you within?" Cuan called. The place was most untidy.
There was a bench and a stool and a makeshift cupboard on
the wall. There seemed to be pieces of paper everywhere, writ-

The Silent People

ten with blackberry ink parts of which had faded. They were on the floor, on the bench, on the window sill. Dualta bent and picked one from the floor. They were words in Irish, a succession of adjectives. They described brightness. The writing was firm and clear and beautifully proportioned. Cuan had gone to the room behind the fireplace. He came down.

"He is not here," he said. "He lives like a pig." He went out the door again, dropping his budget in the middle of the confusion. Dualta took up another page from the bench. It was a part of a completed poem. It was a lament for Uaithne Mór.

Cuan was calling. "McCarthy! McCarthy! McCarthy!" The hills threw off his voice and repeated the name three times. Dualta put down the paper. He felt guilty, like reading the private letters of another person. He followed Cuan into the sunlight. There was a movement at the far end of the valley and a man came into view, stopped to look toward them and then came on. There was a collie dog at his heels. He was a tall man, as tall as Cuan. His hair was wild and he wore a beard which was turning white although his hair was still fairly dark. His clothes were not good. They were badly patched, and his pockets sagged with books, and from all of him pieces of manuscript seemed to be peering in a hopeless jumble. His stockings were falling down on his thin legs and his shoes could do with being repaired. All this Dualta saw as he came toward them, still peering, to discover their identity. He had a big nose and deep blue eyes with a piercing look, perhaps because he was short-sighted, or perhaps because he was used to being alone and looking into the middle distance.

"And that's my brother Flan," said Cuan grimly, as he came toward them. "God be with you, Flan," he said then loudly.

Flan came closer. He looked at his brother.

"It's you," he said. "You are aging. What brings you back to us? I thought never to see your face again."

"You have a soft welcome," said Cuan.

"I did not urge you to go away," said Flan. "What have you been doing? Wild deeds, no doubt. You must tell me and I will sing of them. Who is he? Is he one of the bodachs?"

153

"Since he is a member of the human race, I suppose he is a bodach," said Cuan. "He is Dualta, from the other side of the Bay."

"The Galway men never sang," said Flan.

"They sang for their own," said Dualta. "They didn't sing for posterity."

Flan snorted.

"Poor rhymes," he said, "that died on the air as soon as they were composed, faded from the brain with the fumes of the drink that inspired them. What are you here for?"

"I will stay with you awhile," said Cuan. This didn't seem to please his brother, but he shrugged his shoulders and moved into the house.

"If you must you must," he said.

They went in after him. Almost immediately, Cuan started to tidy things here and there. "Be careful," Flan called. "You live like a pig," said Cuan, continuing to tidy. "Is there something to eat?"

"There are potatoes in the pot," said Flan. He cleared the bench of its papers, by putting them all together and stuffing them into his already stuffed pockets. He got a small packet of salt from the cupboard and put it on the bench. Cuan turned out the potatoes from the pot. They weren't very good potatoes. Dualta thought they must have come from the end of the clamp. He knelt at the bench and reached for one. He was hungry. The other two ate as well. The three pairs of eyes looked at one another and took stock as their jaws chewed. Dualta thought that Cuan had a very peculiar brother.

Suddenly Flan took a bundle of manuscripts from his pocket. He selected one of two pages and handed it to Dualta. "Read that!" he commanded. Dualta wiped his fingers on his trousers and took the script. He was conscious of the eyes of Flan on him as he read.

Grim and dark the plight of the Gael (cried
Flan's song) in his own land.
Blame then be on his own head and heart,

that has all forgot the beginnings—
The Thomond chieftains that lost sweet blood
on the fair south of the Eiscir Riada
Of Conaill, Cutra, great Aengus of Aranmore
and Fiacra of the Flowing hair;
Of Conall dying under the geasa sword of
Cuchulan and covered with his carn;
Of Finn Mac Chumail great in battle and
slaughter at Uinche's reddened ford;
Of Dathi, the great pagan dying for his gods
at the foot of the white-tipped Alps;
Of the great warriors who died defending
hearth and board against Turgesius, the foul Dane.

There were men then who sang them and stout
people who cried them sore—
From the bardic schools of kings and chiefs
poured forth their tender songs.
Like Litanies of the saints they called their
generations back to their beginnings
De Danann, and Firbolg and Formorian they were
the children of Kings, the sons of Milesius;
A race of songsters among them not the least
the O Daly's of O Loughlin;
Donagh Mór, the Ovid sweet of Ireland,
grandson of O Daly of the schools
And silver-songed Geoffrey, chief ollav of
poetry in wide Munster
Carroll the ollav of Corcomroe, Donagh, Aengus,
Farrell and tender-mouthed Teigue.

He came to the end of it. He looked up.
"You see what I mean?" Flan asked.
"No," said Dualta.
"What's wrong with them," said Flan. "A nation of thick-headed louts? How many of them can go back three generations? They have lost their beginnings so they are sunken in poverty

and meanness of mind. It happened the day they abandoned the bards."

"Times change," said Dualta. "The bards brought their fate on their own heads, because they sang above the heads of the people. Now instead of dead dreams you should sing of the flowers on the stalks of the potatoes, the suffering of the evicted, the dreams in the hearts of children."

"Butter ballads," said Flan. "Not poetry."

"I read you," said Dualta. "Brilliant, intellectual, interior rhyming vowels, that stir the beauty hidden in the heart, but for nobody but yourself and the few who can understand you, when you should be singing songs that will raise the people from their knees, fill their hearts with hope and beauty instead of songs of dead heroes, whose dry bones are rustling."

"Commonplace, clodhopper, earth grubber, Galway ignoramus," said Flan.

"You asked me what I thought," said Dualta. "I tell you."

"Cabbage head, turnip top, bog heart, muck-soiled barbarian," said Flan. He hardly raised his voice, but the sound was vicious.

Dualta stood up.

"It seems to me," he said with dignity to Cuan, "that I am not welcome here."

He and Cuan looked at each other and the ridiculous statement suddenly seemed very funny, and they both laughed, and they couldn't stop.

They were like this when the light was darkened at the door and a voice said over the noise: "God bless all here, and may I come in."

They turned and looked then and saw a priest with red hair looking at them with his eyebrows raised.

Flan stood up.

"Come in, priest, and take a seat," he said. "I am sad that I cannot offer you better company than what we have at this time."

"I thank you, File McCarthy," said the priest gravely. He sat on a makeshift stool as if it were a throne, or, as Dualta thought with a grin, as if it would collapse under him. He had given Flan his title of Poet, and it pleased him.

The priest established good relations further.

"Carrol O'Connor recited to me your verses, 'The Lament of the Three Princes,' and I thought them very fine and very moving," said the priest.

"Now," said Flan, "doesn't it take a man of the Church and a man of education to feel the beautiful? If we had not the present company, we could talk about things of the spirit and beyond, but with an ignorant Galway man in our midst and a hater of the bards we can only talk about dung and dirt and ignorant people."

"I am Father Finucane," said the priest. "I am administrating the parish for Father Melican who is disabled."

"I am Dualta Duane," said Dualta. "My birthplace you now know."

The priest looked at Cuan. Cuan looked at him too, but did not speak.

"You are the File's brother," he said then. "I have heard of you." If he expected talk from Cuan he didn't get it. Cuan skinned another potato.

"Were you wanting me, then, Father?" the File asked.

"Not altogether," the priest said. "It is a pleasure to come and see you, even if the road is hard to where you live. And I would enjoy an hour in your company and to hear your songs, but I have something else on my mind."

Dualta looked closely at him. He saw Cuan's shoulder stiffening. There was a slight feeling of tension in the air. The jaw of the priest was strong, but his eyes were calm.

"Birds sing," said the priest. "All communities are composed of individuals essentially. Some are good, some are bad, some are unfortunate, some are peace-loving, but some are not. Some people become part of oath-bound societies. It is an evil of the times. It is hard to stamp out. The way of the authorities is violent. That just breeds violence. My way is to try and nip it in the bud."

Cuan spoke to him then.

"Talk clearly," he said. "You are not a poet."

"It is the custom," said the priest, "if you want something violent done, to send to another district for unknown men who will come and go faster than the swallows, perform a deed of violence, leaving everyone else blameless. It is a good notion, but basically it is evil. I have discovered that two men are expected to come into this valley and that a certain man will suffer. Many people will applaud his suffering. I will not. Because I am a Christian and he is a Christian, and I do not think that this is the way. Also I know this man and his master and afterwards the condition of this valley would be much worse than it is now. So whenever strangers come I think it well to go and say the things I have now said, out loud, in the hope that if the strangers are the right ones, they will hear and understand."

"How many strangers have come into the valley in the past few months?" Cuan asked.

"Many," said the priest. "Packmen, traveling tinkers, chapmen, many strangers."

"And you said this to all of them?" Cuan asked.

"I have done so," said the priest.

"I am not a stranger," said Cuan. "I am one of the people."

"I accuse you of nothing," said the priest. "Perhaps I am awkward, like a blindfolded child playing a game. I am not practiced in subtle designing. I thought this was the way, and I have done what I thought was right. If I have offended you, I hope you will say so, and I will apologize to you as humbly as you wish."

Oh, the clever one, Dualta thought. It was beautifully done, and suddenly he saw that it left Cuan no alternative. Cuan would have to quit. Because he was like that. The night that they assaulted the house of Wilcocks he had been like that. As soon as he saw that plans were going wrong, he called it all off. Dualta watched him closely now. The fierce piercing eyes were looking at the priest. The priest didn't wilt under them, and Dualta's heart started a slow satisfied pound. I didn't want to do it, he thought. I didn't want to do it. I am finished with all that, all that. He knew he was really free from his promise when he saw the twisted smile that came on Cuan's mouth as he said: "Well, there's nothing left for you to do, but to apologize then, humbly."

The priest stood up. He bowed to Cuan.

"If I have offended you with my talk," he said, "I state that I am truly sorry and beg for your forgiveness. It is the larger wish of helping the whole community that made me hurt one of its members."

"That's all right," said Cuan, a little grandly.

"I do not understand all these subterfuges," cried Flan. "What is going on? Like a stream going underground. Explain to me."

"There is nothing to explain," said the priest. "It would be as well for all of us if you stay in the land of poetry. I thank you for your hospitality. I have much to do. The parish is large and the legs of my horse are thin."

"You are nearly talking poetry," said Dualta.

"That is the effect of being in the presence of a poet," said the priest, laughing. "I had no intention of undermining your position, File McCarthy."

"Would you mind if I travel a little way with you, then?" Dualta asked.

The eyebrows of the priest were raised.

"I don't want to press myself on the bard," said Dualta. "I would like to get lodgings in the village. Maybe you would advise me?"

"I will do that," said the priest, looking closely at him.

Dualta took up his budget. He looked at Cuan. Cuan's face was flintlike. Dualta thought of the time they had been together. For a few years now they had rarely been out of each other's company. In a way he had been molded by Cuan, but at many points he had resisted the molding. But you can be with no intelligent person and not get a liking for him. He liked Cuan. But the time had come to part from him. He knew that now. He had known it for some time. One of them would have to bend to the will of the other, and he was still afraid of himself.

"I will not be far away," he said in a kind of apology. "We will meet and talk again."

"Yes," said Cuan.

"I thank you for your limited hospitality," said Dualta to Flan. To his surprise Flan smiled.

"Come again, ignorant fellow," said Flan. "Somewhere you have a brain. If you drink at the well more often, it might awaken."

"Thank you," said Dualta, pleased. "I will come again." Then he went out and didn't turn back. He walked the floor of the valley and turned left at the sort of sheep track. He mounted this and stopped where the priest's horse was cropping at the sparse grass. He waited here. The sky was still cloudless. He could see the Galway coast across the shimmering water of the bay, and the mountains rising blue-tipped from the land, looking tiny from here, like ones painted by children on a sheet of paper. He suddenly felt a longing for them. Would he go there? He would like to talk to his uncle Marcus. Would it be safe to do so? The vicious ones of the Ascendancy had long memories, and long arms.

The priest watched him for a moment, the good-looking clean-cut face with the heavy hair of his head waving in the mountain breeze, a well set up young man with intelligent eyes, and a good clean body, lithe and healthy.

He said, "Do you want to go home there then?"

Dualta didn't turn his head.

"What drove you out in the first place?" the priest asked.

To his own surprise, Dualta told him, a tale stale with repetition but almost meaningless as you aged away from it. Somehow only the pain of Paidi remained in the whole of it; Paidi laughing and the house in the glen with the family and the waving children and their feet bare on the dust of the road and the spades on their shoulders as they journeyed into the strange lands.

He told him all this. Sorting it out for himself in a way more than for the telling of it. But he said nothing about the Wilcockses and his behavior in that place. Somehow he felt that the priest might surmise it. They were walking down the hill, the horse between them.

The Silent People

"Are you like a wisp in the wind then?" the priest asked. "Have you no idea for the future?"

"Only vague," said Dualta. "I want to be one of the people. Isn't that a strange ambition?"

"No," said the priest, "it is a brave one. Stay here awhile. There are good people in this valley. If you become part of the people then, you must wish to add to them, not take away from."

"I do not understand you," said Dualta.

"It is necessary that you give, not take away," said the priest. "You are educated. I can see that. Your uncle Marcus did a sound job on you. You have experience, so there your education is grounded. Now you must use it by giving back to the people what you have got."

"I'm not sure of your meaning," said Dualta.

"Think over it," said the priest. "I'm sure it will come to you. When the old chieftains were being inaugurated in this place there was always a block of stone in which were imprinted the footsteps of the first chieftain. They set their feet in these footprints and with a white wand in their hand they swore to uphold the Brehon laws and the laws of the people and to give rather than to take away. Sometimes the oaths were empty, but sometimes not."

"I see what you mean, I think," said Dualta.

The priest mounted the horse.

"I will go ahead of you," he said. "When you get below you must ask for the house of the Scealaidhe the Storyteller. They will point it out to you. It is the home of Carrol O'Connor. They will find room for you. I will see you again. If you have troubles, I would be honored to look at them for you. Goodbye, and may God bless you, and perhaps undo some of the curses that Flan unloaded on your poor head."

He laughed, and Dualta laughed, and then he waved and the horse picked its way down toward the rough road that ran into the valley.

Dualta looked after him for some time, and then shouldering his budget, he set off into the valley, whistling a song and jumping from stone to stone.

chapter XVII

IN THE DARK OF the moon the revenue cutter had sailed silently into the bay, dropped anchor off the shore and the lieutenant and two men had been rowed to the beach. They had walked left through the silent town, scarcely disturbing the dogs. Then they had headed up into the valley on the shoulders of the hills. Halfway they had paused, until before dawn they were joined by seven men from the other side. The lieutenant was curt with those men. He knew their kind. Hired for a shilling a day, they were the out of work, the misfits, the drunkards, whose assets were physical strength and a certain savage courage. In time they would be hired as bum bailiffs, or tithe proctor's men, or sheriff's assistants. They were available for any unpleasant job that was going.

These were his guides now.

He followed them up the hill and over the hill on the far side. They hugged this, moving by instinct on the barely walkable places in the midst of the millions of rocks. The lieutenant followed easily. He was used to walking awkward places in the dark. His object always was tobacco or silks or brandies, imported by daring men in small boats from the foreign ships that they met with, far out in the bay. If they had not powerful customers, he knew, they could not exist. If they did not exist, the lieutenant would not have his job. So it was a profitable circle. Now he was on a job he did not like, smoking out illicit stills. It always involved cold and wet, and boring, probing, intensive searching. The lieutenant wasn't interested in the morals of the thing, the thousands of people who had become hopeless alcoholics at the easy availability and cheapness of the raw whiskey; of the thousands existing on the bare fringes of poverty who sought ease for their hopelessly worried minds in a few hours of easily attained oblivion. All that was for the clergymen. He acted on information, and when it was clear and patent like now, he had to act on it, plan neatly and swiftly and get the whole thing over before people were properly awake.

The leader of the rough men came back to him.

"We should be opposite the place now," he said. "Let us go over the hill and go down with the dawn. He should be there."

"Right," said the lieutenant. "Let there be ten yards between each man. Move down in a half circle. When we come near the place, close the circle. Don't let anyone get through."

The man nodded and went away. The lieutenant watched them spreading out in a long line, on each side of him. Then he walked and they walked with him until they came to the top of the hill. Here he waited.

The sun would rise at his back, very shortly now. It was July and it rose early. There was an eerie light everywhere now that always came before the sun. The lieutenant had seen many of those. He was grateful that it wasn't raining. Standing here, watching this strange light creeping over the rocks, you could imagine yourself dead and walking a strange place in a strange unknown country. It was a bleak, hard, uninhabited place. No birds sang, and the fitful wind from the sea was stirring the coarse grass against the stones making a sort of sibilant sound, like the scraping on the soles of inumerable bare feet. The lieutenant shivered, wished for a mug of strong tea with sugar, and feeling, rather than seeing the great arc of the sun rising behind him, he gave a low whistle, waved his arm and the line of men advanced. He could see a red light creeping across the land, reaching out toward the ship on the bay which had appeared magically as if someone had waved a wand. Then, more practically, he could see the wisp of blue smoke rising almost from the ground—it seemed some hundred yards ahead of him—and knew that this time he was going to be successful. Most times he got the still and the makings and maybe the filled jars, but rarely was there a human being within miles. It was like *Hamlet* without the Prince.

He stopped and waited, making a circle with his arms. They saw him and moved on, until they ringed the place from which the smoke was rising. He walked then to the smoke. As he came nearer he noticed that there was a sharp fall. He skirted it, walked gently down and was looking into a cave with a narrow opening. Other times the opening would have been closed with the bushes and stones that lay nearby. But now it was open. There was a squatting man in there, looking out at him, with his mouth open in astonishment. The lieutenant wanted to smile. The man's face was red from the light of the fire that was under the boiler of the still. He could see every emotion on it, surprise and dismay and then savage anger as he came to his feet and made for the opening. The lieutenant, who was a small neat man and opposed to violence, took the pistol from his belt and held it in his hand. That stopped the man's mad rush. He slowed, bent down and came erect outside the cave. He was a big gaunt man, with a black beard, black hair. His clothes were soiled, his eyes were flaming and red from the smoke. He rubbed them now with his hands.

Jeering voices came from behind them.

"Ho, Bottle, you come like a cork from a jar."

"Now, Daxon, let us taste your beer. Who will take a jug of the first run?"

He looked around him. He was like a trapped animal. He peered at the faces in the gathering light.

"I will remember you," he said.

"You will have time," a man answered him, and they laughed.

"Tie his hands," the lieutenant said to his own two men who were behind him with guns in their hands. One of them did so. Daxon did not resist him. He kept looking at the other seven as if he wanted to memorize their faces forever. The big man who was the leader of them came closer to him.

"You know me, Bottle," he said.

"Yes, Jack Gately," said Daxon, "I know you. You were a bad customer."

"Now I'm a good customer," said Jack. He laughed.

"I will remember what you owe me," said Daxon.

"I will be living for that when you come out," said Jack, "in ten years or so."

Daxon said nothing more. He stood impassively as they broke up all they had to break up, and took what they had to take for the evidence the lieutenant needed, and then they headed without subterfuge straight down the valley. That was part of the exercise, to display the uselessness of opposing the Revenue, so they set off toward the road across the very rough ground, walking carefully, the seven men from over the hill, laughing and jeering, and waving the thick sticks they held in their hands. The lieutenant walked behind Daxon and his two men one on each side of him. He didn't expect trouble, but he was a bit anxious. All he knew was that no matter what happened, Daxon would end up on the cutter, and then in a court. He would present his evidence, and that was that. It was another job done.

As they came near to the road, all the same, he took precautions. He called to the rough men and they walked three on one side and four on the other. They were big men and formidable. They made the lieutenant and his two sailors look small. Only the towering figure of the man with the tied hands equaled them, and they walked on the road like that until from the lane that led from Daxon's house the small figure of a boy came running, with the sleep barely out of his eyes, a dog at his heels, and he was calling, "Father! Father!"

Dualta and Carrol O'Connor had come early to the hayfields. Carrol had a good place. He was one of the very few in the valley who held his farm on a lease of two lives, the life of himself and his son. As long as he paid his rent he was safe from eviction or rack-renting until the death of his eldest son, who was now fourteen and likely to live to be a hundred. So he could afford to keep his house and lands looking well. The house was a long house, neatly thatched with two big bedrooms apart from the kitchen and an offshoot that was used as the priest's parlor. He had four children, a very hardworking, earnest wife and a golden tongue. He wasn't yet forty. He was brown-haired, broadly built and had a very even temper. He had memorized from his own father an enormous number of stories and songs with which, after persuasion, he regaled the people at wakes and weddings and celebrations. He wasn't a creator as he told Dualta, he was just a storage vessel used to pass on the beautiful native culture by word of mouth in an unbroken line that stretched back to the mists of time. Dualta liked him; he liked living with him, and paid for his board by working in the fields for him. His eldest was a girl and the next to her a girl and the two youngest were sons who, now that a teacher had appeared like a rainbow in the valley, were reluctantly going to school. So, since he owned about thirty acres, and hired out his horse and plow, had many cattle and sheep, he needed help.

They were in on the hayfield, sharpening the scythes, when Carrol straightened himself at the sight of the cutter below in the bay. "Oh, but there will be fluttering in the birdhouses now," he said laughing. He was right about that. When the town woke up and saw the cutter in the bay and the armed sailor guarding the small boat on the shore, as soon as the people had rubbed away the sleep, they scurried about like disturbed rabbits. The owners of the tippling houses hid their unlicensed whiskey and tobacco in stables and thatches. All smuggled goods went underground, the loot from the shipwreck of last winter found new hiding places. It was like a cleaning of consciences.

Dualta laughed. They talked about the reason for the cutter. They couldn't make out why.

The hayfield was near the road, so when they heard the sound of feet, coming down from the hills, they leaned on their scythes to look.

The men were a long way off when Carrol understood.

"It's Daxon, by God," he said. "They have taken Daxon at last. Well, now, who would have ever thought that they would take Daxon?"

"He is the father of the boy Colman?" asked Dualta.

"Yes, the poor little fellow," said Carrol. Everyone was sorry then for the boy, but few liked his father, even if they drank his raw whiskey. He was a dour man. Just plain stupid, Carrol said. He had kidnapped a girl from the other side of the hills.

Her name was Rafteri. He was a big strong good-looking fellow then. Many brides were kidnapped like that. If a father objected, the suitor took her away with help and hid her a night, and since the father didn't know if she was impaired or not, he either made the best of it, or cut her off like a limb from a family tree. Daxon's bride had been cut off. She was only two years married when they found her face down in a stream. She was a person with God anyhow, people said, not quite all in the world. Others said Daxon drove her to it. He was unkind they said. He brought up the boy like a hare.

"So that was why they came," said Carrol.

Dualta heard the voice of the boy then, as the men came closer to the field. He walked down to the stone wall bordering the road. He looked. The procession was approaching. Daxon walked in the middle, his face blank, his hands tied. The seven rough men were looking behind them as they walked. They were laughing. The tallest of them was holding off the boy, who was trying to break through them to his father. He couldn't get through the ring. His plaintive voice came over the sound of them. "Father! O, Father!" Once Daxon spoke. He half turned his head. "Home, boy, go home! I tell you to go home!" he called. It could be the way you would talk to a sheep dog, or it could be that he was moved. Dualta couldn't make out.

"Drive him off," the lieutenant called. "He might lead to a riot."

The big man caught him by the long hair, raised him and hit his backside with the stick. Dualta had often seen a dog thrashed this way. The sight of the boy like that drained the blood from his head. He jumped the wall and ran to the big man and as the stick rose again he unbalanced him with a poke on the head with the handle of the scythe. The dog was barking furiously. The boy fell in the dust. The big man roared and turned waving his stick. His six companions, joyfully moved toward them. Dualta held the gleaming blade of the scythe high in the air. "Come on now," he said.

They paused. His face was white. He was straddling the boy.

The lieutenant turned.

"You can be arrested," he said, "for resisting the Revenue."

"Since when have you started to make war on children?" Dualta asked. "Are you so weak that a boy may frighten you?"

The lieutenant looked at him.

"Close up," he said to the men. "Keep that boy away," he said to Dualta.

Then he turned and walked on. The rest of them followed him, reluctantly, the big man rubbing the side of his head. Dualta watched until they were around a bend in the road. Then he felt movement under him. He dropped the scythe and reached for the boy, but he was too late. He was up and off down the road. Dualta followed him. The boy dodged, calling. Dualta grabbed for him, caught his shirt. The shirt tore. "Colman! Colman! Colman!" he was shouting, pleading. Colman dodged again. Dualta reached a hand and caught his leg. He held on to it. It was like holding a year-old calf. He had to fall on him, to lie on top of him, to quieten him. The dog kept barking at Dualta's heels. Dualta kept saying: "Colman! Colman! Listen to me." The boy was wriggling and calling and crying. His whole face was dirty with dusty tears. Finally he lay still. He turned on his front and lay with his forehead on his arms. Dualta stood, looking down at him helplessly. Then he went on a knee beside him. "You can do no good, Colman," he said. "These criminals will injure you." Dualta thought: I was like that at his age, even if my father was dead. I was alone and I felt desolate, and uncle Marcus found me. It would be worse to have your father go like that. The boy was very thin. He could do with feeding. He stood up. Carrol was beside him.

"What will we do?" he asked.

"The priest is away," said Carrol. "He will be a hard one to manage. You will have to try the schoolteacher. I hear great accounts of her sense. Maybe she could talk to him. I will see what we can all do otherwise."

"We are all passing on the baby," Dualta thought. He felt helpless. He didn't know the boy well enough to be in his confidence. Nobody in the valley knew him really. He was like a hare, they said, peering at you from a covert with his ears up.

"I'll do that," said Dualta.

The boy had stopped sobbing. He was just lying supine. The dog was sitting beside him, now and again licking his ear.

"Colman," said Dualta, "get up and come with me." The boy didn't move. He bent down and raised him to his feet. He stood there his head down.

"It's all I can think of," said Carrol.

"Come on, Colman," said Dualta taking his hand. It was a thin hand. The boy moved with him as he walked. That was all. "I'll be back soon," Dualta said.

Carrol watched them for a while, and then shaking his head and collecting Dualta's scythe, climbed the wall and went back to the field.

It was strange sight for the birds, the stick-waving men ahead with their prisoner. People came from the fields to look at them. Now and again a clod of turf came sailing over a fence to spatter the road and once or twice to hit one of the stick carriers. But that was all. It was only half-hearted. The people of the town stood and watched and only jeered. They threw some dirty remarks, but that was all. The lieutenant could sense that there would be no actual opposition, so he relaxed as they walked toward the shore. After all, there was nothing political about it. It was a civil crime, and Daxon was not particularly liked and there were many more in the valley just as adept as he at firing a still.

Dualta sighed as he turned at the road that led to the school and walked toward it with his most silent partner.

chapter XVIII

Miss MacMahon was absolutely distracted and feeling helpless.

It is always very easy to dream of an ideal. She thought back to the days when she was discussing with Father Joe what she would do with her life; how she had made up her mind inflexibly to devote it to the welfare of the people, and when she thought of teaching, it seemed like an inspired pink dream, like a completed woven tapestry, like a work of art, hanging on a wall. She never really gave thought to how it would be like in practice. Words like "difficult," "hard," "grinding," "out of environment," "sacrifice," "loneliness," are simply words until in practice they acquire meaning. They were meaningful now. She could have taught in a town where conditions would have been better, where there would have been people of her own kind within reach, where she could lean on somebody who would understand. Here she was like an odd bird blown in by a storm, among birds with strange feathers, native birds who were foreign to everything she had been brought up with. The life of a convert is hard anyhow, abandoned by those you have left and ignored by the ones you have joined. It was of little use to say that it was bound to involve sacrifice, that pearls of price must be paid for. All these were words, and most time words contain little comfort.

She looked at her class now and her eyes were a little wild, and she was not aware that strands of her hair had come loose and were waving around her face.

She thought it would be all right if she had only girls to deal with. It was the boys that were defeating her. Just their names alone. She was in a more difficult position than the postmaster in the town. You have to know who John Pat Éamon is, or Tom Bán or Seoirse the son of the shoemaker, or Tomás son of the cooper, Jack Kitty Tomás. Mostly they were not the sons of tradesmen at all, but the sons of cottagers or laborers. The eldest boy was sixteen. He was a tall rough youth with a heavy fuzz on his face. It did not make him look attractive. He was Móra the son of the tinker. His father was not a tinker. He was a laborer for the Bradishes, but he was handy with pots and sometimes fashioned tin lanterns to hold candles. This Móra was a scourge. He was the most illiterate of the lot, stupid and unsettling. If she had been capable of giving him a box in the ear, she would be saved, but she was afraid to do this. For a simple reason, he might hit her back, as his father was well known to do to Móra's mother. He made the other boys unruly.

There was that. The girls she could manage. They were willing. The class was divided into three, readers, spellers, and writers. They were readers if they could afford the books. These were what they called the Reddy May Daisy, *Reading Made Easy*, and the Universal, *The Universal Spelling Book*. They were expensive. They cost three shillings and three shillings and sixpence, from the chapman or the peddlers and hawkers at the fairs. In fact some of the parents had gone as far as Ennis to buy them when the school was started. They sold a firkin of butter or a bag of potatoes, or turf, or pawned a treasured blanket in order to acquire a copy of these or *Gough's Arithmetic*. The books were then carefully covered in strong canvas or lambskin with the woolly side out, and a dangling thumbmark. The scholars carefully carried them at their breast to spare them from the disaster of their playtimes.

If they could not afford the books they were writers. They used quills plucked from a goose for this, with the small earthenware jar of ink made from the juice of boiled briar roots or the juice of the blackberry mixed with indigo. That and precious writing paper, also costly, sometimes consisting of the blank pages torn from old books. At this time there was great stealing also of the lead from lead-paned windows. This lead could be melted and when hot poured on to the tip of a gander's quill to make a fine lead pencil.

For sums they used a slate, smoothed by a sea-stone on which they could put the figures with shaped limestone. Most of the slates were brought to the carpenter who framed them like a picture, and they could be cleaned with a spit and the rub of a sleeve.

When she saw all this she knew she was right. There was a terrible thirst among the people for learning. If they themselves hadn't it, they would do anything so that their children would acquire it. She knew the joy in the house the first day that a scholar could go home and be able to read aloud the American, the letter that had come from an emigrant with the precious ticket in it that could be cashed in the bank in Ennis. All this she heard from the first girl who had done so. How embarrassed they had been before having a letter that meant everything to them, having to have a scholar come in and read it for them, a neighbor but a stranger, very embarrassing and here now was cause for rejoicing, one of their own reading aloud to the manner born: "I take this favorable opportunity of writing these few lines to let you know that I am well and doing well. I work in the day and I get a dollar for this. It is hard but it is not slavery and I am my own man. How I abided it at home I do not know. We eat meat nearly every day but on Fridays, and sugar and tea every day with white bread. I look every man in the eye. I am my own. I do long for home all the same. Sometimes I do cry and I thinking of it. But what use with the great hardship and the hunger there and men no better than slaves to the landlords. Julia O'Brien is well. I do see her now and again. She sends you her best wishes as I do now, with these few dollars which will help to meet the wind for you on Gale Day. If Seán will come out I will save up for the fare for him. He will be well off here even if he will be lonely. There are no gentlemen here. All are one. There is no lords or gentry in this country that you have to put your hand to your hat for. Indeed I do be thinking of ye when ye don't least suspect it. I finish now, hoping this finds ye as it leaves me in good health and happiness your loving son Joe."

Miss MacMahon had read this letter and little Margaret's carefully composed reply, dictated by her mother, admonished to cover every bit of paper as what use was it to send white paper to her son.

Rewarding, thought Miss MacMahon, the fact that she had to work so hard to improve her Irish, so that she could translate English into Irish in order to make them understand the English. Because they all longed to learn English, feeling that it would put them on a better footing, or at the back of their minds the knowledge that someday if things were really bad they would have to emigrate and join the growing band of their race who were scattering all over the world.

That and cleanliness. Most of them were spotlessly clean even if their clothes were very poor. But some of them came from dirty homes and lice walked on them. How did you get them clean then? Did you put them away from the school on that account? How could you do this?

It was very lonely. She saw little of the Bradishes. How she longed now for their goose-feather beds and their fine food. She had no time. She had to cook and clean and make out lessons, and try to improve her house, this barren-looking place that was merely a shelter from the weather, gaunt and cold-looking with its unplastered walls.

Móra the son of the tinker was droning at the back. He was standing. There were three benches. She let them sit in turns. He was droning an arithmetic table. He was making foolish mistakes. He was thickening his tongue to say the unfamiliar English words. There were twelve other boys. They were all being infected by him. The four that were reciting tables were giggling and aping the way he was saying it. She was at the fireplace. She walked to him. Her voice was quite desperate. She had to look up at him.

"Móra," she said, "if you don't behave I will put you out of the school."

"What am I doing wrong then, noble lady?" he asked, his thick-lipped mouth open. "I am only doing what you told me."

"You are not," she said angrily. "You are behaving like an animal."

"I am not an animal, noble lady," he said. "I am only trying to do what you tell me."

"Don't answer me back like that," she said, wishing she could hit him until he became unconscious.

"My father says I must always answer up for meself, noble lady," he said.

"It isn't your father that's at school. It's you," she said. "You are very thick. You should be trying harder than anyone to learn."

"If you were good you could learn me," said Móra. "Isn't it easy to blame me for your own weakness, noble lady?"

"Go out!" she said. "Go outside at once!"

"I will not, then," he said. "Haven't I paid my penny like everyone else? Haven't I brought my sod of turf?"

Now what do I do? she wondered. Should she try physically to get him out. She glared at him, completely helpless, and then this man came in the door, and he said: "You heard what the teacher said then, Móra, so out you go!" Miss MacMahon was looking at him in amazement.

Móra looked at him. He said a rude thing to him. The next minute he was set back on his heels by a blow from an open hand. Then the young man caught him by the seat of his patched trousers and the scruff of the neck and propelled him out the door like a bullet. He threw him out there, and he fell in the yard. Móra looked up at him amazed. "O, what my father will do to you!" he said. "O, what I will do to you," said Dualta, "if you are not on your feet and running in two seconds." He made for him, and Móra, frightened now, got to his feet and stumbled and then ran as Dualta made for him. He ran fast. Dualta called after him; "When you come back, come back like a dog on your knees, tinker's son!"

Then he turned back to the schoolhouse door.

Miss MacMahon was at the door, looking at him with her mouth a little open. There was dawning delight in her face as he went to her. He had never before seen her at such a loss.

"Dualta!" she said "Dualta! Where in the name of God did you come from?"

"Why I came from the field behind, Miss MacMahon," he said his pulse racing. "I brought you. . . ." he looked around for his charge. There was no sign of him. "Oh, God," Dualta groaned. "He's gone again. I will have to chase him. Come after us, Miss MacMahon. I will explain." Then Dualta was gone as soon as he had appeared. She went quickly back into the house. The children were disturbed. "Read and write and use your slates," she said. "I will examine you when I return. If one of you moves from his place I will murder you when I come back or I will get the young man to murder you."

Then she left them. She went around the house. She saw Dualta toiling up the hill behind, chasing the figure of a boy, but in good heart, she hoisted her skirts a little and set off after them.

The real effort was gone out of Colman. His flight was only token. When he came to the wall he stopped. The dog jumped it, and then jumped back again and looked at him, his tongue lolling, his tail wagging. Dualta stopped in front of the boy.

"Anyone would think you were a child instead of a nine-year-old boy," said Dualta.

"I'm ten years," said Colman.

"Isn't that worse?" Dualta asked. "Why are you afraid of me? Would I beat you?"

"You took me to school," said the boy accusingly.

"I did not," said Dualta. "I took you to the schoolmistress."

"Is that different?" Colman asked.

"If it is your desire to remain ignorant," said Dualta, "you may do so. Even wild hares have manners among themselves, and foxes are polite. They do not act like you. You are like a wild cat spurning friendship. Will you listen to wisdom?"

"I do not need help from anyone," Colman said. "I am able to stand on my feet."

His tear-stained face, his bright eyes, belied his statement. Dualta felt sorry for him, but kept his face stern.

"It is good to be independent," he said, "but even the Pope listens to advice from other men. Even a king has counsellors. Are you greater than those?" He looked down the hill. Miss

MacMahon was coming close to them. She looked very well, he thought. Her hair was shining, her cheeks were flushed. Miss MacMahon was pretty, even if she was severely dressed.

"She is young," said Colman in a surprised voice. Dualta thought she would be the same age as himself, turned twenty. What was she doing here, in the name of God, in this valley, with that schoolhouse of children? Was she altogether mad?

They waited for her. She slowed her pace, lowered her dress and stood in front of them.

"Miss MacMahon," said Dualta formally, "this is Colman Daxon. His father has to go away for a time." His eyes drifted down the valley. Miss MacMahon looked too. She saw the knot of men below, small now with distance. But you couldn't mistake the revenue men, nor the unusual sight of the cutter in the bay. "His mother died some years ago. He just wanted to talk to you."

"I'm pleased to meet you, Colman," she said. She spoke in English. This seemed to surprise him. She had a soft voice. He looked at her hand and then stretched out his own. He nodded at her. She sat on a stone.

"You don't come to the school?" she asked.

He shook his head. He couldn't confess this, but he had wanted to go to the school, that was why he avoided it so much. But where would he get a penny a week? And he would be ashamed to be seen in his clothes which were so bad. Most Sundays he avoided Catechism classes after Mass, in case the others would laugh at him.

"No," he said. He looked down. He shuffled his bare feet. The dog was sniffing at Miss MacMahon. He liked what he scented. Suddenly he put his head on her knee. She stroked it. "Why, he likes you," said Colman, as if this was a wonder.

"Why wouldn't he, indeed?" she said. "Amn't I harmless?" She said this in Irish. Her eyes crinkled with laughter. Colman laughed too. He went on his knees beside her.

"I didn't know school people were like you," he said.

"Did you expect me to be like Napoleon?" she asked. "With a wooden leg too?"

This amused him. He shook all over with silent laughter.

"Do you beat the children with a bunch of sally rods?" he asked.

"No," she said. "I am afraid to beat them in case they beat me back."

"Oh, you should hit them," he said. "Some of them are thick."

"I'll try," she said solemnly. "Tell me, Colman, would you ever be able to help me?"

He looked at her in wonder.

"Me help you!" It was almost a snort.

"Yes," she said. "I need help in the worst way. I am on my own. I can't do everything. I wish you would consider this. While your father is away if you would come to me and do little jobs, like the fire and cleaning and many things. I will try to pay you a little. You can sleep by the fire and eat with me. Only if you wish."

"Would I have to be at school?" he asked.

"Not necessarily," she said, "unless you want to listen in."

"Sometimes I mind Moran McCleary's sheep," he said.

"I'm sure you could do that too," she said.

He dropped his head. He was thinking.

"I will go with you for a while," he said then, "to see if I like it. Will that be all right?"

"That's fair," she said.

He stood up. "I will go and get my things now, so," he said. "I will close my father's house. It would be lonely anyhow for a while until I get used to it."

"That's true," she said.

He clicked his fingers at the dog. "Come, Flan," he said.

"What!" exclaimed Dualta, "do you name a dog after the poet?"

Colman laughed. "He knows that," he said. "It is because I admire him."

"Oh, I see," said Dualta. "Some time then I hope you name a dog after me."

The boy looked at him. "We'll see," he said doubtfully. Dualta laughed.

"I will be with you then," Colman said to Miss MacMahon and set off running. He kept his head averted from the road on the right where his father was being taken.

They looked after him for a little, then Dualta turned and looked at her. Her eyes met his firmly.

"You have a way with boys," he said, "and men, Miss Una."

She didn't answer him. She looked steadily at him. Then she spoke. "You will never know how pleased I was to see you come in that door," she said.

He sat beside her.

"Why," he said, "tell me why you have changed your name? Why you are here? What caused it?"

She plucked a blade of grass. She chewed it with her even teeth, small teeth in a determined chin.

"MacMahon was my mother's name," she said.

"It is strange," said Dualta. "One time long ago, there was a MacMahon among us. My uncle Marcus told me of him. He kept a journal. Part of it survived. This amazes me. That it should be your name. But your father? How is he? What does he think?"

"You saw my father last," she said. She left it in the air. Dualta felt his face flaming.

"Yes," he said. "I saw him last."

"I heard all about it," she said. "So you didn't come to our house for a good purpose, did you?"

"I never did anything bad," he said. "I liked your father. He wasn't injured through me."

"I know that too," she said. "Is it all a closed book? Why are you here? Are you still mixed up with violent men?"

He thought over it.

"No," he said. "Sometime I will tell you. No more. That's gone. In a way, it was your father that decided it for me."

"What brought you to this valley?" she asked.

"What brought you?" he reposited. "It's inconceivable, a person like you, with all that you have, to be here. What about your own mother's people? Did you not go to them? Why?"

"You can never understand what happens when you cut your-

self off," she said. "But you must have a purpose. The only
thing to do was to teach. I was well educated. I wanted to pass
this on, if I could, somewhere that it was really needed. That is
why I am here. My friend Father Joe was at Maynooth with
Father Finucane. He knew he wanted to set up a school. That is
why I am here."

"But it is not right," he said. "A girl like you." He took her
hand, turned up the palm. A small hand, it was cracked from
toil. It used to be as smooth as finely ground flour. He remembered the touch of it when he would help her on or off the
carriage. The nails were short and some of them broken. "See,"
he said.

"It's hard," she said. "Just today, it seemed impossible. I
thought, it is no use. I am defeated. I cannot go on with this.
It is beyond me. There is no hope of me being able to hold out
under it. And then at the very worst moment, you walked in. I
was so happy to see you."

"You would have been happy to see a tinker," he said, "as
long as he came from your own valley."

"That's probably true," she said. "But now I am so pleased
there is somebody I can talk to here. You won't be running off
again, will you?"

He laughed.

"No," he said. "This is my last refuge. But there are gentry
in the valley, how about them? Can't they be helpful to you?"

"You must always go up in this world," she said. "You must
never go down, even if you know that in going down you may
be going up. It is all very hard to explain. All I can say is that
it is lonely to be lost in the middle, and that is why I am so
happy to see you."

"I was talking to Father Finucane too," he said. "He has an
odd way of challenging you without saying anything. I am
going to settle here. I am going to build up a small place. I am
going to be part of the people. That's what you must do too.
You only know them through their children. You have to know
themselves, individually, the poet and the storyteller and the
singer and the carpenter, the drunken ones and the sober ones

and the hypocritical ones and the pious ones. You must get a hint of the culture they carry that goes back thousands of years. You see!" He was excited now, on his knees. "You must go to wakes and weddings and funerals. You must shout God Save Ireland, and grumble about the landlords. You must shout Up Daniel O'Connell, and Freedom, and watch the boys hurling in the fields and the girls dancing at the crossroads. You must get behind the curtain they draw between the stranger and the one like themselves. You see! That way you will be able to survive and become part of them since you seem to have thrown in your lot now so completely with them."

"See," she said. "I have set a river flowing."

"And I myself," he wondered, "what can I do? I have knowledge. I had the best teacher in Ireland. I didn't appreciate him then. Well, the best teacher apart from the one in the Valley of the Flowers. So I know a lot of things. I too will pass them on. You see. I will take the boys off your hands. Isn't that an idea? I will teach the boys! I'm not afraid of them hitting me back. I will pound knowledge into them! See! Isn't that an idea? Was that what Finucane meant then? Did he see me like thistledown on the wind, aimless, although thistledown is not aimless since it carries the seed that it will sow. How do you think? Would this please you?"

"Oh, how much, how much!" she said. "If Father Finucane will pass you."

His face went blank.

"Pass me?" he asked.

"Yes," she said. "He is a wise young priest. He will say. How was it humanly possible to preserve the faith in the land when the people had no priest, no altars, when their heads were worth five pounds to an approver? They established the teachers in the hedge schools. They picked highly moral young people who held catechism classes in the woods and on the bleak shores. They made use of the fiber of their teachers. That way the faith was held like a pure stream that always flows sweetly to the sea no matter what obstacles it meets. You see, I'm telling you all this. He will test you."

"I will pass his tests," he said. "Now that I know I can do something that I want to do. If necessary I will take the three vows for him, I swear."

She laughed.

"Don't do that," she said. "You might be sorry." She got to her feet. "I must go back to my crosses," she said. "They will have torn the place apart. I'm so glad you came here, Dualta. I'm so glad we met like this."

"Not as glad as I am," he said. "Things will move now. When I have a little place, I will take Colman off your hands. I will look after him."

They walked together toward the school.

There she held out her hand. He took it. "Come again and talk to me," she said, "when your plans are laid."

"I will," he said. "I will bring you on a journey into the hearts of the people. You will never be lonely again in the valley."

"I'm so glad, so glad, to see you," she said.

He watched her into the school. He was under no illusions, he thought, as he went back toward Carrol and the scythe. She was pleased to see him on account of her loneliness. What a wonderful girl, to do this thing she was doing! But she always had it in her to do something great. Only who would have thought her greatness would have turned in this direction?

She was a lady, he thought, and the flowers of the valley were the more beautiful for her presence.

chapter XIX

N THIS 25TH OF September, three events coincided to make it remarkable. It was a Thursday, and it was fair day, gale day, and mail day. Naturally people remarked on it, and determined weeks in advance to make it more memorable. Nobody was going to work anyhow and everybody was going into the street town, where from two o'clock in the morning the animals were being driven from many miles away, converging on the town. The roads were built in a great Y, west and east and the south coming down through the valley, while the town itself was huddled in the fork of the Y stretching along the rough seacoast. So from early morning as far as your eye could see their winding lengths, the roads were being packed with people and animals and carts.

Una looked at herself in the small mirror that was set in the window stool of her room. It was hard to see her face. Dualta had scraped a lambskin, dried it and inserted it in the wooden frame. The light through it was not as clear as glass. All the same she thought her complection was gone to hell. She looked healthy enough, but her skin was sunburned and had lost its creamy whiteness except under the neckband of her dress, where it had been protected. She contrasted the two, shrugged and rubbed the last of the buttermilk into her hands. It didn't do them much good, but they felt softer. She was afraid Mrs. Bradish would see them and be scandalized, so she went to the rough chest of drawers and pulled out her last pair of long gloves. She smoothed the front of her dress with her hands, lifted her skirt to look at her buckled shoes. They were still respectable. Then taking her reticule in one hand and her hat in the other, she went down to the big room. It was tidy. Colman had swept it, put the benches against the wall, banked the fire, rolled his bag of straw, all this before he departed for the town. She sighed, went out the door, shut it after her on the latch. There was nothing for anyone to steal even if the people were thieves, which they weren't.

It was a nice morning. There had been rain during the night. The aging world looked washed and temporarily revived. Mrs. Bradish had sent her a note, lavender-scented, asking her if she would like to accompany the girls to the town. If she wouldn't mind calling. It was a gentle reminder of her fall from high estate. Una didn't mind. She liked the walk. The rain had settled the dust, so her shoes would not be destroyed. All the same she dodged the many puddles in the potholes of the road. The sun was quite hot, but there was a cool east wind that spoke of more rain. She supposed Dualta would be going to the town. She hoped she would see him there. She didn't see much of him. He came for four hours, and his effect was magical. Before he came and after he went she could always threaten the boys with him.

She opened the gate to the avenue of the Bradishes, and she told herself as she walked toward the house: I am going to enjoy myself. I am not going to let the woman upset me. I have few holidays. I am going to savor this one. I will be like I was at sixteen, a maiden going to a fair, looking for a ribbon favor.

The open car was standing outside the house. She patted the nose of the quiet horse and went up the steps.

All was confusion in the hall. Maids were running in and out carrying things in their hands. One of them screamed up the stairs, "The schoolmistress is here, ma'am!" dropped Una a quick curtsey and departed. Mrs. Bradish came rolling down the stairs, like a sailor Una thought, on a rocking ship.

"Dear Miss MacMahon, how good of you to come. You look very smart," turning her around, feeling the stuff of her dress with her fingers. "But your face, dear, you have let the sun get at it! You'll be like one of those horsewomen." Turning to the stairs: "Girls! Girls! What's keeping you? Miss MacMahon is here!" They answered: "Coming, Mother! Coming, Mother!"

"How you can do it, dear, those awful children. How can you stand it? Are you not tired of it?"

"No, Mrs. Bradish, I love it. I love the children."

"But most of them are so dirty, dear. I haven't anything against the poor, but they can make soap."

"Most of them are very clean, Mrs. Bradish. It's only the few and they will benefit from the good example of the others. That's what education is for. To elevate the mind. Everything else follows."

"But elevate them for what, dear? Why above their station? Will they need arithmetic to feed the pigs, grammar to fork the hay, spelling to manure the potato ridges?"

I must be patient, Una says to herself.

"And now I hear you have a young man down there, teaching the boys as well. An ordinary young man, dear. From the wilds of Galway I hear. Can that be true?"

"Yes," said Helen coming down the stairs, pulling on gloves, "and a very handsome young man too, even if he is from the wilds."

"But where would he get the education, Miss MacMahon? Was it the priest put him in on you?"

"No, Mrs. Bradish," said Una. "He came of his own accord. He is very well educated. Better read than myself. In fact I doubt if there is anyone in this valley, high or low, who could equal him, and nobody who could impart knowledge as he can. I knew him in my father's house."

"Oh," said Mrs. Bradish relieved, "that's different."

"No, Mrs. Bradish, it's not different," said Una. "He drove my father's carriage. He worked in the fields. He helped to make up the accounts."

"You mean he was just like Tom Keane, our handyman?" she asked, with very raised eyebrows.

"Oh, no," said Helen. "Tom Keane is about fifty years old and couldn't spell his own name. This is different. Margaret! Margaret! Please hurry! Margaret is always last. Always last. You look well, Una. Sunburn suits you. If I let the sun at me I'd look like a peeled onion."

"Ah, Miss MacMahon, so pleased to see you," said Bradish

coming down the stairs, his arm around Margaret's shoulders. Margaret was his favorite daughter. You could see that. Perhaps because she was the prettiest. She was slender too, where Helen was becoming plump and would be a walking edition of her mother in time to come. "The girls will take good care of you. I have arranged for lunch to be served to you in Glasby's office. He is my agent you know. I want the girls to keep an eye on him. You can trust nobody. Just because he knows they are there will make him cautious. So I hope you will have a good day."

"Thank you," said Una.

"Let us be off so," said Helen, going out the door.

"Be careful, dear," her mother called after her, "and watch your sister. Don't be late. A lot of drinking goes on. It's disgraceful."

Una was down the steps by now. Placid Tom Keane helped her in. He was a graying man, with a moon face, wearing his best clothes. He smiled at her all the same. She taught his daughter, Margaret, who was very bright and had been the first child to go home and read a letter for her mother. Margaret joined them and they listened for a few moments more to advice and admonitions from Mrs. Bradish before they went on their way.

Mrs. Bradish said: "That girl has changed a lot. The first time I saw her I said, There's a lady if ever I saw one. Now she's beginning to look like a dairymaid."

"Shush, shush, dear," said her husband, and kept waving his hand until they were out of sight.

"Well, she does," said Mrs. Bradish. "She must have had common blood in her all the time."

"Please dear," said Mr. Bradish urging her toward the house.

"Thank God! Thank God! Thank God!" said Margaret. "A whole day to spend on our own, and without Mother. You have saved our lives, Una. If you hadn't come we would have been in a stewpot. Now watch how I am going to make smoke, like a hot fire."

"Margaret, control yourself," said Helen, but her heart wasn't in the rebuke.

Una looked at them. Their eyes were shining. What a dull

life they must have, she thought, when this means so much to them!

The main square of the town was jam-packed. Tom had to roar and beg and beseech and threaten with the whip to get a way cleared for the horse. The confusion and sound were too great to distinguish anything. Finally he got the horse to the gateways of the yard of Donaghue's. He was sweating and grateful when he managed to get the carriage in there, and helped the ladies to alight.

"We will be a few hours, Tom," Helen said. "Don't get too merry."

"I will only grease my throat, Miss," Tom said. "You can be sure of my behavior."

"Drink as much as you like, Tom," Margaret said. "You can sing croppy songs for us on the way home."

"Margaret!" said Helen.

"Pish," said Maragaret. "Una and I will collect the mail, Helen. We will meet you in Glasby's rooms then."

"All right," said Helen. "Don't get into mischief."

They parted at the door of the shop. It was a low-built place. They had to go down steps to get into it. It was a long room, as if the end wall had been taken out of two adjoining houses, to make this shop smelling of meal and spices and leather and whiskey.

Their entry had been noticed all the same. A bald-headed man with rolled sleeves, bright eyes and an energetic manner waved to them. "Ho, Miss Bradish, you are here. Come over that we may open the mails," he said. Margaret was standing on her tiptoes trying to see over the heads of the people to the counter below. "O," she said, "all right, Mister Donaghue!" She went over to him. People made way politely for them. He pulled a heavy leather satchel from under the counter. It was sealed and had a big brass plate in the center stamped with the insignia H.M. Mails. He opened this ceremoniously and took out the tied bundles of letters. Una could feel the people behind them stretching their necks. She noticed some of the yellow envelopes peculiar to American letters. She heard the "O-o-oh" of people, and a voice said: "Caffar, son, is one of the yellow's for MacInerney?" Caffar Donoghue looked up. He was severe. "Have manners now, let you," he said. "Let all be done with order." Outside Una could hear shouts that traveled from one to another for miles. "The mails is open now." But they had to wait. She knew it was as severe a protocol as being presented at Court. Personal gentry first, then in order of precedence, gentlemen's butler, minister's man, priest's servant, policeman, down the line before the ordinary people were serviced. It was amusing to watch. Margaret took her letters and looked at the envelopes, then she came over and took Una's arm and said, "Come down here." Una went with her. This was the serious part of the shop, for the buying and selling. There was a young man here inside a counter, with his sleeves rolled. He could have been Caffar Donoghue except that he had a heavy head of curly hair. They made their way to the counter and when he looked up, she saw that he had a pleasant face. Margaret said: "I want to do some shopping, Eamon, I have a long list." He looked and swallowed and a glaze seemed to come over his eyes. Una was astonished. She looked at Margaret. The girl was looking at him smilingly and her eyes were bright. Good God! thought Una.

"Yes, Miss Margaret," he managed to get out. "Just give me one second, one second, and I'll be with you." He went back to a door and called "Murty! Murty! Come to me! Here, Murty!" Margaret said: "Isn't he a pet?" Then he came back to them. He could see nobody but Margaret. "What can I do for you, Miss Margaret?" he asked.

"I'll be back, Margaret," Una said. She went away. They hardly noticed her going. Oh, what will Mrs. Bradish make of that? she thought with great joy. She had to push her way out of the place. A call was coming from inside. "An American for O'Halloran!" she heard someone say. "Hold it up to the light, Caffar. See if there's a ticket in it." All the way the call preceded her, hurled from place to place. "There's an American for O'Halloran" all away the call until it reached the end of the town and traveled the roads and was lost in the hills.

She walked from one end of the town to the other. Sometimes she didn't walk, but was carried in the press. She did not think there were so many people in Ireland. She had never been in the middle of them like this before. She sat gracefully in a carriage and waited, or drove around the outside roads so that they would not be involved. Now she was involved, in noise above all. Everybody was talking, shouting, singing. She thought that at least one quarter of those present were drunk. This was not pleasant. But the majority were not. They bargained their pigs for the rent money, and their cattle and their firkins of butter and eggs and fowl, and they bought from the chapmen and hucksters and tinkers, from the stalls of all descriptions. And they listened to singers and fiddle players and soft flute players, and gob singers, and watched jugglers, and flame swallowers and fortune tellers. It was a press of people the like of which she had never experienced. She was caught up in them, in the smell of them, of drink and new wool, and polished boots, the smell of fetid breaths and milk and little bits of roasting meat, and fresh baked cakes. She was nearly squeezed to death.

At this time Dualta was fighting for his future.

Carrol had left the house early. He was selling an in-calf heifer, a collop, a pig, and some sheep. The young people were helping him. Dualta drove the horse and cart with Mrs. O'Connor and Sheila. Mrs. O'Connor was selling a firkin of butter, which was four churnings packed into the firkin after being kept cool on a slate in her little dairy. She also had eggs and chickens. She was a tidy woman, well fleshed, fresh-faced with bright eyes and a silent tongue. There are enough talking tongues in the house, she would say. It was true for her. Sheila her daughter made up for her. She was a restless type of girl, moving all the time. Even now in the cart, she was shifting in her seat, moving her feet, grabbing Dualta by the arm. She was dark-haired and one of the prettiest girls in the valley, but she didn't seem to be too aware of it. She waved at people she knew, shouted at some girls that she would meet them at the ribbon stall, and kept up a running advice to Dualta of how he was to handle Clarke.

Clarke was the sort of nemesis hanging over the valley. He was Tewson's agent and he was all-powerful. Dualta had just seen the back of him at Mass. His head looked like one that had been carved out of hard wood, placed on thick shoulders. That's all he knew of him, but every tenant of Sir Vincent's was due to meet him today, gale day, in order to pay up their six-months' rent, or explain why they weren't able to pay, or to give something to stave off eviction.

Dualta knew what he wanted. He wanted something that nobody else did. He knew it would be regarded as an odd thing if a stranger hardly in the valley set himself up for a place that another local man wanted or was due to be evicted from. After advice and some searching he had hit on the Bacach's place which nobody wanted. It was a ruined house. The roof had fallen in. The walls were almost hidden with clumps of briars and winding woodbine. He traced the outlines of the land. They were covered in gorse, the walls fallen, but he saw that five acres of it at least could be made sweet and the other three could be grazed if they were cleared. But it was in a terrible state of neglect. Who would want it? Nobody but a fool. It was that way since Bacach died. He died swinging at the end of a rope from a thorn tree. He had been a lame man with one short leg, an only child. He was slightly hunchbacked as well, so there was nothing but a life of loneliness ahead of him when his mother died. What girl would look at him with all the sound-legged fellows in the place hotly looking for wives? So Bacach died, and his place was a haunt. Children were frightened away from it and only the goats grazed it. When Dualta talked about it, men blessed themselves, then they joked, said that it was a hilly place, and only suited to a Bacach, one leg up and one leg down. But would he get it from Clarke? He was freshly shaved. His hair was washed and neatly tied. He wore his best white shirt, short coat, breeches and buckled shoes. He wanted to look respectable.

"Don't be spiky, then," Sheila was saying, "like you can be. Don't talk over his head like you do over mine when you want to annoy me."

"Good, good," Dualta was saying.

"And I'll meet you afterwards," she said, "and you can be my escort at the fair and all the other girls will be as jealous as old spinsters." She caught his arm again, pressed her face against his shoulder. "Can I tell them all that you are in a fever about me?"

Dualta laughed. Her mother grunted.

"You can if you like," said Dualta, "only that I'm in a fever of annoyance about you. How can you expect to get a husband when you go chasing one?"

"I can get as many as I like," she said, tossing her dark ringletted hair. "I think I'm deciding to pick on you, and if you do get the Bacach's place and make it successful, my father will approve of you. Besides you are handsome, and you know a lot, and you set about educating me."

"What? In the art of love?" he asked.

"Oh, no," she said. "I can train you in that."

"Sheila!" said her mother.

"Innocent love, Mother," Sheila said. Dualta noted with amusement the looks some of the young men cast at him. Sitting beside this beauty, sleeping in the same house as her, and he a stranger too!

He dropped them and their goods in the marketplace. He had to get down and lead the horse through the throng. He parked the cart in Donaghue's yard, tied the horse to the cart and unloosed a bag of hay for him. Then he shouldered and elbowed his way to Clarke's house. There was a small crowd of people lining up patiently waiting their turn. Farther up the road there were people waiting to get into Glasby, who was the Bradish collector, and up the street Cringe held his rent court personally as agent for the glebe lands on the far side of the valley. He was a bitter one. Small, wizened, he was a pint-sized tyrant. Nobody had a good word for him. His latest venture was to set up a small very neatly built school, the other side of the valley, backed by the sinister Kildare Street Society, where he had installed what he called a Catholic teacher, and commanded the children of his tenants to attend his school, under pains of all sorts of penalties. His teacher was a thin-faced young man with skin eruptions on his face who asked the children if they really believed the Blessed Virgin had only one child?

The people were silent going into Clarke's. They were clutching purses, turning their backs and counting money. Dualta finally got into the first room, and finding a vacant stool sat in the corner and watched. He didn't want to see Clarke until the regular tenants had been with him. He watched the procedure. It made him burn with anger, but he swallowed it. There was this room. It was occupied by Clarke's brother-in-law, a thin man with a stringy neck. He was George Shields. Men said he was the long shadow of Clarke, the way a butty powerful man can throw a long shadow when the sun in descending. He sat at a table and smiled and checked off their names. Ah, yes, Tim Mahon and Dave Lynch. He hummed and hawed, and affected to be so surprised when they slipped him a "compliment" of two shillings and sixpence, or five shillings.

After George came Julia. She was Clarke's wife. She was in the next room. She was a fat jolly woman with a broad smile. She, too, was nearly overwhelmed with the compliments. A chicken or a goose or two pats of butter wrapped in cabbage leaves, or eggs, all adding up to sizable sums. So apart from rent of land, rent of house, tithe tax, cess tax, turbary rent, you had also to worry about the "compliments" to the agent's relations. It's part of life, he told himself. There is nothing dishonest about it. People are normally generous. They like out of pure generosity to compliment people.

"I can hear your teeth grinding," said a voice beside him. He turned in surprise. Cuan was standing there. He looked well, but grim. Dualta got to his feet. He took the other's hand, pumped it. "I'm so glad to see you, so glad to see you," he said. Cuan said with raised eyebrows, "We don't live a mile apart."

"I haven't had much time," said Dualta.

"Speak truth," said Cuan.

"Pilate wasn't the only one to ask what is truth," said Dualta.

"You cut me out of your life," said Cuan. "You want to become respectable, forget the past?"

"No," said Dualta. "I want to find myself alone. Then when I am what I am, you and I will meet again."

"You will not be tempted then, later," said Cuan. "When you

are responsible. When you have picked a girl and raised a family on her? I hear you are with Carrol O'Connor's daughter?"

"You are more human," said Dualta. "You listen to gossip now."

Cuan laughed. "I feel better," he said. "I am rested. Whatever stimulation I need I get from my brother Flan, arguing with him. He asked for you. You should see him. Don't become too much of a bogtrotter or a teacher of children. You could decay."

"No," said Dualta. "Children keep your mind alert. They want to know."

"Why are you here?" Cuan asked.

"I am looking to rent a place," said Dualta.

"Oh-ho," said Cuan, "you must have the childbearer picked already. Why are you waiting? Come now. I am here to pay my brother's rent. Come with me!" Orders again. Dualta shrugged, followed him.

"I am McCarthy," said Cuan to George. "I am the brother of Flan. I don't believe in bribery. There's nothing you can do for me." They left George with his mouth open and went into the next room. Here was Mrs. Clarke. She was alone. She was looking around at her compliments. No wonder. They were piled high and a joy to behold.

"Are you Clarke's wife?" Cuan asked her. At this gruffness the joy went out of her face. She was like a child deprived of sugar.

"Yes," she said. "I am Mistress Clarke." She always called herself that. She was unaware of the jokes it gave rise to. She had no children. They said: Perhaps if Clarke had a wife instead of a mistress he would have a family.

"I am the brother of Flan McCarthy," said Cuan. "We have no chickens, butter, eggs, geese. All we can give you is our good wishes and hope for a happy death." He stalked past her to the sanctum and walked in. Dualta thought he was rude. He felt like stopping and consoling the woman whose soft face was becoming blubbery. But the action had started. He followed Cuan.

Clarke was ushering out a tenant by a door that led onto the street. Cuan stood inside the door, Dualta beside him. Clarke turned. Like all butty men he was deceptively tall. He had a strong square face with thick eyebrows. A hard man to daunt, Dualta thought. A man completely assured of his own power. He stood like a tower on the sacred rights of private property. He was always within his rights.

"I am McCarthy," said Cuan. Clarke looked at him. "Ah," he said. "I have heard that name before. Many years ago a bailiff had it beaten into him. Are you the same man?" He went and sat down behind a table. The table was weighted with money-bags.

"Past events have nothing to do with the present," said Cuan. "I have come to pay my brother's rent. Here it is! I wanted to have a look at you."

Clarke emptied the little canvas sack and counted the coins, slowly, meticulously. "It seems all right, for this year," he added. "I wondered if he would be able to scrape it together. I'm not sure I like you living with your brother. You are a trouble-maker. Don't make any trouble in this valley, or you and your brother will go out of it on the back of your necks."

Cuan didn't speak. He leaned both his hands on the table. He bent down in silence until Clarke raised his head and looked at him. Dualta could imagine the look in Cuan's eyes.

"You want to live?" Cuan asked. Clarke didn't blench, but all the same Dualta thought his composure wasn't quite as certain. He was looking into the blazing eyes that meant what they spoke. Dualta knew the look.

He didn't answer Cuan's question.

Cuan said, "I am dangerous, Clarke. I am indifferent to death. I am indifferent to you, and the powers behind you." He walked to the door. Dualta knew from the way he walked that his whole body was stiffened with rage. So did Clarke. He turned at the door.

"I will see you outside, Dualta," he said. He closed the door softly after him. Clarke watched the closed door. Then he turned his eyes to Dualta. Dualta thought, Cuan has really put me in the briars now.

"You are a friend of his?" Clarke asked. Dualta debated.

"Yes," he said.

"You are teaching in the school?" he asked.

"Yes," said Dualta.

"Do you teach the boys treason?" Clarke asked.

"No," said Dualta, "just reading and writing and arithmetic."

"They can be as dangerous as gunpowder," Clarke said. "What do you want from me?"

"I want to rent the Bacach's place," said Dualta. Clarke's eyes opened wide. Then he threw his head back and laughed.

"By God," he said, "that's a good one. What do you want it for?"

"I want to bring it back to life," said Dualta, "so that I can make a living on it."

"You know what it's like?" Clarke asked.

"Yes," said Dualta.

"Do you expect to get it cheap?" Clarke asked.

"Yes," said Dualta.

"You won't," said Clarke. "You will get it at one pound seven shillings an acre." Dualta felt as if he had been kicked in the stomach. How to find rent like that and make enough to eat would be a terrible challenge. Clarke was looking at him. He expected him to refuse.

"If I get a ten-year lease," said Dualta. "I will take it."

"Tenant at will," said Clarke.

"No," said Dualta. "You know it will take at least five years to bring it to anything. After another five it will be something. I don't want to be kicked out of it as soon as I have made it into a decent place. It's that or nothing."

He didn't think he would get away with it. But Clarke thought. He was constantly being pressed from the agent in Dublin who was pressed by Tewson in London. He was being squeezed. This which was earning nothing would now earn something.

"All right," he said. "I'll have the papers drawn. You will have no leeway. Rent will be paid every six months. Miss one gale day and you are out. You understand that?"

"Only too well," said Dualta.

"Right," said Clarke. Then he called. "Send in the next one, Julia." Dualta was dismissed. He walked to the door. He knew Clarke's eyes were on his back. He didn't care. He had got what he wanted.

He stood outside the door in the sun, and while he felt pleased, he also felt that a great burden was now placed on his shoulders. He thought that now he was at the beginning of being a common man.

Una had come up to the town on the opposite side. Having failed to find Dualta, she was going to the inn where Glasby had his rooms. For a few moments, like a calm stretch in the middle of lake ruffled waters, the crowds between her and the other side of the street faded away and she saw Dualta on the street, standing in contemplation, his head bent to one side, his hands on his hips and a furrow between his brows. She watched him. She raised her arm and was just about to shout his name when a girl came running from the right and stood in front of him, one hand on his arm. She saw his face coming from meditation to awareness. She thought he had a mobile and expressive face. The girl was asking him something. She was a most pretty girl. Dualta smiled and answered her and there in the middle of the street, throwing decorum to the winds the girl threw her arms around his neck and hugged him. Dualta seemed to enjoy it. He laughed and didn't avoid her lips. Una lowered her arm. She thought it only right that Dualta should have a girl, particularly a pretty girl like that. She had heard about her, Sheila O'Connor. Their names were being linked. Well, it was time for Dualta to settle down. It would make a man of him, and she was one of his own kind, hardly very bright, she imagined from the look of her, but then what countryman, even a countryman like Dualta, above the average in intelligence and education, wanted a girl to be a genius. As long as she was pretty and knew how to milk cows and rear hens and feed pigs, what more did they want? Una was surprised at the leaden feeling. It was just that she had known him for a long time, it seemed, and he was such a help with the school and she wondered if he became a family man if he would continue to help her. She saw an elderly woman, an old edition of the girl come up, and rap her on the back, and almost pull her away, expostulating, and Dualta begging for forgiveness. The woman was looking around, hoping nobody had seen the shameless behavior of her daughter. But many had and were grinning broadly.

Then Una saw Colman. He was running into the cleared space. His face was red, his thin fists were clenched. There was a man and his companions there in the middle of the street. Talking and laughing. They carried sticks in their hands or under their arms. Colman bent to the ground. He took up a handful of the madder of the street. He shouted "Gately! Gately!" the big man turned and as he did so he got the fistful of dirt straight in the face. Colman didn't stop here. He kept running and he beat at the near-blinded man with his fists, and kicked at him with his bare feet. Then one of his companions reached out and hit the boy on the head with his hand and he fell back on the ground.

Una was already running toward him shouting, "Dualta! Dualta!" but by the time she reached him and bent over him, she was involved in a welter of legs and shouts and clashing sticks. It was as if Colman's cry of "Gately" had been the awaited signal for battle. There were great cries and shouts and drunken huroos as the factions of near-drunken men ran from each side with swinging sticks, and Una, kneeling on the ground over Colman, was suddenly the center of a circle of bloody violence.

Dualta was startled as he heard her calling his name. He looked up. He was in time to see Colman on the ground and Una running toward him. Then he saw the men running from his left and Gately's men lining up, pushing Gately behind them, as both sides met and swung their heavy sticks. He was furious. A faction fight. They were looking for it, of course. They were waiting for it. The curse of God on them, he thought, disgracing their country, shaming their own people. This illiterate desire for senseless violence. Would it ever be rooted out of them? Thinking this as he shoved and pushed his way through them, bending, dodging, holding an arm over his head, receiving a blow on his arm that nearly paralyzed it. He could see their faces, squinting eyes, open mouths. Hear the cursing, the great shouts, the blows of sticks falling on skulls. Spatters of blood fell on the back of his hand. With disgust he rubbed it on his coat. He hit out and used his feet. He could hear the screaming of women, young girls screaming as they ran from the fight in fear, and older women screaming at their husbands, as well they might. Come back! Come back! thinking of the split scalps that would have to be tended, the wounds and the embarrassed shame when the hot blood cooled and the drink fumes left the head.

He bent over her, who was bent over Colman. "God," he shouted at her. "What were you thinking, coming into the middle of this? Come on!" He raised her. He held her in front of him with one hand around her and walked her away. He shouted at Colman: "Hold my coat!" he felt him grasping it and made his way through them. Una couldn't believe what she was seeing. She would never forget the looks on the faces of the men. These men she had been feeling so good about, kindly people, respectful. Faces squinting in hatred, low atavistic growls coming from their throats, the bright blood on the sunburned faces.

He pressed them against a clear space when he reached Clarke's house. He kept them pressed to the wall, holding off the violence behind with his hands held over them.

"Colman," he said. "I could murder you. You see what you started." The boy's eyes were wide. "Look at the shirt I got for you," he went on. It was torn and dirty. His face was close to Una's. He saw the bewilderment and fear on it and complete distaste. "You see what you are living with?" he asked. "Now, won't you go home to your father? What use is it? What use when at the turn of a wrist things like this can arise in all of us?"

"Their children will not be like this," she said. She had to shout. "If we educate them."

"Can you hold back the sea?" he shouted angrily. "Can you bring the hills low?"

"Somebody can," said Una, noting the change in the shouting.

Still protecting them with his arms, Dualta turned his head.

The red-headed priest was fighting his way right into the middle of them. He was shouting. His red hair was flaming, part of his stock had been torn away. His fists were rising and falling like flails. He seemed to be swimming to the center of the disturbance. Shouting "Animals! Creatures! O, animals, stop it! I tell you to stop it!" Where was the policeman? Dualta wondered. Everyone knew where he was. He would be in his house with the door bolted. There was only himself. He would have to send for help to the next town and, if things got very bad, to Ennis or Galway. Now he was in a safe place. Dualta watched.

By sheer force the priest got to the center of them. He held his arms out from him with the knotted fists at the end of each arm and swung around, shouting "Enough! Enough! Enough!" When he had cleared a space they fell back from him. But they were not finished. They were ready to clash again, priest or no priest. He turned his back on the town faction. He faced Gately. He pointed his finger. He walked toward them. "Go back!" he said. "Start going back, or I'll curse you to the seven generations. Are you men? Look at you! Like the slaughtered blood-stained beasts in the shop of a butcher."

Dualta admired him. His anger seemed to give him height. There were lights flashing from his eyes.

"Go home, Gately," he said, "and bring your gang with you. You hear. Don't come near this town again or I'll have you arrested. You hear!" He turned back to the others. "You!" he said, walking toward them. "Are you brutes or respectable married men? Are you Christians or are you pagans? What has become of your faith and your holy religion, or your families and all you are supposed to hold dear?"

He had won. He had created a space. He had created a pause. Dualta saw the madness dying from their faces. Sheepishly some of them wiped away the blood with the palms of their hands. One of them turned and went away. Then another and another. Of the townsmen there were wives waiting for them with arms akimbo. Then the priest turned back to the Gately contingent. He said nothing to them. He just stood there, silently, an angry man with a torn stock, a little color coming back into his face. They shuffled and looked down and then they half-turned and walked away from him. They shouted threats. "We'll get you, men! Don't come over." But when the shouting was started the fighting was over. They pulled away in a body.

The priest turned and came over to them. He looked closely at Una.

He said: "I saw what you did. It was a reckless thing. But you were a brave girl. You, Colman, I will talk to you again." Colman hung his head, shuffled his bare feet. His mouth was a thin line. "You will have to forgive us," the priest said to her. "There are reasons, reasons, so many reasons. Soon these faction fights will be no more. Don't judge us on them. I am afraid you will go away."

"I will not go away, indeed," she said.

"You must take the bad with the good," he said. He sighed. "There is such a lot of bad."

"And such a lot of good," she said, but she was watching the pretty girl who had come back again and was holding Dualta's arm and looking into his face and saying. "O, Dualta, Dualta, are you all right? Did nobody hit you? I hope nobody hit you."

chapter XX

IT IS A LITTLE trickle in a high place that makes a great river flowing to the sea. In the same way, but almost as fast as the journey of the sun across the arc of the sky, men heard before nightfall in this remote place that Daniel O'Connell was going to stand in the election for Clare. The sitting member, Vesey Fitzgerald, was invited into his Cabinet by the Duke of Wellington, known derisively by O'Connell as The Great Captain, and so he would have to stand for reelection. Vesey Fitzgerald, they said, was no more corrupt than any of the others, but he had used the cover name for corruption, patronage, with great skill, so that there was no second or third son in the Army or in places of patronage in the whole of the county, with all their families, who wasn't under geasa, as they say, to his favor. Who would they get to stand against him? There was nobody in the Catholic Association, or no presentable Protestant who would dream of doing it. So O'Connell put himself up and wrote out his address, and it was like a fire burning in a dry field of corn.

Father Melican sent for his administrator. Since his accident with the lightning he lived mostly in his book-lined study sunk in a leather-covered chair with a pair of crutches handy. He had been a big athletic man and sitting so much had made him weighty. He was surrounded by books, magazines, and papers, which were his only extravagance. He was always looking for his papers and never able to find them, because as soon as he had finished with one, the housekeeper Bridie always removed it, and passed it on so that it went the rounds of the place. Newspapers were too expensive for most people, so everyone was grateful to Father Melican for being a subscriber. When the paper had passed through many hands it ended up with the dressmaker who used it for cutting out patterns, so it was cheap at the price.

Father Finucane, who lived in a small house near the church, left his account books, put on his coat and hat (Father Melican insisted that his young priest be properly dressed) and went over to the neat two-story stone house of the parish priest. He paused outside the study door and tidied himself and tried to put a look of gravity on his countenance before he knocked and entered. He saw Father Melican's eyes checking over him.

"You wanted to see me, Father?" he asked.

"Have you heard about O'Connell?" Father Melican asked.

"I have indeed," said Father Finucane. "Isn't it wonderful? Isn't it the best thing that has happened in history? I hardly slept last night thinking of the excitement and the wonder of it."

"Your attitude is wrong, Father," said the old priest. His lips were tight. The spontaneous joy went out of the young priest's face.

"In what way, Father?" he asked.

"It's nothing to do with us," said Father Melican. "It can do nothing but bring trouble and confusion on the whole county. It will excite men to foolish dreams, and turn tenants against their landlords, dangerously. You see this. We must stay out of it."

Father Finucane looked at him. He sat carefully down on a chair, his hat in his hands.

"Father," he said gently, "we cannot stay out of it."

"We are here to care for men's souls," the priest said. "Do you think we should be like the Wexford priests leading men with pikes in their hands to death and destruction? I have thought over this, Father Finucane. We must stay out of it."

"If O'Connell wins this election," said Father Finucane slowly and carefully, "we will get Catholic Emancipation."

"We will get that without the demagogue," said the priest. "It will evolve. Time we couldn't put a steeple on a church. Now we can. Time we lived in the hedges and the woods. Now look at us. It will improve. It must not be forced."

Father Finucane looked at him. Father Melican had been

ordained on the Continent. There, he had been indoctrinated with the terrible lessons of the French Revolution. He was for passive peace, quiet advance, slow evolution. Father Finucane could understand him, but he found it hard to sympathize with him.

"Father," he said. "I do not agree with you. Ninety per cent of the people want to live quiet and peaceful lives. It is always a small minority that can excite them to blood. It has happened before. They are wary of violent men. Of seven million people at least two-thirds are living in wretched conditions of poverty and hopelessness. This man has arisen. He doesn't want their blood. All he wants from them is courage and resolution. If he can get seven million people to say Yes, all together, just peacefully saying together, We want change, then change will have to come. This is his testing time. He is the first Catholic to stand up and talk back. He is the first one to test their laws and find loopholes in them. This is a chance for the seven million to find their voice. We must not stop them. We must be with them."

"No," said Father Melican vigorously, "you will leave this alone."

"There is scarcely a priest in the whole county who will not urge them to do the brave thing," said Father Finucane.

"What the rest of them do is nothing to do with us," said the old priest. He bent down. He got a poker and banged the smouldering turf in the hearth. "I absolutely forbid you to encourage revolt against the landlords," he said.

Father Finucane put his hand into his pocket and took out a letter. It had been written by himself.

"Here, Father," he said, "is my resignation as administrator. It is addressed to you. I am also sending one to the Bishop."

The old man craned his neck to look at him. His heavy face got red under his head of white hair.

"You wouldn't do that?" he asked.

"I would," said the young priest. "Also, when I have resigned, I will consider it my duty as an Irishman to encourage them, in my private capacity."

The old priest looked at his resolute face and the letter in his hand. He shook his head. He put his hand up to his forehead.

"This is sad," he said. "We are generations apart. How can we communicate? Tell me, your contemporaries from Maynooth, do they feel like you too?"

"Most of them feel like I do," said Father Finucane. "O'Connell is the man, and this is the acceptable time."

"I don't understand," the priest said. "When he was young O'Connell was a rationalist. Hume, Godwin, Voltaire, Rousseau, and Paine were better known to him than the Book of Genesis. He has killed a man in a duel. He is a man who plays on people's emotions with the power of words. He has insulted institutions and men of high station with farmyard invective. And you say this is the man for the acceptable time."

"Have you met him, heard him speak, Father?" the young priest asked.

"No! No! No!" said the old priest vigorously.

"Then don't judge him," said Father Finucane. "You want to see him. He is the yeast in a mass of dough. You can see the cake baking. People know. They cannot tell you why, but they know. He is the man that is making them a nation and he wants nobody to die for him. They have never seen his like before and probably they never will again."

"I cannot accept your resignation," the old priest shouted.

"You will have to, Father," he said. "I am determined."

"Not because of that," the old man said. "It's because I like you. You are a good young man. How could I get better than you? Go away! Do what you like! I am not to be responsible! People must know that. I have nothing to do with it. I didn't approve of it. We are not here to build temporal kingdoms." He took up a book. He was agitated. The book was wrong side up, Father Finucane saw. "But don't blame me afterwards. You know where I stand. I want to hear nothing. Know nothing. Now! You have heard me! Go away. And don't neglect your duties. Get that woman Bridie to bring me my tea. She spends more time gossiping than working. Tell her the fire is going out, like my own. I am old. I cannot remember when the blood was hot in my veins. Do what you like! Disobey your parish priest. That's right. Off with you. That's the kind of men Maynooth is turning out. No culture, if you ask me. None of the finer things of life."

When he looked up, Father Finucane was gone. The old priest let the book drop in his lap. He looked at the smouldering turf, and sighed, and then called, "Bridie! Bridie!"

Looking for Dualta, Father Finucane tied his horse under the famous thorn tree. It was the first time for many years that anyone could get that close to it, not to mind tying a horse off it, he thought with a grin. The jungle of briars and hazel had been cleared all around the approaches to the house, opening up a wide yard. He could see the round black spots where the great piles had been burned. The collapsed roof had been cleared away, some of the black beams salvaged and erected with bright new ones. These had been branched and scrawed ready for the pointed sticks of the thatcher. He was curious. He went into the house. There was a new frame but no door as yet. It had been a good house. It was completely bare. Light was still coming through the scraws. But it was wide and roomy. There was a room behind the open fireplace, a big comfortable room, and another smaller one off the kitchen at the other side. He came out to the door again. He was looking across the valley. It was at his feet and the rocky hills on the other side were level with his eyes. The sea was on his left. There was a heavy rain cloud scudding across it like a rippling cloth. He went around the back of the house. The yard was cleared. There were three small houses, for a pig and a cow and a small dairy. They had been cleaned out, roofed afresh with scraws, and whitewashed. He went through the yard and looked up the hill. He could see the figure of Dualta in a small field way up. He could see the fields that he had already passed through, with great labor, he judged, all cleared of scrub, stone walls rebuilt. It seemed impossible that one man could have rescued so much from wilderness and decay.

He started to walk up the hill through the fields. The sun was blotted out. The squall of rain caught him, but it was June and the rain was warm. He got within a few yards of Dualta. Watched him. He was uprooting young hazels with a matlock. He was wet from the rain but he was intent on his job. Three tools he had, a matlock, a spade, and a crowbar. The exposed parts of him were browned by the sun.

"You'll kill yourself, Dualta," said Father Finucane.

Dualta straightened himself and turned.

"I will not," he said. "You have only to do this once, and then you keep it clean with little labor. In two weeks Carrol will give me his horse and plow and I will turn it to the sun for the first time in twelve years. A little more labor and it will be as fruitful as a tinker woman. Then I will rest and just look at it."

"You have done great work," said Father Finucane. "I hope you don't lose it all again."

"I won't lose it," said Dualta.

"Daniel O'Connell is standing for Clare," said the priest.

Dualta's eyes widened. "He is! Is this true? Where did you hear it? This is of great account! Is it true?"

"It is true," said Father Finucane, "and you are a forty-shilling freeholder. You have a vote."

Dualta looked at him closely. "Now I see what you meant," he said.

"It will be a terrible fight," said the priest. "How do you feel?"

Dualta dropped his head. He put the handle of the implement under his arm. He leaned on it. After a while he looked up.

"My heart went cold," he said.

"Many men's hearts will go the same," said the priest. "Tell me why? What will they do?"

"It meant little to me before," said Dualta. "Now, with all this!" He waved his hand at the reclaimed land. "It's easy to be free when you have nothing to lose."

"But you are safe, you have a lease," said the priest.

"I have a lease," said Dualta, "with a lot of small writing in it. Don't forget the landlords interpret the law. They are the judge and jury. They can read the writing whatever way suits them. I think of this and I am afraid. Most men will be. O'Connell is asking a lot of them!"

"I am glad to see you have changed to a cautious man," said Father Finucane.

Dualta laughed. "Only a part of me. I remember. I saw forty-shilling freeholders being driven to the vote like cattle to a fair. We jeered at them. We baaed at them like sheep. Now I know how they felt. I will not feel this way. But will I be on my own? How many will come with me? Can you say?"

"No," said Father Finucane. "There are eighty-seven voters in the valley. They will have to fight their fear. We must help them. There is not a lot of time. This is Monday. Next Monday will be nomination day and the polling will start on Tuesday. It leaves us little time. It is the opportunity of a lifetime. We must grasp it."

"Then let us start now, in the name of God," said Dualta. He picked up the spade and the crowbar. The rain squall passed and the sun burst on the valley, for a moment reflecting from millions of raindrops, almost blindingly.

"The sun has come out," said Dualta. "That's a good sign. What will we do? Will we talk to everyone? Do all men know?"

"They will know by now," said Father Finucane. "They will be bursting with talk. They must get a lead. You are a good talker. You have won your way into their affections with your teaching of their children. You see! They will trust your word. They have seen what you are doing with this property."

"Carrol O'Connor and Moran McCleary will be with us," said Dualta. "They have a lease of two lives."

"It is the men that have everything to lose that we must persuade," said the priest.

Dualta put his tools into the empty house. He took his coat from there and pulled it on.

"You have done great work," the priest said. "Nobody but you knew what a grand place this was. You will live on a high hill. You must not be like the poor Bacach. You must marry and make the place bright with the laughter of children."

Dualta laughed.

"Nobody will have me," he said. "I am too literate for some, and too foreign for others. I will be like the poor Bacach, biting my nails waiting for a princess to come in the door."

"I know many girls would be glad of you," the priest said, as he untied the horse.

"When they get to know me better," said Dualta, "they shy away like colts. I have no magic attraction."

The priest mounted. "Get up behind me," he said. "You won't be a bachelor." Dualta leaped up behind him. The horse was gentle. He ambled off with his double load. "You are doing good work. Do you feel the better for it? Do you remember our first conversation."

"I remember," said Dualta. "I feel good."

"I see the children's games," said the priest. "Now they play at school. The teacher and the children. The man teacher, the master, always speaks with a Galway accent, and the mistress speaks in parody the beautiful precise English of Miss Mac-Mahon. You like Miss MacMahon?"

"I like Miss MacMahon very much," said Dualta.

"You had met her before, then?" the priest asked. Now, how did he figure that out, Dualta wondered.

"Yes," he said, "I had met her before."

"And yet you are not too friendly?" said the priest.

"Oh, yes, we are," said Dualta. "I work a lot. Running for a few hours to the school and running back to the fields and the house, it is little time I have."

"And Sheila O'Connor is a nice pretty girl," said the priest. Dualta laughed at him.

"Are you a matchmaker then?" he asked.

"I want to keep you in the valley," he said. "You are good for it, like Miss MacMahon. She is worth harvests. She does not know her value. Life is hard on her away from people of her own kind. She would be a great loss."

"Let us think about the election," said Dualta.

"We'll divide the valley," said the priest. "You take the west and I'll take the east. Parcel the place. We must be victorious, here anyhow, whatever happens in other places. Sunday after

Mass will be the testing time. We will see the fruit of our work. I'll drop you here at O'Connor's. God guide you. Be eloquent. You have a good cause. Use it. On to victory!" He waved his hand and galloped away. Dualta watched him for a time and then he started to run into O'Connor's yard and he was shouting: "Wake up! Wake up, the O'Connor clan. O'Connell is standing for Clare!" He frightened the chickens and the grubbing pig and brought a bark from the dog and the astonished face of Mrs. O'Connor from the dairy.

It was a small chapel. Two pointed windows in each sidewall, a pointed window behind the altar, and a square doorway. It was built of rubble and mortar. Inside it was peeling. It was damp. Patching could never save it. There would have to be a new one. Each family in the parish was paying a halfpenny a week into a fund for one. It would take a long time before it would reach the stage where they might begin. It didn't hold half the people. The rest were outside at the door, around the windows, which were open to let the voice of the priest and the sound of the little bell bring solemnity into the air. Father Finucane knew it was too small. Every year there were more and more children being born. That was part of the trouble. If a family had half an acre they could grow enough potatoes to feed them for a year. So when sons and daughters were marriageable, they got married. Their fathers cut off another bit of their holding, they built a small house and they were away. It was rare in the parish for anyone not to be married before they were twenty-one. It was good for morals, he knew, but bad for congestion. Half the holdings in the valley were sublet and sub-sublet. No wonder a third of the people couldn't fit into the chapel.

He was trying to divert his mind from his worries thinking about these things when he had finished Mass and was about to turn and address them. He debated if he would take off his vestments first or not and decided not to. Vested he might appear to have more authority.

He turned to them abruptly. The coughing shushed. They

shissed the people outside. Young men clambered up on the windows. The first people his eyes found were the Bradishes, sitting in the front seat. The face of Mr. Bradish was grim. Over in the other front seat, Clarke sat with his family. His hands were folded across his chest. One thick leg was crossed over the other. It wasn't a good attitude, but it was typical of him.

"You have searched your hearts," he said. "You know the cause. There is a Catholic standing for Clare. You are Catholics. If he was a bad Catholic, you would know. He is not. He is a good man. He is the first one for many years who is capable of bringing you freedom for the practice of your religion. You have a measure of freedom now, but not in law. He will make your freedom lawful. You must pay for all good things. Nothing good can be gained without sacrifice. You are afraid. You must conquer your fear and do what is right. Many elections there have been no contests. Powerful men have come together and said: Such a one will be the member for Clare. And so it has been. Now there is a contest. You have the privilege of exercising your vote, eighty-seven of you. You can be eighty-seven heroes, honest men, able to live with yourselves whatever the consequences, or you can be eighty-seven weak men who will have to live with the knowledge that you have voted against history. We will start the march for Ennis tomorrow morning. It is a long way to go. It is a sacrifice. I will be at the crossroads. I will lead whoever is going to vote for the Catholic candidate. The others can follow their landlord's representative. For my part I will never by word or deed or look or act condemn any man whose conscience or fear makes him vote at the dictates of his landlord."

He was interrupted. "No, then, but we will!" a voice shouted from outside. Dualta had been listening. He was at the doorway. The voice came from behind him. He knew it. The voice of Cuan. He turned to look. Cuan was with Moran McCleary and his wife. She spoke then: "Hurrah for O'Connell!" she shouted. She was a dark-haired woman, with heavy hair pulled back on her head. She had a strong handsome face. "O'Connell and freedom!" her husband Moran shouted. People were surprised. Moran was known as a quiet man.

"Deeds speak louder than words," said the priest. "You have until tomorrow morning to think over it. Think over it prayerfully. I will be waiting at the crossroads." He had spoken very quietly. That was against his nature because he was impulsive and quick enough to anger with the red hair. Dualta thought his words had been telling. There were only a few seats in the church. People were rising to go. There was shuffling at the back. It was customary for the ordinary people to make a lane and let the gentry out first before they followed.

"You will wait a minute!" said the voice of Clarke. He was standing up facing them. His voice brought tension into the chapel. Father Finucane went on disrobing at the altar.

"I didn't think a priest would use the altar for politics," said Clarke. "Since he has and I am a member of this church, I think I have the same right. A priest may be a good guide to heaven but he can't claim to be a good guide to the House of Commons. Priests should stick to their prayer books. That is my opinion. I'm not afraid to state it. I have here a letter from your benefactor, the man who has provided you with fields and land and food for over a hundred years. You will listen to it." He cleared his throat. He rustled the paper of the letter. "My dear tenants," he read. "Here in London I have heard with dismay that that good man Vesey Fitzgerald is being opposed by Counsellor O'Connell. I wish you to understand that Vesey Fitzgerald is a good friend and a powerful politician. With a seat in the Cabinet, he will be in an extraordinary position of bringing benefits to the whole of the county. Therefore it is my wish that you go en masse and vote for him. I know you will listen to my counsel as you have always done. ("Like sheep!" said a voice from outside. Clarke stopped for a moment. His hands trembled with anger.) "O'Connells come and go but the families of Vesey Fitzgerald go on forever." ("Until they are shot," said the voice.) "I have always been a benevolent landlord." ("That's a damn lie!" said the voice.) "I have treated you well, cared for you like my father and grandfather before me.

I may say I have loved you all." ("Like his strumpets," said the voice.) "I have never been a stern father to you" ("He fathered half London," said the voice), "but if you proceed on a course of electing this powerless demagogue I will have no option but . . ." ("Ah, close your gob, Clarke," said the voice, "you are catching flies.")

Clarke couldn't go on. People started tittering. There were a few hurroos and laughter. He stood there, the letter clenched in his fist, his face red.

"By God, if you won't listen to him, you will listen to me," he said. "You will do what you are told. Let any man listening to me who is on a hanging gale tremble in his shoes. I tell you that. People have been hanging on to land that they owe for seven times over. If they want to keep it they will do what they are told. I will be at the crossroads on Monday too. If you want to live without fear you will follow me. If you don't you can look out for the results."

He walked out. If they didn't get out of his way quickly enough he pushed them aside with his hands. Outside he stood. He was hemmed in. It didn't frighten him. Dualta thought he was without fear.

"Who was that voice?" he asked.

"It was a bird," he was answered. "It was a sheep," said another. "It was the landlord's get," said a third. "It was the fairies," said another. "Hurrah for O'Connell!" "Hurrah for Tewson's fair ladies." From all sides they came, remarks loud and clear or whispered. It had never happened before. Clarke stood there, his jaws tight. "Come into the open," he said. "I will bet that no voice with a vote spoke. You'll regret it! I promise you!"

He went through them. He walked out the gate and turned down toward the town. His back was tight with anger and menace.

Mr. Bradish was at the door. He was talking. They listened to him.

"I want my tenants not to vote for O'Connell," he said. "You already see the sinister design. These men want to come between the landlords and the tenants. Don't let them do it. It will lead to strife and violence. That is their object. Don't let them do it. Do what you have always done. You have more to gain. I am a Catholic too. Now I tell you to vote for a Protestant gentleman, a literate civilized man who has always been on the side of Catholic Emancipation, and who is in a better position to gain it than a man like O'Connell."

They said nothing. He ushered his wife and the two girls out to the gate. The girls were pale. Mrs. Bradish was silent. (That's the first miracle someone remarked.) The carriage drew up at the gate. They went in. It moved off and the people started to go home. They were talking in groups. The young men were laughing. Some of the people who knew no English were saying: "What did he say? What was the letter about?"

Dualta was leaning against the wall of the church. He was looking at Cuan. Cuan caught his eye. He winked sardonically. Cuan was a leaven too, working in the valley. Dualta ought to have known that he wouldn't be quiet. He was going away. He waved an arm. "See, Dualta," he called, "how I am working for O'Connell. He has won me over. Are you pleased?"

Dualta said nothing. Just kept looking at him. They were gone. Father Finucane stood beside him.

"Have we won, Dualta?" he asked.

"I don't know," said Dualta. "Only tomorrow morning will tell."

"Then let it come quickly," said the priest.

chapter XXI

THE PRIEST SAT on his horse at the crossroads. The rain was dripping in streams from his hat. The cloak he wore was sodden from the rain. The mane of the horse was sodden, his appearance woebegone. The sun was risen. It was completely obscured by the gray pregnant clouds that lay helpless on the hills. He was at the town side of the crossroads. On the other side there was Clarke's carriage. It contained Clarke and his wife and his brother-in-law. Buach, Clarke's strong field bailiff was mounted on a horse beside them. Buach was very big. He had a mashed face that appeared as if it had been crushed between two rocks. Another bailiff, Páid, barefooted, ragged, but muscular, held the reins of the carriage horses, moving impatiently in his wet clothes. He was called Páid Monuar, because every time he had to carry out an unpleasant chore for Clarke, he would say "Mo nuar! Mo nuar!" but carry it out he would all the same.

Now and again Clarke poked his head out of the carriage window, looked down the empty road, and withdrew again impatiently.

It was some time before the silence was broken by anything except the splash of the big raindrops in the puddles of the pot-holes, then from faraway there came the thin sound of a boy's voice singing. It was a strange sound to hear on the leaden air. Even the priest's horse cocked his ears for a little at the strange-ness of it. You could make out no words, just the sound. It had an odd refrain like the quick lilting notes of a dance tune. It brought pleasure into the gray day, the priest thought, as he turned his head to look. He saw the man and the boy coming to the crossroads through the fields. His heart lifted. He recognized Dualta and Colman. When Dualta saw his turned head, he waved an arm. They were barefooted, the collars of their coats turned up against the rain. Dualta wore his shoes around his neck and on his shoulder carried a small budget tied to a stick.

As they came nearer Father Finucane found his fingers tapping the pommel of the saddle in rhythm to the boy's clear tune. He was singing in Irish. Father Finucane had never heard it before. As they came nearer he could translate the words, which were repeated over and over, the boy jigging in the heavy grass to the sound of his own mouth. He sang:

> Down near the fall by the willow tree
> On a stone by the well, did he wait for me,
> With shoes of gold and a shining light
> Which he stole from the stars in the dark of night.
>
> Then he danced and he sang like the good people can,
> Over the trees and the streams of the glann,
> Fol-dil-di-diddle, fol-dil-di-diddle,
> This was the song of the small little man.

Dualta jumped the wall with Colman behind him.

"It's a right good morning, Father," he said. "Are we the first to join you? Colman hasn't the vote but he comes to prepare himself for the day."

"Where did you get the song, then, Colman?" the priest asked.

"He made it himself to an old tune," said Dualta. "Isn't he a one for you?"

"It's a very good song," said the priest. "My love to you. I didn't know you had it in you."

"I'll make better than that," said Colman casually. Dualta and the priest laughed loudly at him, the way he said it. It brought Clarke's head out of the carriage. He looked over at them. Then he pulled back again.

"Is there much movement in the town?" the priest asked.

"We came by the fields," said Dualta. "To tell you the truth

I was afraid to go the other way, in case." The rain was streaming off his hair and his face. "Don't worry," said the priest. "You have done all you can. Here is the first of them now and it is a poor omen."

The procession had come from the other side. They were Cringe and his people. The priest knew he had lost them. There was no joy in them. Cringe rode at their head, a small cock of a man on a black horse. His bailiff, McInerney, rode a rough pony behind him, and then came the schoolmaster, the pimply-faced one riding an ass. Very suitable, the priest thought, and chided himself. After them came ten male tenants. They walked heavy-footed, dourly, with secret faces. They were dressed in their best clothes. They weren't talking. They avoided the eyes of the priest. None of the ten had leases. They were all tenants at will. He could see them at home in their houses, looking at their few possessions, their small fields for which they had given so much of their sweat and toil, the tears of their wives, the stomachs of their children. He felt no anger.

Cringe stopped at the carriage.

"Your people come yet, Clarke?" he asked.

"Not yet," Clarke told him.

"If they don't come, go in and round them up," said Cringe. "That's what I did with my lot. We'll go on then. You can catch us up. On men, to the hustings." He waved his arm. The wet procession straggled after him. As he passed the priest, he raised his black hat, politely. There was no sneer in it, just politeness. Father Finucane nodded his head at him and kept his eyes from the tenants. They were sad enough without making them sadder. The last of them had hardly passed before the strains of distant music came from the town road. The horse again cocked his ears. The priest and Dualta held their breaths as they listened. The band was ragged. It was playing an Irish marching tune. The priest turned the horse's head to face the sound. From where it was coming there was a break in the overcast. It seemed as if the ill-assorted sounds had broken through the clouds and dispersed them, bringing brightness with the noise. He could distinguish the sounds of what they called the soft flute, that would pierce the ears of a flying bat, and fiddles, and tin whistles and the loud bang on a skin drum. As he watched they came around the bend of the road. The band was up on Carrol O'Connor's cart, sawing and blowing and banging, and behind them came people on carts, and donkeys and horses, women behind men, and children danced and laughed beside them and most of them had fresh tree branches in their hands which they waved and two men carried a green banner on two ash poles and written on the banner in words of gold were O'CONNELL FOR CLARE, and another one had the words THE MAN OF THE PEOPLE. They were all dressed in their best, the girls in gay fresh cotton skirts, skipping barefooted on the road. There were seventy-seven voters there, walking or riding or holding the reins of the carts, and with them were their wives, and their daughters and their sons, and every single person in the townland he would say and from every house in the valley.

He just stood there petrified, shivers running up and down his back, whether from the awful martial music or just from joy he did not know. He looked at Dualta. Dualta's eyes were shining. He reached up and pressed the priest's arm. The procession swung on to the road to Ennis.

Carrol O'Connor shouted.

"Well, then, Father, are you ready to lead us or must we go alone? It's a long road and you should be ahead to bless it."

Father Finucane laughed and swung the horse out in front of the cart, raised his arm like a general going into battle, shouted, "Forward for freedom, then!" There were loud cheers, and calls and boys' voices breaking as they sang the words of the band's song. It was a brave colorful sight and it was only right that the sun should shine on it, Dualta thought as he took Colman's hand and joined in the procession and soon Clarke, standing on the road, was looking at the tail of the procession and his wife was frightened at the look on his face. It availed him nothing. Not one of the people had given him even a second glance.

Una sat in the body of the Courthouse and wondered. She had come to Ennis the day before with the Bradishes. They were staying in a house a few miles outside the town with a distant relative of Mrs. Bradish. Margaret said her mother brought them to Ennis because the town was ringed with three thousand soldiers and stiff with policemen and all the aristocracy of Clare and if her mother couldn't find husbands for them at all the election routs, then they were doomed to be old maids. Her mother heard her. She claimed it was their duty to be there to give backing to Vesey Fitzgerald. Una had been taken along to act as unpaid maid to the woman and the girls. She didn't mind. She wanted to see. She thought the price she had to pay was high but it was worth it. They had difficulty coming through the streets this morning. Nobody would have recognized the town. Banners hung from every window. About thirty thousand people were already crushed into the narrow streets. People said in the big houses: Where will it all end? O'Connell had come like a king. He had been passed from county to county, from town to town by bands, bonfires and hundreds of horsemen carrying torches to light up the night.

And no disorder. That was why the aristocrats were perturbed. They didn't know the order that had gone out. Every man coming into Ennis was under a pledge to drink no whiskey, to raise no hand against a fellow. They were pledged under the direst threats. The first man found drunk was to be thrown into the Fergus. In all, sixty thousand people were expected to crowd into the place. There will be riots, they said, drink, and faction fights. So throw in the army, one soldier to twenty men and all the policemen in the county. When they start, break them up, swiftly, ruthlessly. Clear the town. Get as many voters as possible in jail or thrown out of the town quite legitimately, and there is no doubt about the election.

But there were no riots. People bowed respectfully, got out of your way elaborately if you were well dressed, touched their hats to you, maybe they licked their lips at the sight of the whiskey houses, but there was no disorder. So people said:

Where will it all end? and a little doubt about the result may have bent their complacency.

The cause of it all stood up there beside the sheriff. He was alone. He held his hands in front of him. He was dressed in a blue coat with a black velvet collar, yellow waistcoat, white breeches and he wore a gilt button on his shoulder as a sign of his leadership. He had a powerful face, its strength leavened by the snub nose, the curly hair touched with gray. Vesey Fitzgerald, surrounded by all the gentry of the county, clean, very well dressed, pomaded, a small man with a round face, hazel eyes and gentle almost effeminate gestures. O'Connell in his stillness and calm looked equal to the lot of them, she thought, even if she disliked the notion. "Look at him! Look at him!" Mrs. Bradish kept saying in a whisper as if she was telling you to look at the devil. The gallery was crowded with the people and priests.

For Vesey Fitzgerald, Sir Edmond O'Brien spoke. He was one of the most powerful landlords in the county. He looked powerful. His speech was taken up more with the ingratitude of his tenants who had deserted him, stolen by the priests in this grave hour, than with Fitzgerald. He wanted to know if the country was any longer fit for a gentleman to live in when property lost all its influence and things were brought to such a pass. He produced tears but they affected very few, Una saw, since he was well known to be able to cry at the drop of a hat. But he dropped a few words of menace for his tenants after the tears. He was applauded by his own side. Other men spoke, she didn't know, and the strange O'Gorman Mahon for O'Connell and a "villain called Steele" said Mrs. Bradish.

The gentle Vesey then spoke. He spoke more powerfully than his appearance would lead you to believe. But he was a practiced politician. He spoke of his dying father's fight against the Union, of his own efforts to establish Maynooth. He spoke of his father. How they were afraid to tell him that his son was actually being opposed in an election lest the blow would prove fatal. He turned away to wipe tears from his eyes. Una was amazed to see how he had affected everyone about her. His speech seemed to leave behind him a wave of genuine sympathy, even among the people in the gallery.

She was impatient. Do they realize, she wondered, who they are up against? The big silent figure of O'Connell with an immovable countenance. Do they think a man like that is to be defeated by tears? He wasn't.

He annihilated them, she thought. It wasn't his actual words. The very moment he opened his mouth, power seemed to emanate from him. The words themselves were nothing, they were like the instruments that play the notes. She could feel it herself, this attention he drew from you. Even if from her and all about her, it was a sort of distaste, a sort of fear that a man who was opposed to your beliefs should have such power in him. The actual things he was saying were not more insulting than the usual political insults, but it was the way he said them that made them deadly like a blunt instrument hitting you on the top of the head. It was small wonder that he was hated, she thought.

One of Fitzgerald's supporters a Mister Gore had acquired his property at the time of Cromwell. It was said this ancestor had been a nailor in the Puritan massacre squads. So O'Connell spoke about Gore "striking a nail on the head" or putting a "nail in a coffin" and each time he drew a shout of pure glee from the balcony, while poor Mister Gore shrank in his clothes. He tackled Fitzgerald's other supporters and then turned on Fitzgerald himself. He had a deep voice. You couldn't miss a word of it. It was musical. It was like being insulted with thick rich wine instead of water. Now and again Fitzgerald stood up and said: "Is this fair?" He heard the words repeated that he was a friend of the people. What? A man who had enrolled under the banner of bloody Perceval a friend of the people? This friend of the people is also a friend of Peel—the bloody Perceval and the candid and manly Peel—he is our friend! He is everybody's friend. The friend of the Catholic was the friend of the bloody Perceval and the friend of the candid and manly Peel.

Monstrous, Mrs. Bradish was muttering, monstrous. Why

doesn't somebody do something? There wasn't a landlord who wouldn't like to murder him, Una thought. She thought she could understand some of the pattern of his insulting language. It was as if he were saying: "Look, all your life you have to touch your hat and bow your head when one of the Ascendancy pass by. Open your mouth and you get a whiplash across the face. Now look at me. See how easy it is. Talk up to them. Show them what you feel. Assert your independence of speech. They have reduced you by cartoon and ridicule in everything they write about you. (She remembered suddenly Dualta's anger as he looked at the drawing in a magazine long ago.) From the highest to the lowest they had felt the lash of his speaking, his lack of respect for their pride and their wealth, their position and power, and being a lawyer who knew their laws and could drive a coach and four through them, he remained immune, like a flying bull dropping dung on them, someone said.

He had the place in a frenzy. They were shouting and cheering and calling. "Where will it all end?" she even heard Fitzgerald say as they made their way out of the courthouse. It was impossible. Gentlemen had their fists clenched on their walking canes. But what could they do? It was an election. There had to be freedom of expression. But not this, O God, not this! Wouldn't you think God would strike him dumb? There was no malice in his eyes, she saw. It was the words, the love of words and the way he could play on the emotions of people, like a great musician. He was looking for effects and getting them in the best way possible, reducing men to helpless fury or to wild adulation.

By the time they got their carriage the square outside was jammed with people cheering him. Good-looking handsome women leaned out of the top windows of the tall houses in the narrow streets and waved handerchiefs with the figure of O'Connell stamped on them.

He was staying in a house across the square from the courthouse and from this house a platform had been run out and decorated with fresh tree branches and ribbons and banners and favors. When they were coming back, slowly making their way in the carriage through the densely packed cheering crowds, Una thought that O'Connell might have known that Mr. Bradish was passing by. He was on the platform. Unfortunately he was talking about Catholic landlords. They had all gone over to Vesey Fitzgerald in a body. He hoped their tenants would not be so foolish as to follow their example.

"What are they?" he asked in his glorious voice, "orange Papists, they are!"

"Drive on, Tom! Drive on!" said Mr. Bradish leaning out of the carriage window.

"I'm trying, sir, but it's hard," said Tom. "Make way! Make way!"

And they got out of his way, hardly giving a look at the people in the carriage, their eyes glued to the big man on the platform, but it was slow going and as they went they heard a lot of what he was saying. Mr. Bradish was gripping a strap, his knuckles white, his breathing heavy.

"Byron had a word for them," said O'Connell. "Let them hear it now." You would think he was talking especially to Bradish, that he knew he was there:

" 'And thus they plod in sluggish misery,
Rotting from sire to son, from age to age,
Proud of their trampled nature, and so die,
Bequeathing their hereditary rage
To the new race of inborn slaves, who wage
War for their chains. . . .' "

"Oh no, it's insufferable!" said Mrs. Bradish. "It's insufferable! What are the police doing? What are the army doing?"

"It's a good job you have no sons, Father," said Margaret, "or they would be inborn slaves too." She giggled.

"Silence," said Mrs. Bradish. "Silence!"

They left his voice and the laughter behind them.

Dualta savored it. There could never be a time like it again, he felt. It was the joy of people who threw off their chains for however short a time, said tomorrow the consequences, but we do not care. Everyone seemed to be uplifted. The long tramp to Ennis, taking many long hours, the rain falling on the whole of them for an hour at a time and then hot sun for another hour steaming them. He got secondhand joy through Colman's naïve wonder. Colman had never been abroad from the valley before. From many villages they were joined by others, or had to wait until the road was clear. There were bands and banners and waving branches. There was laughter and song and wild shouting that should only have come from a drunken people. But they were not drunk.

As they got near the town, they could almost hear it heaving. All the roads into it were black with people, who shouted and cheered and made a way for them, and armed them with fresh laurel branches, smooth dark green and shiny with rain.

Around they went and into the long narrow Gaol Street, that led into the square of the Courthouse. Cheering people leaning from windows, waving and calling. They stood in front of the green-bowered platform in the square, with Father Finucane at their head and all the people around called "O'Connell! O'Connell!" and when they saw him emerge from the house and walk onto the platform, and raise his arm in greeting, even Dualta couldn't help the roar that burst from his throat as he held Colman on his shoulder to see him. It was the same man he had last seen on the hillside of the hares, but he wasn't carelessly dressed. His eyes twinkled at them. He was smiling.

"We are for you, O'Connell!" they shouted all around and "Talk to us! Talk to us!" they called.

He said, "I need lungs of brass, and a tongue of iron. There are no words left to me. We have freedom in our grasp. You can provide it. I see your priest at your head. I know you are for me. Tomorrow the vote. That will be your voice. We will lay them low." That was all he said to them. You would think he had been dropping jewels in their path. They cheered and roared, and he went in and they passed on through more streets and around again until they came to the great fields by the winding Fergus. Here they set up their tents, like the tabernacles of the Israelites, Father Finucane said, before he left them.

Dualta helped Carrol O'Connor to drape sacks around the cart so that underneath it provided a shelter for them. He saw the McClearys doing the same thing with their cart. Other people copied the tinkers and piled stuff around bent branches stuck into the ground. Many big fires were lighted, and people dried their clothes around them, and danced around them and ate around them, while pipers and fiddlers played themselves into a state of exhaustion. He would long remember the packed fields with the makeshift tents, and the great blazing fires almost throwing shadows on the clouds.

He danced with Sheila. She was as light as a feather and as gay as if she had taken of an herbal drug. Later he roved the town with her and Colman. Colman was wide-eyed, looking in at the windows of the candle-lighted shops, bookshops and cookshops and clothes shops. Only the whiskey shops were empty, some despondent owners standing and saying: "Won't you come in and take just a small one. Sure it won't break the pledge!"

The sight of a big man in the square standing tall and straight and a little man hammering on his chest with small fists, and the big man praying aloud to God in the moonlighted sky, "Temper me, God," he was asking. "Don't let me hit him. Hold my temper on me until the voting is finished. I made a promise. After that I will squash him into the earth like I would a beetle with my big toe. Only let me hold my temper until then!" Everyone laughing, the little man leaving his futile chest-beating, throwing his hat on the ground and stamping around calling, "Come to me! Come to me until I pulverize you! Come to me until I half-sole your eye!"

It was good. Sleeping under the stars.

The voting was slow and wearisome, but nobody faltered. To delay it the authorities decided that all voters must take the oath singly. A ridiculous oath, going back to something about the Pretender. But there were protests and loud calls and finally they were lined up twenty-five at a time against four walls and they took the silly oath and then they went in a great body to one or other of the fifteen polling booths and in a loud voice they declared "Daniel O'Connell for Clare." There were many who didn't. Poor men under the spell of fear and free men who were doing what they thought was the best thing to do and did it fearlessly and were willing to argue their vote and willing to fight for it if the oath of restraint was not on the others and kept them from boiling over into battle.

Dualta wandered. He feasted his eyes on the color and movement. He lost Colman who went to look at the soldiers, gaudily attired. Dualta remembered a few things.

The priest and the man talking to O'Connell. O'Connell walked around from booth to booth, from place to place. Anyone could talk to him. He had a word for everyone, but sometimes the press of adulators made him withdraw from sight.

This man was saying to the priest: "Father John, I think I rounded up everyone to the vote. All except one, that fellow called O'Connell. What else could you expect from a man with that name? The bastard comes from Kerry too, and I never knew a man from there that was worth a pinch of dust."

Dualta was watching O'Connell's face. It broke up into creases as he laughed. The man then suddenly thought of what he had been saying and put his hand in front of his mouth and looked over it with wild eyes. This made O'Connell and the priest laugh even more.

At night he worked his way into Carmody's hotel where they were eating after the long day. Father Finucane was in the lower place. He had sent a message to Dualta that he wanted him. There were many freeholders with priests there. The talk was loud. Father Finucane saw him. He made his way to him. "Are the people hungry?" he asked. "Did they bring enough food?" "Yes, they are," said Dualta, "and no they didn't bring enough food. Some of them will only be able to vote tomorrow. The swearing took too long."

"I'm trying to get something done about it," said the priest. "Father Murphy," he called. "Father Murphy! Will we be able to get something to eat for them."

The tall priest turned. He had a long face like a Tipperary man. He said: "We will, Father! We will indeed, and we will do it now." He went out of the door calling in a loud voice that hushed the great noise into silence: "The wolf is on the walk! The wolf is on the walk! Shepherds of the people what are you doing here? Should you stuff yourself while the freeholders are unprovided for and temptation in the shape of famine among them. Rise up! Rise up! the wolf, the wolf is on the walk." They heard him going up the stairs where the eating was, and the call of the wolf brought a burst of officials with tickets and orders to the priests to provide meat and beer, but no whiskey, to the freeholders who were far from home and food.

The people of the valley ate then in a great warehouse where huge pots steamed. Bread and meat and beer. They needed it because the poll of the first day was O'Connell 850 Vesey Fitzgerald 538. Eat and vote! Eat and vote for tomorrow is the day. Tomorrow we will let them see. Today is too close, too close for comfort.

Tomorrow would be the day indeed and it was to mean a lot to Dualta, as well as to Daniel O'Connell.

chapter XXII

THE DISILLU-sion of Una's set in slowly. You cannot go back, the small voice said in her ear at odd moments. When she discovered that her one really good dress that she had been saving had mothholes which she carefully patched and darned. They were scarcely noticeable, but she knew they were there. She wore long gloves to cover the coarseness of her hands. She had no scent, nor powder to whiten her suntanned face. She was a friend of the Bradishes, which was the only cachet she possessed, the schoolteacher (this with a lifted eyebrow) which negatived the cachet. She had lost the offhand way of dealing with people. She had become too interested in people as people.

There was a ball this evening of the first polling. It was held in the big living room from which most of the furniture had been removed. In the dining room there was a long table groaning under the weight of food and claret cups. Liveried men and neatly dressed servants moved about with trays.

She danced once or twice with a young lieutenant. He had fair hair and fair whiskers, combed out. He liked those. He fondled them often. He had blue eyes and a young face. He smelled nicely of wine and tobacco. She would never know his name, but she would remember him. Small talk. Yes, she was a schoolteacher. Yes, she taught the natives, not genteel ladies. She liked it! Oh yes, she did. If the country was to advance it could only begin to advance by climbing the ladder of the alphabet and mathematics. Books and science. No, indeed, she found them brighter than children who were better off than they. They had a need. They had a desire, the others had neither, except some. She agreed that O'Connell was crude, but powerful. She was not sorry there had been no violence. She did not agree that the people were incapable of continence. She was glad the army had no chance to intervene in the election.

She walked with him down the steps into the garden. It was so hot in the crowded dancing place. And she knew her status when he immediately reached for her with his hands. No preliminaries at all, you see, no fending off, bright eyes over the top of a fan. It was a crude attack. It showed her her position with great exactitude, so she was glad of her hard work when she hit him in the nose with her clenched fist. She was proud of that, that she drew claret. It gave her satisfaction to see his look of outrage over the hand holding his bleeding nose. She walked away from him, pulling on her glove. Perhaps it was the glove because she had taken it off to cool her warm hand and he had felt, not the powdered smoothness of delicate skin, but the hardness of a working hand. Perhaps he had thought she was a milk girl in disguise or a hearty horsewoman with the morals of an animal.

She went in the back way, her face white under the tan, ignoring the looks of the kitchen scullions. She went up to her room and sat on the bed, thinking. If it was different my father would shoot him, or he would horsewhip him. If it was different it would not have happened. I would be treated with deference. She thought of the many decent young men who had once danced attendance on her, for her own sake and for the sake of her father. Now she saw the change in herself, that she had chosen a life that left her open to this just because she was wandering in the twilight between two worlds. For several painful minutes she longed for her father, and all that he had meant to her, for the magic wand of his presence that would change her status in the twinkling of an eye like the story of the Princess of Ireland that Carrol O'Connor told.

She tried to get rid of her misery by saying her prayers and climbing into the soft bed, but she was very depressed. There was no one on whom she could release the torrent of her depression. She wondered if she was altogether mad to be doing what she was doing. If she went back to her father, if she pleaded with him, would he not welcome her and embrace her and cry over her bent head? Deeply she knew he wouldn't unless she would say: Father I have sinned against your religion. Take me back into it and you.

In the morning she had a headache. She knew she couldn't face Mrs. Bradish. She wore her other dress, the second best one. If only people knew it was also neatly patched and darned. She was darned all the way in, she thought lightly. She walked the mile to the town. On all sides there were people and talk. They were camping at the side of the road, in the fields, under trees, everywhere. They seemed happy. They did not seem to have lost their lust for life. They greeted her politely, got out of her road when they had blocked her way. She came into the streets of the town. They were packed with people. The banners were limp and discolored after a night's rain, but they still shouted and called, and in the square they were packed in front of the platform calling, "O'Connell! O'Connell! Come forth!" They smelled of wet wool and sleeping in close quarters, and sweaty excitement. There was no sense of anticlimax about them. The musicians were even playing. Stalls were abounding, selling their wares and calling them loudly. The shops were packed, mostly with people looking and now and again a woman was coming into the light gazing deeply into the crevices of her water-wheel purse.

She was past the square and walking down another less crowded street when she came face to face with her father. They were both shocked. She knew the two gentlemen with him. They were walking from a house to a carriage that was down a side street. She felt as if she had been kicked in the heart. He had aged. He was using a walking cane. His hair under his hat was much whiter. He had a port wine flush on his face. She saw his shock, his face paling. She saw his eyes devouring her and then a look of coldness come into them as he looked from her face to her shoes all the way up and down, assessing her as she was. He looked in her eyes again. Was he looking for a lowered flag? for a glint of encouragement? She didn't know. But he didn't find it. He remained a gentleman. He raised his hat and turned toward the side street. The two gentlemen with him paused, found their hands awkward, went to speak, could find nothing to say, looked painfully embarrassed, and then followed after him.

She stood there, listening to the sound of the closing carriage door and the sound of the turning wheels on the cobblestones, and then as a blinding flood of tears came into her eyes, she lowered her head, quickened her pace and walked without direction. She ought to have known he would come, like all the many gentlemen of Tipperary. She ought to have known and remained where she was. Now he would know. He would inquire until he found out, and he would know what she was doing. It would puzzle him until he died.

She didn't know where she went, nor did she notice the looks of people who stood aside to let her pass, watching her tear-stained face. Over the humped bridge and right by the river and a little way along there was a ring of boys and girls, dancing and laughing to the sounds of a soft flute. She brushed by them her head lowered, seeming to find it the crowning blow of all that one of the dancers was Dualta and that he saw her and caught the look on her face before she averted it, nor that he cried out and called. A lot he cared, lecturing about the hidden people and the secret people, that you must find, working slowly to discover a new land that was so much more lively and dramatic than the other, even if it was hidden under a veil of poverty and dirt and lice. They were there all right, she thought viciously, there was no mistake about that. But where were the great songs and the laughter and the poetry and the music and the heartwarming neighborliness, the people who would die for you to save you from a heartache, the people who would take your burdens on their back and carry them for pure love, because there was nothing to gain?

"Miss MacMahon!" she heard him call behind her, "Miss MacMahon!"

"Leave me alone! Leave me alone!" she called back over her shoulder. She jumped over a stone wall of low size and headed across the cropped field toward the rushes that grew at the wind of the river. There were no camps here, just the water and the green grass and a curious cow that looked at her with enormous eyes. She went on her knees there and she sat on her heels and covered her face with her hands.

She heard his feet on the grass behind her. She heard his heavy breathing. He had run fast.

"Let me help you, Miss MacMahon," said his voice to the side of her. "Please let me help you!"

"Don't call me Miss MacMahon!" she said. "I am not Miss MacMahon!"

This nonplussed Dualta. He scratched his head.

"All right, Miss Wilcocks," he said.

"Don't use that name!" she said. "Don't dare use that name!"

"All right, Miss," said Dualta, sighing patiently.

"How dare you be patient with me!" she said. She turned on him then. He was on one knee looking at her. It was so strange to see tears in her eyes, mixed with a flaming anger that seemed to be directed at himself. "I have met my father," she said. "Do you hear that? And he passed me by! Do you hear that? My own father!" Her head went down again.

"Lord, I'm sorry," he said.

"I don't want your sympathy," she told him. "Go back to the bridge and dance with the pretty girls."

"I would dance with you, if you would dance," he said.

"It's your fault," she said. "You and that O'Connell man. What do I care about him? What do I care about you? I wouldn't have come at all but for that. I wouldn't have been insulted. What do you think my father would have done to that lieutenant in decent times, when I was decent and normal?"

"What lieutenant?" Dualta asked.

"What he did to me," she said. "O, if only my father was there!"

"What lieutenant?" asked Dualta. "Who was he? What did he do to you? I'll cripple him if you will point him out to me!"

"What does it matter to you?" she asked, facing him, her eyes blazing. "What do you care about me, or what happens to me? Your life is cleaning scruffy fields and dancing and flirting with pretty girls."

"I wasn't flirting with anyone," said Dualta. "I'll leave that to your fine feathered friends."

"You see," she said. "You are making a distinction of me! You will never accept me. I am set apart from one side and the other. I have nowhere to go."

"You can come to me if you like," Dualta shouted. "I'll be a better father than your own father if that's what you want."

"I don't want you to be my father," she shouted.

"Well dammit, I'll be your grandmother so," said Dualta.

"Now you are making a joke of me," she said, tearful again.

"Oh God," said Dualta. "I love you. I want to marry you. I wanted to marry you from the first minute I set eyes on you, but what chance was there for me?"

"What are you saying?" she asked.

"See," he said, "you are sneering at me. You become the lady of the big house when I say this."

"What did you say?" she asked. "Just say it again."

"I love you," Dualta shouted loud enough to startle the cow. "I have always loved you. From the beginning I have loved you. The last time I was in your house, I sat in your vacant room and I smelled your presence and my heart nearly broke."

"Dualta," she said, "you are joking. You are only being kind to me because I am sad."

"What do I have to do?" he asked the sky. "Do I have to eat grass? Do I have to strip myself bare? What chance was there for me to say it until you are reduced to what you are feeling now? What would you have said to me at other times? Just answer me that?"

"Why," she said, "I would have said, What took you so long to say it? That's what I would have said."

"You're joking me," said Dualta.

"I am not," she said.

"You mean you felt the way I felt? You couldn't."

"Oh, yes I could."

"You mean this?"

"Would I be saying it if I didn't mean it?"

"You mean back in your father's house you knew?"

"Not altogether then. I thought I just had a sick stomach."

They both laughed now.

"You were as high as the sky from me," he said. "See how you have been brought to my level?"

"It was you that was high," she said. "I have come up, and I haven't gone down."

"Do you believe this?" he asked.

"What do you want me to believe?" she asked. She was close to him. He could feel the warmth from her body.

"Believe me," he said.

"I believe you," she said.

He wiped the tears from her face with his rough fingers, and the cow, no longer curious, went back to the grass.

For them the day then passed like a bright dream. There was heavy rain but they sheltered in shops and arched doorways. They bought halfpenny rolls of bread, and little pieces of cooked meat on sticks and they ate them on the tombstones in the ruins of the old monastery, the great window of the church bereft of glass rising to the sky as sublime as their feelings.

She waited while he bought her a favor. Normally it would be a ribbon for her hair, but he came from a dark shop and gave her a small bottle of scent. The apothecary thought he was mad. No wonder the country was going to hell, with countrymen buying scent! Great God, where would it all end with upstarts like O'Connell outfacing the gentry? Back to your sty, boy, back to your sty and shake it on the pigs!

Una was so pleased. "How thoughtful!" "It will probably have to last you a lifetime," Dualta told her, and they laughed. "We will make our own scent," he told her, "from the flowers and the herbs." "But it was such a thought," she said. "Who else would have thought of such a foolish thing but a person like Dualta?"

They met O'Connell. Near the square. "Watch," said Dualta.

"Just watch." And he stood there with Una and he waited patiently until the eyes of O'Connell swiveled around in his direction. He saw the eyes rest on him and pass on. He waited. They came back again. They focused on him, a frown between them and then they brightened and he left his companions and he came across to them, his hand out. "The hares," he said, "the hares on the hill. I remember. Odd name. Odd name. Don't tell me! Dualta. See! Am I right?" "You are right," said Dualta proudly. "You are still paying your halfpenny to my welfare, then?" he asked laughing. "Oh, yes! Oh, yes!" said Dualta. "See where they have led, all the halfpennies," he said. "I am pleased to see you. You didn't come back to talk to me." "I will," said Dualta. "I will. This is Miss MacMahon." He took off his hat. He bowed over her hand. She felt his magnetism, his shrewdness as he assessed her. He was smiling. "Are you a convert to the cause?" he asked. "No," said Una. "I am on the other side. It is in my blood. I don't like invective." "Even when it is dramatic?" he asked. "You do not desire my victory then?" "I don't know," she said. "Are you afraid of change?" he asked. She thought over this. She and Dualta. That was change enough for anyone? "No," she said, "I embrace change." He saw their eyes meeting. "I envy you," he said. "What happened to your dark violent friend, then? the brooding man? Has he changed?" "No," said Dualta, "he has not changed." "He never will," the man said. "He is like the other side of a penny. He and I will always be at odds." He was fingering his lower lip. He seemed to have left them. "They are the conflict of the Irish character. He and I. I have not forgotten him. In ways he is a greater enemy to me than the ones I oppose. He will be eternal, unforgiving. War or peace. You see?" "Yes," said Dualta. "Will you win this one then?" A wave of his hand. "O yes, Vesey Fitzgerald is done. It won't be long until the bells ring out for Emancipation. You watch. You have done it. Don't forget that. You and your halfpenny. Don't forget that. It could not have been done without." "Mister O'Connell! Mister O'Connell!" they were calling him urgently. He looked at them again, his eyes bright, and then he went away.

"See," said Dualta. "He remembered after one meeting. That's what power means. That's what leadership means, to remember the faces of the little people."

"You are not little," said Una.

He laughed and they searched for Colman. They found him in a state of wonder. Soldiers, uniforms, shops. "A policeman knuckled me on the head," he said. "I was doing nothing. May he roast in hell." They fed him. He didn't notice anything different about them. He was too busy absorbing sights and sounds. Dualta bought an ass from a tinker. There was tremendous bargaining over the ass. He needed one for carting seaweed from the shore, and many things about the house. He got him in the end for three shillings and ninepence. He was a young sturdy ass. Una wrote a note to Mrs. Bradish: "Dear Mrs. Bradish, I am going home by another method of conveyance. Please bring my few belongings home with you and oblige your servant." They laughed a lot over that. Mrs. Bradish would think she had met a gent who was returning her in a carriage, perhaps after disgraceful interludes. She wouldn't know that Miss MacMahon was going home sitting on the back of an ass with a sack of straw under her.

They left the town while the place was bursting with the results of the day's poll: O'Connell 1,820; Vesey Fitzgerald 842. The place was a maelstrom of delirium, people embracing in the streets, a continuous and prolonged shout of joy and noise. For good or ill, it proclaimed the reign of the Liberator, a demagogue, a thief, a scoundrel, a saint, a hypocrite, according to your impressions. But here and now he was a never-ending shout of joy and release that followed them far from the town into the fresh air of the evening, over a long trip on muddy and potholed roads that seemed to them as soft as cotton, as short as a happy dream, as promising as if it was paved with gold.

And Colman sang and skipped and made up odd songs about the wonders of Ennis, and none of them was afraid of the future.

chapteR XXIII

FLAN MCCARTHY came to the wedding. He sang. This was his song, sung in a quavering off key voice thin and clear:

> Let me sing of the sons of the King,
> Of Murcha and Conchubar and Flan
> So dear to the heart of Brian.
> Let the strings break with
> the wet of my tears
> when I recall them.
>
> Young and fair with shield and sword
> they fought the sea-borne men.
> (In northern lands the hearths were cold
> and widows of beauty ashed
> their long fair hair.)
>
> O, well might Brian cry
> as he prayed in a shaded tent
> foreknowledged of the loss of his lions;
> well welcome death with
> his three brave sons.
>
> In the Kingdom of God they reign
> the three fair princes of Brian,
> Murcha and Conchubar and Flan
> riding the winds of the world
> sons of the New King.

They cheered him. Now you talk to us, Flan the Poet, they called. Now we understand you. You are the last of the Bards.

He was ridiculously pleased, shedding bits of paper from many pockets, smoking a pipe. He sang another song for them. It was obscure, but they pretended it was even better than the other one. He basked in their praise. Moran McCleary danced on his own. He was a big man, but he was as light on his feet as the feather of a duck. His wife Sabina, the regal-looking woman danced with him then. It was song and dance and story for many hours. It was not unruly. Outside, when it became too crowded, young people made their own dance in the yard with young men playing the rhythm of the dance blowing with their mouth on green leaves.

Una met the eyes of her husband on several occasions. See they seemed to say, will you get entertainment like this in the ballrooms of great houses. She smiled her pleasure at him.

It was a great night. People said it was one of the best nights they could ever remember, and it would be long until they saw another like it.

It was really too good to last. It was abruptly ended by Cuan McCarthy.

Una had missed his sardonic presence from the kitchen.

Suddenly he was there dominating it.

"Stop the dancing! Stop the music!" he called. He stood in front of the fire, a tall thin man with fire in his eyes.

"Tewson is here," he said. "The house is a blaze of lights. Tomorrow they are going to call in the hanging gales."

He had succeeded in sobering them. There was none didn't get a cold feeling in his spine. There was three months to go to gale day. That meant there was three months' rent owing, since all of them were in arrears. It meant before the harvest was in, before the potatoes were up or the corn, or pigs ready for the market or turf or eggs or butter, that they would have to find three months' rent on demand.

"How do you know, Cuan?" Dualta asked.

"I know," say Cuan. "I have sources of information. We will have to stop them. And stop them now. He waited a long time. Now he is going to leap for the votes for O'Connell."

The Silent People

"Have you a notion what we can do, Cuan?" Moran McCleary asked him.

"I have," said Cuan. "I want a hundred men with me, who will get their spades and in the light of the moon we will turn up ten acres of their grassland. That will give them pause. That will set them back."

"It's a brave notion," said Moran McCleary.

"It is not," said Dualta. "It's a bad notion. If you are being made to pay for the voting, what do you think will happen after this?"

Una noted with a beating heart that a coldness had descended in the joyful atmosphere, and a lot of it was being directed at Dualta.

"Nobody asks you to dig on your wedding night," said Cuan. "If you don't want to!"

"That has nothing to do with it," said Dualta. "Many men will not be able to afford the hanging gales. Let us go in a deputation to Tewson and plead for them. If that fails let those of us who have a few shillings pledge ourselves to find the rent for those who haven't. Let us sell what we possess to help our neighbor."

Una looked around at them. They dropped their eyes from Dualta's challenge.

Sabina McCleary said. "Turn up the land. We have been too long lying down under them. Let us awaken the valley. If ye are men let ye go and turn up the grasslands."

"You are wrong," said Dualta.

"You weren't long changing from a man to a woman, Dualta," said Cuan. "Has a patch of land made you a coward then?"

"Experience has made me see that what you want is wrong," said Dualta. "Patience and sacrifice are more important than violence."

"The priest has trained you well," said Cuan.

"Life has trained me," said Dualta. "Has O'Connell taught you nothing?"

"No," said Cuan. "Forty-shilling freeholders were to be pro-

237

tected. Where are their votes? Dead. Where are the ones that were to be saved from eviction? They are evicted. Now here. They threaten us. We strike back. That is the way. Who is coming with us? The young men are gathering their spades. This is a testing time. We can stop them. Let us stop them now and not wait until caution clears our heads."

"Don't do it," said Dualta. "Let us have time. Let us educate your sons. Let us be patient, for the love of God. We are too many. We will force them eventually by opinion, by being educated. You see your children, what different people they are. Let us train them to win for you while we hold on with patience and perseverance. I appeal to you. Don't listen to Cuan. He is my friend and I tell you that."

"I am no longer your friend," said Cuan. "Come men, any of you that have the courage to come with me."

He walked to the door.

The people felt hurt. There was hurt in their eyes as they silently left. Because they were outraging hospitality, breaking a thread of happiness. Very soon they were all gone, except the fiddler who was staying for the night, and Napoleon in a drunken sleep in a corner and Carrol O'Connor and his wife and Sheila and Flan McCarthy.

Una thought, what a thin thread there is between complete happiness and gloomy dismay.

"You cannot talk to the wind, Dualta," said Carrol O'Connor.

"My talk is true," said Dualta. "They are wrong."

"Time will tell," said Mrs. O'Connor.

Flan rose to his feet. He walked toward the door. He talked to the sky.

> "We are the silent people.
> How long must we be still,
> to nurse in secret at our breast
> an ancient culture?
>
> Let us arise and cry then;
> call from the sleeping ashes

of destiny a chieftain who
will be our voice.

He will strike the brass
and we will erupt
from our hidden caves
into the golden light of newborn day."

Dualta went to him. "Flan," he said, "isn't he here if they
will listen to him?"

"Tainted," said Flan. "Will he stand at the ford with a
bronze shield and a warlike spear? Will he call the bards from
their poverty?"

"You can teach wisdom," said Dualta. "They will listen to
you!"

"No," said Flan, "tillers of the soil! War with spades! It
becomes the men of turf to make war with spades. Let me go
home. I am sick of men. Come and see me, Dualta. I am not
unaware of life. I grieve that your wedding night has been put
in upon. You have won yourself a fair bride. Enjoy her before
the tears. Come and see me. I wish you well. I have no power.
I am impatient of men." He went across the yard. He started
again to sing his song of the three sons of Brian, his voice quavering on the night air. Dualta felt Una beside him. She put her
hand on his arm. Below in the valley through the trees, they
could see lights in the windows of the big house. The unusual
lights seemed very menacing.

"No good will come of it," said Dualta. "They are wrong."

"You are not longer alone to argue it with yourself, Dualta,"
she said. "Remember, I am here now. Forever."

He looked at her.

"I am sorry I forgot," he said. "You are worth everything."

The O'Connors came into the night. Dualta helped him to
tackle the horse to the cart.

They were silent. When they were going Carrol said: "I
am your friend, Dualta. I am not the only one. You must not
forget this."

"Don't let them altogether spoil your wedding night," said Mrs. O'Connor. "Tomorrow I will come and give you a hand to clean up."

They went away.

Una and Dualta stood there. It was a soft night. He had been on the point of winning the friendship of the whole valley.

"It is like Cuan to wreck this day of our life," he said.

"You mustn't let him," she said.

"It is difficult to think of hard-earned acres of grass being turned up to the light of the moon," he said. "Now that I know how hard it is to make a single field, I grieve at the loss of made ones. It will stop Clarke for a time, but time is on their side. They can afford to wait."

"You will have to weigh my love against the loss of the green fields," said Una.

"The scales are weighted," said Dualta. "You have no competition. But my heart is sore."

"I will balm it for you," said Una. "Remember me, I am a stranger. I am far from home. I feel sad. You will have to comfort me. You will have to console me. Don't let them win you. I want you."

"You have me," said Dualta, turning her determinedly toward the house. "Let them dig their own folly. We will bed Napoleon and the Fiddler and then we will blot out the night."

"Now you are saying something worthwhile," said Una. "You must remember that you are no longer alone."

chapter XXIV

QUALTA WAS molding his lumpers and felt depressed. The stalks were thick, the plants were healthy, soon they would be in flower. He had planted two kinds of potatoes, lumpers and Irish Apple. The lumpers were big and fruitful, the Irish Apple small and much tastier, but they grew those only for sale. He thought of the immense amount of labor that had gone into the saving of this potato field, cleaning and burning and the first year setting it out in lazy beds, ridges about six feet wide. Then the field in the following year had to be manured with bog, or mold, lime clay and, when he had it, dung and seaweed. All costly. Lime had to be burned with turf and one barrel of it went to a perch of land. He found that when God threw seaweed from the deep that it would be taken away laboriously with the donkey and baskets at the cost of 4/2 per ton, and if you wanted sea sand to liven the soil you had to pay from 5/– to 10/–. If seaweed and sand weren't free in the world weren't all men slaves?

But the soil was improving, he told himself, as he took some of it in his hand. It was becoming more powdery, even if it was very stony, but that allowed air to travel in it, so perhaps stones were good too.

He straightened his back and leaned on the spade and was suddenly pleased to see the figure of Una, far below, coming out of the house with the basket in her hand and starting to walk through the fields. Almost he could hear her humming.

He kept his worries from her; the cold wind of fear that blew on the back of his neck when gale day began to loom up. Only now after all those years he could feel genuine sympathy with the forty-shilling freeholders going in like sheep to vote in Galway. The loss of a cow or the failure of one crop was all that stood between you and beggary. In the three years since he had the place the only thing that saved them was the few pounds that Una got for teaching school. At a penny per pupil per week this amounted to about six pounds per year. Many children could not afford to pay the penny at all. It was a poor parish. It had to support two priests. Father Finucane himself seemed to live on very little, and his supplement to the school fund would be about five pounds per year.

There was a fair wind. It was ruffling the green shoots of the oats.

He dropped the spade and went down to meet her. He jumped the wall of the potato field, walked the headland of the oatfield feeling the texture of the green shoots with his palm. He came to rest in the next field sitting with his back to a sweet-smelling cock of first crop hay. Here he waited for her. He knew where she would come. First he would see the top of her head and then her eyes and then her smiling mouth and then the rest of her. She would be happy. She seemed to be always happy since the day they were married, as if she had said: Here now, you are my husband. You will bear all the burdens. I will be happy. He looked forward to seeing her every time they were separated, even for short periods, as if he were seeing her again after a long absence.

He saw her head, the sun shining on her hair, uncovered. She always wore it that way, and then her eyes, deep-sunken and crinkling as soon as they alighted on him and her smiling mouth. She was singing tra-la-la. She always sang in English, even if she was becoming very expert with the speaking of Irish. He thought: What does all the rest matter when I have her? The basket was swinging in her hand. She was thinner, finer than when he had known her long ago. Her body was lithe and the fine bones of her face more obvious, but a healthy fineness she had. She wore shoes. She couldn't use her bare feet. She had tried. Anything but that she said, so the cobbler had to come for a week with all his paraphernalia, to measure her feet and make her shoes on his lap-stone. In all the shoes cost seven shillings and fourpence. They were made of harder leather than she was used to, but he could mend them himself and with care they would last a year.

She got on her knees between his legs and she put the basket aside and bent forward and kissed him.

"God be with you, o man," she said.

He held on to her hands.

"You will never learn to be of the people," he said.

"In what am I lacking?" she asked.

"You must never show you love your husband in public," he said.

"Who can see but the birds?" she asked.

"It is the spirit of the thing," he said. "When you are of the people you are not expected to have finer emotions. You must be like an animal, a little higher-class animal. You eat, you sleep, you love when hunger arises in you."

"I am hungry," she said leaning forward and kissing him again, "and you are bitter. Don't be bitter."

Her hands were very small. They were very roughened too. He looked at them.

"Why wouldn't I be bitter?" he asked. "No matter how hard we work, your hands will never be smooth again. They are right to regard us as animals, except that animals have a certain measure of freedom. We have none at all."

"You better eat," she said. "Your stomach is upset." She took her hands from him, and lifted the cloth from the basket. It was simple fare: potatoes freed from their skins, a bottle of buttermilk and a coolin, a halfpenny salted herring. The smell of them made him hungry, but the sight of her picking at a potato with her even white teeth and taking up a fingerful of the boiled herring daintily, made his heart sink as he saw her in a picnic setting as he had once seen her. All those delicacies.

"It's not right!" he said. She laughed at him over the potato.

"How long will it be," she asked, "before you lose your pride? I am happy, Dualta. How can I make you see this, totally happy. I am married to a man I love, and I am doing things that I feel are fruitful. There is nothing that can cause me dismay, only sadness in you. So please don't be sad. Are you grieving because I haven't given you a son?"

"You mustn't say that!" he exploded. "Down there in the school you have many sons and daughters. They are important. It may be that God does not want us to have any of our own until we have dealt with those. You must not worry over this."

"I won't," she said, "if you will stop worrying over my lost white hands. What use were they anyhow?"

"They were beautiful," he said, "even if they are just as beautiful now."

She bent forward. She rubbed the finger of her left hand between his brows.

"You have a growing furrow there," she said. "What causes it?"

He sighed.

"Do you understand about tithes?" he said.

She thought over it.

"Mr. Glasby is the tithe valuator," she said. "Clarke is the tithe proctor. Glasby comes and looks at everything we own. He sets one tenth value on everything we might sell."

Dualta saw the list: Hearth tax 4/– (2 hearths)

Potatoes	5/9
Corn	3/6
Turf	1/7½
Hay	4/10
Poultry	8
Pig	5/–
Small dues	5/5

It all amounted to a sizable sum. It took gathering. It was the price of one good pig or a year's supply of tobacco. That was the joke. They said a man smoked a pig a year if he used tobacco.

"You know why they make us pay tithes?" he asked.

"Yes," she said. "Tithes is for the support of the Church of Ireland, for the upkeep of Protestant Bishops and ministers, and cess tax is for the erection and repair of Protestant edifices and the expense of its services. I know that."

"Most people in this valley have never even seen a Protestant minister," he said. "Is it fair that Catholics should have to pay for the upkeep of a religion that is contrary to all they believe?"

"It is an unjust law," she said. "That is obvious."

"There is trouble in the land," he said. "Last month thirteen people were shot dead in Newtownmountbarry and twenty were wounded at tithe sales. In Carrickshock a process server and twelve police were slaughtered with scythes, spades and pitchforks. Now there is trouble in our valley. Police have been brought into the town. There have been letters flying round, warnings, notices signed by Lady Clare and the Terry Alts and Captain Moonlight. I am afraid."

"Why, Dualta?" she asked.

"I do not want to pay tithes," he said. "Even O'Connell said don't pay tithes. He was not going to pay them himself. It is all right for him. What happens to us?"

"What happens?" she asked.

"The process server comes," he said, "and he will take away our cow. She will be brought to the town, and she will be auctioned. Most of the violence has arisen from these forced tithe sales. I do not want to pay these tithes, but I do not want to lose my cow. I do not know for sure but I feel that I am a coward. Now that I have something, I do not want to lose it. When I had nothing to lose I was not a coward. You know what they say: Use the whip on another man's horse."

She thought.

"Will everyone in the valley refuse to pay?" she asked.

"That's the point," he said. "They won't. If they did there would be no problem. They couldn't take a cow from everyone in the valley. The weak will pay. Will I be among the weak?"

"Maybe they are strong, not weak," she said. "Why will you seek violence?"

"There comes a time when oppression becomes too hard to bear," he said, "and men must assert themselves."

"Don't Father Finucane's sermons against violence mean anything to you?"

"Yes, unfortunately," he said, "but in this case I am in doubt."

"If the law is unjust," she said, "it will be changed, but violence only breeds violence."

"Who will change the law?" he asked.

"Why, those boys and girls down in the schoolhouse," she said. "We will make them change the law. We will educate them to justice by perseverance and the force of their literate opinions. It's a long-term plan but it is the most important."

"You think I should pay then?" he asked.

"Whose head is on the coin?" she asked.

"The image and inscription of Caesar," he said. He got to his feet. He reached for her hand. He pulled her to her feet. He put his arms around her. "You are the most valuable possession in the world," he said. "If I had to pay tithes on you there would not be enough gold and silver in the world to meet the tax."

She laughed at him, and then as his eyes were caught by a movement in the valley, she felt him stiffening. "What is it, Dualta," she asked.

"Look," he said, pointing down. "The police are moving in on Moran McCleary. See, that's what they do. Take one person and make an example of him. I hope to God Moran pays, but I am in doubt. Cuan has been working on him."

He left her. He started to run.

"Dualta! Dualta!" she said.

"I'm going down," he called. "Stay at home. It doesn't feel right. You see the sun glinting on the bayonets. Who do they think we are!"

Then he turned and was gone. She called after him again: "Dualta! Dualta!" then, unrewarded, she gathered the fragments and put them in the basket and lifting the skirt of the cotton dress, she ran down after him.

As a small swallow hole in the water attracts to its core all the flotsam that floats on the surface, so the band of men who set out from the town toward the farm of Moran McCleary attracted the young people of the town and the lazy ones and the wretched ones from the cottages, and the farmers from the fields, a silent crowd that followed on the rough dusty road behind them, or moved through the hedgerows and over the walls like a scattering of mice leaving a depleted corn stack.

Clarke was mounted. Buach, who was the process server walked at his stirrup armed with a heavy stick. Páid Monuar with the soft pleading eyes walked at the other stirrup. There were six policemen with the constable from the town. They carried guns and the bayonets were fixed to them and glinted in the sun. Only one man was a Peeler. The others were baronial policemen, rough-and-ready boys without the proper policeman's neatness of dress and carriage. They were burly men and they were apprehensive. They were slightly dismayed by the gathering of people all around them, and the man at the end would turn now and again and say to them "Back there! Keep back there, now!"

Clarke looked neither to the left nor the right. It was left to him to choose the man who would be an example for the valley and he had chosen McCleary. It was a daring thing to do, because McCleary was one of the few with a two-life lease on his farm and therefore independent. But Clarke didn't like him. He told himself this was legitimate. He was sure McCleary was behind the revolt in the valley, that would have to be ended. McCleary had made a very good farm out of his acres. Clarke would have liked to give this farm to a more honorable man, but he was balked by the lease. But as a tithe proctor he could harass him and this he was determined to do. His duty compelled him to it, he told himself.

So they turned off the road into the track that led to McCleary's house. It lay on a plateau, a smiling property. He could afford to keep it well, as improvements couldn't mean extra rent for him. It shone in the sun, gleaming white with a new gold-colored thatch, a long house with flower beds under the windows and on each side of the yard stables and dairy and pig house, all clean and gleaming with wash. Behind the house there was a fruitful kitchen garden and an orchard.

Clarke admired the place as he came into it. It was well kept. A lot of labor had gone into the making of it. He thought it was too good for the rent that the estate was getting out of it.

He stopped out from the door.

Moran came from the kitchen. He was in his bare feet, breeches and shirt with his big chest straining the cloth of it. He was a fair-haired man with blue eyes and his mouth was grim over a square chin.

"Stop there now, Clarke," he said. "Come no farther. Speak what you have to say and then go away."

"Hand him the process, Buach," said Clarke.

Buach went up to Moran with the paper in his hand. His stick was across his shoulder, a smile on his mashed face.

"I serve this on you," he said, "in the name of the Sheriff of the County. Take heed of it and obey it."

Moran took it from him. He crushed it, unopened, and threw it on the ground.

"I will not pay tithes," he said. "That is all."

"Then we have no option," said Clarke, "but to take possession of a cow of our choosing. It will be auctioned in the town on a day to be stated in payment of the tithes owing. Do we have to take possession of the animal peacefully or do we take it forcibly? You can decide."

"You will get away from here," said Moran, "as fast as you are able. The first man to lay a hand on a beast of mine, policeman, proctor or bullyboy will be stretched on the yard."

"What's come over you, Moran?" Buach pleaded. "Will you fight the whole world?" He put his hand on his shoulder. Moran threw it away so forcibly that Buach staggered.

"Weary of taxes, rack rent, tithes, cess, of the the whole lot," shouted Moran. "This is the last of it. I will not pay! You hear that, Clarke? And I will defend my possessions until I am dead. You hear that, Clarke?"

Clarke signaled to the police.

"Restrain him then," he said to the Peeler. This man signaled and two of the rough-and-ready boys moved on Moran, their guns held across their chests.

"Now, come easy man," one of them said. "We have no wish to hurt you."

The action was probably instigated by Buach. He was behind Moran. He reached a hand for his shoulder. The big man sensed this, swung around and hit him on the neck with his fist. Buach roared and fell. The two policemen moved in quickly, but

Moran caught one of them, and in a flaming rage threw him at the other. The gun fell from the man's hand and Moran reached for it, as Dualta came running panting into the yard.

"Now go! Now go, by God!" Moran shouted taking the gun into his hands. Someone shouted. It was like a command. The Peeler shouted: "No! No! Don't shoot! Don't shoot!" But two of them had leveled their guns and had shot, probably in a panic. They were not disciplined men and all the people in the yard saw the bullets hitting Moran's chest, heard the shout strangled in his throat, saw the two blood roses appearing on the cloth of his shirt, just before he fell, heard the scream from his wife Sabina who was standing behind at the door. For a few seconds everyone stood there, almost petrified and then shouting, the people all around reached to the ground for whatever was handy, clods or dung or stones and hurled them at the officers bunched in the yard. Under the hail of missiles, Clarke turned the horse and with his free arm over his head, galloped from the yard.

The Peeler rallied his men, got them moving, shouting: "Don't shoot! Don't shoot!" One of them did shoot but he hit the barrel of the gun and deflected the shot into the air. Dualta himself was bending and groping and firing, inarticulate sounds coming out of him. The band of men got out of the yard, their arms over their heads. Stones hit them, clods dirtied them. Clarke came back and put the horse between the people and the policeman while the Peeler got some order into them. Clarke was shouting: "Enough now! Enough now! Hold off, or the men will shoot! This is the law! This is the law!"

Gradually they got on to the main road.

As quickly as it had started the noise ceased. The people stopped still, suddenly aware of a tragedy. You could hear a bird singing in the quiet, Dualta thought. It seemed to him an indecent sound.

"Pull away quietly now," the Peeler said. "Just walk along the road slowly, under the hedge."

They did so. He could hear their heavy breathing, smell the sweat off them. He was an ex-soldier. He hated them.

"That pair of bloody fools didn't have to fire," he said. "I told you warning shots would serve. You didn't have to shoot the man!"

"They did right," said Clarke loudly. "He would have used the gun."

"That's right, that's right," the fat sweaty one of them said, "he would have used the gun. I saw his finger on the trigger."

"It was his own fault," said Clarke. "The men did no wrong. They shot in defense of the rest of us."

The Peeler looked up at him. "There was no need to shoot," he said.

"If that is your opinion, it's not mine," said Clarke.

"Will you get a medal for them then?" the Peeler asked.

"Be careful with your tongue," said Clarke. "I am the Sheriff's representative. They did no wrong. They probably saved all our lives. You saw how we were attacked. See the blood they drew from some of the men."

"They'll live," said the Peeler looking at the bleeding scratches. "But the shot man won't."

"That's enough," said Clarke. He pulled the head of the horse around and set off on the road. The others followed him. He found his hands were shaking. It is a pity, he thought, about Moran. He should have had sense. Wasn't it better to pay a few pounds than to lose your life? An odd thing. A two-life lease and here was one of the lease lives gone. It was a pity. Why should a man have to die over a few pounds of money?

They heard the clattering of hooves coming around the bend of the road. Clarke stopped. He waited. Then the horse and the young priest came into view. He had no hat, such was his hurry. His stock was untied. Clarke thought primly that priests shouldn't be seen abroad like that. The priest pulled up his horse.

"What happened?" he asked. "I heard shooting."

"Moran resisted," said Clarke. "He grabbed a gun. Some of the men fired in defense. He was hit."

"You are very calm," said the priest.

"I have nothing on my conscience," Clarke shouted. "He seemed to go mad. There was nothing to do."

"I hope God takes as easy a view of it," said Father Finucane. He urged his horse past them and set him galloping again. Clarke looked after him. I'll complain to the Bishop, he decided. He is too cocky to be an administrator. He will have to be taught manners.

When Dualta turned back into the yard again, it seemed to him that all of the people had become statues. They just stood where they were looking at the man lying in the yard. His wife was still outside the door her hand up to her mouth. But the man on the ground was not alone. Una was kneeling beside him. She had raised his head and shoulders on to her knees. She was trying to stem the flow of blood from his chest. He walked to her. She looked at him. Her face was pale, her eyes were desperate. He got on his knees beside them.

"Is he alive?" he asked.

"Only just," she said. There was sound coming from the wounds as if he was breathing through the holes. "Oh, Dualta, what will we do?"

"We'll have to get him in," said Dualta. He stood up. He looked around at the people ringing them helplessly. "Get a board," he called. "Someone get a board, we'll take him in."

It broke the spell that held them. They moved then, paused when they heard the sound of the horse coming back, tensed and waited until they saw it was the priest. Dualta was relieved. He went to him. "It's bad, bad," he said.

"All right," said the priest. He went to Moran. He was surprised to see that it was Una who held him. "How is he?" he asked.

"Not good," said Una. "He is dying." He wondered at her knowledge. She had seen two men dying of wounds from guns, young men who fought in duels for an intangible and stupid thing called honor. She knew Moran was shot in the lungs.

"Go to Sabina," said the priest. "Look after her. Get the children away from here. We will take care of Moran." He took off his coat. He put it under the big fair head as Una withdrew her knees. Her dress was stained with the blood that flowed from his back. It had soaked into her. She could feel its moistness on her knees. She walked to the woman as Dualta and the men came with a door they had pulled from the stable.

Una said: "Sabina, get the children out of the house. We will send them to a neighbor. Sabina! You hear me!" She took the hand that was covering her mouth and held it. She shook it a little as she called her name. "Sabina!" She saw then the shock dying out of Sabina's face and a little of the strength but none of the color coming back into it. She turned her. They went into the house. There were six children in the kitchen. The eldest boy and the girl she knew well from teaching. The boy Fiacra was twelve. He was bright and intelligent. She spoke to him.

"Fiacra," she said, "take the children, go out the back way and bring them to O'Connors. You hear me?"

"Yes," he said. "I'll do that. But I must come back myself."

"All right," she said. "You come back then."

Fiacra collected them. The youngest, a flaxen-haired boy wearing a petticoat didn't want to go. The girl Julia took him in her arms. He protested. He cried. The girl put her hand over his mouth. But he kept crying. They went out the back way. They could hear his crying for a long time. Sabina sat on a stool in the corner. She rubbed her forehead with the back of her hand.

"Soon, I will be all right," she said. "So quick. I do not understand. What happened?"

"Where is the bedroom?" Una asked. Sabina pointed. Una went up there. It was a neat room with a five-shilling bedstead covered with a white quilt. It was ready for Moran. There was nothing she could do. She went down again and stood in front of Sabina as they brought him into the kitchen and worked him into the bedroom. Then the three men and Dualta came down and left the priest with him. They stood awkwardly in the kitchen. All of them seemed incapable of movement. Outside she could see the people standing in the yard close to the house. They were not talking. There was a terrible shocked silence which you felt you ought to break by screaming. The priest came down. He was taking the stole from around his neck.

"Moran is dead," he said. His face was stricken. His words reached to the outside. There was a loud wail from a woman. It seemed to bring Sabina to life.

"Mrs. Duane," she said to Una, "you must change that dress. Come with me. You will have my Sunday dress." She walked up to the room on the other side. Una followed her.

Father Finucane stood looking at them. They were watching for him. What could he do? The only thing he knew about. He said, "We will pray," and he took out his rosary beads and got to his knees and faced toward the door of the dead man and the men in the kitchen and the people in the yard got to their knees and the only rival sound to the music of their voices was the song of the birds.

And they got ready for a wake and a funeral. He was washed and dressed in a cotton nightshirt and he looked very handsome, and the people came and the provisions came but he had a quiet wake and he would be buried with the wailing of pipes and the flying of flags and it was so sudden and so shocking that it would take time for them to believe that it had happened.

It was two in the morning when Dualta and Una were walking home. They had no words. What could they say? A decent man was shot to death over a few shillings. He wouldn't get the benefit of a Coroner's Court. There was a Coercion Act in force. He was legitimately dead. He didn't matter. He wasn't even a footnote in history.

A voice called from the shadow of the hedge.

"Dualta! Dualta!" Una felt his arm stiffening. She knew the way the wrinkles of determination would form at the right side of his mouth. He was striding on. He wasn't going to wait. She held him.

"It's Cuan," said Una. He stopped.

"Are you happy, Cuan?" Dualta asked. "Now you are right! Here is Moran dead. Good man, Cuan! Now you can really go to work."

"No, Dualta," said his voice. "I would give my own life for him. This is wrong, Dualta. Listen to me."

Dualta went close to the hedge. He couldn't see his face. It was just a blur.

"I have listened to you too long, Cuan," he said. "You will always bring death. Only death to other people. That is what the great patriots do. They are like the generals. They are always safe behind the battles while they incite the innocent to die."

"Dualta," said Cuan. "I didn't mean Moran to die. He was too fine to die. He was a big man. He makes a protest and others follow him."

"They have a bloody way to follow him now," said Dualta.

"You must tell me what I can do," said Cuan.

"Go to hell," said Dualta.

"Dualta! Dualta!" said Una.

"I cannot tell you how I feel," said the voice of Cuan, "because I have never felt this before. I am truly desolate, Dualta."

Una heard the pain in his voice. She went forward a little and caught his arm. She pressed it.

"I don't know what to do," said Cuan. "What would you do, Dualta, tell me. Just tell me."

"Replace him," said Dualta. "That's what I would do. I would take on the burden of his life, that's what I would do. But all the great patriots do is to write a penny pamphlet and a song."

"How can I take on his burdens, tell me," Cuan persisted.

"Go to his wife and children," said Dualta. "Say to them: I am responsible for the death of your father."

"That's not true," said Cuan.

"It's the way I see it," shouted Dualta.

"Please, Dualta," said Una.

"Say: I will be your father, to the children, and I will be your husband to the mother. Take all the burdens of a great broad-shouldered man on your thin back. Plant and sow and reap and mow, day after day, week after week, and pay the rent and sell the crops. You think you are able for that! It's so much easier to talk and incite, rapparees and burning thatches."

"You think I should do this then? Would they receive me?"

Dualta laughed. "You is it? They would prefer Buach or Páid Monuar or Clarke himself or one of the policemen that shot him. They would be of more use than you."

"Don't mind him, Cuan," said Una. "Go and talk to them."

"I do not know what to say to them, how to express myself; what they will say to me?"

"They will be kinder to you than Dualta," said Una. "They might even understand your pain."

"I will do that so," said Cuan. "I didn't want this to happen. I didn't think it would happen like this. Thank you, Una. You are a person of the people. I am very sad."

They stood and watched him walk away, from the shadows of the hedge into the light of the moon. His shoulders were bowed and his head bent as he made his way toward the house of Moran.

"A lot of good he'll be," said Dualta. Una walked away from him. He went after her. "You are displeased with me?" he asked.

She didn't answer him.

"If you knew all the pain he is responsible for," said Dualta. "I only know it now."

"Kindness costs nothing," she said. "He feels it deeply."

"Late has it come to him then," he said.

"It's harder for him to be humble than you to be kind," she said.

"You take his side against me?" he asked.

"Dualta," she said, "don't be righteous. It does not become you."

"Now you are aristocratic," he said.

"Must I suffer because you are mixed up?" she asked.

He was silent. Until they got to the house and found that the candles were lighted in the window and the door opened and in the kitchen Colman was waiting for them, and sitting on a stool in the corner was his father, Bottle, unshaven, with prison pallor still on him, his clothes very ragged and grinning at them over a mug of buttermilk. Colman was exalted.

"See," he shouted, "my father is home again. I said that one day he would come home. He is let out. Isn't it a great day?"

Dualta's heart sank, as he saw the boy with the lanky hair falling into his eyes. He was tall. His eyes were shining as if he had found a crock of gold. Did we mean so little to him, he wondered, thinking of the training, the coaxing to give his bright brain a disciplined education? Did he really prefer this dirty illiterate maker of illicit whiskey to them?

"You are welcome, man," he said to Colman's father.

"This is your wife," said Bottle. "It was decent of you to care for Colman. He turned into a fine young fellow. He will be a great help to me now."

"You are going back home, then?" Una asked.

"Yes," said Colman. "I have been keeping the house above warm. One day, my father will come home, I said. Now he is home. Isn't this great news? What greater news could happen in the valley." He knelt by the stool. He put his thin arm around the old man's shoulders.

Una was looking at Dualta's face.

"You will stay with us tonight at least," she said to Bottle.

"No trouble," said Bottle. "I'll doss in the ashes."

"I knew one day it would happen," said Colman. "I was watching the road. I saw him way below coming over the hill. I said: That is my father coming over the hill. I traveled the rocks like a goat until I came to him."

"I'm glad you are so glad, Colman," said Dualta.

"You got him to read and write too, and make up sums," Bottle said. "Imagine that? It was a brave task."

"He's not finished being educated," said Dualta. "He still has a lot to learn."

"He knows enough now," said Bottle. "Isn't he a scholar? He will have little time for the books now. We have to build up the place again. It will be more important for him now to learn how to fire a still. I must have been sorely missed in the valley."

Colman laughed. "You hear that? I will have a place of my own again. Won't that be a great thing? We will be living near to Flan too. I will blind him with my songs."

Una said: "You ought to get more schooling, Colman."

"I will. I will," said Colman. "Now you have seen him, I will spread a bed for him near the fire. Tomorrow we will move on. It will be a great adventure."

Dualta and Una wished them well and went to their room. They didn't take a candle. They undressed in the dark. They lay silently untouching in the bed. She could almost feel the depth of Dualta's suffering.

"He is his father," she said.

"All we did and we mean so little to him," said Dualta. "He casts us off like a worn-out kerchief."

"He is his father," she said.

"But what a father," said Dualta.

"You see now, maybe," she said, "that Cuan was really in sorrow."

He didn't reply.

"Oh, Dualta," she said. "I will give you a son. I swear I will give you a son."

He pressed her hand. Lying on his back. All he could hear was the sad wailing of the pipes that would follow a shouldered coffin.

"I will! I will! I will!" she said.

part four

chapter XXV

YOU SAY TO A person: You have ten years. When you are twenty, ten years seems as long as eternity. When you are thirty, ten years past seem as short as a pleasant dream.

In this September Dualta shaved himself in the piece of broken mirror and discovered two gray hairs. He had to search for them but he found them. Why, he thought, I am getting old, I am a man. He looked more closely at his face. It was lined, he saw in some amazement. Wrinkles on his forehead and between his eyes and by his mouth could be pressed out with his finger, but they returned.

He was dressed in his best clothes. A new body coat of frieze costing 16 shillings and elevenpence. It would have to last three years. A new cotton shirt 2/–, breeches 7/4, stockings 1/–, a waistcoat 1/8 and stout shoes 6/–. He had come to the stage that everything had a price. It had to. You had to know if you could afford it and if you couldn't afford it now that maybe you could afford it next year.

He gathered the money on the table and put it in the canvas sack. It was exact. For here was another gale day, and he thought grimly as he tied the mouth of the sack, it might be his last gale day. His ten-year lease was up. Next week, if Clarke so wished he could be thrown out on his head.

That would be a pity, he thought, as he looked around. It was a pleasant house now. There were curtained windows and painted furniture that he had made himself, many cupboards, a collection of delf, harness for a pony hanging on wooden pegs.

He threw ashes on the turf fire to rake it. Then he went out and closed the door after him. He walked out of the yard and turned to look back at his property. It was pretty. Men had said to him: Don't make it look pretty on the outside. You will suffer. Put your dung heap outside the front door. Don't whitewash. Don't paint. Let it look as poor as possible. You will pay for your cleanliness. You will attract covetous eyes. It doesn't pay to be clean. He didn't listen. It was a neat place, it was clean. There was a flower patch under the windows and wild roses were trained to climb to the thatch. Even the fearsome thorn tree had a seat built around it and neighbors had lost their fear of it, and gathered there some evenings smoking and telling tales and spreading news. Behind the house his clean fields climbed the hills, seeming with their neatness to be holding back the wild lands. All right. He had worked for it. He had earned it. It would be a strong man who would take it from him. Even if he died now they could say: The Galwayman achieved something.

He whistled to raise his heart. Then he discovered that it was one of Colman's songs. So he stopped whistling it. His heart dropped always when he thought of Colman. He had never come back to school. He was a young man now, a tattered lanky young man who sang songs and sold whiskey for his father. Clever too. Bottle had never been caught since. He provided a need and so he was protected. Publicans who held a license were pleased to mix his with their legitimate brew. He was the mainstay of the whiskey cabins, who needed him as the land needed water. But Colman could have been so different.

He liked going to school. The few hours he spent there seemed to refresh him. It was a great thing to see children becoming literate. There were always the stupid ones. So difficult to put anything into their heads. But there were the bright ones who soaked knowledge. They had affected a visible change in the valley. Mainly due to Una. He himself forced knowledge into the children, but she inculcated culture. Cleanliness and manners and faith, and they went home to the poor houses and they spread this like gospelers. Una was the most popular person in the valley.

Before he went into the school he tried to cast the worry out of his face. He had cause for worry but it was for himself.

There were voices droning from inside. He could hear the

spellers chorusing over and over again the English word "procras-tin-ation." He went in. He expected Una to be there. She wasn't. There was a smell of homemade ink, confined young bodies. They twisted the whites of their eyes on him. Those who were sitting on the forms stood and chorused: "God with you, Mas-ter." The spellers chanted their word louder than ever. He said: "With you too, sit down." The door of the other room was closed. He walked toward it. He thought that the place looked like a school now. The stones were mortared and whitewashed. Cupboards held books. There was a map of Ireland and a map of Europe on the wall. There was a bright fire burning in the open fireplace. It needed a fire. It was a cold September. It had been a wet summer.

He opened the door and went in. Una was standing there with her back to him. She was talking to little Finola Mogue. She turned her head when she heard him come in and he was shocked at her face. It was drawn and white and as sad as the face of a painted Madonna.

Finola was a small girl dressed in a poor frock that was well patched. Her feet were bare. She was about twelve. She was Una's favorite scholar. She had stopped her in the town last year, plucked her dress and said: "I want to go to school, I have no penny." She was a small little one. She was not pretty. Her dark hair was straight. She had a small nose, small eyes and thin lips, but when she smiled her face lighted up like a candle in dark-ness. She lived with her father and family in one of the cottages.

Una, of course, got her to school. She was bright, she said. A quick little brain. She answered to affection as if she were starved of it. Before Dualta could say anything, Una caught the little girl by the hand and led her to the door.

"Just go to your place, Finola," she said. "I will be with you. You are all right now."

She watched her down, closed the door after her, leaned against it and said: "Little Finola is pregnant."

"In the name of God what are you saying?" he exclaimed.

"I didn't want to believe it," she said, "but it's true. How low, how beastlike can people become?"

Dualta had to sit on a stool. He put his head in his hands,

tried to think. Of people like the Mogues. By May or June their potatoes would be finished. They would have their turf cut. So they would put the latch on the door and take to the roads, during what men called the hungry meal months. They would wander and beg and work where they could get it, the mother for fourpence a day, the children for their food. From June to September the whole land seemed to be swarming with beggars, living in the open or in squalid suburbs near the towns where they erected makeshift shelters, nearly a million people living on the verge of starvation until the tubers grew and swelled in the ground and they could tramp home again and dig their potatoes.

"It cannot be," he said. "You are mistaken. There are ugly ways they seek to live but not this. It is not so."

"It is," she said. "We have to face it. They went away in June. She spoke of her father. He is fond of drink. She spoke of money passing. Of grass under trees. Of funny men smelling who did things to her. She doesn't even understand. She cried out. Her father said it was all right, all right. You hear that! Her father. He should be killed. He should be killed slowly. If I was a man I would kill him. I would flay him to death. Oh, Dualta, I cannot stand this. This is too much. That child!"

He rose to her. He held her. "Easy, easy," he said patting her, but he had a cold feeling in his stomach. This child. Great God! "I'll do something, Una," he said, at last. "Leave it to me. I'll do something."

"What can you do, Dualta?" she asked. She was furiously rubbing her wet eyes. "This is something for which there is no cure. This is final. How do you tell Finola what's wrong with her? How do you explain?"

"Leave it," he said. "For a time. I have to go to the town. I will see her father. I will be calm. I will bring no weapon. You cannot take the whole world on your back. This is terrible. But it will resolve itself. We'll find a way. It does something for me. It makes Clarke seem less important."

"This is the day then," she said. "I forgot. I should be with you. I cannot think. Let God go with you. Don't lose your temper with Clarke. That's all. We can't afford it. But now it seems to me that the whole valley is smudged. What is the use of trying? A thing like this. Is the world filled with monsters?"

"No," he said. "Most people are good. You have to think of the good people. If it wasn't for them God would have the world wiped out long ago. Stay here for a while. I will go. You see, you are doing good. Think of all the fine young people you have turned out from the valley school. Finola's father was not a pupil of yours."

"I will go down," she said. She wiped her eyes with her palms and the sleeve of her gown (6/–). Here was his mind turning again on costs. Cloak 9/6, three shifts 3/9. Aprons and handkerchiefs she made herself like all the other things. Just the price of the stuff. In dress she was no longer a lady, just a lady in her face, that was maturing like his own settling into the groove of life, being carved benevolently by the years. He put his hand on her cheek.

"You are a wonder," he said. "Don't suffer too much over it."

She went ahead of him. There was a scurrying as some of them ran back to their places. A louder hum from the spellers. Dualta walked out. He patted Finola on the shoulder as he passed. A thin shoulder, a child just coming into bud. He felt his jaws tightening with rage as she smiled up at him. An unaffected smile. Her small teeth were sharp-pointed. They gave her smile a peculiar charm.

"Be good scholars," he said, and he went out the door. He went for the pony.

He saw what Una felt, the smudge on the valley. Although the sun was shining on it, on the harvested fields, on the wet rock mountains, on the sea, it seemed that it had been smudged with a dirty thumb. Yet it was nothing, one little girl among millions. Who would care? They would say high up: Well? Is this the kind of people you want to be free, selling their own daughters for the price of a drink in a tavern? Ignorant, illiterate, dirty, unscrupulous, wallowing in enjoyable wretchedness. He thought of Flan's picture, of benevolent chieftains, ruling a clan, every member of which belonged, important. This was a dream of nostalgia. It probably wasn't like that at all. It was why people believed or pretended to believe in fairies, or listened to stories of giants who could do impossible things. All you wanted was to find a crock of gold at the end of a rainbow, or from the hidden store of a small green cobbler. Then your troubles would be over. All afflicted people would turn to a dream world to get away from the harsh reality of bleak oppression, of helpless wretchedness.

In the town he felt he hated them. They roared and shouted and sang, chapmen and bakers and buyers and sellers, a deafening noise arising from them. This was in the mass. You had to look closely at each separate face then to see that they were not like the sound of them. Friendly, kind, cruel, brutal faces, and the brutal faces would probably belong to kind people and the kind faces to brutal people. Flan's silent people indeed. And yet he knew what he meant, that the louder they were, the more silent they were. They would shout to hide themselves.

He paid his compliments to Clarke's brother-in-law and to his fat frightened wife. Frightened because by a strange chance Cuan was there at Clarke's house with him, Cuan and Fiacra McCleary, a stocky youth with very fair hair and blue eyes. Cuan was thin. The ferocity had never left his face, but he could smile. Dualta didn't see him often. He was running Moran's place better than the dead man had done it. This won the wonder of everyone in the valley. But then he had married Sabina. People said they didn't sleep together. There were no fresh children. Dualta could believe this. If Cuan had decided to do a thing he would do it with dedication. If he married Sabina it would be to protect her name, he thought. Since Moran died there had been no upheavals in the valley.

"We do not see you, Dualta," Cuan said.

"Who sees anyone?" Dualta asked. "Life is too hard. Unless we bury the dead or bed the wed, we do not meet. Will we have time to meet then when we are old?"

"If we have life," said Cuan. "Fiacra, pay the little gentleman five shillings. That's necessary. It's a sort of bribe, but it is as well to go with the customs of the people."

"Now, McCarthy," said little George Shields.

"He has his eye on your place, Fiacra," said Cuan. "There is nothing between his getting of it except your life. You must remember that. You must stay alive for his funeral."

"Now, now, McCarthy," said George. Dualta laughed.

He went and handed his box of eggs to Mrs. Clarke. "I do appreciate it, Mister Duane," she said. She was the only one in the valley to call people Mister.

"Here's a hen, ma'am," said Fiacra. "It is a young hen. My mother sends it with her compliments."

"See how polite the boy is, ma'am," said Cuan fixing her with a cold eye that made her shudder.

"Well, well," said Clarke, leaning back in his chair when he saw Dualta.

"I know you have been waiting for this for ten years," said Dualta. "Another day it would have mattered to me. It doesn't matter now, Clarke. Here is your money. You can play with me. I haven't time. I have something to do."

"You know that I could put you out of the place tomorrow?" Clarke asked.

"I do," said Dualta. "I also know that there would be trouble in doing so. I don't want trouble. I know that I am a hard worker, that I have brought something from nothing. But I am at the greatest strain to make it pay. If I cannot make it pay, nobody else will. You know that. Your money is safe from me. But don't stretch me too far or there will be no money."

"I like straight talking," said Clarke. "You people don't understand my position. Private property is sacred. It must earn. It cannot lie fallow. The estate must pay, or Sir Vincent will get an agent who will make it pay. Probably a meaner man than I am. You will be a tenant at will."

"No lease?" asked Dualta.

"No lease," said Clarke. "You have had your lease. You made a nice house out of the Bacach's place. There was no rent on it in the lease. Now we will settle for three pounds rent on the house. I won't increase the rent on the land. I think I am being decent. Now that the tithes have been put on the landlords we will put a rent of two pounds ten shillings spread over the eight acres. This will take care of the tithes you used to pay. So you will have to find five pounds ten shillings extra. This is not a great burden."

"So we lost the battle for the tithes," said Dualta.

"No, you won," said Clarke. "Didn't you know? Parliament have abolished the tithes. They have put the burden on the landlords."

"Who put the burden on us," said Dualta.

"But you won the battle," said Clarke. "The people will always prevail. O'Connell won the tithes battle, didn't he?"

"I have to accept your terms," said Dualta. "I can't do anything else. It will take finding, all this. It represents the earnings of one hundred and forty days extra. Do you know that?"

"Hard work never killed anyone," said Clarke. "You have no family to support. It's not like as if you had."

Another time, Dualta might have hit him and destroyed everything. Now Clarke sardonically watched the white on the knuckles of his fists. He knew tenants at will could not afford displays of temper. He felt that he had won a measure of respect from the disrespect of this independent stranger.

"That's all, Duane," he said. "I'll see you next gale day." He called. His face clouded when he saw Cuan and young Fiacra coming into the room.

Dualta left. He breathed hard outside, and then, recovered, he went into Donaghue's shop. No change. Mail day crowds, smells of spirits and spices. The only change was young Mrs. Eamon Donaghue sitting on a high chair at the far counter. Once Margaret Bradish. They knew she was going to marry Eamon when Mrs. Bradish came in her carriage to the school and in front of the scholars and much to their delight, told the schoolmistress what she thought of her. She had lowered herself to marry a common spade man from Galway. Was it any wonder that the valley was infected? Her own daughter Margaret announcing that she was marrying the son of a merchant. Margaret had told her mother if she didn't get her permission she would live with him in the open (more to Eamon's dismay than his mother's, Una thought). So they were married and the only one who really suffered was Tom Keane who had to drive many weary miles to the next town for provisions, since Mrs. Bradish wouldn't deal with the commoner who had captured a queen. Maybe old man Donaghue suffered too. Margaret reigned in the business like a queen. She was improving everything, including old Donaghue. Sometimes he was proud of his son's bride, but other times he wished he had married the daughter of a tinker or a tailor.

Dualta thought of all this as Margaret treated him distantly. Oddly enough she seemed to be more of a snob now than when she had sort of cause to be one.

So he left there and loaded the pony, tied him in Donaghue's yard, and grimly set off down the town toward the cottages to seek out Mogue, the father of Finola.

He answered greetings mechanically. He passed his way through the mobs of people almost unconsciously. Where the houses of the town gave way to the clustered cottages near the sea, he paused. The cottages were built like flies in summer swarm around the eyes of cattle. But between the town houses and the cottages there were four better-type houses near the road roughly walled off with slab rocks. He paused, then went into the second of these. At the door he called: "Sheila! Sheila! my darling, are you within?" There was a pause and then a shout of glee and Sheila O'Connor erupted from the house, threw wet hands about his neck and kissed him.

"Dualta! Dualta!" she said holding him back to look at him and then kissing him vigorously again.

"Hi, hi, hi!" Dualta exclaimed.

"Are you finished fondling my wife, Duane?" said the man who came to the door behind her.

"Come in! Come in! Come in!" said Sheila, "we'll boil an egg."

"Is it a cuckoo's egg we'll give him then?" her husband asked.

Dualta laughed. He went in. Three children swarmed around him calling "Dualta! Dualta! Dualta!" Dualta raised them and kissed them, and said, "You might find things in my pocket." So they screeched and put their small hands in his pockets and pulled out the few boiled sweets that always rested there. It was the mark of a childless man they said, always to carry boiled sweets in his pocket for children.

"We are pleased to see you, Dualta," said Sheila. "So pleased. How are they all in the valley?"

He thought: What a relief to see happiness. He looked at her husband, a tall, very dark man, dark hair, dark eyebrows, always looking unshaven, with a thin handsome face and a lithe body. He was the son of the cobbler, Mac an tSiuneara, just that. His name was Tom Walsh but people rarely used his name. He had kidnapped Sheila a few years ago. Farmers did not like tradesmen. They did not like their children to mate with them. So one night poor Carrol O'Connor came home to find his daughter gone and a letter from the cobbler's son saying he had taken her away as he loved her, and if Carrol gave his consent to their nuptials she would be returned to him intact. Usually the farmers consented. Even if she had not lost her virginity, how would you ever be sure? But not Carrol. She was his favorite child. The loss of her like that was a terrible blow to him. But he did nothing. He did not give his consent. So they were wed without it, and they settled in this small place in the town. Cobblers could earn about one shilling and sixpence a day if they were good cobblers, and Tom was, but the better you made the shoes the less call there was for your services and in summer most people used their bare feet anyhow, so they found it hard to live, but as he looked at them, he realized that hardship was as you made it. The house was neat and clean; the children, two girls and a boy, had only playing dirt on them. The few years had matured Sheila, but had not hurt her gaiety. Tom was kind. He was an athlete, a great runner and jumper. She fell in love with his long legs, and his face like a black donkey, she said when she saw him running at the parish sports meetings or playing mighty hurling in the fields.

"My father? My father?" she asked. "How is he?"

"He has not come to see you then?"

"No. No." She was sad for a second. "God is good. What brings you? You will eat with us? How is Una?"

"I'll not stay with you," he said. "I have a mission. I am seeking a man called Mogue. Can you tell me where to go?"

"Oh," said Tom, "he is a bad one. What business have you with him? You better seal your pockets."

He wouldn't tell them. It should be told from the tops of houses so that people would beat him and drive him away. But what about Finola herself? No. People must not know.

"We like his daughter Finola," he said. "We want to know if he will let her stay with us for a while."

"That would be good for her," said Tom. "Do not despair. You can buy her from him for sixpence. He is a drinking man." He spat in the ashes of the fire.

"Let me go so," said Dualta standing. "I will come back again."

"No, no, no," said Sheila.

"No, no, no!" said the children holding his legs.

"I am jealous of their affection for you," said Tom. "Leave him be, children. He has a mission."

"But you will come back," said Sheila, holding his arm.

"Don't I always come back to you, Sheila?" he asked.

"Such talk," said Tom.

"I saw her before you," said Dualta. "Let me go. I swear I will come back. Not today, but another day. Visiting you is like clover fields in the summertime or the warm wash of the cleansing sea."

"You must, you must come back," Sheila said, as they went to the door with him, holding on to him, the small jaws of the children bulging with the hard sweets.

"I will be back," he said, "as sure as God."

He got away from them. Tom walked a piece of the road with him.

"There is something moving you, Dualta?" he asked.

"Yes," said Dualta. "It will pass. You are happy, man. Hold your happiness. You have something precious."

"Sheila aches for her father," said Tom.

"One day he will come," said Dualta. "Just men are very severe on themselves."

"I want nothing from him," said Tom. "He must know that."

"If he searched the world," said Dualta, "he could not have found a better son-in-law. One day, he will know."

"You turn into the second lane," said Tom pointing, "and go first right and first left and the dirtiest and most smelling house is the one of Mogue. Come to us again."

"I will," said Dualta. "Your happiness refreshes me."

"God bless you," said Tom, and watched him go into the lane. The houses were thrown at one another. The dirt ways between were muddy and smelled vilely of pigs and the dirt of dogs and the leavings of humans. Most of the houses wanted re-thatching. They were green with moss and decay, and the walls were stained green. Few of them had chimneys. The smoke came out the open doors, along with screeching chickens chased from the houses, so that the women could come and look at the stranger, their heather brooms in their hands. Many children sucked thumbs as he passed. Very poorly dressed, almost naked, extremely dirty. How had a flower like Finola come from such a place? One or two of the houses were well kept in the midst of the general poverty. Whose fault? They lived on a few roods of potatoes, a few days' work during the year. Made enough to pay an exorbitant rent on the patch of land and the terrible houses. Sometimes they rarely saw an actual penny. They used their labor to pay their rent and when that ran out, they took to the roads, like migrating sparrows. Whose fault? They rarely blamed God.

He found Mogue's. He recognized two children sitting on a dung heap. They had the odd sharp features of Finola, the big hungry eyes.

"Is your father within?" he asked them. They just looked at him. They didn't answer. He went to the door. He was standing in a puddle of mud. The place was wreathed in blue smoke that made his eyes ache. It was dark. The two openings in the walls were deep and narrow without glass or stuffed rags. "God bless all here," he said. He waited for a word. He didn't hear any. A sort of grunt perhaps. He bent his head and went in. There was a man sitting at a badly made table which was merely a potato cish standing on a three legged pot. His eyes were the part of him most easily visible. The rest was a mat of tangled hair, tangled beard. He was a big-bodied man covered in places with old, oddly patched clothes. He was eating potatoes.

"You are Mogue?" Dualta asked. He had to rub his aching eyes with the back of his hand. They started to stream.

"Sit down," said the man. He had a deep voice. Dualta felt wood behind him. He turned. A woman was holding a stool at his knees. "Thank you, ma'am," he said. She was a thin-faced woman. Her face was grimed from the smoke. "You are welcome, sir," she said in a small voice. Dualta had never been called "sir" before.

"Eat," said the man Mogue, waving a dirty hand at the cish of peeling-littered potatoes.

"I thank you. I have eaten," said Dualta.

"You don't like our salt," the man said.

"I will eat a potato," said Dualta, taking one and starting to peel it with his nails. "You have good potatoes."

"New," said the man. "What do you want? You are the man of the Mistress?"

"Yes," said Dualta. "It's about Finola."

"She is bold, hammer her," said Mogue. Dualta saw that his eyes were red-rimmed, from smoke, and the whites bloodshot from drink. He was a most unprepossessing man. How could he be the father of Finola?

"She is good," he said. "Will you let her stay with us?"

"Keep her. She is yours," he said.

This reply maddened Dualta. He had been holding on to his temper. He knew the people. The poorer they were, then the more precious were their children to them. It was always the way. When you could create nothing else, to create a child of your own was as precious as discovering a jewel in a turnip field.

"She means so little to you! Would you sell her then? If I offer you sixpence for her will that be enough? Is it so little she means to you?"

"Don't insult me," said the man. "What is under you?"

"You!" shouted Dualta. He was standing. "Have you no feeling? Are you an animal. What have you done to her? You took her away? What did you do to her? Are you human? You take her away and sell her body to a tinker for the price of a glass of whiskey. How many? May the great God rot you! May the worms eat you! May the pigs feed on you!"

The man Mogue kicked the pot and rose to his feet. He was very big. He was nearly touching the roof. He hit Dualta in the face with his two fists held in front of him. Dualta went down in the dirt and the man fell on top of him. His breath was fetid. His clothes smelled. Dualta was smothered. He heard a cry from the woman. He wriggled from under the great weight of him, grabbed the stool he had been sitting on, and raised it up to bash the man on the head. The woman's voice stopped him. "No! No!" she said. Dualta lowered the stool. The man lay on the floor. He turned over on his back. "He is drunk," she said. "He does not know what he is doing."

She bent to him. Dualta put down the stool and helped her. They put him sitting on a stool. He leaned back against the wall, his big head lolling.

"You will come outside," she said. He went with her. He breathed the outside air into his lungs. She was rubbing a sack apron to her eyes. He couldn't make out if she was crying or if it was the smoke. The two children kept looking at them.

"You will look after Finola," she said. "God reward you. Here is no place for her."

"You know what way she is?" he asked.

"No, no, no, please God, not that, not what you said," she said. "It cannot be. Just to look after her. She is a good girl. She will work hard for you."

He looked at her. She was very thin. She was a young woman but very old beyond her years. What was the use?

"All right, ma'am," he said.

"He was a good man," she said. "You must believe. We were put off three years ago by Cringe. He wouldn't send the children to that school. So we were put off. We had to come down here. He was a good man. His place was fine. He lost his heart. He was a good man, a good man."

Who is good? wondered Dualta. Who is good? But he still wanted to kill him. He wanted to tear him to pieces. He took two half crowns from his purse. "These are for you," he said, "for you. Not for him. You hear?"

"God reward you," she said. "God reward you." He felt in his pockets. There were four boiled sweets remaining. He gave two each to the children. They looked at them a long time before they shyly took them. They sucked them then, and their faces lighted up with pleasure.

He turned and left. Mogue would probably get the money anyhow, he thought. But what did it matter? The day was still smudged. The palms of his hands were almost cut from the way he clenched his nails into them. But it was good to feel the clean air from the sea blowing on his face.

When he got home Father Finucane was sitting on the seat under the thorn tree. Dualta went over toward him. The priest's head was in his hands, and it was only when he got near to him that Dualta knew the priest was crying. He looked up then and saw Dualta. He turned his face away as he reached for a handkerchief. Dualta sat beside him.

"It is good that you have tears," he said. "I saw her father."

"Did you kill him?" Father Finucane asked.

"No," said Dualta.

"I would," said the priest.

"No, you wouldn't," said Dualta. "He has stopped being human."

"You work and you work and you work," said the priest. "So much goodness. So much humor. Hardships borne smilingly. A thing like this is beyond comprehension. It wounds the world."

"Una! Una! Una!" Dualta called. They watched. She came to the door. The girl was with her. "Come over here with you both," he said.

They came; he took Finola's hands and pulled her between his knees.

"Your father wants you to stay with us, Finola," he said.

He saw her breast rising and falling fast. He felt the clasp of her small hands tightening on his own. "He does?" she asked. "To stay with you? Always or for now?"

"It will be for always," he said. "If God is good. Your mother wishes you to stay with us. Will you be able to abide us, do you think?"

"Oh, yes, yes, yes," she said.

"This is a gift," he said, taking the satin-dressed doll from under his coat. "It is for you. I got it at a stall." It cost three shillings and ninepence out of his tight stores. It was worth eight times that sum to see the light in her face. A girl expecting a baby, overjoyed by the possession of a rag doll? This is the world. He looked at Una over the top of her head.

"We have a daughter," he said. "Not a son."

"He will come," said Una.

Father Finucane stood up.

"You are blessed," he said. "I will not go near the cottages for a year. I have not your patience. You are a better man than I am, Dualta."

"That is a plain lie," said Dualta.

"God bless you," said the priest, and walked away.

God was good. She didn't carry the embryo, so she didn't know, and Dualta had a daughter, and a spoiled daughter she became, but Una longed for a son, and she got him at a peculiar time.

chapter XXVI

FATHER FINU-
cane spent the
Friday night at
Maynooth. He had
been several days on the road, feeling guilty at leaving his parish
even though he was a sort of official Repeal Association em-
issary from the valley. He hadn't had a holiday since he was
ordained. He felt like a schoolboy released from school, jogging
on his horse to Dublin. It was October and the harvest had been
good and nobody talked about anything but O'Connell and the
great monster rally that had been called at Clontarf on Sunday
next. Men said it would be the greatest meeting until the Last
Judgment. O'Connell had called thirty-one great meetings between March and August. Each of them was bigger than the last.
The one at Tara in August was still spoken of with awe. From
thirty miles away on the western road he had passed thousands
of people who were on their way by foot to Clontarf, their silken
banners rolled, camping cheerfully in fields and ditches, singing
and dancing at night by the campfires. He had thought the hosts
at the Clare Election were big, but they would be nothing to
the crowds that would be gathered at Clontarf.

He stayed with his friend Father Pat in the college. He greeted
him joyfully. They had been in the same ordination class together. They could talk over many things, past times and
what had happened to all the men who had been ordained with
them.

It was a bit of painful nostalgia to see the old corridors, the
old lecture rooms, to think of the fire of fervor, the heated dia-
logues, wanting to convert the world overnight; the sad awak-
ening, growing old. He saw his own age in the features of Father

Pat who was a lecturer. They smoked pipes sitting on leather-covered chairs in the book-lined room.

Father Pat was filled with O'Connell.

"Yes, I was at Tara," he said. "And it is true about the crowds. If you said a million people you would be near the mark. There wasn't a coach or carriage or four-footed beast left in Dublin. If you could stand on the mound at Tara you couldn't see a blade of grass with the bodies of men, women and children. I have never seen anything like it. Never will again. There were people stretching from Tara to the Hill of Slane, I declare. Bands without number, banners, bunting. It was a riot of color. It was unforgettable."

"How did he take it?" Father Finucane asked.

"He is a master of mobs," said Father Pat. "There isn't another man living in the world who could handle a million people. It's just amazing. He is sixty-eight and he looks young. Standing up there his voice reaches out to the horizon. He plays tunes on the spines of people, like a great fiddler. He tells them this is the year of Repeal. We will get Repeal. We will get our own Parliament back where it belongs, the one that Pitt stole from us forty-three years ago. They believe him."

"Will he get it?" Father Finucane asked.

"No one else will," said Father Pat. "He is ruling Ireland. Such a master of symbols. Tara of the Kings. It belonged to the High Kings. They feasted there, called the great fairs there for hundreds of years. Here was O'Connell standing on Tara. As far as the people were concerned he was their descendant, crowned and all. And Clontarf. You see. That was where Brian Boru won his great victory over the Northmen. This is where Daniel O'Connell is going to win his great victory over Peel and the Englishmen. How can any Government ignore the moral pressure of a million people gathered on one place saying, We want Repeal? Before they said: We want Emancipation. They had to get it. Since the beginning of history there had never been peaceful pressure like this brought to bear on a single subject. I tell you, I am a fairly cold analytical man, and there at Tara I felt myself burning, and all without bloodshed. That will be his great strength if he succeeds, that he succeeded without bloodshed."

Later some of the young students came and sat on the floor. They reminded Father Finucane of his lost youth.

"O'Connell is a bluffer," one young redhead said. "If I was Peel I would call his bluff."

"Man, listen to the politician," one jeered at him.

It heated the redheaded one.

"Who wants a Parliament back like it was before?" he asked. "What good was it to the people only to pass laws repressing them, and feathering their own nests. A bunch of unprincipled scoundrels is all they were, social criminals."

"Oh, oh, oh!" they called him.

"It's true," he said. "You get nowhere with soft words and bluff."

"He has been reading *The Nation*," another one said.

"Why not?" he asked. "Davis is a better man than O'Connell. O'Connell is gone soft in the head. He won't be contradicted. The Young Irelanders are the ones for me, building a national ideal, with power instead of blather."

"Listen to him! Listen to him!" they said, and piled on top of him, smothering him, laughing and tumbling until Father Pat put them all out.

It was a nice interlude. Father Finucane was sorry in the morning when he had to leave. Yes, he would come back again, sometime. When would sometime be? Pity, he thought, as he looked back once, that you cannot always remain behind those sheltering walls, loving the theory, not knowing the reality. Talking your head off, settling all the affairs of your country in an evening's passioned oratory.

The people were piling into Dublin. I must remember all that I see, he thought. I will be questioned so closely sitting under the thorn tree. He crossed a bridge and went his way by the Liberties near St. Patrick's. The thoroughfares were filthy here, the tall delapidated houses jam-packed with people. They lived, he saw, in the most appalling poverty. Thousands of children were playing in the gutters, dogs barking, draymen cursing.

Was there a difference, he wondered, between the poverty of the small towns and the poverty of the great towns? It was only in towns of any size that you saw why the country was called a nation of beggars and O'Connell was their king.

He went up the good shopping street. Here were carriages and coaches and liveried footmen, sellers calling wares, and beggars, little children pulling at his gaiters. He had nothing for them. His pouch was empty. He was getting by on charity himself. So all he could give them was his blessing. Into the Green with its fetid stench where the people discarded rubbish and dead dogs in the trench surrounding it. Coming to the house of his friend near the Church. Thinking of them all: Father Pat, Father Joe who had sent him Una, Father Pete, Father Mike. And here was Father Phil.

Wide-eyed. "Fin! Fin! Where did you come from? I thought you were dead."

"Not dead," he said laughing, "I'm in Clare."

"Same thing," said the Dublinman. "The culchies will be the death of you. Come in. I'm so happy to see you. And why are you here?"

"I am here for Clontarf," said Father Finucane going in with him. He had tied the horse to the railings outside.

"Oh, man, this will be it," said Father Phil. "It will be the greatest day in history. Have you been at any of the great meetings at all?"

"I was at Ballycoree," said Father Finucane. "Repeal Police, white staves in their hands, ribbons on their hats. Great order. People in parishes and counties. And no drinking. That's what makes you think the people are so serious. Whoever heard of ten thousand Irishmen together and not a drop of whiskey between them?"

"It's a wonder, man," said Father Phil. "Father Matthew came at the right time, but even if he hadn't, they wouldn't. They listen to O'Connell's voice. If he said, Take the country with your bare hands, they would do it."

"You are all for him, then?" Father Finucane asked.

"He is the greatest Irishman that ever lived," said Father Phil.

"Now I got my answer," said Father Finucane laughing.

They were not properly in the house when the great knocking came on the door. It was very urgent knocking.

"At this time," said Father Phil. "Sit down and wait. I will be back."

He went out of the room. Father Finucane sat on the arm of a chair. He had hardly seated himself when he heard himself being called. "Come down! Come down!" He went. Father Phil was taking off his soutane. There was a big man with a ribbon in his hat standing at the door. Father Phil's face was pale.

"Peel has proclaimed Clontarf," he said.

"It's not true!" said Father Finucane.

"As true as day," said the man. "They are calling it out with the handbells. The posters are going up."

"I will have to go over to the Hall," said Father Phil. "Will you come? What will O'Connell do?" he asked.

"He will let the meeting go on," said the man. His jaw was hard. "Will they massacre a million men?"

Father Phil gave orders for the horse to be brought around to the yard and then they hurried away through the streets. It was not far. There was a tremendous babel of noise arising. They saw one of the notices going up. So that was true. And they heard the bellringer calling it, so that was true as well.

Father Finucane was glad of Father Phil. The Repeal Police at the Hall knew him. They let him through. Thousands of people were milling around outside now. They were calling for O'Connell. Inside, the stairs and the passages were jammed with sweating men. Their faces were red. They were angry. They were bewildered. The man pushed a way through for them. The police at the door to the room opened it for them and they were inside. There were not many there. O'Connell was facing them. He was pale. Father Finucane was shocked at his appearance. He had his hands behind his back. Why, he thought, the man looks his age. He was ringed by men. They were hitting the table with their hands.

"He cannot get away with it," they were saying. "They daren't fire. We can match them."

"How?" O'Connell suddenly shouted. That silenced them. He spoke in a lower key. "They have brought in thirty-five thousand troops. The Martello Towers are fortified. There are three men-of-war in the Bay with their guns cleared. On Clontarf they have the 60th Rifles and the 5th Dragoons; the 54th Foot and the 11th Hussars are on Conquer Hill. They have the Royal Horse Artillery with four six-pounder guns unlimbered and ready for action."

"It's bluff," a tall thin man with a fierce moustache shouted at him. "There are Irishmen among those soldiers. They will never fire their guns on other Irishmen. They will not kill their own."

"They have killed their own before this," said O'Connell. "They will do it again."

"You must not call off the meeting!" the man said.

"I am an old man," said O'Connell. He stopped as if he was listening to what he had just said. His body sagged. He sat into a chair. "I am an old man," he repeated. "In a terrifyingly short time to come I am to meet God. It would be easy to be a hero!" He shouted this at their faces. "I could say, Come! and they would come. They would walk into the mouths of the cannon. I could die with them. It is a wonderful picture. I would live forever. It is a great temptation. Can't you see that? It is a great moment. But I won't face God with the blood of innocent people on my hands. Make what you will of it! That is all. Call off the meeting. Send men out on horseback to every road. Turn them back. Just turn them back."

"So Peel has won the victory over you," said the tall one with a terrible taunting.

Father Finucane watched him fascinated. Peel and he. The one he had called Orange Peel, "his smile is like the glint of the plate on the lid of a coffin," he had said. The patient Peel who had been willing to wait long years for his revenge.

"He may have won a battle," said O'Connell, "but he has lost the war. What is the alternative to me? Did he think of that?

Leave me alone for a while now. Just leave me alone. Later I will talk to the people before I am arrested. He will have to do that. He can't have one without the other."

Father Finucane thought he would never forget O'Connell's face as it looked at that time.

He told them all these things sitting under the thorn tree.

"He had the greatest opportunity of any man in history," said Cuan, "and he rubbed his name out of the books talking like a pious old woman. Even if a thousand had been killed, wouldn't it have been worth the sacrifice?"

"He wouldn't think so," said Dualta.

"I don't think you understand, Cuan," said the priest. "Many mistook his attitude for fear. It will be long debated. I don't think he was ever greater than at that moment. His decision was worthy of a great poem. Do you think so, Flan?"

"No," said Flan. "He was not the voice. How can you raise a million people to the stars and then dash them down? He was not worthy."

Flan rose from the seat. He spat on the ground and walked away from them softly humming the song of the sons of the King. They listened to him until they could hear him no longer. Their mood was as depressed as the fog in the valley.

"He has a point," said the priest. "How can you raise the hopes of the people so high, and then dash them? There has to be something to fill a vacuum. There are angry voices writing in *The Nation*. They say they are Young Ireland."

"Their voice has a truer appeal," said Cuan.

He rose too and walked away.

"O'Connell had nearly won him," said Dualta.

"O'Connell is in jail," said the priest. "When he comes out he will die. He has left too much undone, unraveled. Explosive material."

"Only God knows what will happen," said Dualta.

"It's His mystery," said the priest, rising.

Shortly now, the mystery was to be revealed.

chapter XXVII

YOU CAN PURchase satisfaction in a field. Why do men till if there is no satisfaction? It cannot be expressed. It would be foolish and a cause of laughter to say: I love the flowers on the potato stalks. Who would not laugh if you said that a healthy potato field is like a poem, a song, a painting, a cathedral? There is creative satisfaction and a sense of frustration attached to all those things. But the potato field has an added quality—you can eat it. You cannot eat a poem or a song or a cathedral. Life would be empty without these beautiful things, but you could survive without them. If your belly is empty, then you will die, so in a way, a potato field is of higher cultural value than a poem or a song or a cathedral.

Dualta was laughing at these fancies as he jogged home from the town on the pony. His head was slightly light. He had been drinking whiskey, for Paidi the smith had pulled a back tooth out of his head. Dualta thought it had not been too bad. Thinking about it had been worse than the actual thing. It had been an admirable strong tooth with a root like an oak tree, said Paidi, as he waved it in the pincers. Dualta had to drink whiskey in order to stop the bleeding and to restore feeling to his legs which had been shaky. He kept putting the tip of his tongue back to feel the empty space in his jaw, tenderly. Getting a tooth pulled like that made you feel you were really getting old, he thought. Part of you was gone from you forever. As you got older and older, he supposed, more and more of you was pulled out or fell out.

The men had laughed at him, but it was the sort of protective laughter that paled when he reminded them that one day, they too would have to pay a visit to the forge, not to get shoes on their horse, or to get an iron band on their wheel, but to have a strong tooth pulled from their jaw with an iron pincers, the Lord save us. Drink up there, for God's sake, and we'll have another one.

For it was a beautiful July day. This was remarkable. This year had been one of the strangest any of them could remember. They were used to rain, but not the kind of rain they had, that sent the grass growing hip-high. One week it would be clammy weather with the clouds down on your head. It was like living in a baker's oven. Then next week there would be hailstones and you would be shivering with cold. This happened in June. It was remarkable that there was not much wind. In the valley they were used to wind. You cursed it but you missed it when it was not sweeping up the valley so that you could taste salt on your lips. And now here was a day that was scalding hot, almost burning. The heat in the forge from the charcoal had been unbearable so that the operation took place in the street outside to the awe, sympathy and laughter of the people. People didn't mind the hot sun. They were sick and tired of the awesome rain clouds that seemed to depress the spirit and portend evil.

Going to the town he had remarked on the potato fields. He had said it to the men, what a great crop there would be this year. Since most of their food depended on the crop, everyone was pleased with this and said even if the weather was depressing it was great for the crops, all the warm humidity. You could hear the tubers growing below the ground, they said, and it was as well. By Garlick Sunday, the first of August, last year's crop of lumpers would be uneatable, and the meal months would begin.

He was pleased with his own fields. He thought how you cursed the back-breaking labor. A week to bring seaweed and sand from the shore, and burnt lime from the kiln, digging, manuring sparsely from the dunghill at the stable, the careful cutting of the seed and the way the planting of them with the stihín or the dipple stick made the muscles of your back ache.

All that hard labor, that seemed it would never end, but you knew that one day the fields would be as they are now, that your labor was not in vain.

He was near Carrol O'Connor's when he was disturbed by the smell. First he thought it might be from his mouth. The smith had held the tooth under his nose when he pulled it and said: Smell that now. Smell the decay of it. You are well without it. Dualta could have murdered him.

What he smelled now was like that. But it couldn't be. Mists always rise at evening from wet land after a hot day. It was happening now. It was bright, only eight of the clock, but this smell seemed to be rising from the ground with the mist. He sniffed around him. It was the smell of decay, like an unburied animal, say? Some people were careless with dead dogs, but then that couldn't be it either. You would smell a dead animal just passing it by. You would close your nostrils for a few minutes and when you opened them again the smell would be gone. Now he tried this, but the smell remained. He was suddenly very disturbed. He looked at the road all around him. The road was clear. There was nothing dead under the hedges of fuchsia and blackberry all coming heavy with fruit. He went to an opening in the hedge where a field was barred off by the road by withered thorn bushes.

He looked in here. He wondered what strange crop could have been grown in the field. He smelled. The stench came from the field. He left the reins of the horse tangle in the thorn bush and went into the field. It was a sloping field overlooking the valley.

He examined the crop. He didn't want to believe it. He had passed this way in the morning after all. It was a potato field then with blooming flowers. Now it was nothing. It was a brown soggy mass of corruption. The whole field. He wouldn't have believed it was potatoes but here and there a green stalk still stood, but the green leaves were being devoured with brown spots, like animals, like locusts eating into the green, fouling it with the touch of their breath. He looked down then. Everywhere there were potato fields the brown corruption was resting, only emphasized by the odd few stalks that stood green and pitiful in the welter of decay.

He felt his stomach go cold. He shook his head. Maybe it was the whiskey. He bent then. He scooped under the rotten stalk, and scrabbled with his hands, feeling for the tubers. His hands were wetted and sticky with a glaucous substance that couldn't be potatoes. He was on his knees then. He scraped at the rich ground. He tore up a yard of it. The potatoes were rotten. There were one or two muddy white little balls looking forlorn, in the middle of the wet stickiness. He stood up. This was the field of Carrol O'Connor. He went out to the road again. He untangled the reins from the bushes. He mounted the pony. The pony felt his disturbance. He danced on the road before Dualta could control him, then he galloped up the hilly road until they reached the turn off to O'Connor's. On all sides of him was the smell. The fields were brown. The oats stood tall and green in a terrible comparison, the hay was cocked in the fields. He raced into O'Connor's yard.

He didn't go any farther. Carrol was there in his shirt sleeves and Mrs. O'Connor and Carrol's son, a good young man of solid build like his father.

Dualta pulled up. They looked at each other.

It was Carrol who said the word. "You see it?" he asked. "It is the blight. It is over the world."

Dualta looked at them with his eyes wide. What could he say? All over the valley by now, men would be out looking, staring, at the fields. He turned the head of the pony and he went away. For he was thinking of his own fields climbing the hill. They were high up. They might not have been hit. They were up in the clear air. He cut across the fields before he reached his house. He kept his eyes half closed. He thought, surely, surely they are green. The pony was laboring. He was kicking him with his heels, leaping the stone walls.

His fields of potatoes were a brown mass.

He had to sit on the wall, his hands between his legs saying: "No! No! Oh, no! This is not so. This cannot be so." The pony cropped the after grass of the meadow with joy.

Hearing distant calling, he raised his heavy head. Tiny figures on the top of the rocky hill, waving, calling. That was Colman and Finola. Another time he might have worried about Finola seeing so much of Colman, a ragged young man; you could use him as a scarecrow, the hair on his face never shaved since it started to grow, a wispy fair beard. He has songs, said Finola. Such songs. He dances like a goat on the stones. He makes me laugh so.

He saw Una near the house. She waved to him. She started toward him. He couldn't bear that. He mounted the pony, having to drag his muzzle from the soft green grass and he went down to the house. Gaining time, he took the reins and bit from the pony and turned him into the field behind the house. He heard her calling then: "Dualta! Dualta!" He thought how funny it was that he still got pleasure from hearing the sound of his name on her lips.

He ran from the back of the house by the gable. She was running the other way. He stopped her. "Una!" he said. "Una!" He thought she must have seen, that she was as coldly fearful as himself. But to his surprise there was joy in her face. Her eyes were alight. She came running to him, with her arms wide. He had to spread his own arms to hold her.

"Dualta!" she said. "Oh, Dualta! Now you know! Now you can know. I knew. We are going to have a child. You are going to have a son." She put her head on his chest, squeezed his body with her arms. He tightened his arms around her, looking over her head at the blasted fields which had not got her attention. He turned her toward the house. Let it wait a time, he thought. Let there be joy in my heart instead of fear.

"O, my woman," he said, "you have picked a wonderful time for a noble deed."

"You are pleased, Dualta?" she asked. "Say you are pleased? Say the long waiting has not made you sad?"

"Oh, I am pleased," he said. "Only God knows my pleasure. You have left me without words. I love you with all my heart. You are the most wonderful person who was ever created."

Lighten my heart, he prayed. Please lighten my heart, for now your long-awaited child will be born in the middle of a famine.

It takes only three weeks to starve. This is for the poor. Dualta knew this. That was why he was on his way to the house of Finola's people. You have a little oats growing as well as the potatoes. Fine, but you can harvest only one quarter of that, or draw one quarter of your turf from the bog. You are forbidden to move the rest until you have your rent paid in September. The landlord requires a mortgage on your ability to pay. Clarke hired extra stewards to see that only a quarter of either was harvested before September. The oats and the pig paid your rent. What did you feed the pig on if you had no potatoes or offal? If you weren't wise enough to kill the pig and eat him, he would die. They were very susceptible to cholera. Then you could eat a diseased pig before you were evicted. It was the law. It was legal. You may have thought it unjust, but you understood it was the law. How could the world function otherwise if things weren't paid for? You grew cabbage. That was good. So you ate boiled cabbage. Or turnip boxty called champ. This was mashed turnips mixed with the roots of fern or dandelion. This and also boiled crushed roasted leaves of dock sorrel. Put in nettles and you had an exotic-tasting dish. You could go at night and steal a pint of milk from the udder of a richer man's cow, or you could nick a vein in an animal's neck and extract a quart of blood. You could cook this with mushrooms and cabbage and you had a dish called relish cake. This did not last long because men with cows or cattle took to housing them at night or setting a guard on them, or selling them off altogether before they were bled to death.

Then you could turn to the sea for the fruit of the shore, seaweed and shellfish, and later on as other sources dried up, you could cook snails, frogs, hedgehogs baked in clay, and after that crows or blackbirds which you picked from the hedges at night with a light to blind them. But even the birds became cute. Later you found that your strength was not as good as it was, and that a journey to the shore to search for bairneachs or cockles or even seaweed was wearing on your strength. So you took to eating what they called laughingly the scadan caoc, or blind herring, that is, one that wasn't there but existed in your imagination. And all the time, in the poor cottages by the sea, their determination was to survive until the spring, find some seed for the planting of the new crop of potatoes, hang on somehow and next year would be all right. Eat anything, anything at all. Some of them took to the roads, as they had always done in the meal months. Some of them weren't strong enough. They had to stay. Some of them went into the poorhouse in Ennis, hoping their strength would stay with them until they reached it, even if death was there.

For you can survive on nettles and dandelions and seaweed, grass, roots, as long as you have the strength to look for them. If you are not struck by the fever. No famine, no fever, they said. Dualta found the fever.

He had Carrol O'Connor's horse and cart. He had been many miles to the mill for the last three days. Three-quarters of his oat crop he had sold raw. From this money and what he had got from a calf, he had enough to pay his rent. For himself he had four sacks of oaten meal. They were hidden in the cart. There was turf loaded on top of them. Besides his own four he had one belonging to Carrol O'Connor that was to be delivered to Carrol's daughter. He didn't like any of this. He kept his eyes fixed on the fat rump of the horse. He had to force himself to think of his own needs and his dependants. He didn't let his mind think of next March, another gale day, where they would find the rent, the money for new seed. That was tomorrow. Let us survive until then.

In the town he noticed the emptiness of the streets, the closed doors. He wondered at this. Many of them had locks on the doors. The people were gone.

Not Sheila. Not yet. But she was going. He stood and looked at it. It was bare. Tom was on his knees tying the neck of a sack. Sheila was tying a ribbon in the hair of her eldest daughter.

He said, "God bless all here!"

They turned and looked at him. His heart sank. The eyes of the children were big with hunger. Sheila wasn't plump. The face of Tom was cavernous.

"You are welcome," said Sheila in a subdued voice. She was not exuberant. She did not run to kiss him.

"Your father sent me with some meal for you," he said.

They looked at each other.

"Tell him," said Sheila, "to give it to somebody who really needs it. We are going away."

"Where are you going?" he asked, his heart falling.

"We are going to America," she said. "Tom sold all his tools. We sold the furniture we had. Most of the clothes on our back. We are walking to Galway to get a ship. We have our oatcake. We are beholden to nobody. We are taking the emigration."

"Your father doesn't know," he said.

"It won't worry him," she said. "He didn't know we were here. We could have died. All he cared about is his two-life lease and his eldest son. He will be happy to know we are away from his conscience."

"Don't say that," said Dualta.

"Take the meal to the cottages, Dualta," said Tom. "I hear there is fever down there. They need it. See, we are happy to be leaving it all behind us. It is death to remain. Who wants new shoes or mended shoes? It is better to go. This is a miserable land."

"You won't win it by leaving it," said Dualta.

"Who wants to?" said Tom. "It belongs to them. You cannot snare a rabbit, cut a tree. You cannot even own the fresh air."

"Things will change. They won't change if everybody goes away," said Dualta.

"Don't be mad, Dualta," said Sheila. "Everybody will die. I don't want my children to die."

"People have died on the American ships," he said.

"We won't," said Sheila. "We won't."

"Won't you go and say goodbye to your mother even, Sheila?" he asked.

"I tried," said Sheila. "They are afraid of the fever. She had to talk to me from behind the closed door."

There was nothing more for him to say. The change in them was a symptom of the change in the land. People were hungry. They were afraid. You had to look after yourself. Who would do it for you if you didn't? Wait until next year. Just hold out until next year. He felt like crying. That was weakness induced by hunger, because he was on low rations himself, counting every bit that went into his mouth, watching Una, her growing body, making sure that she got more than she knew.

He left the cart near the cottages. They were all silent. Smoke was coming from some of the chimneys but all the doors were closed. There was a terrible smell about the place.

He stopped outside the door of the house of Finola's father. It was closed. He tried the door. It was bolted from the inside. He called. There was no reply. He turned and went to a house where smoke was coming from the chimney. He banged on the door. "Where are the Mogues?" he called. "Tell me where are the Mogues?" There was a call from the house. Then a woman's voice spoke. "Go away, amac," she said. "We have the fever. Go away!" He pulled back from the house.

Then he went back again to the Mogue place. He looked at the door. Suddenly he put his shoulder against it and pressed. It was frail. The door opened. He was in the kitchen.

They were all dead. All four of them. The turf fire was out. There had been a pot on the fire. Its contents had been burned black. The two children and the father were on the straw. The children were heads and points. Their limbs and faces were black, their lips drawn back from their teeth which were white. The father was naked from the waist, his body a mass of purple marks. The woman was lying on her face near the cold fire. She had her hand stretched out to the pot. He turned her. Her face was yellow and purple. He was back again in his terrified youth with fever and dysentery and scurvy; Irish ague, bloody flux, with all its symptoms and its smells and its appalling terror. He was tempted to light a fire and burn the whole place, bodies and all. He didn't. He lifted the woman. She was as light as a feather. He placed her by the side of the children. Then he left the place and ran out. He didn't take the cart. He ran.

Outside Father Finucane's house the people, women and children, rested their backs against the wall, or sat on the ground, listlessly, the row of them went from the road to the open door.

He was there.

He was measuring meal. To each person three pounds of meal.

Dualta stood away from him and called. He looked up.

"Come," said Dualta. He left the measuring to the blacksmith who was there. "No more, no less," he said. "I'll watch it," said the smith.

"The Mogues are dead, the four of them," said Dualta.

"Oh, no," said the priest.

"It's the fever," said Dualta.

"God spare us," said the priest. "They are the first."

"There are more of them in the cottages," said Dualta.

"What can we do? What can we do?" the priest asked. "I have sold all I possessed. The only thing left to me are the sacred vessels."

"We will have to bury them," said Dualta. "If we leave them over the ground more and more will get it."

"Leave it until night then," said the priest. "I will get a grave dug. We will be wanting graves. Nobody is doing anything. Don't they know what's happening? Don't they know it's a disaster? What's going to become of us, Dualta?"

"I don't know," said Dualta. "I will go to the carpenter. I will get some coffins made."

He did this. The coffins weren't dear. The carpenter was making cheap ones out of inferior timber. He had the wit to know what was coming.

Nobody came near them. The priest and Dualta put them in the coffins with their own hands. They carried them to the cart. Dualta drove the cart and the priest walked in front saying prayers from his book. It wasn't an Irish funeral. Where were the banners and the slow march of the wailing pipes, the jammed mourners? The people watched them from behind closed doors.

The smith and the carpenter filled in the grave while Father Finucane prayed. It was moonlight, so they could see. Afterwards, Dualta went to the sea, and he washed himself in the cold water. He was afraid. Was he to bring home the breath of fever? Was he foolish to have done the things he had done? He scrubbed his hands with sea sand.

They were waiting up for him.

"You are safe then," said Una. "You were so late. We were afraid?"

"I am all right," said Dualta.

"Did you see them?" Finola asked. "Did they get the meal? How is my mother?"

"They did not get the meal," he said. "Many people have gone away. They have gone away." He put his arm around her thin shoulders. "They are well away," he said. She would know soon enough. They had the distinction of being the first to die.

chapter XXVIII

He was dig-ging the last blighted area in the potato field. Behind him Una and Finola worked. It was early December and it was very cold. The ground was hard. It was slow digging for him. He felt that if the ground was turned up to the frost, and not left until the spring, that the blight in the earth would be turned away. If blight came from the ground. No man knew where it came from. Over the few months in half an acre they had gathered a basket of not altogether blighted potatoes. They were not good, but if they were grated, soaked in water, and the bad matter skimmed off it could be made into a sort of boxty bread—if a handful of oaten meal was added to it. It didn't taste good but it might ward off scurvy. Men knew that potatoes kept scurvy away for some reason. Many people were suffering from scurvy. If they got scurvy and the fever they couldn't live. They called it blackleg because when you were dead your legs were completely black up to the middle of the thigh, your teeth had fallen out and your body was covered with blood blotches.

He rested on the spade and looked at the two in his care. They didn't look too bad. Finola was very thin and her eyes were bigger, but Una looked less drawn. That was the cow and the milk. Now the cow was dry and would not be giving milk for a few months. The cow would have to be giving milk when his son was born. He was aiming for that, varying her diet of hay which was all they had with a few turnips which they wanted themselves, some roots and herbs from the hill. She was a spoiled cow, but she was necessary for their life.

He told himself: They will live. Una will have my son.

From the hill behind they heard the thin sound of the singing.

It was like a call of a bird from a great distance. Finola's head came up at once, a pleased light in her eyes, her pointed teeth showing in a smile. Then she saw Dualta looking at her and she dropped her head in confusion.

"Why don't you take a walk up the hill, Finola," said Una.

"Will I do that?" Finola asked.

"Do that," said Una. Finola looked at Dualta. He smiled. Then she rose and brushed off the front of her heavy skirt and set off up the hills walking slowly, pausing to let the breath settle in her breast. It would take her a long time to climb the hill, but there he would be huddled in the sheep shelter, waiting for her, wondering if she would come.

"Don't worry," said Una, looking at Dualta. "He treats her like a precious china cup, or a songbird with a wounded wing. There is so little light left in the world."

"It's just that you have become attached to her," said Dualta. "You don't want anything more to happen to her. She is frail."

"Nothing will happen to her from Colman," she said. "Listen!" The thin sound seemed to be part of the frost air. Una hummed. She sang the Irish words to the lilt of the old melody.

"I found a bird in the hazel tree
O sing, sweet bird, so sing for me.
I will shelter you round with ribbon and string
From the blight of the night and the hawk
    on the wing
In my breast you will rest like the child
    of a king,
So sing, little bird, o, sing, sing, sing!"

"They are too young to know what is on top of us," said Dualta.

"They are as well off," said Una. "Soon enough they will know."

He spat on his hands. He finished digging the ridge. They looked at the basket with its light load. If you didn't know better you would think you were looking at a dozen lumps of earth.

"We'll go down," said Dualta. He helped her to her feet. "You feel well?" he asked. "You don't feel tired? Is your head clear?"

She laughed. "Don't worry, Dualta," she said. "I will not die. Everything is going to be all right. You must believe this."

"I believe," he said. He put the spade on his shoulder. He carried the basket in his other hand. She held on to his arm. They walked down slowly. He could feel warmth coming from her. Her face was flushed. He wished with all his heart that suddenly, as quick as a thought, he could transport her to a safe valley of lush land where there was no blight, no famine, no death. Was there a place like this anywhere in the world.

"O," he said, "if only you knew what you were letting yourself in for! If only you had sense at the right time."

She laughed at him.

"If only you had remained single," she said. "You could be far away. With nobody to care for. Are you sorry then for your marriage bargain?"

"You know," he said.

Father Finucane was sitting tiredly on his horse in the yard in front of the house. They stopped when they saw him. Then they walked over toward him.

"Don't come too close," he said. "I have been with the dying again today." As he saw Dualta's face hardening, he turned the horse away from his approach. "If you don't think of yourself, think of Una," he said. That stopped Dualta.

"I had the fever when I was a child," said Dualta. "They say it does not hit you again."

"Did anybody come back from the dead to prove this?" the priest asked.

Una thought back to the day she had first met the red-haired priest. He was so different. He had gone speckled white the way red-haired people do. He was very thin. His stock was loose on his neck, the hands that held the reins were all bone.

"You want me?" Dualta asked.

"Yes," said the priest. He dismounted from the horse. He stood away from them. "Something will have to be done, Dualta. Things are very bad."

"I would give my life," said Dualta, "to stop it all."

"As of today," said the priest, "there are ninety-seven dead in the parish. They don't seem to care. Governments move slowly, I know. There is a Relief Committee founded. No priests are allowed on this committee, so how is the true tale to be told? There is American meal being sent on American ships. Depots are being set up. There is not one in our town. Soon, they say, soon. You hear? They cannot sell this meal, until all local supplies are used up. Then it must be sold at the price prevailing in the district. Where will the people get three shillings for a stone of meal? If you own any land at all, you are not supposed to be poor. The poorhouses are crowded. They are dying like flies there. You cannot get into the poorhouse if you are a tenant of land. The Board of Works is setting up task jobs. When will they be here? Soon, soon, they say."

He took a newspaper clipping from his pocket.

"In the Government, they speak of us. One fellow says that the famine is not as bad as the Irish members make it out to be, that they are shamelessly exaggerating for low political purposes. Here is what a Royal Duke says: 'I understand that rotten potatoes and seaweed and even grass, properly mixed, afford a very wholesome food. We all know Irishmen can live on anything, and there is plenty of grass in the fields even if the potato crop should fail.' You hear. Many people in England are pouring their pennies into a Famine Fund. None of this has reached us. Dualta, we have no voice."

"What can I do? Who would listen to me?" Dualta was shouting.

"O'Connell would listen to you," said the priest. "You must go to him."

"But he knows, he must know," said Dualta.

"He knows," said the priest. "But you must go to him. You must tell him to talk louder. It's no use talking from Kerry. He must go to the place where his voice will reverberate. Why isn't he going there?"

"They say he is sick," said Dualta.

"He must drag himself on one leg," said the priest. "We will be wiped out, Dualta. Before the new crop of potatoes comes in next July at the earliest the most of us will be dead. There is no help for us. The Bradishes have locked up and fled. Clarke has pulled into the big house. You cannot approach them. You must do this, Dualta."

"You think too big of me," said Dualta.

"Once a week a carriage comes in from outside," said the priest. "They set up a soup kitchen in Cringe's school. This is Friday, so they make meat soup. You see? So none of the people go. Because it is Friday and it is meat soup. The Quakers are coming, they say. They are good people. But not yet. They haven't come yet. We have to have a voice, Dualta. You must go. Let him write a letter, anything. But you must go."

"I will go," said Dualta.

The priest relaxed. "I knew you would," he said. "You will want sustenance on the way. Here are two shillings. This will buy your food. It is a long way." He saw the face in front of him. "You are a rich man, then? You have stores of money hidden away? You do not need this humble subsidy? You are proud?"

Dualta dumbly held out his hand. The two-shilling piece landed in it.

"You are just part of something, Dualta," said the priest. "I am writing letters to the papers, to the Grand Jury, to the magistrates, to the landlords. We are at the end of our own resources. If we do not get help then we will all die." He was back on the horse.

"If you don't take it easy, you'll be dead for sure," said Dualta. "Will you be of use dead, Father Finucane?"

"I won't die," said the priest. "There is too much to be done." His teeth were clenched.

He turned away from them. He waved a hand, then he slumped down in the saddle. He was like an old man.

Dualta was looking at the ground. His hand was clenched on the two-shilling piece. Una was watching him.

He said: "There are cracks in your shoes. Tonight I will have to mend them before I go." She looked at her shoes.

"I will bake oaten cakes for you," she said.

"Only one," said Dualta. "One will do. You must be careful. Don't let people in. Keep the door closed. You have to shut your heart. They might bring the fever. You will promise this?"

"I will be careful," she said.

They walked toward the house.

The pony was strong. He had hay to eat. There was plenty of hay along the road. There were few animals left to eat it. The people who moved on the road were like walking skeletons. He had to stop his eyes sending messages of intelligence to his brain. They were all on their way to the towns or the poorhouses, unencumbered by anything except their tattered clothes. They had already sold their best clothes to buy food, their blankets, shoes, furniture, anything at all. Peddlers with their four-wheeled carts were gobbling all the raiment in the land. The warehouses of the pawnbrokers were bulging. He couldn't stop remembering the time he had traveled this road to the Clare election. Think of the bands and the banners and the songs and the great jollity and the cooking fires. It was a terrible contrast. He had to let himself think of that much. Now there was only the silence of shuffling bare feet on the frostbitten road. Feet raw and thin, dirty and red with the burn of the frost, and they were without greeting. This was a terrible thing. They didn't look up at him. Their eyes never came farther than the lively body of the pony. Were they thinking then how nice a chunk of the pony would be boiled in a pot? Some men were carrying old women on their backs, walking a few paces, stopping, going on again. Some men were wheeling their thin children in turf barrows.

He galloped the pony, and then he stopped galloping him, because it seemed to him that he was disturbing this silence. He longed with his whole heart for this thin stream of shuffling people to be ended. But it was never-ending. A free mile and then there would be more.

He was near the town when he saw the man and the woman and the three children. The woman was supporting the man. The children were holding onto her tattered skirt. In front and behind there were no others. It was coming toward evening. The sky was a pitiless steel blue and there were white banked snow clouds on the horizon, being tinted with a fiery heavy red color.

He got off the pony. He didn't greet them. They looked at him from their enormous eyes. He took the man from the woman. He was no weight. His breath on Dualta's cheek smelt of the smell he knew so well, the smell of the shrinking stomach. The man would have been big one time. He had big bones. Dualta got him on to the horse. He put two of the children in front of him and the other behind him. The pony was restless. Dualta went to his head and led him. The woman was by his side. She had no words. This is the worst thing about it, he thought. It has brought silence down on us.

When they could see spires ahead of them they passed a turnip field. In the fading light he saw movement in it. Then he saw it was covered with people. They were standing or sitting or squatting. They were eating the raw turnips. The field had been pulled. They were eating what had been left, some soft with frost, some half eaten by birds or rats. All you could see in the sunset was their eyes as they stopped to look at the people on the road. Some of them were nearly naked. Dualta hurriedly moved on.

It was that way to the town. Every turnip field had squads of people gleaning it.

He knew why when he got to the poorhouse. There was no admittance. The man there held the gates shut. There were hundreds of people lying and sitting and standing along the walls outside the gates. Their faces were lighted by the yellow glow from the glass light at the gate.

The gateman was loud and he was fat. Dualta would always remember that about him. He was so fat. No! No! No! In the morning. Not now. In the morning when they counted the number of the dead. Could you put a gallon into a pint? It can't be done.

Dualta heard a voice say: "They have a coffin with a bottom on a hinge. They drop you into the pit and they can use the coffin again." Tomorrow! Tomorrow! Tomorrow!

He left his people by the wall. Into the woman's hand he placed the two-shilling piece. She looked at it listlessly. What could you buy with it! How long would it stave off the inevitable?

He went away. It was dark, but he had to get away from the town, as far as he could, as far away, wishing that the pony could grow wings and take to the air, so that you could see nothing, nothing, nothing at all on the ground.

By the light of the moon, he found an empty house with a sagging door, black within. He didn't go in there. He found the garden haycock. He pulled hay for the pony, and he pulled some for a bed for himself. He took out his oaten bread, but he couldn't eat it. In the morning I will eat, he thought. In the morning. He pulled his coat about him. He was thankful to sleep.

He went in the long avenue, the back way. He had shaved himself at an icy mountain stream. He was so cold that he had dismounted and walked. He had had a feeling that by the time he reached Darrynane the cloak of the Liberator would have thrown an invisible and magical protection around his own land. It was not so. He had seen unburied bodies. In one deserted village he had found a man who had died crawling toward the graveyard. In another house he had found a dead woman who had succeeded in burying her husband and two children in the dirt floor of the place before she died. His inclination had been to stop and bury the people, but if he did that he might spend his whole life at it. His brain was numb. He felt that he was empty of all emotion. He wondered what he was doing this for or why, or what difference it made.

He tied the pony and walked toward the kitchen door. It reminded him of long ago, of the house of Una's father. There was no great difference. The yard and the out-offices and the servants' quarters and the carriage houses and the cooking quarters. And around the front the carriage drive. There would be a pleasant library looking on the sea and the mountains.

He knocked at the door and nearly fainted when it opened and the smell of cooking came to his nostrils and made his stomach ache. He had to bend forward to stop it.

A woman stood there, a plump woman with a soup ladle in her hand. "Well," says she. "I want to see O'Connell," he said. "I have come from far away."

She snorted. "Have you indeed? Well you can go back the way you came. He is not seeing anybody. He is not a well man."

"I am staying here until I see him," said Dualta. He said it politely.

"Are you now?" she asked. "We'll see about that then!" She went back and called: "Party! Party!" She turned to Dualta again. "Now we'll see how long you will last," she said. Dualta waited patiently. A man came into the kitchen. He was the very big man they had met on the mountain with O'Connell long ago. But he had been dusted with years. He stood in front of Dualta, towering over him. He said nothing. Just looked at him, bent forward. "I have seen you before." He spoke in Irish. "Yes," said Dualta. "You were chasing hares." The man shook his head. "I cannot remember. But your face I do. What do you want of himself?"

"I was sent from Clare by the priest to talk to him," said Dualta. "He is not a well man," said Party. "Come in!" Dualta went into the kitchen. "You," said Party to the woman. "Pour the man a bowl of soup while he waits. I will see. I begin to remember you now. It is long ago." He went out another door. Dualta looked at the soup pots.

There was a long scrubbed table.

"Sit down," the woman said. He sat at the table. She ladled out soup from the sweet-smelling copper pot. She placed it in front of him. He kept his hands under the table in case she would see them shaking. The smell rising from the bowl was almost overpowering. She cut off a chunk from a wheaten loaf and put it there too. Slowly he brought his hands from under the table. In one he took the big pewter spoon and in the other the bread, and he forced himself to eat slowly, slowly.

She was watching him, a thin-faced man with fine eyes, and his tied hair growing gray at the sides. A handsome fellow if you liked them, lithe, she thought. Maybe dangerous. She hadn't liked the firm way he looked at her. He thought it might be a dream that this rich meat and vegetable soup was going into his stomach. He thought of them at home, how they would appreciate this. He thought of the many thousands who would literally give an arm or an eye for it. If he kept thinking that way he wouldn't finish it. So he finished it, slowly, carefully.

Party came back with a woman. She was a low-sized woman with brown hair. She was plump. He wondered at how you noticed plump people now.

"Have you had fever?" she asked.

He paused.

"No," he said. "I am free of fever." She blushed under his gaze then.

"We have to take precautions," she said. "What was your name?"

"Dualta," he said. "He might remember that."

"I'll see," she said. She went out. Party sat at the table.

"Things are bad with you?" he asked.

"Things are bad with everybody," said Dualta.

"That is true," said Party. "Wait until the O'Connell is his own man again. He'll make things well. We must have patience."

"We have nothing else," said Dualta.

"Is it bad abroad?" Party asked.

"It is death abroad," said Dualta.

"Aye, aye," said Party rubbing his thick thatch with a large hand. "Wait until the O'Connell is well. He will wipe it all out."

They sat there thinking until the woman came back.

"All right," she said. "Not for long. He is expecting people. You must not tire him."

He didn't answer her. She was uneasy with him. She turned

and walked. He followed her. He walked carefully on the polished floors. He had rubbed his shoes with the bottom of his coat. He smelled of damp wool, and of good soup, he thought with pleasure.

They went into the room on the left. There were many windows. On the right the estuary and the islands in the sea. Ahead of him the looming mountains. There would be less smoke from the thatched cottages.

He was sitting in a big chair in front of the turf fire. He had a woolen thing around his shoulders. Dualta was shocked, as the pale, almost yellow face turned to him. He had been in jail. He was sixty-nine. Now he would be seventy. Before he went to jail he hadn't looked like this. He had looked eternal, Dualta thought, hearing of him before Clontarf. Being in jail and being freed by the Lords on appeal, the ones he had called the soaped pigs of society. Now he looked older than his years. "Come down!" he ordered. Dualta went toward him. O'Connell closed one eye to look at him. He smiled. The flesh was loose on his face. That was the thing about him that was lost. He had filled himself. Now his jowls were loose. There was a slight shake in the hand that rested on the chair.

"I'm glad to see you, sir," said Dualta.

He pointed a finger at him. It was the hand of an old man. The flesh was loose at his wrist.

"Dualta," he said. "You see. Not forgotten." He turned to the woman. "All right. He will not shoot me." Showing his yellowed teeth. "Go!" She was going to protest. She didn't. She left. They heard the door closing after her. The walls were lined with books.

"You have trouble?" asked O'Connell. "The world has trouble. There is no end of it. You come from where?"

Dualta told him. About Father Finucane. About what was happening to them.

"All for Repeal," he answered. "If we had a parliament in Dublin, they would not let an ounce of food leave the country. You see. All for Repeal. I will get Repeal. I will get it. Without it we are dead. Like now. If we had Repeal would the oats be leaving the country while the Indian meal was coming from America? Socialism. You must not give something for nothing. I will make them see."

"You are going to talk to them?" Dualta asked.

"After the Christmas," said O'Connell. "You'll see. I feel. In here. How can I abide it? Along the coast they die. I do what I can. I am emptying my granaries. What I have. Like a spoonful of seawater to the sea."

"You will rouse them, sir," said Dualta. "You will rouse them, but soon, sir, soon."

"In 1800, I said it to them, at the Royal Exchange," he said. "Have I changed since? Have I said any different? I told them what would happen. Did they listen? They listened. Now that this happens, am I a prophet? No Repeal, famine, pestilence. It had to be. They should stop the ships. Feed the people. Forget famine. Forget rights. Forget finance. Anarchy, they say." He put his head back. His eyes were still blue, Dualta saw, but they were as if they had been misted over. The brilliance had been scraped away. To Dualta's eyes, this great man, this O'Connell had what the people called the smell of the earth from him. He was due for death. The very vague hope in Dualta's heart withered away.

Weak tears forced their way from O'Connell's eyes.

"There is only one for each person. I talk of a friend, of a companion of the soul, for a soul. Gone. She was Mary the name of the Mother of God. Where do you find balance, love, silence, restraint? I could have been Robespierre. Bloody! Agnostic! Filled with Paine." He chuckled now. Raised his head again. Dualta wasn't sure if he saw him at all, even if he was looking at him. "That is a pun. Rousseau, Voltaire, Hume, Paine, Godwin. Like racehorses in your veins. When you are young. Mountain torrents. Uncontrolled. Head in the clouds. Heart red with anger. But she saw. You take an idea from one and the other. The good ones. The moral ones. They do not understand God. All good ideas come from God. Like a good stew, these are mixed, you see, and the evil parts skimmed away. She could see. So she goes and there is a deep hole at your feet. You will be buried. Is there use in going on? Only for Repeal. Hauled back from the sea of sorrow. For that. Noble."

He leaned forward. He was looking at the blaze in the turf fire, unseeingly.

"I am in a grave. Before they close this grave, they will come and spit into it. The others and my own too. These rash young men. They are wanting in guile. They are wanting in wisdom. They will not learn. Let them listen to me. I held back the tide. With my arms. I held back the red tide. I am building barricades of peace. You have to see this. Repeal is the last gap. If this is filled, then there is peace. It is the damming of the tide. Will they break my arms? If they do, who will be there? I have stood like the Skelligs. Can they see this? I have baked a cake. Where is the leaven now? Who will savor salt?"

He put his head back in the chair again. His eyes were closed. There was sweat on his forehead.

Dualta rose to his feet.

"I will go now, sir," he said.

O'Connell nodded. He did not open his eyes. Dualta thought that he was nodding to a speech in his own mind. He took one last look at him and then he walked out the door, turned right and went down the long corridor and into the kitchen. He didn't look at the people there. He walked into the yard. He took his pony and he mounted him. And he was crying. For what else could he do?

See this man towering on a platform, the strong planes of his face lighted by torches, alive, vibrant, the golden voice propelling words that sent shivers up your spine.

He was sorry he had come. There was no hope. Now the people were really on their own. The voice was silent. It was weak and dying, it was ten, twenty years too old, and the black horseman could ride unreined.

chapter XXIX

WHILE DU-alta rode the long road home, he was impressed by the great silence. No dogs barked. People did not eat their dogs. They drowned them. They had to do this, because in their hunger the dogs became vicious, or they started to eat unburied corpses. The two sounds you would always associate with the land, the bark of the dog and the crow of the cock, were no longer to be heard. He would always remember the silence. It was so profound that he could not have heard anyhow the sound of the other horseman who rode ahead of him.

For ten days, Finola had left her chores to go into the yard at the back and look up at the hill. Sometimes she brought knitting with her and faced up the hill while her bone needles clicked. She could not stay too long. Her limbs would become stiff with the cold, even cutting through the blanket she wore around her. No tall figure was seen on the hill. She heard no shrill song.

Una would say: "Do not worry. He is all right. He is doing things for his father."

"I suppose so," said Finola. "He would not be sick, you think?"

"You would know," said Una.

They had not much to do. The school was closed. Who could study on an empty stomach? Some of the children were dead. Una didn't want to think about this. So all they had to do was look after the cow and cook their measure of meal, keep a bright fire burning in the hearth, spin a little wool saved from the sheep they once owned, six of them, that had been sold. So they had time on their hands to watch the roads. Una watched one and Finola watched the other while they knitted gray-white woolen garments for the small body of the son of Dualta, ready for him when he came. Una was sure that he would come, that he would be a son, and that he would need the woolen garments.

Finola saw the column of black smoke rising in the frosty air one morning. There was no wind, so it was like a black finger poking into the merciless hazy blue of the cold December sky. Her heart started beating fast for some reason. The smoke was rising from the direction of Colman's house. It needn't be his. There were many poor houses in the folds of the rocky fields up there. It could be from the house of Flan McCarthy, but she thought that would have been a little higher and to the south.

She went into the house. She caught Una's hand. Una came with her. "Look!" she said pointing. "What is that?"

Una looked at it. Who would be burning in December? What would they be burning? Later on, the bog lands were burned so that the green sedge would grow better for the sheep. Or men burned land if they were carving a new potato field from the heather. The hand Una held was trembling. "I am afraid," said Finola. By now, Una thought, we should be saturated with fear. There should be no more fear left in us.

"Go and see," she said. "You will not be satisfied. Go and see."

Finola left her. She kept the column of smoke in her eye like a beckoning beacon. She crossed the fields of Dualta's land and got into the wild reaches of rock. She paused often as she climbed. They were nearly always hungry. She realized this. They were living on oatmeal and that alone. Two times a day. One potato would be better. It would put strength in you. There were no potatoes. There was cold sweat on her forehead. She had to pause and lean on a rock, panting. Little by little she made her way to the top of the hill. Then she looked down. She had to hold her arm against her breast to ease the racing of her heart. Because it was Colman's house and it was burning.

She got her strength back and she ran down into the valley. She had to climb another hill then, a shorter one, and go into another valley and climb another hill. Each valley held a mountain stream. They were not spated. They were partly frozen.

She came on the last hill, and the burning house was at her feet. There was a man sitting on a stone looking down at the house. She closed her eyes, and opened them again. A ragged man. Ragged hair, ragged clothes, the breeches torn, the feet bare and cracked with the frost. His head was hanging, and his long thin hands were listless.

She got on her knees beside him.

"Colman," she said, "O, Colman!" He turned his face to her. Her hand was on his arm. His eyes were red from weeping.

He looked at her as if she were his enemy.

"He is there," he said. "I piled straw around him and I lighted it from the coals of the fire."

"It is your father?" she asked. "O Colman."

"It is my father," he said. "Eight days he took to die. He withered in my eyes. I brought him roots and little birds. I stole two chickens from the big house and eggs. I milked a cow. It was no good to him. My father died."

"You should have brought him the priest," she said.

"Did they care for him?" he asked. "They did not care for him. They made him live alone. They took from him what they wanted and they did not like him in return. They will not come near him when he is dead. He has a fit grave in the flames. He will belong to the earth."

"Colman, please, Colman," she said.

"They do not know," he said. "He was a good man. He was abrupt. My mother died on me when I was born. He brought me from that, like a baby rabbit. Sometimes he hit me, like you would for good. He had silent laughter. He knew the sky and the birds. You think he had no love in him. He loved my mother. Life went out of him when she died. He looked a dark man without feeling or wit. He was not. To me he revealed himself. My father is gone and the world is empty for me!"

He buried his head in his arms.

She put her two hands on his arm. Tears were easy in her eyes.

"The world is not empty while somebody loves you," she

said. "It is when nobody loves you that the world is empty and
you are better dead." It took a little while for this to reach his
mind. He turned his head and looked at her, a girl with straight
dark hair and a thin face. You would say a face without beauty.

He said: "You are like a bird. Sometimes you have a face
like a hare. You know that, or a little creature, or a likeness
made from hazel twigs, or a reflection of a cloud in a bog pool."

"I am a girl," she said. "I have a soul and a heart. I would
give all I possess, which is only my life, to save you from suffering. I am sad I did not know your father."

"I will tell you of him," he said.

"Come home with me," she said, rising to her feet.

"You have no home," he said. "Now I have no home either."

"I have a home," she said. She said it with a little anger.

"Is charity a home?" he asked.

"No," she said. "A heart is a home. Has Dualta no heart then
or Una? Are they monsters? Do they gain riches by loving me
and loving you? But for them, would I ever have met you?
Would you have sung songs to me?"

He rose to his feet abruptly.

"I will go with you," he said. He looked down at the house.
The flames were coming out of the window and curling up to
the burning thatch. She caught his hand. She tugged at him.
He gradually came with her.

"I will sing no more," he said. "My song is dead."

She said nothing. She thought: You will sing again, Colman.
I will cause you to sing.

"I want to see the priest," said Dualta to Father Finucane's
girl. She was a virgin of about sixty and notoriously cantanker-
ous.

"Then you'll have to go to the graveyard," she said. She saw
the shock in his face. "No, no," she said, "he's not dead, yet,
but he will be if ye keep after him, mark me. He's gone to the
Carrol O'Connor funeral."

"Carrol O'Connor is not dead," said Dualta.

"His son is," she said. "Big funeral. Biggest since the deaths started. Rattle his bones over the stones, he's a pauper that nobody owns. Not for the O'Connors. Everyone else goes down in the famine pit."

He was not listening to her. He turned away. Which son, he wondered. Carrol O'Connor had shut himself and his family away from contagion. As if he was besieged. It had made no difference then. The fever had crept into his fortress. Dualta knew now that there was no keeping it out. He had seen big funerals of wealthy people on his way. All the trappings had been there, black coaches and widow's weeds, white handkerchiefs. At least they could afford dignified death. It was strange, like an anachronism, to see a real funeral.

He was horseback sore, so he left the pony and walked to the church.

They were coming out with the coffin when he got there, four men carrying it on two white sheets. There were not many people. The smith was carrying the coffin sharing a sheet with Cuan and Fiacra and Carrol's son Seán. That meant that Bercan was the dead one. Bercan was Carrol's eldest son. Bercan was the half of a two-life lease, he thought. Now there was only the life of Carrol himself to hold the lease.

He held himself straight, but his face was ravaged, he saw, as he came out of the church putting on his hat, Mrs. O'Connor and the youngest girl, Fiona. Their state was predictable. He couldn't help thinking how well nurtured they were in comparison to the thin haggard people who waited outside the walls to pay their respects.

They walked to the graveyard. It was not far. He was surprised at the amount of disturbed earth that was in it now. They were going to bury Bercan at a big stone that marked the resting place of Carrol's people. He helped them to let down the coffin into the ground. He could see the few rotted remains of the coffins that had gone in there many years ago. Mostly they were dust.

Father Finucane said the prayers. They knelt and said a decade of the Rosary. They covered him in. Nobody was talking. They were all avoiding one another's eyes.

Dualta went to Carrol. He took his hand. Empty eyes that focused and then settled on him.

"There was no need for him to die," said Carrol. His voice carried on the quiet air. "He should have stayed at home. He was going down to the town after a girl. You hear. He should have stayed at home. He was protected. He bought the fever himself then."

"Father," said his son Seán, "come on home."

"He was my eldest son," said Carrol. "He should have protected himself."

"Come home, Father," said Seán. "He is not himself," he said to Dualta.

Seán caught his arm, and walked him away. They watched him out of the place and then Father Finucane came and took Dualta's arm.

"You are back, Dualta," he said. "Tell us, did you see him?"

"I saw him," said Dualta.

"Did he send a thousand pounds for relief?" Cuan asked.

"No," said Dualta. "But he will talk. He is going over there to talk."

"One talk from him in the right place will be worth more than a thousand pounds," said Father Finucane.

"Can you eat talk?" asked Cuan. "Did you tell him how bad things are with us, Dualta?"

"I told him," said Dualta. "But things are bad everywhere. We are even a little better off than most."

"There are less of us to die," said Cuan.

"As long as he talks," said the priest. "As long as we got to him and he will talk."

"He will talk," said Dualta.

"Can the dead hear?" asked Cuan.

"I did what I could," said Dualta, suddenly angry. "It is a long way. I went that way. It was like a journey into hell. I can absorb no more sights. No more talk. I am sick of it, Cuan. Words."

"Let us do deeds then," said Cuan. "Let us band together and attack the grain carts. Will any of you do that with me?"

"You cannot cure a fever with the prick of a pin," said Dualta.

"You are tired, Dualta," said Father Finucane. "Go on home. It is Christmas Eve. Maybe in the new year they will move."

"Is it Christmas Eve?" Dualta asked.

"Yes," said the priest. They walked to the gate. They stood there. "I must go now and see Mary Greevy," said the priest. "She was Bercan's choice. His father did not approve of her. That was why Bercan had to sneak away to see her. Carrol didn't learn the lesson from Sheila after all. I do not know about people. Is Carrol grieved for the loss of his son or the loss of half his lease? I'm sorry. I shouldn't have said that. But the girl's heart is broken. Bercan would have got the fever if he was shut up in a glass cage. Go home, Dualta. You have our gratitude. You have tried. The day he speaks, the whole world will come awake to our plight."

Oh, no, Dualta thought, it will not, as he walked to the town. They will see this old man speaking in a cracked voice. He will have no command. They will greet him with a great silence. His thoughts will not be incisive. His magic will be gone. His enemies will gloat and the hearts of his friends will quail. But how could he say any of this?

"You have not much hope, Dualta," said Cuan beside him. Dualta looked at him.

"You look well, Cuan," he said. "You are eating well?"

"You reproach me?" asked Cuan angrily.

"You know I do not," said Dualta. "All your care is well?"

"They are all well," said Cuan. "They will stay well."

"The sorrow is gone out of death," said Dualta. "That is a terrible thing, that even death can become commonplace and you cannot share in the sadness of your friends. I look at Carrol and my heart is cold. I think of Bercan, and I do not cry. Isn't that a terrible thing to happen to us?"

"You were always soft, Dualta," said Cuan. "You spent more time thinking of other people than your own plight. Are you hungry? Have you enough food at home?"

"We are not hungry," said Dualta. "We have enough food. We can live until the next harvest."

"If you need," said Cuan, "I will give you what we can spare. It is even becoming tight with us and our forty acres. Don't be hungry, Dualta."

"No," said Dualta. "I must go into the shop. I didn't know it was Christmas Eve." They looked at the deserted street. "What this would be like on another Christmas Eve," he said.

"It will be again," said Cuan.

"Never again," said Dualta.

"We can make it," said Cuan. "If we were on our own we could make it."

"Is Flan well?" Dualta asked.

"We keep him fed," said Cuan.

"That is good," said Dualta. "For he would be a greater loss than any of the rest of us."

"Sometimes I don't know what to make of you," said Cuan.

"It is the lightness you get in the head in times of hunger," said Dualta. "I wish you a happy Christmas, Cuan, and all belonging to you. Next Christmas we will meet and we will talk over this one. We will rejoice."

"Let us live until then," said Cuan.

Dualta went into the shop.

It was changed. He knew that Caffar was dead. People said his funeral was the most notable of the famine. His son put him down well.

Eamon was taking no chances of the fever now. The counters were almost barricaded. Eamon peered at you through slotted timber. There was no contact. It was almost empty. His turn came.

"I want," he began, but Eamon looked away. He was looking down below where Margaret was, Dualta knew. She must have shook her head.

"Sorry, Dualta," he said. "Things are very bad with us. How can people buy when they have nothing to buy with? I cannot give you more credit. You have three pounds on the books."

"I wanted to pay," said Dualta, feeling his slim purse.

"You understand how it is," said Eamon. "And if they start giving out free Indian meal, where will we be? Don't we have to live too as well as the poor?"

"You do," said Dualta. "I want four ounces of Twankey tea. I want one pound of priest's sugar. I want six salt herrings. That is one shilling and elevenpence. Here is the money."

He pushed it under the barricade. He took his little parcel through the square hole. He wasn't even angry. He didn't care. He was thinking: Tomorrow, Christmas Day. They said: Two days in the year are good for the belly, Easter Sunday and Christmas Day. Because people ate meat on those days and they had tea and sugar.

"You understand how it is," Eamon was saying. "We are up to our ears in debt. Everyone wants credit. We have to pay for the things we buy." He was still looking for sympathy when Dualta left.

He forgot Eamon and Margaret as he started on the road out of the town. He was weary, but his heart lightened a little as he thought of Una and Finola. There would be a bright fire. The kitchen would be clean. He would have a real bed to rest on. His heart was bitter as he weighed the little purchases. But some people couldn't even have a salt herring for Christmas Day, he knew, so really if you thought of tea and sugar and salt herring with an oaten meal cake, in comparison to some they would be eating like kings.

They met him out in the lane. Una's arms were wide. She didn't care if the whole valley was looking at her as she embraced him. Una embracing him in front and Finola with her arms around his waist at the back.

It was a great pleasure. It was nearly worth going away. Her skin was as soft as rose petals. Her face was a little fatter from the baby she was carrying. He could get lost in her eyes and forget all he had seen. He could lose his sense of hopelessness in her courage.

They walked to the house. The pony trailed after them, nuzzling at Una's back, he feeling neglected, so they walked one side of him and he felt better.

"You must know," said Finola going ahead of him, turning and walking backwards as she spoke, anxiously looking at his face, "that Colman's father died and we brought him into the house with us."

Her head was on one side, like a sparrow, waiting for a crumb.

"I am sorry," he said. "Colman must be fierce sad."

"Oh yes, he is," said Finola. "His heart is broken. You do not mind because we took him into the house?"

"I do not mind," said Dualta. "I told him when he was a little boy that what we had belonged to him. I do not go back on my words."

"You are wonderful," said Finola. "You are a saint. You are a hero. I am pleased that Una married you. I will run and get him. He was inclined to fear when we saw you on the road."

She turned and ran away, skipping. Dualta had to laugh. He was amazed at himself. I am laughing.

"She is like a fairy," he said.

"It is good to hear you laugh," said Una.

He stopped. "I laugh because I am home again, and you are here and nothing happened to you," he said. "All the things I saw, I feared for what I might find at home. I am sad because I have nothing to give you. And it is Christmas. I did not even know this until I was told."

"You give me yourself," she said. "You are home. Now I am happy."

They were in the kitchen when Finola came back. Her eyes were bright.

"Here he is," she said.

Colman came in. He looked at Dualta. Dualta thought: Why this boy has become a man. Seemingly in the same ragged clothes in which he had first seen him. He was looking at Dualta as if he expected to see unwelcome in his face.

"I am sad about your father, Colman, I truly am," said Dualta. "I would be pleased if you would spend some time with us, until things are right again."

"Look what he has! Show them what you have, Colman," said Finola.

She held up his hands. There was a dead rabbit in each one of them.

"See," said Finola. "Now we have Christmas. Who will be eating rabbits for Christmas except us? Isn't Colman clever?"

Dualta laughed.

"Man, you are rich, Colman," he said. "We will eat like princes. You could get six months in jail for the two rabbits. You are a criminal. We will eat your sins."

Colman looked down at the rabbits.

"It was sad to kill them," he said. "I didn't really like to kill them. But it is Christmas."

"That's right," said Dualta. "It is Christmas, so we will boil the kettle and we will make tea."

"You have tea!" exclaimed Una.

"Yes," said Dualta.

"This will be a wonderful Christmas," she said. "I will boil the kettle."

They laughed. Why they didn't know. But they laughed. There is great hope in laughter. Even Colman's sad face broke into a smile.

chapter xxx

OUALTA LEANED against the lintel of the doorway and looked down the valley. Sometimes he moved his eyes from the valley to the figure of Una, sitting on the seat under the tree, knitting the gray wool. She was heavy with the child now. There was a shine from her hair. The March sun was unusually warm. He thought: Love is not what you imagine. It is like a seed planted in good soil, cared for and attended to. It will grow slowly like a hardwood tree. He thought: Each day that passes I love her more. Without her there would be no point in my life. He sighed. His breeches nearly fell down his hips. He laughed, thinking: I will have to put another notch in my belt or I will lose my breeches. He had given up thinking of the succulent things you could eat. That only occurred in the early hunger stages. Finola was standing out from him looking down into the valley. She was standing on one leg like a crane, the free foot wound around the standing one. She was chewing a blade of grass.

"You think Colman will find the peddler?" he called.

She looked over at him. She nodded her head.

Dualta laughed. "You are so sure," he said.

"Colman will bring him," she said.

"Come here to me," said Dualta. She walked toward him, her arms behind her back. She was thin. The bones on her face were too defined. She came close to him.

"You think Colman is wonderful?" he asked.

Her face flamed but she did not drop her eyes. She nodded her head.

Dualta laughed. "You must be married," he said. "One evening I saw you walking the hill. You walked close together. You know what people say: They walked so close together that if the priest was at hand, all was lost."

She laughed then, her thin hands up to her mouth.

"Does Colman wish to wed you?" he asked.

"Colman says: If I had a blanket to cover her I would marry the girl I love." She said this, looking at him from the corner of her eyes. She made him laugh. Then she went on. "It is a dream. We have nothing."

"When the new harvest comes, things will be different," said Dualta. "You'll see. There are many holdings vacant now. We will get you one. I will loan Colman a blanket." They laughed again. Then he sobered. He put his hands on her shoulders. "You will be married. I tell you this. You will be like a little candle of hope lighted in the valley."

"I think I hear wheels," she said. She walked away from him out to the rough road. She stood there.

Dualta thought of seed. What it would be like to see real potato seed. If he had enough to bargain for them, he saw the four of them carefully cutting them, putting the verdant eyes on one side and the unrewarding remains another. What was left could be eaten. Put in a pot and boiled, and drained and mashed with a little of the precious butter from the cow.

You could buy Indian meal. It was three shillings a stone. The Poor Relief Act was in force, but not for people like Dualta. Owing to a fellow called Gregory, may his name be blessed, there was what men called an exterminating clause in the Act by which if you held one-fourth acre of land you were not eligible for relief. Men wanted their little plot of land. It would grow enough potatoes to feed them in the future when the famine was over. But Gregory and his kind thought there were too many small holdings and they wanted them eradicated. So if you wanted relief you had to forfeit your holdings. Relief was two pounds of mixed meal, one-fourth oat meal and three-fourths Indian meal per person, per week. It was little but it would sustain life if you were not fever-ridden. If you wanted this you had to abandon your little holding. It was hard for men seeing their family starving to death. If you could hold out with remittances from America, you would leave them their poor relief. If you had nothing else, you had to abandon, so many thousands dragged themselves to the meal depots or to the poorhouses, where, if they were healthy, they were liable to get the fever. But their homes were lost.

First the Indian meal came raw. There were no mills to grind it in penny packets, so people who knew nothing about this strange corn didn't know how to cook it, and they ate it half raw, and many of them died from gripe, wondering how it was that food could kill you. This strange stuff spat as it was boiled so men called it Peel's brimstone. Men like Dualta with their few acres were supposed to be able to look after themselves. He could manage, half-starved, until the harvest. Everyone had his hopes pinned on the harvest. Early seed potatoes planted in April should come in six weeks later if the weather was suitable. So by July they should be eating well again, God grant.

He moved out to the road as the heavy four-wheeled cart came toward the yard. It was pulled by two jennets. Colman was sitting in front with the peddler. "I got him! I got him!" he called as the heavy cart turned into the yard. Colman jumped down.

"Whoa! Whoa!" said the peddler. "He got me all right. Do you think it pays me to climb the mountains?"

He was a tall thin man. He wore a three-cornered hat from a past age, and a sort of military coat with a few pieces of blackened braid still sticking to it. "Oh, the things that Jack does for the people," he said as he let himself down to the ground. He always called himself Jack. Who knew his real name? Did he know it himself? He was an alternative to the pawnbroker. If you went to the pawnbroker you generally went surreptitiously. You had to go a long way. To Ennis. The pawnbroker charged you 25 per cent interest on every pound. You paid a penny for every pound ticket. You had twelve months to redeem. But pawnbrokers didn't travel and people were ashamed to be seen dealing with them.

His cart was piled with clothes and blankets and pieces of furniture. It made Dualta's heart sink to see these things. It meant that people were stripping themselves of all their best possessions to get seed. Girls' Sunday dresses and women's cloaks that had been in the family for generations, improving with age, and shoes and boots and men's good Sunday clothes.

"You are welcome, Jack," he said automatically.

"So well Jack should," said the peddler. "Amn't I a bene-factor? Wouldn't half the people of the land be dead next year if it wasn't for me? I greet you, ma'am," he said then, taking off his hat with a flourish as Una came over toward them.

"Won't you come into the house?" said Una as if she was welcoming a lord.

"I thank you, ma'am," said Jack. "Jack will be pleasured. Ye don't look so bad," he went on walking behind her. "Ye look far from death, God bless ye. Not like others. They have a soldiers' tent below in the town for the fevers, with a real doc-tor. Times are hard. Time a man would be asked to throw his straw in the corner and eat his sup. Now they have you to get rid of you. People are afraid now. What has happened to hospi-tality then? Isn't it the greatest victim of the famine." Dualta took the hint. He got the bottle from the cupboard and poured a half mug of it.

"It is Bottle's make," he said, looking apologetically at Col-man who stood inside the door.

"God rest him," said Jack, "he had the best right hand of any man in Ireland. I wish ye health." He drained the mug. "God! Now what have ye for Jack, that ye try to rob him? What seed do you need, then?"

"We need half a sack for an early crop," said Dualta, "and four for the main crop."

"Oh, you are riding high," said Jack. "Have you a notion of the price of seed? It has to be imported, no less. Look what they do with the Indian meal. They buy it at £13 a ton and sell it at £19. Where does the difference go? Aren't there people that'd rob their own mothers? The land is desolate. The seed is three pound a sack."

Dualta drew in his breath.

"It is high," he said.

"Is it Jack that makes it high?" the other asked. He hit his breast. "I am favoring you. I am giving it to the people at what it cost me. Won't they erect a monument to me in every village in the land when this is over?"

"As well as seed," said Dualta. "I have to find the rent for the end of this month."

"Will you sell the whole house then?" Jack asked. "I am a poor man. I will help you all I can."

"Here are two best blankets," said Dualta. They were made from sixteen pounds of clean wool, woven in Ennis, making two blankets five yards long and two yards wide. They cost ten shillings and tenpence. Jack felt them. "They are worth five shillings," he said. Dualta's heart sank. How are we going to do business at this rate, he wondered?

"They are worth more," he said.

"To you they are. Not to me," said Jack. "I would not bargain with you. Jack does not bargain. Fair is fair."

"All right," said Dualta. He put them aside. "Here is my greatcoat," he said. "It is one year old, and my trusty. This is two years old." New they had both cost together five pounds ten shillings. Jack felt them. "They are worth half a sack of seed," he said.

Dualta felt like saying, Get up from there and get out of my house! Of course he didn't say it. Jack knew that he couldn't say it.

Una was looking at Dualta, at the sweat on his face, forcing himself to keep his temper. She went up to the room. She brought down her two best dresses. She had been looking forward to wearing them again when she would be slender.

"No," said Dualta.

"Yes," said Una.

"Fifteen shillings," said Jack.

"Each," she said.

"For the two," said Jack.

At this point Colman left. Finola followed him. Colman was ashamed he had brought Jack.

So they bargained. There was no bargain. Dualta's best

shoes, and his Sunday clothes, smallcoat and vest and breeches. Two solid stools he had made himself, the table. They were still short. They shouldn't have been. But Jack was doing them a favor. Where would they get a better bargain? He walked out with the clothes.

"I should kill him, you know," said Dualta. "I should leave my mark on him."

Una put her hand on his taut arm.

"Clothes and furniture we can get again, Dualta," she said. "We cannot buy a harvest. Let these things go. He is the small man."

"I have not enough," he said. "We cannot pay Clarke yet."

"Maybe he will let it hang," she said.

"You do not know him," said Dualta. "He will not let it hang." He went out. They took down the sacks of potatoes from the back of the cart. Dualta let Jack load the stuff himself. He would not put a hand on them.

"Colman," he said then, "go and get the pony."

"No," said Una.

"It has to be," said Dualta. Colman looked at him and walked away around the back of the house. It doesn't matter, Dualta told himself. I have worked him. The seaweed and the sea sand and the lime were drawn to the fields, and the manure. It meant he would have to spread it now with a basket, but that could be done.

"This is a good pony," Dualta said. "If you do not give me a fair price for him, I will not let him go. I will sell him in the town, or in Corofin, or I will even go to Ballinasloe. So make your price fair if you want him."

"My price is fair, always fair," said Jack. "You farmers do not understand figures. What it costs to go from place to place. What it costs to sell the things I buy. When will they be sold? Is there a crossed halfpenny in the country to buy these things from Jack? Isn't seed potatoes worth your life?"

They looked at the pony. The pony looked at them. He was in good condition. He was beginning to lose his winter coat. Where he had lost it, he was shining brown. Una went back into

the house. Finola followed her. The pony was sold for £6. 10.
0. Dualta knew that feeling about animals was only sentiment.
He kept telling himself this. Jack paid out the money over and
above the value, his value, of the seed potatoes. Mostly greasy
notes and well worn coins. Dualta didn't put a hand on the
pony. Colman tied him with a rope to the back of the cart. Then
he stood beside Dualta as the peddler got up and turned the
heads of the jennets in the yard and out on the road. The pony
kept turning his head toward Dualta. He was wondering.
Wouldn't any pony? What have I done? Where am I going?
Dualta kept his face hard, and kept telling himself that people
like themselves had no sentiment for animals. They just did
what had to be done. They were only animals. It would be a
sin to think of them as having intelligence.

And then they were gone and there was only the sound of
the heavy cart wheels on the rough road. Colman broke away
from him and went to the seat under the tree. Colman is a
singer, thought Dualta. He has the heart of a singer. He can
see this far more clearly than I can. That is why he can cry for
a sold pony. But I am not a singer. I am a man who needs seed
to feed my people, to pay my rent, to live until the harvest.

So, a strong unfeeling man, he went back into the house, but
when he saw Una and Finalo he had to defend himself.

"I had to do it!" he said. "I had to do it! It was us or the
pony. You understand that? It was us or the pony!"

Dualta was paying his rent on the twenty-seventh when
Colman caught up with him.

Clarke had barricaded himself from contagion. You had to
kneel in front of a window and talk to him through a small
opening. This meant the end of the compliments, but he was
lucky to get anything at all. Dualta was reluctant to hand over
the money. It would mean absolute security until the harvest.
He thought in terms of the food it would buy and his heart was
sore.

"No," said Clarke. "I cannot let it hang. Do you know the
state we are in? How many have not paid their rents? Where

do we find money to keep going ourselves? Free meal! Who pays for it? We do. The Poor Relief is only loans. For us it is poor rates and cess and tax. Where are we to find it? Aren't half the people of Ireland eating off the Poor Rates? Where are they coming from? Who is paying for the poorhouses and the infirmaries and the extra doctors?"

"I do not wish to be lectured on social things," said Dualta. "All I want is a little time. Will you take half then and the rest with the September gales?"

"No," said Clarke. "No! No! I can find a tenant for your place easy enough."

Dualta handed over the money. He took his receipt. There was no great rush to kneel in front of Clarke's window. Dualta sat there with his back against the wall. Everywhere there were posted notices. If the rents on the estate were not paid, drastic action would be taken. He hadn't talked to a soul. Undernourished, the passersby just looked at one another. To talk was too much of an effort. What was there to talk about? Most people, in their old patched clothes looked like beggars. That's all we are, Dualta thought, a nation of beggars. So low we have come. He thought of the planted seed. They would be sprouting in the ground. Next month the green shoots would be over the soil. That was all you could hope for. That was the vision you longed for.

Then he saw Colman walking toward him. Colman had been running. Now he had stopped running. His face was expressive. Dualta's heart started a slow pound. "Sit beside me, Colman," said Dualta. Colman sat beside him on the cold ground. He was panting. It took time for his breathing to become normal. He didn't speak.

"Something is wrong," said Dualta. "Something bad."

Colman didn't speak. Oh God, thought Dualta, so you cannot ward it off just by saying It won't happen to us! It won't happen to us! Three people, Una, Finola or the baby that was not born, or was it born and was it now dead. "Tell me, Colman," he said savagely.

"Una has the fever," said Colman.

Dualta's head dropped on his arms that were resting on his knees. He didn't want to do anything. He thought it would be nice to go to sleep for two weeks and when you woke up, somebody would say: It's all right, Una did not have the fever. He knew it was the hunger that sapped the energy in him. He wanted to weep, helplessly.

"When?" he asked. "She didn't have it this morning."

"She didn't say to you," said Colman. "She has been having the headache for a few days. She didn't say. She hoped. And the mist."

"She is clever, clever," said Dualta. "I didn't see." How could he see? Colman and himself in the fields all day, planting. The effort it required to walk up the hill to the fields alone, weakening, so that when they came home in the near dark all they wanted to do was sleep.

He rose to his feet, after he thought.

"Come," he said, "we will try this doctor."

He knew there was little chance of him. When they came to the field where the dirty brown bivouac was set up, he made Colman stay outside. "No," said Colman. "Stay," said Dualta. "If I was to get it I would have got it from my father," said Colman. "Stay here!" Dualta commanded him.

There was a terrible smell in the tent. The people were lying on straw covered by blankets. The brown canvas did not let in much light. Over the other side of the town they were building makeshift places where they put the sick and they gave them their food with long-handled ladles through an opening in the earth walls. Clarke's people were burning many of the cottages down by the shore. Dualta thought he would prefer to die in the open air than in this tent.

"The doctor! The doctor!" he called. He pulled back from the place. He seemed to be enveloped in a tangible mist emanating from it, groans and cries and moaning and the terrible smell of the dysentery and the famine dropsy.

This man came out. His face was sweating. He was a big gray-haired man, like a soldier. He had a gray moustache. His eyes were bloodshot.

"My wife," said Dualta. "She is expecting. She has the fever. Will you come?"

"Man, you are mad," said the doctor. "I am serving three towns. I sleep in the carriage between the towns. Bring your wife here."

"No," said Dualta. "No! No!"

The doctor shrugged.

"I will pay," said Dualta, who had no money. He would get it.

"No," said the doctor. "It's no good. It's time. No time. No time to live. Doctors die too, young man. One in every fourteen is dying."

"Next month she is expecting the baby."

"She will not carry it," said the doctor.

"For God's sake," said Dualta.

"I can't help you," the doctor shouted. "Keep her warm. Give her the cure of the Irish nurses, milk heated and whey and whiskey. I know. I have seen. What you need is a miracle. Seventy out of a hundred the baby is born with the disease if the mother has it. Fifty out of a hundred get it from the milk of the mother. What can I do for you. I am not God. Get your priest, you will need him."

"O, Doctor," said Dualta.

"She is only one in many millions," said the doctor. "I cannot help you. You must see. I will send the priest to you."

He was gone. Dualta stood there. For the first time in his life, he was without an idea, without a plan.

"Dualta," said Father Finucane. He came from the tent. He looked like an old man. There was sweat on his face.

"She is going to die," said Dualta. "She has the fever."

"She does not have to die, Dualta," said the priest.

"If she does not die on me the baby will," said Dualta. "It is too much. I have lived to here. I have seen many things. I have brought great suffering on her. She would be safe if I had not seen her. This is too much. I cannot abide it."

"Who says she will die, that the baby will die?" the priest

asked. "Have you spoken to God about this that you are so sure?"

"I know this is the end of the road," said Dualta.

"Come on, Dualta," said the priest. He caught him by the arm. He walked out of the field. "Is it the slow or the fast fever?" he asked Colman.

"It came slow," said Colman.

"It could be worse. The yellow fever is worse, I see," said the priest. He turned into the church.

"Where are you going?" Dualta asked.

"We are going to pray," said the priest.

Dualta laughed. "You look around you and you still say this? How many have you dead now? How many people are without graves. They have been eaten by the dogs. How many more are due? They prayed. Who heard them? We were faithful. We didn't turn. We didn't jump. We didn't take soup. And we are stricken. We are being wiped out. Is this our reward? I will not pray."

"Come with me, Colman," said the priest. Colman looked at Dualta and he followed the priest. Dualta just stood there, and watched them go into the door of the church. He thought dully: What ráiméis? It was like throwing buttons down a holy well.

Colman felt awkward in the church kneeling down behind the priest. There was only one colored window. The priest's head was sunk in his hands. He was as thin as the handle of a hayfork. Colman thought: Dualta has been good to us. He has been good to Finola. If it wasn't for him would we be here? He thought: Would I be willing to sacrifice Finola so that Una would live or that Dualta could have his long-awaited baby? This was a very hard thought. Have I enough gratitude to be able to say this: Is this carrying gratitude too far? When my father was dying and I waited on him, I cried and said, I would give my life for you, Father. Nobody heard me then. Well, can I do the same now? Who will see Finola through the world if I am gone? Why, Dualta will. That would be sure. So if it will balance the earth that Una stays and I go, then I want to go to repay a great friendship. Amen. I mean that. I hope with all my heart I mean that.

The priest thought: This woman sacrificed many things. She came to the valley at a time when she was needed. She had put into many heads ideas and thoughts that would one day be fruitful. It seems now that this is all gone, wiped out, but it is not so. Some remain. They will be fruit. There are many millions. If it is not necessary, do not let her go. Let there be one gleam of light in the midst of all this death and decay and hunger and pestilence. She sent many children into the world. Let her have one of her own. Life and death must balance. Who knows why?

"I will not die, Dualta," she said, every time she was aware of him, bending over her, sitting beside her, making her take two-milk whey. This was new milk, with boiled skim milk added to it. He made her drink this and eat the whey with a spoon he held to her mouth. She kept it from him, the frightful sickness of the head that seemed as if your skull were being sawed, the shivering fits, the aching in every joint. Until the day he went to pay the rent and she could hold it no more. She knew she had the typhus mist, seeing all through a dreamy white cloud. She had seen his face when he came back. She had heard him shouting at Finola and Colman. You must go and live in the school the pair of you. You must stay away. You hear. You must stay away. You must not get it too. She wondered what happened about them. They didn't seem to go. Sometimes Dualta was her father and she would explain to him why she had done all these things, why she had abandoned so much for the seeming sake of so little. Not so. There is the hidden life of the people. A real race. Not made up by words distorted on white pages. You hear new songs and poetry that in a line here and there can be sublime. Sometimes she taught the children. Dirty. Licey. Only some. You saw the difference. Bright brains. Needlelike intelligence. One or two had written from America. They said: Oh, so much you did for us. What it meant to count and add and write. She was walking in the woods with fair-haired young men who smelled of pomade. All

the clean things of life. But they didn't know the other. The
secret joy of being handicapped. The secret pleasure of abandoning. The tinkle of the harpsichord. The smell of wine. Her
father's face looming over her. Not understanding. Why? Why?
Why? Sometimes she felt as if she were drunk. She was aware
of the red rash that broke out all over her. In lucid moments
she touched herself to feel the child. She would cry then. Was
the child moving? He would wipe off her tears. She could see
him do this. I will not die. He bathed her forehead with cold
water. She never became lucid and found him absent. Oh, my
poor Dualta. So bewildered. So seeing. All the things he saw.
She knew she was delirious. She knew she was sinking into
stupor. She knew the day that she was like as if her body rested
in a river of moisture, floating on a stream of flower-strewn
water like an etching of Ophelia. She knew all this.

And she knew when she awoke, and she could see. There
was morning light coming through the window. It was clear
morning. She saw Dualta. He was squatting beside her, his legs
crossed, his head bowed, asleep like the statue of Buddha. She
reached her arm. She saw it was white. It was free of rash. She
remembered the cool touch of the bathing that Dualta had used
on it. She rested her hand on his hand. My hand is so much
thinner, she thought. She thought she said: It is all right, Dualta.
It is all right. She didn't. But he awoke.

She saw the intelligence coming into his face. He unwound
himself. He caught her hand. He pressed it. "You see me, Una?"
he asked. "You see me?" "I see you, my beloved," she said. He
put his hand on her face. She could feel its coarseness. He called,
"Colman! Colman! Finola! She sees me! She sees me!" She saw
them come in the door. She would greet them, but for the
pain. This was not the same. It was the other. So she said:
"Dualta, Mrs. O'Connor! You must get Mrs. O'Connor." And
he looked at her and he was gone and Finola was beside her
holding her hand. "We prayed and we prayed and we prayed,"
said Finola.

"Keep away! Keep away! Keep away!" Carrol O'Connor was
shouting at him from inside the locked door. "She wants her!

The fever is over! For God's sake Carrol, let her come. There is no more danger of the fever."

"No! No!" he shouted, "I have lost too much. I will not lose any more."

"For the love of Christ, Carrol, I pray you!"

"No," said Carrol. "No! No! Go away, Dualta. I ask you do not bring us the fever. I have had enough now. I am the last life. I will not be killed. I am the last life!"

Helpless, he stood. How far are we driven from all the good things of our race?

But Finola knew. She had been with her mother at a tender age. She knew. And it was a son. Was it any wonder the sun shone? And they had a cow giving milk, to take the place of the absent milk of the mother. And they could scrape sixpence to buy a pound of sugar to give strength to the milk. They could fight for the life of the child and they could win. Now that they had got this far, they would not be beaten.

This was good. And the green shoots were sprouting in the potato fields.

chapter XXXI

NO PLANT IN the world then was watched over with greater care nor got more attention than the potato plant of this year. Each separate plant was molded and remolded with devotion, its color commented on. They were all of a good color. The summer came with great heat, hotter than men had remembered for a long time. But the dew was heavy in the night and the plants seemed to thrive. And the sturdier the stalks grew and the greener was their color, the lighter the hearts of the people became. Soon now, they saw, the plants would be in flower and their troubles would be at an end, for once they could eat with abandon, they could work with ease. When bellies were full the fever would lose its force and die away.

Dualta and Colman were at task work for a few weeks when the weather broke.

They had to take it up. They were almost at the end of their own resources. It meant going to the town and lining up to get a work ticket. This came from an Inspector of Works and the Engineer in charge. He was expected to ask how much land they owned, what was their ratable valuation; were they in receipt of meal under the Poor Relief Act? Many questions. The Engineer just asked their names and gave them tickets.

So they moved to the mountain behind Tewson's and helped to build a road. They got tenpence a day if they could supply their own implements. They could, a spade and a shovel. People who could not supply an implement got fourpence halfpenny a day. It wasn't hard work. Climbing the hill on a half-empty stomach was the hardest part of it. The road seemed to be starting nowhere and going nowhere. Its eventual end would be the bog. They dug a ditch on each side and they threw the dirt in the middle. This was covered with broken stones delivered by the horse carts of Fiacra McCleary and Seán O'Connor from a roadside quarry where men beat the stones between their legs with hammers and tried to keep the chips from blinding them. A lot of them were successful in this. Over the stones would go a thin layer of clay and over that would go a heavy layer of gravel.

Dualta and Colman were at the gravel pit, digging and chopping, making a cliff that would fall on them if they didn't keep an eye on it. They loaded this gravel into the carts. There were many people working. There were women, whose husbands and sons had been killed off by the fever. They wheeled barrows of earth, with determined faces, their bare feet slipping and sliding. There were young girls. There were young boys. These were the children of people who were not entitled to poorhouse porridge.

There were many men in charge of the work, gaffers and gaugers and clerks. These were ex-policemen or men appointed by the bailiffs or the javelin men who were assistants to the High Sheriff and whom he was rewarding. Dualta thought the staff was top-heavy, but this was to be understood in all government work. It was patronage. It was all right. It was part of life. They were well paid, these men. They drove pegs and watched. They kept you up to the mark. If a man was too weak to work, they made him rest for an hour and knocked a penny farthing off his pay. The worst thing Dualta had against them was that they were strong and well fed and looked it. At midday, the dinnertime, they took and ate from fat hampers, bread and butter and meat. They were not consciously cruel in this. It is understandable that the satisfied never understand the emaciated. For few people on the work could eat. They ate in the morning before they came and they ate when they got home after the long day. In a week each man could earn the price of a stone of meal. With caution, it would last his family for a week, but it left little over for himself. So no matter how hard he tried, his work was slow, and capable of being reproved.

He hated the pay clerk. He was a small white-faced man

with a pinched mouth who came with the money tied on his horse. Sometimes he didn't come with the money. There was a shortage of coins, or the order hadn't come through. This happened two or three times. One time they waited three weeks for their wages. But he was kind, this pay clerk. He loaned people money out of his own pocket and then when the wages came it was understandable that he should charge 25 per cent interest. Without his kindness they wouldn't have had any meal at all.

Dualta liked the engineer. He was interested in his work. He would work himself. He was as kind as he could be. You couldn't be too kind. Dualta would help a woman with a barrow, or he would carry a large stone for a girl or shovel a hard part in the ditch for a thin panting man. You couldn't keep this up, because each time you did it, the lost time was deducted from your pay. This was understandable. If everybody did somebody else's work, no work would ever be done.

What work?

"You must be proud of your work," said Dualta to the engineer. He was inspecting the gravel pit.

The man looked at him under his eyes.

"Well, you are building a good road," said Dualta, "even if it is going nowhere."

"It is going to a bog," said the engineer. "Someday it can be used to draw turf from the bog."

"In five years," said Dualta, "the soft spots will be buried as deep as hell. There will be no road."

"Why should you complain?" the engineer asked. "You are getting meal for your belly out of it?"

"I was just wondering if you were happy driving roads to nowhere," said Dualta. It was dinnertime. The engineer got the saddlebags from his horse. He took out bread and meat wrapped in a linen cloth and a bottle of porter. He sat on a flat stone.

"Would you join me in my meal?" he asked.

Dualta could smell it, even if he was ten feet away.

"Thank you," he said. "I am not hungry."

The engineer shrugged. He was about thirty years old. He had a thick body and black hair on the backs of his hands. But he had clear eyes. He ate his meal.

"Task work is under the direction of Poor Relief Committees," he said. "They pay the piper. They call the tune. We know this. So a landlord wants a road to a bog. He gets it. A man wants a high wall built around his demesne. This is task work too. He gets it. There are more high walls being built around demesnes at the present day that contain enough stone to build the pyramids of Egypt. But," he paused to take a drink from the bottle of porter, "here and there," he went on as he wiped his mouth, "there is a harbor wall going up, or there is a useful road going where no road ever went. So you see, by stealth we in the Board of Works are getting some things done that would never have been done."

"That is true," said Dualta. "There are so many beautiful roads being built to carry the bare feet of beggars."

The engineer stopped eating to look at him.

"Also for coaches and carts," he said. "The price of transport will be cut. Whatever you feel, a road is a good thing. It is there, it must be kept. The quicker a thing is brought from the farm to the port, the cheaper it will be. Everybody will benefit."

Dualta laughed heartily. The engineer didn't lose his temper.

"You'll see," he said. He got to his feet. "Meanwhile it is time to continue this road to nowhere."

He looked closely at Dualta. Dualta's eyes didn't shift.

"People like you are dangerous," said the engineer. "Don't let others hear your thinking. They might not agree with you as I do."

Then he mounted his horse and left. Dualta heard Colman sighing.

"You should have taken one lump of bread from him," he said. "Even if you are not hungry, I am."

"There is little left to us except pride," said Dualta.

"I would exchange that for four ounces of mutton," said Colman.

They laughed then and spat on their hands and dug gravel.

So in July the hot weather broke. The cloudless misty skies became like cauldrons of black clouds shot through with the red-tinged ones of thunder, and the rain was driven on the land from the southwest, roaring in swathes across the valley, bending the strong shoots of the potatoes, bowing them to the soil. And in a morning when Dualta and Colman came from the house, unprotected from the rain (for who had protection when it was sold long ago for seed?), and set off across the hills to work on the road going to nowhere, even above the whistling of the wind, they heard a cry on the side opposite them. They looked, wiping the rain from their faces, and there was a man standing in a field with his arms to the sky looking like a figure dressed to scare the crows. And he was crying, "They are gone! They are gone!" The replies to him were like an echo in the valley. They saw other men in the fields. It was five o'clock in the morning. It took them time to get to the task work. The sun was somewhere behind the clouds. And they paused and heard and turned away and ran to their own fields behind the house, and could not believe their eyes. For the green fields were blasted to death. The strong stalks and the broad leaves were lying like brown muck on the ground, and the same smell was with them that had been there last year. They were blighted to death. Every single stalk. It was no use going digging with your fingers. You didn't have to look under the stalks to know. You knew what was there. It couldn't be true. Not now? After all the sacrifice? After all the pain? After all the beggary? Not again.

There was a silent wail went up from the valley that would have drowned the highest wind, if men had the strength to shout it. He thought of the baby in the house, the feel of the soles of his fat feet under his finger.

"We will not go back to the house," he said to Colman. "It is too painful. We will go to the road."

They set off. They joined the straggle of tattered thin people who were climbing the hill, looking back, standing, shaking their heads. It cannot be so. Where was God, they asked? What is He doing to us? What have we done to deserve this? Wasn't one year enough? Were there not enough of us eliminated from the face of the earth like muck scraped off with a shovel?

They would not forget this day.

Nor the news at the top of the hill.

The pay clerk was waiting for them. They were to be paid off. The task work was over. The harvest was in. It was ready to be garnered. That was the law.

They laughed, those of them who had strength. Are they mad? Don't they know? What will we do? Where will we get food? See our fields. Smell them from here!

It is not our fault. That is the law. There was a date set for the end of the task work. It is here. It is the law.

The engineer was white-faced.

"I will do my best. I knew it was too early. There was always the chance. Who could predict a second blight? The wheels will move again. But it will take time. I will move heaven and earth. I will do all that I can. In a few weeks. Just a few weeks." He was genuinely disturbed.

"In a few weeks we will all be dead!"

"No, no, hold on! You'll see. I will ride tonight to the county town. I will explain. They will do something. You'll see. Just hold on. Hold on!"

They walked down from the road. They trailed shovels and spades and wheelbarrows. It was like a silent group of the damned. There were no words from them. Only silence, beyond tears. Beyond hope, it seemed. How could you live until another harvest a year away when you had expended everything you possessed for this one? Dualta thought of the work put into the fields, of what they had paid for the seed.

He stopped at Moran's whiskey cabin on the hill outside the town. "Go home," he said to Colman, "I am going in here."

"It is a foolish solution," said Colman.

"Go home," said Dualta.

"Have you lost your wits?" asked Colman.

"Do not advise me," said Dualta. "Just go home. Leave me alone! I am on my own. Go away!" He went in. Many of the men were there too. They were counting their coins. Their wet clothes dripped with the rain. They smelled. The atmosphere was fetid. Colman did not go home. He pulled himself under the overshoot of the thatch where the rain would not reach him and he squatted on the ground.

It was nearly dark when he was rewarded. Dualta came out. He was not as bad as Colman expected him to be. Dualta was no man for whiskey, he knew. So he let him walk down the road. Then he padded after him.

Dualta heard him. He stopped. He turned.

"I told you to go home, Colman," he said. "You should have bought meal and gone home. Have you no respect for me?"

"I will go home now with you," said Colman, "if you are satisfied."

"I will not go home," said Dualta. "I must wear out my wits. I will not go home."

"You are like that ship out there," said Colman. "Even a big ship has to run for shelter. Where will you get shelter but in your own home?"

Dualta looked at the bay. There was a three-masted ship anchored in the bay below them. It was laden you could see, riding, and it would have been one that set out from Galway across the way, and unable to beat out against the southwest wind turned in here for shelter.

"A ship," said Dualta. He looked at it. He shook the rain out of his eyes. He shaded them with his hands. "A ship," he said. "God sent it." He started to run. "Come on, Colman, we will not starve. We will hold off the day." He started to run carefully, finding holes under his feet that were not really there.

"Where are you going?" Colman asked. "What are you going to do?"

"Come with me and find out," said Dualta. "You'll see. By God, you'll see!"

Cuan came to them from one of the outhouses which was lighted by a couple of tin lanterns. If Dualta had been normal he might have remarked on this. It was raining very hard. Cuan peered at them from the dim light. Somewhere behind the dark weeping clouds there was a moon.

"Cuan," said Dualta, "now is your time. You must come with us."

"What's up?" Cuan asked. "Where are you going?" His eyes adjusted to the darkness, he could see Paidi the smith and McGreavy the carpenter and even the thin pale face of Slowey the weaver, and Colman. They were all very wet.

"There is a ship in the bay," said Dualta, "we are going to get food from it."

"You are in drink," said Cuan. "A night like this."

"Do you fear then?" Dualta asked. "You have always urged us to action. You have sneered at me for timidity."

"That is not true," said Cuan. "How will you take a ship? Are you strong enough? Can you overcome a well-fed crew? Have you given thought to a deed like this? Will you walk into disaster because you do not plan?"

"You will not talk me out of it," said Dualta. "We are the men in the middle. Nothing for us, except take what we want. It is under our hands. We will go and take it. We will need your horse and cart and we will need you, if you have the heart to come. If you have not the heart say so and give us the cart."

"It's not that I am afraid, Dualta. It is something else altogether," said Cuan.

"What is more important?" Dualta asked. "Tomorrow the ship will be gone. We cannot wait. You must say. Will you come? Will you not come?"

"Do you know what you are doing?" Cuan asked. He was surprised that Dualta had talked these men into such an adventure.

"What have we to lose?" the smith asked. "With the second blight we are in poor shape. If we succeed we will have staved off the hunger."

Cuan thought.

"All right," he said, "I will go. The horse is in the stable. Harness him to the cart. I will be with you."

He turned to go to the lighted shed again.

"Bring a weapon," said Dualta.

Cuan turned to him. "You are like a man with the rup-rap, Dualta," he said. "All right. I will bring a weapon." Dualta seemed to be in a fever. He got the horse and they harnessed him to the heavy cart and they waited impatiently for Cuan, who came to them carrying a sickle. Cuan drove the horse. Colman sat in the cart with him and the weaver. The others walked. They were silent, drenched by the rain.

Dualta felt his head as clear as spring water. He knew exactly what he would do.

They left the cart at the shore. The wind outside the harbor was strong. The harbor was free of the wind but there was a backlash from the stormy sea outside. Moghan and his son were waiting at the shore with the four-oared heavy boat. They had a job launching it into the water. Dualta was the last to haul himself aboard. He had been in the water up to his neck. It was a change to feel the salt on his lips. They kept themselves from the oars. Dualta stood in the bow. Cuan was behind him.

"Will we kill, Dualta?" he asked.

"What are you saying?" said Dualta.

"Have you decided?" Cuan asked. "If they oppose us, if we can get on board in the first place, will we kill them to get the food?"

"We'll face that when it comes," said Dualta, shouting.

"You better face it now," said Cuan. "You have to know. If you will not fight you cannot win."

"We will fight," said Dualta. He was clutching a makeshift pike belonging to the smith.

"As long as I know," said Cuan. "I will wait for you to strike the first blow."

"If I have to, I will strike the first blow," said Dualta. "You go with Colman and the weaver to the hatch of the seamen. The rest of us will go to the captain's cabin."

"All right," said Cuan.

The ship was anchored quite near the shore, about a quarter of a mile. They could hardly see it until they were almost on top of it. Then they saw it looming, looking much bigger when it was viewed from here. It was a three-masted ship. The sails were tied. The wind was whistling in the riggings. It was creaking and groaning, smelling of fresh tar. The rope ladder was hanging. Even if it wasn't it was well loaded and low in the water. They would have no trouble getting aboard. Dualta gripped the side and climbed until his head was free of the boat. He looked closely. He could see no figure of a man against the dark sky. He could see a light coming up from the hatch in the center and near the middle mast there was a light from the superstructure, through round portholes. He climbed over. He whispered to the Moghans, "You hold the boat. The rest of you come." Then he sat crouched until they joined him. The big ship was rocking gently, waving away from its anchor. For a moment Dualta wondered; What in the name of God am I doing here? There was no sign of a watchman. They should have had one. Maybe he had gone below for something. He pointed at the hatch leading below, the stairs covered from the weather by a half circle. "Go now," he said to Cuan. He walked himself toward the cabin under the wheelhouse. He paused a moment until he felt the others about him, the smith with an old blunderbuss, the carpenter with a pitchfork. Oh, he thought, Oh, and then he opened the door and went in with the pike held in front of him.

There were two men at a bolted-down table. They turned to look. He saw the utter surprise coming into their eyes as they saw three wet scarecrows facing them, dripping water onto the white scrubbed floor. One was a big man. He wore a beard. The other wore oil clothes that were gleaming in the light of the tin lantern.

The big man coughed.

"Are you the revenue men?" he asked. They saw his teeth as he smiled.

"No," said Dualta. "We want food. We intend to have it. You have plenty of it. There will be enough left over for your destination."

The captain considered this. He wondered if he and the mate would be able to overpower them if they rushed at them. It was possible. The three men didn't look well fed. The one who spoke was a small man, with a lithe body. But the captain didn't like the glitter in his eyes. He didn't like the blunderbuss in the hands of the muscular one with the black and gray bristles on his face.

"Is that gun loaded?" he asked the smith.

"There's nails in it," the smith said.

"You could get seven years' transportation," said the captain, "if you were caught with that."

"You could get death," the smith said, "if you try to take it from me."

The captain looked at the mate. The mate was tensed. The captain shook his head. He thought. If this had happened in a port he would not have been surprised. He often wondered why the starving men who loaded his cargo didn't do something like this. Of course they filched from the cargo. That was understood.

"This is a sort of piracy," he said then. "If you are caught you could be hanged."

"First we will eat," said Dualta. "And then we will hang. At least we will hang on full bellies."

"It's better that way," said the captain. "The blight is with you too then?"

"It is," said Dualta.

The captain didn't think deeply about economics. He was a simple man with a hard fist who brought manufactured goods to an Irish port and brought back food. A simple exchange. He thought it odd that he should be going out with Irish grain and meet American ships coming in with grain and holds filled with clothes gathered by famine committees. But then, if grain did not go to England the poor people who made the goods in the factories would starve, and you would have two famines instead of one. The men who sold the grain for transportation said that if they did not sell their produce where would they get the money to pay the taxes and rates for the Poor Laws? It was all very complicated. But he wasn't a hard man. He had seen terrible destitution and death. He wondered for a moment: If I were starving and had a family, would I risk an adventure like this for food? He thought he would.

"I'll tell you," he said. "You can take as much as you can carry. Each man."

Dualta looked closely at him.

"You are trying to trick us," he said.

"No," said the captain. "I am not. We could fight you. We might defeat you, even with our bare hands, but then we might have to spill our blood trying. So it is easier to let each man carry what he can, and let the police recover it afterwards, if they can. Is this a fair bargain?"

"We do not want pity," said Dualta, feeling deflated.

"Who pities you?" the captain asked. "We are giving in to force. Would you use that weapon in your hand?"

Dualta tried to look fierce.

"I think I would," he said then, beginning to feel desolate thinking that the effects of the whiskey were wearing away from him, wondering what Una would say if she could see him now, what Father Finucane would say if he were standing at his shoulder.

"We won't test you," said the captain. "This is what we will do. Mister Pendrive, my mate, will go down in the hold and tie a rope around as many bags of grain as you can carry. Is this fair? How many of you are there?"

Dualta felt everything was being taken out of his hands. He counted. "Three and two, five, and two, seven," he said. "Seven."

"You can have seven sacks of grain," said the captain. "Let us set about it." He walked toward the door. Dualta barred his way and then stepped aside. "You are not trying to trick us?" he asked again.

"No," said the captain. Dualta let him by. Pendrive came after him. Pendrive looked scornfully at them as he passed. They followed him. The captain stopped at the steps leading to the crew's quarters. He saw the three men standing there.

"You better stay there," he said to them. "Don't let them up.

They might get wet. They should have been standing watch."
He walked on.

"What is it?" asked Cuan surprised.

"I don't know," said Dualta. "He is either a Christian or a deceiver. Stay there."

The captain and Pendrive unlashed the tarpaulin covering the hatch. They loosened some of the heavy timber. Pendrive got a coiled rope, threw it over his shoulder and prepared to go down. Dualta stopped him.

"Are you deceiving us?" he asked. "Can he get to the men's quarters from below?"

The captain sighed.

"You are like all pirates," he said. "You wouldn't trust your own mother. There is no way out of that hold. Down you go, Mister."

He took an end of the rope. "Now," he said, as he took the weight of it. Dualta used one hand to help him and the smith, bewildered, did the same and they hauled up a sack. They did this seven times. Then they moved the sacks over to the side and they lowered them to the Moghans waiting below. The captain took charge of the whole operation. He advised the Moghans where to stow the sacks in that tossing boat below. Then one by one the others went down into the boat while the captain watched them. He was smiling broadly. Dualta could see his face in the rain and the clouded moonlight, his teeth gleaming.

Before he went over, he said, "Why?"

"I told you," said the captain. "You forced me. Go away. I will send a boat after you to report to the police. I must do this. I hope you eat well."

"Have you a name?" Dualta asked.

"Have you?" the captain asked. When Dualta was silent, he went on: "Ships pass in the night. You look decent men. I think you must be badly off to do a thing like this."

"You will go to heaven," said Dualta.

The captain jeered. "Won't the devil be disappointed," he shouted.

They pushed off. The Moghans rowed away. Dualta kept looking back at the ship. It was an adventure, he thought. What happened to it?

"We could get the dory out," said Pendrive, "and be there before them."

"We could," said the captain, "but we won't."

"Are you going soft in the head?" asked Pendrive. "Will you let them get away with this?"

"Our people are not going to miss the grain," said the captain. "The rats eat more than that on a voyage. Leave them be. The wind is dying outside. Get those lazy bastards up from below. They could have stolen the sails and they wouldn't notice. We will get under weigh."

"I do not understand you, man," Pendrive shouted.

"My wife always says that too," said the captain. "She is Irish. She came from around those parts somewhere. I met her in Bristol."

"Oh," said Pendrive.

"Rouse out, ye lazy devils," the captain was shouting down the hatch. "Rouse out! Hoist sail! We are on our way."

Dualta and the others heard his voice over the waters. The Moghans bent to the oars. They listened for sounds of pursuit. When the boat grounded they very quickly unloaded it, and piled the sacks on the cart.

"Put the boat away," said Dualta to the Moghans. "Deny you were ever out. We will drop your share at the house. Your family can hide it."

They nodded. They were quiet men. They had been sick. They were not strong. Now they were better they could fish again, that the fever had not killed them.

They separated as they went, dropping off the grain at the houses on the way.

They left Cuan's sack at his house.

"Take the cart," he said to Dualta.

"You did not tell me I was a fool," said Dualta. He had been waiting all the time, his stomach tight, for Cuan's sneers. I am not a leader, he had thought, I am not even a man to do things out of the common mold. What madness brought me to this? He knew it was the whiskey.

"Why would I say you were a fool?" Cuan asked. "By their fruits you shall know them. You were successful."

"But not for the right reasons," said Dualta. "You heard that man out there. He made me feel like a child. I am a mature man."

"Do not worry, Dualta," said Cuan. "I did not want to go with you because Fiacra has the fever. He is in the shed. He is not good. I am afraid he will not live. He has the yellow fever."

"Oh, Cuan," said Dualta.

"You must not be sad," said Cuan. "That is the way things happen. I am beginning to think we cannot help our fate. We are moved around like twigs in a rushing river. God speed you. You can bring back the cart." He left them.

Colman had to drive the horse. After a while, he said to the silent man beside him.

"Do not grieve," he said, "you did not know, Dualta."

"I should not have been a fool," said Dualta.

"A man is entitled to be a fool some times in his life," said Colman. "They will be pleased with the grain, you'll see."

"I wish it was at the bottom of that ship," said Dualta. "I am a mature man with the heart of a boy. I wish with all my heart that Fiacra doesn't die. If Fiacra dies I will never feel the same."

"God is good," said Colman. He clicked at the horse with his tongue and slapped her on the flanks with the reins. The rain was ended. There were clouds rushing across the face of the moon, and Dualta felt sad.

chapteR XXXII

IT WAS DIFFERENT this time. Last time there had been clods and stones flying. The policemen were cowering. Lines of people were running from the far fields.

Now there was just Clarke, sitting on his horse, ordering from the saddle, terrified of infection. He kept putting a handkerchief soaked in mint juice to his face. The only force was the constable and the new subconstable. Even those weren't needed. They were just used as a gesture to show that the McClearys were leaving by law.

Father Finucane helped Dualta to carry Cuan to the cart. It was Cuan himself, fighting the typhus mist, who had ordered this. They carried him from the shed where Fiacra had died, with his life terminating a lease which Clarke would not renew. The two blond McCleary boys were herding the cattle and the sheep, and had driven them ahead. They had spent two days emptying the house of its effects, and the outoffices of the implements.

They placed Cuan on the straw-strewn bottom of the cart and put two blankets over him.

Then Father Finucane got on his horse and led the way. Dualta sat on the seat and started the horse. The cart rumbled out of the yard. Father Finucane paused as he passed Clarke. Their eyes met. Then the priest went past him. He knew it was no use. The only concession he would make was that when the fields of oats and rye were ripe that the McClearys could come back and harvest them. They could also take the saved hay. He pointed out what a concession this was. Most landlords would have claimed the growing crops on the expiration of a lease.

It would have been different, Dualta thought, if Cuan had been well. Or would it? They all remembered too clearly how Moran had died. Would they have been able to resist this?

He pulled up the cart while Sabina came out of the door. She stood and looked at the house. It had been a great credit to her. It was always cleanly thatched and whitewashed. She had been proud of it, the small kitchen garden, and the little orchard. She remembered the time she had come to wed into it. She remembered Moran. She remembered the children coming and growing. She remembered great evenings of songs and house dances and merriment. But all that went with Moran. She thought that that had really for her, been the end of the place. She wasn't sorry to leave it now. She was brokenhearted for her sons who were being deprived of it, but when Fiacra died, the last of her attachment went with it.

She went to mount the cart. She threw the last of the things she carried in a blanket in beside Cuan. She met his gaze.

"You are comfortable now, McCarthy?" she asked. He nodded. He wetted his yellow lips with a white tongue. "Drive on, Dualta," she said. "Stop now for a minute," she said as they came close to Clarke.

"You will have no luck with it, Clarke," she said. "I don't know who you want it for, probably one of your own, but you will have no luck with it."

"That's no way for a Christian woman to talk," said Clarke.

Cuan thought: Oh, if only I were well. He had imagined this day coming, as we all anticipate disaster. It would have been different. He would have killed Clarke. He knew this. He would have spitted him on a hayfork, before he himself was killed. It was the last debt he owed the McClearys and he would have paid it. He groaned. Now he could not even lift his head to blaze hatred from his eyes.

"Are you all right, Cuan?" Dualta asked.

"There was blood spilled in the yard," she said. "Your horse is standing on the spot. From now you will not pass it without a shake in your soul. You will get no benefit from the place. It will wither, Clarke, like potato stalks under the blight."

He moved his horse from the spot. He couldn't help his eyes flicking down to the ground.

"Be on your way now," he said.

"Go now, Dualta," said Sabina.

When they were gone, Clarke came down from the horse. He walked to the house. He looked in the windows. Like all empty houses it looked bleak, but it was clean and spacious. He was pleased with its condition. He walked around the back. He looked into the stables. He lifted the latch on the door of the small cool dairy under the sycamore tree. He admired it. It was a good sound place. It was worth four times what the McClearys had been paying for it. It was too good for them, he thought. It was above their station. It would be very lucrative. Everything comes to those who are patient, he thought. Normally Moran McCleary and his sons would have lived for a hundred years and more between them. So it is an ill wind that blows nobody good.

He walked around to the front. He saw the cart turning out onto the road. It would be a change for them, he thought, to be trying to live in Flan McCarthy's cabin. Where would they find grazing for the cattle? They would have to ask him for grazing rights on the commonage. The old lady shouldn't have said things like that to him. She would still have to beg for favors. He didn't approve of the priest going with them like this, as if Clarke had done something unlawful. He would speak to the parish priest, an old white-haired doddering man, weeping weakly at the decimation of his parish. Anyhow if Finucane kept going and burying the fever-stricken he wouldn't last long.

He looked and saw where he was standing, and he couldn't help himself. The hair rose on the back of his neck and he felt a chill in his spine. The warm July day seemed suddenly cold. It is pishreoges he said, just pishreoges. I am a good Catholic. I do not believe in superstitions."

"You will have to keep watch for a few days," he said to the constable. "You never know. These people might be bad enough to come down and set fire to the place. From meanness. You never can tell with people like those."

Then he jogged away. He doubted if they would do that. After all, he had left them the standing harvest. That had been tactical. It was a clever move, like buying off destruction, even if he regretted it.

Well, anyhow, Sir Vincent will be pleased with me, he thought. Bit by bit I am improving his property, making it successful. He thought of the uneconomic holdings that had been taken over, the filthy cabins destroyed. The famine had been a help. You had to admit that. It was a calamity, but most of them who hadn't died were taking the roads to the ports. It was the best thing that ever happened in the country to get them off the bits and pieces of land, to divide it into economic holdings. Most people admitted this. There was a certain hardship involved admittedly, but it was all for the eventual good, and why would the good God have permitted it all to happen like this, if it wasn't meant to be? You had to be practical. That was good Christianity. You couldn't be sentimental. There was too much sentiment. Not enough common sense about all this. The fittest would have to survive. When it was all over, it would be a tranquil country. It would have been cleansed of the parasites. Things would be ordered, like a good estate. He was redrawing the holdings in his head, adding here, amalgamating, drawing a blueprint of a smiling healthy valley. This kept him happy. He did not wish anyone bad luck who had interfered with him. Where was O'Connell now, the man who had stolen the voters? He was dead, dying in a foreign place called Genoa, saying: I have it here in a box. I have Repeal here in a box. He had it in a box, all right, Clarke thought, a wooden one, and there it would be. He knew Cuan McCarthy had turned up the beautiful fields, the green fields. He would never forget the sense of desecration he had felt as he saw those fields, like somebody spitting in the face of Christ. Where was Cuan McCarthy now and the men who went out with their spades? Cuan was in a cart with the yellow fever. So it was that all men who used violence would perish. If only they would see this! If only they would understand this.

He thought of his dinner. He felt hunger. He set the horse galloping.

The McClearys had built a shelter for Cuan away from the house into the steep side of the hill in the rock-strewn valley where Flan lived. They had done this at Cuan's command. He ordered that none of the young people were to come near him. He ordered Sabina to send in his needs on a long shovel. Nobody knew how you got the fever from another person, just to keep away from them. Sabina paid no attention to this command. It was a good shelter, covered and bound with scraws, and drained around outside. He was lying on thick straw.

Dualta thought that Cuan looked older than his brother Flan. He had always been thin. Now his face was yellow. His eyes were very big and burning with the fever. They were bloodshot. The bristles on his face were almost white. He was sitting beside him. Through the square opening he could see the sun shining, and the well-fed cattle on the hill moving impatiently from place to place searching for sparse grass. Now and again, as the great beads of sweat formed on Cuan's forehead he would wipe them away with the wet cloth. His white hair was soaked with sweat. He moved restlessly, his tongue trying to dampen his dry lips. Dualta would put another wet cloth to his lips. Cuan would suck at it.

"I have never been sick," said Cuan. "People like me are only sick once."

"It is a chance to make you lie on your back," said Dualta.

"Too much thought," said Cuan. "Time to remember. You were wrong, Dualta."

"How?" Dualta asked.

"About him, O'Connell," said Cuan. "Spoke the wrong things. He should have called them out. Clontarf. Before. Millions to fight with bare hands. They would have done so. He held them. He had the power. Now you see. They could not have killed millions. Clean death and victory. Not like this, this way. By the roadside. In the ditches. Smelly stinking death. What came

of peace? This. All this came of peace. Turning away wrath."
The opening was darkened. He sensed it even with his eyes
closed. "Who is that?" he asked.

"It is Flan," said Dualta.

"Go away, Flan," said Cuan. "Keep away. You must not catch
it."

"Talk," said Flan, coming. He sat the other side of Dualta.
"Not far away from it, I am not, already. It doesn't matter."

"Remember down in Tipperary," said Cuan. "Good times,
Dualta. Planning. Action. You see. That is the way. Not oratory.
One doer better than forty talkers."

"Too late," said Flan. "By long. The pattern was set from
long ago. Not now. The longer you wait, the harder it is. The
people bring this on their own heads. They betrayed their
beginnings."

"No," said Cuan. "They were betrayed. No leaders."

"They forgot," said Flan. "They turned their backs on their
precious possessions."

"I am tired," said Cuan. "I will sleep. You will come again,
Dualta. You are immune to death."

"No," said Dualta. "I am not. I will come again."

"What will you do now, Dualta? What will become of you?"

"I don't know," said Dualta. "Just that I will survive. Me
and my wife and my son, Dominick. We will survive."

"Not here," said Cuan. "It is too late. It will never rise."

"You are in fever, Cuan," said Dualta. "You do not mean
this."

"You have seen," said Cuan. "What nation could survive?
Who will bring hope? Who cares? You are right. I am in fever.
Tell the priest to come to me later. Eh?"

"Yes," said Dualta.

"I am so tired," said Cuan. "I got tired the day they killed
Moran. You remember."

"You have well paid for that," said Dualta.

"No," said Cuan. "Wrong effect. That was wrong. Blunder-
ing. Not necessary. Think of me, Dualta. I meant well. First
time I saw you in the marketplace. Young eyes. So bold. Bring

up your son that way. Don't let them tramp on you. Go away. Leave me alone now."

Dualta wiped the sweat from his forehead again. Then he rose and went out of the shelter. Flan stayed looking closely at the face of his brother. Then he rose and came into the sunshine.

"I didn't know him," he said. "I do not know him now. It is like looking at the face of a stranger. He had violence in him. I, in words. Just words on paper. Visions and dreams, beyond the understanding of men."

"You must keep them and put them on the paper," said Dualta. "Someday they will be understood."

"No," said Flan. "Too late now. I am bewildered. So many people in my house. They make it clean. They make it like a house. I do not know what to do. I am like a dry well."

"You must give me some of the papers," said Dualta. "I will learn them. I will teach them to young ones who will carry them in their heads, and mingle them with their own dreams."

"You might as well have them as others," said Flan. "It will be no good. You too will forget. You will put them in a box, and someday they will be used to light bonfires. Come."

He went to the house. Dualta followed him. It was a small house. The furniture the McClearys had put into it made it smaller. One of the girls was sweeping vigorously with a heather broom. One was hanging curtains on the window. Another girl was wielding a whitewash brush. They stopped and looked curiously at Flan. He scratched his head. "My box! My box," he said tumbling his thin white hair with his hands.

"Here," said one of the girls. "We put it in the loft out of the way." She stood on a chair. She reached for the box. She brought it down. She put it in his hands. He held it, looking at it. Weak tears came into his eyes. He went out into the air again.

"You see," he said. "I am dead." He sat on the long stone outside, the box on his knees. He jumbled the papers. "Here and here and here," he said. He put manuscripts into Dualta's hands. Dualta glanced at the neat script, then put them inside his shirt. Flan himself was reading now, caught up, showing his few teeth in a smile, saying "Hum," and "Ah, now." He became completely absorbed.

Dualta left him and walked toward Sabina, who was coming from the river with a bucket of water.

"I am going now," he said. "I will come back again."

"You have been kind to McCarthy," she said. She looked at Flan. "I am sorry for Flan," she said. "We have ruined his way of life."

"What will you do now?" asked Dualta.

"Later we will look for another place to rent, out of this valley," she said. "We can live until the harvest. You do not think McCarthy will recover?"

Dualta looked at her. He thought of Cuan. Was there ever anything of tenderness between them, he wondered. Had she just married a need in a time of need? Had she never grown soft toward him?

"I am not a doctor," he said. "I do not know."

"He was a good man," she said. "He came in our hour of need. God will reward him."

Dualta wondered: Why shouldn't people reward him? Was Cuan so constructed that he could not be truly loved by people?

"I hope he does not die," said Dualta. "With all my heart I hope he does not die."

"God's will be done," she said. He looked at her. A tall woman with big bones and a face that was aging well. There seemed to be no softness in her. Was it because she couldn't disclose it or because she did not feel it? He did not know. Suddenly he wanted to be at home.

"I will come back," he said. "I will send the priest. Cuan is sleeping."

"Sleep is a good cure," she said.

He walked away. He stopped at the opening of the shelter. He looked in. Cuan's mouth was open. He was getting his breathing hard.

He walked over the hills, remembering when he and Cuan had come into the valley. That day they had met Colman, a young, bold boy with a dog.

Cuan had been different then. I had been different then. We were younger. Too many things happen. You grow away from people. You grow old. That was it, you grow old.

Una saw him sitting on the seat under the tree. His head was in his hands. She left him for a while, and then she came out to him. She sat down beside him. She knew he was crying. She could understand this. He turned away from her and angrily rubbed his eyes on the sleeve of his shirt.

"It is the hunger that makes you weak," he said. "Cuan will die."

"Here," she said then, and put the baby into his hands.

He was surprised at the weight of the boy. He was a healthy-looking baby. His eyes were opening. He was looking up at his father. He was dribbling at his small fists with a red-lipped wet mouth. Dualta rubbed a finger on his cheek. It felt like velvet.

"It is he that matters," said Una.

"That's right," said Dualta. "It is he that matters. All like him who are born and survive. It is they that matter. You must get Finola and you must start baking oatcakes. You will bake them three times until they are hard. You must bake enough of them from what meal we have to last for four weeks."

"We are going away then?" she asked.

"We can do nothing else," he said. "We cannot pay the rent next September. We have nothing more to sell for seed. We are at the end of the road. We will walk to Galway. We will sell our books and our last possessions. We will buy passage on a ship to America."

"This is what you want?" she asked.

"There is no other way," he said. "You have read the letters. There is work. There is land that you can own outside the cities. It is good virgin land. Where else will we find freedom? It must be so."

She did not sigh. She rose. She put her hand on his head.

Her son was smiling up at him. People said it was not a smile, but wind in his stomach. Dualta did not believe this. He believed his baby was smiling at him.

"We will bake the oaten cakes," she said. She went toward the house.

Dualta raised the baby, so that he could see the waters of the ocean below.

"Out there," he said. "On a ship. It will have tall black sails. It will sail across the world. You will never know the things we knew and you will be the better for not knowing them."

The baby clapped its small hands, and Dualta put his lips against the silky hair.

chapter XXXIII

THEY WERE married by Father Finucane on this August morning. He might have been marrying a prince and his bride. He wore his best vestments. There were bunches of wild flowers decorating the altar. Dualta and Una stood for them, best man, bridesmaid, father and mother. Before the Mass he married them. They knelt at the altar then while he said Mass, a small town-boy serving him.

Behind in a seat Dualta sat beside Una. She was holding the baby. The baby was saying "Ah-ah-ah" and varying that by making sounds with his small fingers pulling at his mouth. The sounds of the baby's mouth, and the intonation of the Latin of Father Finucane, did not seem incongruous.

It was not a too tattered wedding. Colman looked almost leanly handsome, with his lanky hair cut and tied back. He was shaved. He wore a blue coat that almost fitted him. It was good cloth, breeches of white, stockings and shoes. Finola was wearing a cotton dress with flowers printed on it, blue stockings and shoes and a hat that had once graced Una's head.

They got the secondhand clothes from the Quakers. They were afraid of Dualta, what he would say because they had gone to the Quakers for the clothes. They said: Just while we are wed, and then we will give them back. He had to turn away from their eyes, and then say: You must think of me as a beast. They said: No. No. The Quakers are good. They do not want anyone to spit on the Blessed Virgin. He said: Not that! Why wouldn't you go to them for clothes? I am pleased that you went to them for clothes when I have no clothes for you. They are good people to give you the clothes.

He glanced out the side of his eyes at Una. She was very

intent on the Mass. Her lips were moving. There were Rosary beads in her hands. She looked well. The fever had left its effect only in her hair which was turning. Her clothes were not good, but her dress was neatly patched. She wore a kerchief on her head.

They were alone in the church except for a few old ladies who knelt at the back, and sighed loudly and prayed audibly. Dualta didn't want it to end. It was peaceful here. It was full of comfort. He felt shut in from the outside and what lay ahead of them. He did not want to part from Father Finucane. He felt as if he were abandoning him when he needed him. Not that he could do anything. And Father Finucane could not come with them.

Too fast it ended, and the priest took off his vestments and they went into the tiny sacristy to sign the book. Marriage, Birth and Death. The Death Register was open. It was the most used book. Dualta looked at it while the others signed the Marriage Register. He could make out the names in Father Finucane's uneasy script. Each name he read was like a kick in the heart. It made the erasing of people so final to see their names recorded in a book. At the end of the year he had written in a line in a despairing hand: *One hundred and nineteen people died in this parish last year.* What would he put down next year, with the Poor Relief Laws suspended because the harvest would be in and none to come? He shut the book quickly. It was no reading for now.

They were all silent. He could imagine the feelings in the heart of Colman, could envy the light in his eyes, the flush on the thin face of Finola. It made no difference to them that there were no gifts, no wedding spree, with food and drink freely flowing, and dancing, and songs and storytelling, and the fiddler and the piper, and young people courting in the haggard.

Una hadn't the heart to say goodbye now to the priest. She walked out of the church and stood waiting by the slide cart.

Father Finucane looked after her wistfully.

He said to Colman and Finola: "You will never forget me, because I was the one who joined you. You are in my keeping.

I will not forget you while I live. You must have faith. Every-thing will go well for you. I look at you and I know this. You are like a shaft of sunlight breaking through dark clouds." They shook his hand and walked away, past Una, on the road out of the town holding hands.

"If you did nothing else in your life, Dualta," said the priest, "these two should be your reward."

"I gave them little," said Dualta. "They even had to get wed-ding clothes at second hand from the Quakers."

"They look well in them," said Father Finucane.

They were silent then.

"You do not approve of me leaving," said Dualta. "You know I could not stay. We have nothing left to pay. I have to go."

"Go where your head leads you," said the priest.

"Can you tell me why it happened, all this terrible thing?" Dualta asked. "Why He permitted it all? Can you tell me?"

"No," said Father Finucane, "only that it is meant. I do not know. O'Connell had raised the expectations of the millions to a high height. There would have been an eruption, I think, a violent one, after the dashing of the hopes. I think it was just anticipated by the famine. Was that the purpose? I do not know. Was it to wake people to the contempt in which they are held in the eyes of the wealthy? I do not know. The crowded emigrant ships have a reason. There is purpose, some-where, there is purpose, but I do not know what it is. Each time I anoint a dying man, I say, Why? Why? Why? Such good people. What have they done? They wanted so little from life. They were content with so little. I do not know."

"I will write to you," said Dualta.

"I will watch for your hand," said the priest.

"You must take care of yourself," said Dualta.

"One day at the other end of the parish," said the priest, "I was very tired. I was in despair. So much death. So much starva-tion. I stopped the horse near a wood and I went in to pray. I prayed out loud. Why? And Spare us! And Give me the strength. Give me the means! And it seemed to me that a voice echoed my prayer. I listened. There was a voice. I rose and

The Silent People

walked through the woods. There I saw another priest from the next parish. He was kneeling on the pine needles. He saw me. We clasped hands. We sat on a fallen tree trunk and we smoked a pipe. He had the pipe. I had none. And then we parted. We were stronger. I don't know why this is."

Dualta held out his hand.

"May God be with you," said the priest. "I will miss you, that is understood. One day we may meet again, who knows?"

Dualta said nothing. He turned away. He went to the slide cart. It held their remaining possessions, not very much, spade and fork and scythe and implements, what few rags of clothes they had and books and the food for the journey. This slide cart he had used behind the pony to bring turf over the soft bog, or manure or seaweed up to the high hills. It was a wooden sleigh with iron runners. He took the rope and tightened it against his chest.

"We will go," he said softly to Una, who was facing away from him. The road was soft. There had been much rain. Now the sun was shining. There were many white clouds in the blue sky.

He pulled and the slide car came with him. It was not a great weight. He was glad of having something to do.

When they were out of the place a bit he said, "Look back and see if he is still there."

She looked and turned back quickly.

"He is still there," she said.

Later he said, "Look again." She looked. "He is gone," she said. So Dualta stopped to look back at the Valley of the Flowers. He could see the many broken houses of the town with their roofs knocked in, and many houses on the Bradish place and Tewson's place, where no smoke rose from the chimneys. The brown blighted fields, and the green fields of growing oats and barley, soon to ripen. And on the far hill he could see his own fields where he had plowed the high hills, the ridges distinct. Soon, he thought, the heather will come back and the gorse and the scrub. But the ridges and the shape of them, grassed over, will remain, so that in a hundred years men will look and wonder why people plowed so high in such poor land; so much labor for so little gain. He turned and walked on, taking the weight of the car.

Colman and Finola were sitting on the grass by the road. They had taken off their shoes and stockings.

"We must preserve those," said Colman. "They are our dowry. They will have to be well walked before they can be replaced."

"You show great wisdom," said Dualta.

"Besides," said Colman, "the damn things are hurting my feet."

They laughed as if he had made a witty remark. It was a relief to laugh.

"Have we lost our cow, then?" Dualta asked, suddenly remembering her. "She is Dominick's dairy." This made them laugh again. They looked and found the cow. She was ahead of them, cropping the grass.

"She has found food on the long meadow," said Dualta. "Let us go."

They slept one night in a deserted holding, at the gable end of a house. Dualta and Una slept here on heaped hay. They were in sight of the sea at this place. Colman and Finola did not sleep until late. They sat with their backs against a haycock, in this field: They chewed on the hard oaten meal cake, and they drank milk, warm from the cow, and they could look down on the moon-lighted waters of the bay below them. They slept and the strangest thing of all, they were awakened by the song of a girl.

This is so. She was in a field below them. She was collecting charlock and dandelion and dock leaves and nettles. They saw this and she was singing. It was the song of a Munster poet. He met a maid by the wide flowing river, strange and beautiful was she, her braided hair a river of silver kissing the ground at the feet of him. A golden robe and a belt of diamonds around her waist and her eyes so sad. She looked at him with pity and he called out, lying he was wounded there, the blood from his breast flowing free, and he said You have the power with your tears so bright to give me back my green fields. My green fields, oh, my green fields.

They stood there holding hands, wondering if they were hearing or imagining her in the early morning mist. She stopped then, and she was only a girl gathering charlock, and they went back to the house. Una and Dualta were standing there too, as if they had been listening.

"Did you hear?" Colman asked. "We heard a girl singing."

"We heard that," said Dualta. "It was more beautiful than the birds."

"It is a great thing that somebody can sing," said Colman.

"Someday we will sing too," said Finola.

Their elation did not last long. They came on more people as they came to the town. They were all silent people. They carried baskets and babies. They were like the snails carrying their possessions on their backs.

Some of them carried the fever-ridden in carts.

They knew the reason for this when they came in the Bohermore and saw the crowds lying on the road sitting against the walls crowding around the County Infirmary. It was a big tall bleak building, ugly enough to inspire terror in the beholder and the people were packed around it like flies around a wound.

At the Fair Green Dualta left them.

"I will not be long," he said. "Do not move away. I will come back for you."

The town had a smell of sickness, even if they were keeping the famished outside the crumbling walls. The streets were potholed and the potholes filled with water from the recent rains. Dualta was glad he was in his bare feet. He carried on his back a sack with books and some of his implements. He could sell the cow. He wanted this to be the last thing on account of Dominick. He remembered the town the last time he had seen it, with the election and the markets, the fine fed people and the beasts. This was no more. The principal thing now was rags and dirt, and an all-pervading misery. Only when he broke out on the ship quay from the fish market and walked the Long Walk through the Spanish Parade, and he smelled the river and the rising tide, could he unclamp his nostrils. The walk was crowded with people making for the dock, carrying baskets and sacks, women and children. They were not people of the town but country people, most of them with pinched hungry faces. Now he could even pick out the people who had had the fever and had recovered.

He had to push his way. He marveled again at the silence of them. Never before could you have been in an Irish crowd like this and not been greeted and shouted at. There would be jokes and obscenities flying. Calling and shouting.

He stopped a man with a sailor's jersey.

"Can you tell me of a ship to America?" he asked. This was a middle-aged man. He was smoking a clay pipe. His skin was dark from sea exposure. He looked well fed.

"Be careful," he said. "Careful, man. If you go, go with Pat Maloney. He runs a good ship. She is a three-masted ship in the Eyre's Dock. Tell him Lynch sent you. He will know."

Dualta went on. There was a confusion of ships. Across the way on the Rintinane beach he could see many fishing boats and coracles drawn up, and brown nets drying in the sun. On his left at the dock the ships were bigger.

Here there was a gaunt man, badly dressed, standing on a barrel. He was saying, "Don't go! Turn back. I have been. You can walk on drowned corpses from the Aran Islands to Grosse Island in Quebec. I left my wife and child dead in the lazaretto in Quebec. You will die, I say. Turn back. Do not go on the coffin ships. There is a road of skeletons, shifting with the tide from here to Ellis Island. Go back! Do not go! You are sailing with death."

There were many people here sitting and lying. There were many gathered around a tall sailor man who was giving out yellow tickets. He was saying "Pat Maloney runs a good ship. You will have sweet water and space. The ship is sound. She will run as sweetly as a bird. In three weeks you will be in the land of freedom."

"One and a half pounds," a man was bargaining. "For me

and my wife and my son. It is all we have for each head. You will take us for that, man?"

"No, I will not," he said. "It would not pay for the water. Go to Dublin. Go to Liverpool. Five pounds a skull you will pay, with rancid water and people packed like salt herrings in a barrel. Two pounds ten shillings is the price of freedom and filled granaries, where you can eat enough to burst for twopence."

"Do not go! Go back!" said the man on the barrel. "It is death to go."

Dualta pushed his way to Maloney. "Have you room for four, then?" he asked.

"I carry one hundred and fifty," Maloney said. "Head to toe, there will be room for all. You'll find. Bring your own food. There will be no food in the locker, just sweet water and a good sailor to bring you safe over the sea."

"Give me four tickets," said Dualta. "I will be back then and pay."

"High tide in two hours," said Maloney. "Money before you board. Here are the tickets. Go and look at the ship. She is well found. She is a better ship than Columbus had when he sailed."

He laughed at this sally. Then he called out again. "Sweet water and space and a sound bottom to sail to freedom."

Dualta looked at the yellow tickets. They were numbered 146, 147, 148, 149. He went to the wall. The ship was almost level with it on the rising tide. He stepped on board of her. The hatches were open. The decks were clean. He went and looked down into the hatches. Already there were people down there, some of them eating oatcake, others of them just lying wearily, their dirty bare feet turned up to the sky. There was a smell rising from the hold already. He could imagine what it would be like after a few weeks.

He went on the quay again.

"Only the sound," the man was saying. "Only the sound can sail. If you have the fever, go to the Infirmary. Only the sound can sail."

Dualta went past him, hefting his sack. As he passed, the man of the barrel jumped down and walked beside him.

"You look a wise man," he said. "Don't use the tickets. It's a plot. They want us all to die. I have seen the corpses. No man since the history of the world began has seen so many corpses. It is pure death. The yellow tickets are the tickets to death. Don't use them, friend. Listen to one who knows. Grosse Island, Partridge Island, Ellis Island, they are the Islands of the Damned and the Dead. Listen to me."

"There is a choice of death here or death abroad," said Dualta trying to shake off the grip on his arm. The man's eyes were wild. He was dribbling. He was hoarse. "It is case equal."

"Not so," said the man. "To die on the green fields with the Irish sky over you, that is bliss. Listen, I know."

"Leave me be! Leave me be!" said Dualta and shook him off.

"Poor man! Poor man! Poor blind man!" he called after him.

Up from the docks he found a pawnbroker. He was a thin yellow-faced man. He bargained with him. His books and his implements, also the spade and the fork and the slide car he described, on all these things after hard bargaining he would get five pounds five shillings, when they were all delivered. He gave him a piece of paper making this bargain which would be sealed on the delivery of all the goods.

Then he walked slowly toward the Fair Green. He was thinking. He could appreciate the eagerness of the people to seek the ships. It was as if all of them were in the grip of a frenzy. Once they had said: Let us go. There is no hope here. As if the whole land was imbued with this idea and had to carry it out at any cost. Some landlords were giving five pounds to families to help them toward the ships. It would pay to get rid of them this way since they were now uneconomic. In the papers they were praised for their generosity. What would happen if every single person in the country would seek the ships? How many of them would survive into freedom? He thought of some men in the valley, holding to their land, like Carrol O'Connor, battening down a house besieged, determined to hold on and survive with his own lease life. Others too. Grim-faced, scouring the blighted fields for the scrapings of the bad potatoes that would keep them alive, even going to the soup kitchens to take the soup and turn their backs on their fathers' faith. To survive, to hold on. Not to be driven.

At the Fair Green there was a black-dressed man talking from a mound. "Repent! Repent!" he called. "For now you see. The famine and the pestilence are God's vengeance for Catholic Emancipation. Now you must see this. Turn your eyes away from the Roman whore and fix them on the Bible of Christ. Repent! Repent!" Nobody cursed him.

His family looked at him anxiously.

He sat beside them on the grass.

"I will not go," he said. He watched their faces. Colman's eyes widening in surprise. Finola not minding. Come or go, she was happy, he saw. She was still holding Colman's hand.

And Una. No change in her features. Just smiling at him. Wait for him. You don't know what in the name of God Dualta will do.

"I have four tickets for the ship," said Dualta. "I have a ticket from a pawnshop man who will give us five pounds five shillings. This will pay for the fare of two people with a little money over. I tell you this, Colman, because you are now a man. You can go on the ship or you can come with me."

"Where are you going?" Colman asked.

"I am going back to my own hills," said Dualta. "I am going back to see my uncle Marcus. We will go there. We will survive there. We will resist death."

"If your uncle Marcus is not alive?" Una asked gently.

"I would know if he was dead," said Dualta. "Somehow I would know. Even if he was, there are some of us there. We cannot all be gone. So you see, Colman, you are your own man. You have taken a wife. You can make your choice."

"I will take the ship," said Colman.

They looked at him in surprise.

"There is nothing here for me," he said. "I see stone walls and blighted fields. I want to be where the birds will sing over fat meadows. I want to be free. You have educated me to this.

I want to be on my own. My own man. I have leaned on you too long. Not any more. I will be my own man. I was like a hare on the hills. I was happy with this. Now it is not enough for me. I think Finola and I will be well out of this land. I think now that I hate it. It has lost my song. You see. Do you understand?"

"You have about an hour and a half," said Dualta. "The ship sails on the tide. It is a clean ship. We will divide the food. You will take the slide car to this selling man whose name is on the docket. He will give you the money. You will pay for two of the tickets at the dock. You will ask for Pat Maloney. Tell him the other two are not going. You understand this?"

"This is clear," said Colman, rising from the grass.

From the car Dualta took only a spade and clothes and some of the hard cakes. He put those in a sack for himself. Then he handed the rope of the slide car to Colman.

"Go now," he said. "Let us part at speed. We know what is in our hearts. There have been too many tears. When you are settled you will write to us from wherever you are in care of the Post Office at Clifden. It will reach to us. When your first child is born, you must warn us."

He caught Finola by the shoulders and pressed her to him. He felt her trembling, so he released her fast. Then he heard her crying with Una and the baby.

He said to Colman: "Take the car, for God's sake, and be on your way. We will all be broken if you do not go."

Colman said: "Come on, Finola." He took her arm and started to haul on the rope. She held on to him. Dualta could hear her crying as they went across the Green. He gritted his teeth. He started to stuff things into the sack. Think of something, of the body of O'Connell coming home on this day. Muffled drums. Black drapes. He died when too many were dying. But his dying was exceptional. It was the end of hope. The death of an era. Now there would have to be a new one rising from the pus of death and famine and emigrant ships, with enemies and his own too, spitting into his grave, small-minded men making crimes of his failings, mortal sins of his faults, and burying his greatness under a stone monument. Let me cry for that rather than Colman and Finola.

When he looked now, the opening of the street had swallowed them. "I will take the baby," he said to Una. "You drive the cow." He didn't look at her. He knew what way she would look. So he took the baby in one arm, swung the sack and the spade on his shoulder and set off. He saw the road clearly before him, winding toward the strong mountains. The intense man was still shouting "Repent! Repent!" to a tired and hopeless and indifferent mass of ragged people, as they moved to walk through the town.

L'envoi

THEY WERE CLEAR of the town. They were sitting at the side of the road. They were breasting a current of people who were walking wearily toward where they had come from. They were almost the only people on the road who were going west.

They could see down into the Bay.

They watched the three-masted ship tacking out toward the Aran Islands. They could see white water at the prow.

The passing people looked at them indifferently, a woman and a man and a baby sitting by the side of the road.

A carriage passed them. It was loaded with trunks and cases and it was pulled by four horses. There were two well-dressed ladies in it and a man with a gray beaver hat. Their glances rested on them, then passed on.

"We will go now," said Dualta.

She rose. She carried the baby.

"On now," said Dualta to the cow. The cow stopped grazing the free grass and walked ahead of them, her udder swinging.

"Long ago I came this road," said Dualta. "I had a spade and some shillings. Now I am going back this road and do you know, I am a wealthy man."

"Is that so?" she asked.

"Yes," he said. "I have a wife and a son and a cow and a spade. My people will see us and they will welcome us and they will say: Why, Dualta, you left us a poor man and here you are, coming back with great wealth. You are happy I did not take the ship?"

"Oh, yes," she said. "I am very happy you did not take the ship."

"Would you be happy then if I had taken the ship?"

"I would be happy if you had taken the ship."

"Why is this?" he asked.

"Because where you want to go, I want to go," she said.

"Then there is no fear of us, or of my son," said Dualta. "We will survive."

Historical Notes

The Irish House of Commons, although a sectarian and unrepresentative Assembly, was still an Irish voice. It was destroyed by William Pitt, who succeeded in having the Act of Union passed in 1800. From January 1, 1801, Ireland was represented in the United Kingdom Parliament by 100 members in the House of Commons and 32 Peers in the House of Lords. No Catholic could be a Member of Parliament, although four-fifths of the Irish nation were of that faith.

O'Connell was always opposed to the Union. When elected to Parliament, after the passing of the Catholic Emancipation Act in 1829, he devoted the remaining part of his life to the Repeal of the Act of Union, hoping once again to see an Irish Parliament sitting in Dublin.

CATHOLIC RENT

The expenses of organization being overwhelming, the Catholic Rent was inaugurated. Each person paid one farthing a week, or one shilling a year, to the Rent, which was collected at Parish level. By this means O'Connell (who was earning £8,000 at the Bar in 1828) could abandon the law and devote all his time to the cause of Catholic Emancipation. When this succeeded the same device was later used to support the cause of the Repeal of the Union.